Charming the Troublemaker

Pepper Basham

Bling!
Romance

Lighthouse Publishing of the Carolinas

CHARMING THE TROUBLEMAKER BY PEPPER BASHAM
Published by Bling! Romance
an imprint of Lighthouse Publishing of the Carolinas
2333 Barton Oaks Dr., Raleigh, NC 27614

ISBN: 978-1-946016-30-0
Copyright © 2017 by Pepper Basham
Cover design by Elaina Lee
Interior design by AtriTeX Technologies P Ltd

Available in print from your local bookstore, online, or from the publisher at:
lpcbooks.com

For more information on this book and the author visit: https://pepperdbasham.com/

Brought to you by the creative team at Lighthouse Publishing of the Carolinas:
Marisa Deshaies, Eddie Jones, Shonda Savage, Marcie Bridges

Library of Congress Cataloging-in-Publication Data
Basham, Pepper.
Charming the Troublemaker / Pepper Basham 1st ed.

Acknowledgments

Despite popular belief, writing a novel always takes more than an author and her imaginary friends. The process involves lots of people who are long-suffering, kind, detail-oriented, and love story … and love me. I'm certain I won't be able to list everyone whom I owe "thanks" to for this fun book, but know that I'm grateful for you all.

Marisa Deshaies and Meghan Gorecki, you ladies are such fun to work with and amazing encouragers. THANK YOU for helping me bring this story to life. Marisa, you put up with my Appalachian writing dialect so well!

Rachel Dixon, my virtual assistant and all-round superwoman. This writing journey wouldn't be half as fun without you. Thank you for putting up with my craziness. Love you!

Carrie Schmidt, thank you for reading this book as I wrote it to help encourage me along the way. I'm so glad you fell in love with #AdorkableAlex too.

Thank you to my readers who've made *A Twist of Faith* such a great success in my venture into contemporary romance. Y'all have been such an encouragement to me, and I certainly hope you will find this next visit to Mitchell's Crossroads as much fun (or even better) than the last.

To my wonderful former colleagues at ETSU—Teresa, Lindsay, Marie, and Kerry—thanks for inspiring and loving me, our students, and our clients. You all have taught me so much, and I'm thankful beyond words for you.

Thanks to my agent, Julie Gwinn, who continues to champion my many story ideas.

My Amazing Alleycats, thank you for your support and love for all these years. What an amazing journey we've been given the opportunity to experience together. And Amy Leigh Simpson, thanks for making sure my teensy bit of suspense writing didn't fall flat! Love you, friend.

My Dream Team is a remarkable group of ladies who make this writing journey all the more fun, sweet, and sparkly. You will never know how much I appreciate you!

To my large, wonderful, and slightly crazy Spencer family. So many story ideas and family-closeness I write about stems from growing up with a bunch of wonderful people like you. Aunt Penny and Aunt Tonda, thank you so much for championing these stories the way you do!

Thanks to my dad, who not only loves me and my stories, but was a wonderful resource in finding out more information about police protection of witnesses. Mom and Dad, you are such great encouragers in this dream.

As always, where would I be without my amazing family who inspire me, change me, help me grow, and encourage me with their love. Dwight, Ben, Aaron, Lydia, Samuel, and Phoebe, I'm so glad I get to do life with you!

And to the One who brings us out of our trouble into His remarkable love—Jesus Christ, I am eternally grateful that the story of my life, with all of its brokenness, joys, and wrong choices ends in an eternal happily-ever-after because of God's grace. To Him be all glory forever.

Dedication

To my brother Dustin—one of the sweetest troublemakers I know, with one of the biggest hearts on the planet. I'm so thankful for you, bro.

Chapter One

Loser ex-husbands and freezing January afternoons left a nasty chill. Rainey Mitchell grimaced against the thought of Gray's most recent e-mail, another hesitant response to her request for child support.

So she'd resorted to threatening ... a little.

Single parenting wasn't cheap, and despite that she wanted to see him less than he wanted to see her, most likely, she couldn't keep ignoring his irresponsibility.

"Mama, why can't we touch rainbows?"

Rainey stifled a tired chuckle and glanced in the rearview mirror at her golden-headed five-year-old in the back seat. Those bright blue eyes, wide and curious, blinked from behind her darker-blue-rimmed glasses. Sarah was, easily, the best thing Gray gave her.

"Because a rainbow is made out of light, like sunshine, so we can't really touch it."

"Oh." Silence.

But the silence wouldn't last long. Sarah filled almost every waking moment with questions. "Why" being her favorite, but her daughter's chipper little voice proved a welcome distraction from thoughts of ex-husbands, dwindling finances, and an inevitable meeting about both.

Not that laying eyes on her ex-husband was ever a hardship. He had the tall, dark, and handsome descriptors down to a "T," but if Granny's saying about "pretty is as pretty does" was true, Gray's insides resembled what the cows left behind.

Except for the blood running through Sarah's veins, Gray Randall had no right to see his daughter. He'd forfeited that particular honor with two affairs and a rotten disposition—not to mention an overall lifestyle that made Ebenezer Scrooge look warm and fuzzy. But the softer spot within her wanted Sarah to know the sweetness of a loving father.

She inwardly groaned and held the self-flailing at bay. Sifting through regrets failed to help the present or brighten the future.

"Why is a rainbow called a rain*bow*?" Sarah's sweet voice called again, another welcome interference to Rainey's disgruntled musings. "It don't look nothing like a hair bow."

"Maybe not a hair bow, but it looks a lot like Uncle Trigg's hunting bow, don't you think?"

Sarah pushed her glasses further onto her scrunched nose. "Oh, right."

Momentary silence followed as Rainey pulled her jeep into the faculty parking lot of Blue Ridge University. If Dr. Godfrey recommended Sarah for a speech-language evaluation one more time, Rainey would be tempted to scream into the sweet pediatrician's stethoscope. Just because Sarah barely spoke to anyone outside the family didn't mean she couldn't talk. Good heavens, the girl could chat the bark off a tree.

"Mama, why does God sneeze so much?"

"God sneezing?"

The sudden appearance of a cherry-red Mercedes in the faculty parking lot diverted Rainey from Sarah's strange question. Who on earth drove a Mercedes in Ransom? Was this some sort of joke? She pulled her farm-worn jeep alongside the shiny red dream, trying to place the high-class car with a possible prof in her department. Or even in nursing upstairs?

No one came to mind.

Most of the people she knew drove sensible cars and couldn't afford the drool-worthy jewel to her left. She opened her jeep door, careful not to come close to dinging the Mercedes. Its sleek design, all new and gorgeous, evoked the temptation to slide her hand across the smooth body, just to say she'd actually touched such a high-dollar car.

She shook her head and turned back to her jeep, opening Sarah's door. Sensible over dreamy.

Kept everything in the best and safest perspective.

The little princess fired another comment. "I don't reckon He has a cold, being God and all."

Rainey blinked out of her thoughts and turned to her daughter, taking her outstretched hand. "What makes you think God sneezes so much?"

Sarah sighed as if her mama was the dumbest human on the planet. Some days, Rainey agreed. "'Cause we're always saying, 'Bless you, Lord.'"

Rainey laughed and scooped Sarah close, placing a kiss into her soft blond curls. "No sneezes from the Most High, sweetheart, but we can certainly bless Him for bringing such pretty scenery our way today."

Rainey set Sarah on her feet and nodded toward the distance. Even in barren winter, the indigo and azure mountains rose to meet the fading golden hues of dusk in an amazing display of untiring beauty. "Cold and pretty."

Sarah shivered. "I'm cold all the way to my Cat boots."

Rainey knelt close and rubbed Sarah's shoulders, grinning at her daughter's affinity for naming her shoes. "Tell ya what. We'll run in quick enough to pick up my papers and give directions to the new guy staying in Papa's house, then we can head over to Daphne's for some hot chocolate. What do you say?"

"With whipped cream and syrup?" The blue in the rim of Sarah's glasses brought out the piercing shade of her eyes. Paired with those golden curls, she looked angelic. How could Gray ever think his daughter wasn't beautiful?

Rainey sighed into another cherub hug, hoping Sarah had been too young to remember Gray's criticisms. No one needed hateful and mean around. Add arrogant and her ex was the Bermuda Triangle of male traits.

And although Gray always had a weakness for pretty things, he never recognized the beauty in the people who mattered most.

"Definitely with whipped cream and chocolate syrup!"

Rainey sent another appreciative glance to the Mercedes and then walked to her building.

"Is the new guy staying in Papa's house for a long time? Will he like Haus like Miss Doc does?"

Rainey took her time answering, her grin growing at the thought of her grandparents' dog, who basically came along with the house for any new tenant. Somehow, the mutt's creepy smile and relaxed demeanor won over the previous occupant, Dee Roseland. But Dr. Alexander Murdock, the newest renter? Rainey rolled her eyes heavenward, offering God her most exasperated look.

God wouldn't mind. He'd seen it plenty. "Who wouldn't love Papa's house … or Haus?"

Except maybe Dr. Murdock. Rainey kept her gaze forward so Sarah couldn't see the truth on her face. Dr. Murdock didn't seem the sort to stay long in any place. She'd met him a few times when Dee, her friend and colleague, rented the farmhouse. He had "flirt" tattooed all over his high-watt grin, and from those brief interactions, Rainey knew to steer clear.

She grimaced. *Stop it, Rainey.* She could almost hear her mother's reprimand in the back of her mind, the gentle Appalachian drawl easing over the words. *Breathe grace. We all need it.*

Two years of frustrating long-distance conversations with Gray gathered on her shoulders like a heavy cloak, dimming her overall mood—and Alex Murdock's presence, or what she remembered about his Casanova-like, devil-may-care attitude, hit her in the aftershocks of Gray's recent e-mail.

Why, oh why, did Dee have to move to Charlottesville and leave Dr. Murdock in her place? *People and their big-city dreams.*

But Rainey couldn't fault her friend, even though it meant Rainey's brother would follow his future bride up to Charlottesville. Both of them shared dreams, the best kind. It made sense for Dee and Reese to follow those dreams together. And there was something beautiful about romance in the right way. God's way.

Funny how He worked, bringing two totally different personalities like Dr. Adelina Roseland and Rainey's farmer brother, Reese, into a perfect blend of rightness when they least expected it. Almost fairytale-ish ... and a great story to *observe* ... and only observe.

Romance carried a frightful amount of mindlessness with it. And change. And the possibility of life-altering mistakes.

She rolled the tension from her shoulders and squeezed Sarah's hand to redirect her attitude. Alex Murdock, however he might be, didn't deserve a backlash from her grumpy mood and two years of hard-won resentment. He needed a country welcome, as Rainey would give to anyone else moving to the neighborhood.

Sarah hugged closer to Rainey's side as they entered the building, the usual introvert coming out and stealing her happy chatter. Polly, the receptionist, smiled and greeted them. Sarah buried her face into Rainey's thigh but offered a tiny wave—definite progress. Rainey couldn't pinpoint an exact moment when Sarah went from carefree to overly careful, but it started about the time Gray left.

Rainey nursed the worry for a second longer, then pushed it back behind the residual hurt. Other than her highly selective communication skills, Sarah was perfect, and, along with her crazy family, all Rainey needed.

Once they cleared the front desk, Sarah returned to her happy self, skipping around the office as Rainey gathered her class preparation papers and new student roster. With a deep breath, she turned toward her next goal. Alex Murdock.

The other office doors were closed, everyone gone for the last long weekend before spring classes began—all the doors except one. Dee's old office.

"Sweets, let's go see if Dr. Murdock is in his office so we can leave the directions to Papa's house for him."

Sarah's skipping stopped and she edged against Rainey as they neared the open office door. The gentle strum of guitar music shot a mismatched picture through Rainey's head. She paused at the door, leaning closer to listen. The Alex Murdock she met last fall gave off all kinds of "rock star" vibes, not instrumental guitar. Maybe she had the wrong office.

With the quietest motions, she peeked her head around the doorway and scanned the room. Last time she'd seen Dr. Murdock, he'd been in a top-notch suit, head high, with enough condescension on his brow to impress Mr. Darcy. He'd lathered on the charm as thick as his cologne.

Definitely not the best first impression.

But the golden-haired man hunched over a box of books as acoustic music played a comforting melody through the dimly lit room appeared to be a different sort of guy. He wore a V-neck T-shirt and jeans, a vision at odds with her last sight of him.

He hadn't been impressed with her small university and even smaller town—and if what Dee had told her was accurate, his move to Ransom had been more of a demotion than a choice.

A forced decision like that had to hit anyone in the pride.

Especially a guy.

Rainey's annoyance ebbed with a swell of compassion. Being alone, and in a new place, was hard for anyone.

He brought his head up at her gentle rap on the door, and the unique green shade of his eyes paused her brain in the same way it had the first time she'd seen him. A seafoam hue. The kind of color to cause a second look.

"So, how are things going?"

The surprise on his face took a quick spin into "interested." He unfolded to stand, showing off a solid, lean frame, and rested his palms on his hips. "Better now."

Another sigh waited for release. Yep, it was the same guy. The flirt emerged complete with devilish grin.

The communication disorders department already housed a resident flirt in Dr. Khatri. Rainey wasn't sure she could handle another one ... and only three doors down from her own office.

"I'm sure it will keep improving once you get to your rental house. Mama has a meal waiting for you, and one of my brothers has already started a fire in the stove to warm up the place by the time you get there."

"Are you my personal guide?" He slid a step closer, green eyes sparkling with a mischief she tried to ignore like a migraine. "Please say yes."

Obvious much? This unrestrained flirting needed to be nipped in the bud quickly. Stepping into the room, Rainey pulled the directions from her pocket, took his hand, and slapped them into his outstretched palm. "Actually, I'm more like the delivery girl."

His smile fell as he opened up the handwritten note and deciphered the page. He looked back up, a darker glint deepening his gaze. "We've had enough conversations for you to know I'm fun company, Rainey. Promise I'll be good."

Rainey's throat closed around a rude reply, and she nodded toward the paper in his palm. "Make sure you don't stay too long at the office or your supper will get cold." She tagged on a tense smile. "And you really don't want to miss Mama's cookin.'"

The pressure at Rainey's leg alerted her that Sarah had finally edged into the room behind her. Rainey placed her hand on her daughter's head and started to leave.

"And who is this?" The most spellbinding transformation tempered Alex's flirty expression with a look of genuine pleasure. Rainey's mental snark stuttered in confusion.

"Um ... my daughter, Sarah."

Sarah's entire body stiffened against Rainey, but Alex didn't seem to notice. He reached on the shelf near him and grabbed a piece of printer paper, the gentle appeal in those eyes almost mesmerizing. Even Rainey's thoughts came to a halt in utter shock.

With a few twists of his hands, he transformed the paper into a white flower and held it out to Sarah in anticipation. "It's magic, you see? I can only make flowers from paper when I meet a princess."

And the eye roll commenced. This guy had enough charm to create his own Disney movie. Sarah would never fall for...

Her daughter released her hold on Rainey's leg and reached out for the paper flower.

"Ah, I knew it! You *are* a princess." Alex bowed his head as Sarah took the flower from his hand and to Rainey's utter astonishment ... her little cherub giggled.

Rainey stared at the scene, her poor attempt at deciphering the current enigma evident from the slow processing speed of the picture before her. How on earth had he managed to win over her recalcitrant little girl in a matter of seconds? She didn't have much time to unravel the puzzle because a sudden commotion at the end of the hall snagged her attention.

"You can't go back there. I'll call the police." Polly's voice carried the frantic command just before a sickeningly familiar man rounded the corner of the hallway.

Liquid fire flamed up through Rainey's chest at the sight of the scoundrel, and every protective fiber in her body flamed to the attack.

How dare Dan Edwards show his face back in this clinic! And worse yet, how did he know she was even here on a vacation day? Was he stalking her like he tried to do to his poor wife and children?

A sudden chill attempted to creep up her spine, but she shook it off, kneeling by her daughter instead. "Stay with Dr. Murdock. I'll be back in a minute." She stood and shot Alex a look. "Keep her safe, okay?"

Was it the best choice to leave her sweet little daughter with a man whose teeth probably cost more than her house? Compared to the tyrant barreling toward her, she'd take the sweet-talkin' charmer any day. Alex Murdock probably left only a trail of broken hearts, not broken bones, like Dan's wife and eight-year-old autistic son experienced at the hands of the man coming her way.

Rainey nudged Sarah toward Alex and pulled the office door to a firm snap, keeping her body as a shield to entry.

"There you are, Rainey Mitchell."

She braced herself, palms to her hips, ready to block Dan should he prove stupid enough to assault her. "Are you trying to add stalking to your list of offenses? I'm pretty sure you've been warned by the police about showing your face in this clinic again. Especially since last time you had to be forcefully removed."

He stepped so close, the heat of his pungent breath singed her skin. The vile man wielded intimidation like his fists. Rainey refused to cower and even leaned in to take the challenge.

"I know you're the one who reported those lies to Social Services. I know you're the one who took my wife and child away." His words slurred, tainted with cheap whiskey.

Lucky for him, she spoke fluent jerk.

"I didn't take anyone from you, Mr. Edwards. Your abuse of your family did that on its own. Now, if you don't want to go to jail before your time, I'd suggest you leave this building. I'm sure Polly has already alerted the authorities you're violating the court order."

He glanced behind him and took a few steps back. Rainey loosened her fists at her sides.

"You think you have it all figured out, don't you, woman?"

"No, Mr. Edwards. I don't pretend to figure out a man like you. Outwardly pretending to be respectable but inside the privacy of your home, an abusive monster?"

"More lies. You have no right to keep my family from me."

"That is for the judge to decide. Not me. But breaking the court order isn't going to make the judge like you any better."

"You may be surprised how many friends I have in high places."

Rainey squelched a shudder and offered a nonchalant shrug. "And you may be surprised how unimpressed I am with your threats."

His grin turned lethal and he moved a few more steps down the hallway. "You don't know who you're messing with. I'd keep watch over your shoulder if I was you, Rainey Mitchell. This is a small town, and everybody knows where everybody else lives in a small town."

His gaze burned with a warning Rainey felt all the way down her stiff spine. Her shaking knees twinged as soon as he turned the corner, and she leaned back against the cold, cinderblock wall.

Threats. Only threats.

Dan Edwards wouldn't really risk losing more by hurting her, would he? She sent another wary look in the direction he'd disappeared. She'd make a phone call to her cousin, Andy, at the police station just in case. Threats had a dangerous tendency to sprout feet.

How Alex Murdock went from mourning the loss of his prestigious career at UVA-Charlottesville to entertaining an adorable five-year-old at a university in the middle of nowhere, he wasn't quite sure. But from the sound of the raised voices outside, it was a good thing Sarah was as far from the confrontation as possible.

Her eyes, wide and blue behind adorable glasses, stared up at him as if she might break into tears any moment. And he couldn't let that happen. Despite his many blunders, he'd always managed to get along with kids, and little girls' tears? Nothing broke his will like a few well-placed sobs. His niece, Lily, had been able to convince him to do about anything with a wobbly bottom lip and watery doe eyes.

Somehow little kids always seemed to give Alex a better chance than adults did. His father pawned it off as Alex never growing up, and maybe that was partially true, but Alex took the challenge as a "clean slate" with each child he met. He could be the hero for them, even if everyone else saw him as a clown, flirt, or failure.

Adults had presuppositions and expectations. Kids took you as you were.

"You know your mom wouldn't have left you with me if she didn't think I was safe." Alex relaxed down onto the floor and ignored his lie. The look in Rainey Mitchell's aqua eyes laced uncertainty with a healthy bit of annoyance. "So maybe you could help me a little."

She blinked but didn't move.

A deep voice came from the other side of the door, somewhat muffled but enough for Alex to get a gist of the conversation. Rainey kept a father from seeing his child? With police?

Alex moved forward in defense, but Sarah's whimper brought his attention back to the golden-haired fairy at his knees. She moved a little closer to him.

His heart puddled to mush.

Think. Think. What did little girls like? What would Lily have talked about? At the thought of his niece, his chest tightened. He worked the next words through a tense throat.

"Sarah, have you watched *My Little Pony*?"

Sarah's eyes widened further, and the whimpering came to a complete stop. She moved even closer.

Home run.

A burst of protection rose within Alex's chest with surprising force. He might not be great at a lot of things, but he believed in protecting kids, in helping them feel important. Heaven knew he'd needed someone to do that for him in his childhood.

"I used to draw Pinkie Pie for my niece. That was Lily's favorite pony." He offered his hand. "Let's sit at my desk and I'll show you."

Her large, trusting gaze flickered from his face to his hand, hopeful. He held his breath as if this one connection meant the last straw in his long line of failures.

With the tiniest hitch, she put her little hand into his, and for the first time since being reassigned to this tiny university in the heart of the Blue Ridge Mountains, he didn't feel as alone ... or as stupid.

Oh boy, did he play the butt of the universe's jokes or what!

Why did doing the right thing always backfire on him? How was he supposed to know promoting a colleague meant she'd gain the promotion to his position and he'd take her spot here? Even choosing a job as a speech-language pathologist to serve others over buying into his father's corporation seemed like a bad choice at the moment.

Well, not exactly at *this* moment. Keeping Sarah safe and happy felt right.

He settled into his chair and carefully drew her onto his knee, waiting for her to protest. She stayed stiff from golden hair to pink tennis shoes, but she didn't push him away. He placed his arms on either side of her to reach the desk and made a quick sketch of the pink, somewhat neurotic pony from the children's cartoon.

As he drew, Sarah's little body relaxed. Her soft curls even tickled the edge of his chin and smelled of honeysuckles. Memories of his sweet niece nearly choked him. He resisted the urge to hug Sarah a little closer for comfort.

"Don't forget her cutie mark." The sweet timbre of her voice filtered into Alex's gray thoughts. She tapped the back of the pony where the powerful tattoo was supposed to go.

He smiled down at her head, his voice unpredictable. "Balloons, right?"

Sarah tilted her head up to him and examined his face, the previous apprehension in her expression replaced with unprejudiced curiosity. She looked even more adorable with those blue-framed glasses. He'd made a vow to himself when he'd gotten the news about his transfer that he'd steer clear of any serious connections with people in "Mayberry," but it was hard to fight this immediate connection with a little girl who reminded him so much of someone he loved. Someone who couldn't be with him anymore.

"What do you think?" He lifted the sketch for her to get a clearer view.

She gasped and pulled her clasped hands into her chest. "It's wonderful." That blue gaze glittered up to his. "You're a very good drawer."

Warmth started deep in Alex's chest and branched into a smile. How long had it been since someone thought there was anything good about him? He held to the simple adoration like a starving man.

Maybe starting over, a clean slate, was exactly what he needed.

The door swung open and Rainey stormed in openmouthed and ready for some sassy retort, if his people-reading radar worked. She froze in the doorway, her pale gaze flitting from the little girl on his knee and back to his face. An unguarded look of surprise replaced whatever statement she'd planned to make, eyes wide and a flush of rose dusting her pale cheeks.

Unguarded suited her.

"Wh ... what is going on in here?"

"He drew me a Pinky Pie picture, Mama. Look!" Sarah flashed the drawing toward her mother.

"She's my favorite." Sarah looked up at him, a dimple dipping into each cheek, and Alex's heart leapt right out of his chest and landed in her tiny little fingers.

Rainey stared at her daughter for a full five seconds before apparently snapping back to motion. "Um ... well, that was nice of him."

"And he even knows about her cutie mark too." Sarah patted his shoulder. "Most boys don't know about cutie marks."

"You know about cutie marks?"

He shrugged one shoulder, trying to find an explanation that didn't sound as lame as the truth, but Rainey's direct gaze called for an equally direct answer. "*This* boy has been surrounded by girls his whole life, so his mind is full of surprisingly pink information."

"Surrounded by girls? Right." Rainey's response moved as slowly as the turn of her head, back and forth from him to Sarah.

"Well, not *that* way." He fumbled with his words. What was wrong with him? "I was the only boy in a family full of girls."

She continued to stare, the pucker in her brow deepening with each silent second.

He'd guess Rainey Mitchell didn't meet tongue-tied too often. The idea notched up his confidence a little more. She examined him with a deeper layer of uncertainty and then cleared her throat. "Well, that was very sweet of you."

She beckoned Sarah forward.

Sarah got off his lap and turned. "Thank you, Mr. Doctor."

He tapped her nose. "Alex."

"Dr. Murdock," Rainey corrected, attention fastened on him, mama-warning at full alert.

"Dr. Alex Murdock," Sarah repeated, her smile inciting another flicker of dimples. "Do you want to get hot chocolate with us?"

"Sarah." Rainey stepped forward and took Sarah's hand, tugging her toward the door. "I'm sure Dr. Murdock has plenty to do. We've taken up enough of his time this afternoon."

Rainey's pointed look said he'd better agree, but the troublemaker in him flared to full rebellion. It's true he had plenty of mourning to do about the loss of his position at UVA, and he still had a few resumes to send out in hopes of getting out of Ransom as quickly as possible, but...

Sarah's expectant smile spurned the rebel into motion, and with a flicker of victory to the fiery blonde, he replied, "Hot chocolate sounds like a great idea."

Chapter Two

This day was quickly taking a severe nosedive.

Rainey helped Sarah out of her coat and hung it on a little peg by the booth seats in Daphne's Café. First Gray, then Dan, and now hot chocolate with Alex Murdock?

Lord, what hideous sin have I committed lately?

She shrugged out of her jacket and hung it near Sarah's, a flash of red catching her eye out the restaurant window. The Mercedes. Of course, Alex Murdock owned the Mercedes.

Within a few seconds the restaurant door swung open, and he walked in, black wool coat wrapped around him, sending off all sorts of swoony vibes. Wind-swept blond hair, interesting green eyes, perfect smile? She'd probably like him better if he didn't look so good.

Handsome carried loads of distasteful baggage, in her experience.

He took in the room, a look of pure appreciation dawning on his face like a kid's at Christmas. That was it! He reminded Rainey of a little boy in an adult's body—an uncommonly handsome adult body.

His gaze landed on hers, and he sauntered forward, his thick-scented cologne hitting her before he reached the table. "I love the smell of this place."

"Daphne and Emma do keep it toasty and tasty in here." Oh, how stupid did she sound? *Toasty and tasty?* "It's one of the best spots in town for good food."

"Well, I'll certainly be by often. I'm a horrible cook."

The conversation stalled, so Rainey chimed in with another reaction. "So … you drive the Mercedes?"

He slipped out of his jacket, his strong, lean lines moving beneath the folds of his shirt. Rainey trained her focus on his marble-like green eyes. His blond brow edged up. "I do. She was my consolation prize. She's my favorite color, drives like a dream, and smells like Christmas."

"She? Your what?"

"My consolation prize for the move to Ransom." He slid into the booth. "Blue Ridge University wasn't on my bucket list of hopeful employers, as you can imagine."

Rainey's spine stiffened with some homespun pride. "Just so you know, BRU has a great reputation among small liberal arts schools."

"Small being the operative word there."

She tried not to grit her teeth behind her fake grin. "I wouldn't be too quick to judge a book by its cover, Dr. Murdock. Usually there's an unearthed story hiding to alter your impression."

He stared at her, conceding with a tilt to his head. "True. Very true. And I'd really like to make a fresh start somewhere."

She stifled a groan. *Please, not in Ransom.*

"My car's name isn't Mercedes, by the way."

"Oh, really?" The sarcasm jumped out before she could catch it. He made it too easy. "What did you choose instead? My precious?"

He laughed. *Laughed.* And for some reason, her lips were tempted to curl in reply. "Oh, come on. That is so impersonal. The best things in life need a name."

"Is it a girl's name?" Sarah conveniently moved right into the conversation.

"Something that gorgeous has to have a girl's name, don't you think?"

Good grief! Rainey's internal warning radar spiked back to bright red. She didn't even attempt to hide her eye roll. "Of course."

Sarah giggled. "A princess name?"

Alex looked over at Sarah, leaning close, his attention so tender Rainey almost softened to the view. A handsome man talking princesses and showing kindness to her sweet daughter?

The sweet sight glitched against her distrust much too easily.

Her sensible heart reared back from the temptation to ask him about his past, his "consolation." All she needed from Alex Murdock was a professional working relationship. Not friendship. Besides, she'd learned the hard way flirty and sincere rarely lived in the same body—and handsome smiles only went teeth deep.

"Well, not quite, but I think of her as a princess. I named her Marilyn."

"As in Monroe?" And the base predictability flared back to life.

His body tensed at Rainey's reaction, but he never moved his gaze from Sarah's. Another motherly nudge sounded off in her head. Yep, she was being a complete jerk. *Stop it, Rainey!*

"After my favorite princess." He tapped Sarah's nose. "My mom."

Rainey's mouth swung open a little, not enough to welcome flies but enough to give her preconceptions a good dousing. Maybe ... maybe Alex wasn't as fake as Aunt Louisa's eyebrows.

Could flirty and sweet live in the same body? Ugh. The combination left a post-betrayal pang in her stomach. Rainey cleared her throat. "Just to prepare you, the farmhouse is out in the middle of the country, a twenty-minute drive from town. For those of us who enjoy peace and quiet, it's a great sanctuary."

"I've never tried it, so I'm not sure how I'll do."

"You may be surprised then." She attempted a smile to ease the stilted conversation. "It's on family land, beautiful countryside. Great for walks or runs." She relaxed a little as she spoke of home. "Winter isn't as pretty as spring and fall, but once the buds start blooming, oh, the views and the smells make you want to sit on your front porch and breathe in the quiet."

He studied her with such an intense expression that she looked away, checking for a waitress ... praying for a waitress. "And Mama's house is just over the hill from yours."

"Ours is right next door," Sarah chimed in.

What happened to her sweet, don't-talk-to-strangers little girl? Rainey's eyes squeezed closed.

"So, you're my neighbors?" His gaze shifted to Rainey, and his lips twisted into the flirty tilt again. "Well, that does put a sheen on the situation."

"Oh, gracious, Alex. Tone the gallant a little, okay? My sensible head is starting to hurt."

His brows did the shimmy. "Number one, I'm trying to make lemonade from lemons." He looked back at her, his grin perching higher. "And number two, there's nothing wrong with being friendly."

"I don't know that I'm interested in your kind of friendly."

"I'm happy to try your kind of friendly if you'll give me the inside scoop on how."

She challenged his statement with a lifted brow, but his honest expression had her second-guessing her assumptions again. Was he serious? With two straightforward brothers and a jerk for an ex-husband, she couldn't quite imagine this as another personality option. But something in the way he looked at her, a sliver of tenderness woven between the arrogance, pricked at her misconceptions like a wholesome conviction. *Exactly who was Alex Murdock?*

One step from the cold January day into the warm aura of Daphne's and the intoxicating scent of fresh-baked goodness mixed with a sense of rural appeal lit his dim perspective with … welcome.

He paused to appreciate the unique blend of sweet warmth and country charm, surprisingly appealing against the backdrop of his Fairfax upbringing. Though he'd made advances in UVA—particularly with his own research, apart from what he'd supervised for his colleague, Dee—he lost his focus about a year ago, for good reason.

A life-changing reason.

He firmed his chin with purpose. Somehow, he had to make this work for now.

As he sat across the booth from two beautiful blondes, even one with an edge to her smile, he couldn't tame the thoughts of his sister and niece infiltrating his well-practiced control. He missed them, ached for them … and the few moments with Sarah resurrected the ache with enough pain to have him pulling out all the flirty stops.

Rainey's description of home only fanned the longing he'd nurtured for years. The search for a place to belong. And there was something about her, her intense personality, that challenged him to unearth her smile.

He'd keep trying.

"Oh, my. What do we have here?"

A young woman he'd seen in Daphne's before stepped forward, an apron hugging her slender frame. Her hazel eyes danced between Alex and Rainey, mischief carved in her perfect smirk. He liked her already.

"Could this be a … date?"

"No." Rainey answered with such force that Sarah's eyes widened at her mother's response.

Alex offered the lovely waitress a wink. "No is such a definitive answer, don't you think? I wouldn't close out the possibility altogether."

He could feel the red-heated glare from Rainey's general direction without even looking. Maybe this little venture into the wilds of the Blue Ridge had its perks. "Unless you're available to take her place?"

"You've got to be kidding me." Rainey's exasperation broadened his grin.

"Not today, obviously. She's working." He swung his attention back to the waitress. Too young for his tastes, but if it riled sparks from his tablemate, he'd play the game. It was a good distraction from heavier thoughts. "But I'm sure she has days off."

The waitress laughed and offered her hand to Alex. "Don't know if you remember me, handsome, but I'm Emma, Rainey's sister, and you just became one of my favorite people."

He soaked in the admiration and took her hand. "Oh, I remember you, Emma. Your charm is fairly unforgettable."

One of Emma's brows shot high with her burgeoning smile to her sister. "See, Rainey. At least someone recognizes how charming I am." Emma cupped her palm with her mouth to temper the words but still spoke loudly enough for Rainey to hear. "Clearly, only one sister got the charm. The other got the stubbornness."

"The other got the sense," Rainey interjected, pinching her pink lips tight. "And evidently, the work ethic." She waved toward the patrons at other tables. "Don't you have some orders to take?"

Emma offered a one-shouldered shrug. "I can take *your* orders if you're ready."

"Two small, regular hot chocolates for us, with whipped cream *and* syrup," Rainey answered and motioned to Alex.

He leaned his chin on his elbow and moved a little closer to Emma. "What would you suggest, Emma?"

"Good grief," came the mumble from the disgruntled blonde across the table.

"The hot chocolate supreme, if you're going for the gold, Dr. Murdock."

"Oh," he said, his grin etched widely with a waiting laugh. "I always go for the gold."

Emma topped her infectious laugh off with a nod as she turned to walk away. "Life just got a whole lot more interesting around Mitchell's Crossroads, that's for sure."

"Oh no, no, no, Alex Murdock." Rainey's harsh whisper carried across the table. "Don't you dare look at my sister that way."

His arms came up in innocence. "What way?"

"The 'she'd be a cute date' kind of way."

"She *would* be a cute date." Alex relaxed back against the wood. "But she's not exactly my type."

"That's a mercy anyhow. You just got here. You don't even know us."

He leaned toward her, brows wiggling. "Well, a date is certainly one way to get to know you better."

Her eyes shot wide. "Me?"

"You're right. I think I'd much rather be on a date with your daughter than you right now, so maybe you could go to another table and drink *your* hot chocolate."

Rainey's bottom lip dropped open in an adorably distracting way. Speechless suited her quite well. Sarah giggled.

"You know that advice you gave me about the story underneath a book's cover and all?" A sudden rush of pink coated her cheeks. He liked it a little too much. "What do you know about me, Rainey? Just because my brand of friendly looks different than yours doesn't mean it's wrong."

Sarah peeked around her mother's side, and Alex winked at her. She rewarded him with a wrinkled-nosed grin, which lessened the sting of Rainey's doubt a little.

He deserved some of the doubt, probably. His string of girlfriends—none very serious since Beth—gave him companionship but stayed an arm's length away. He liked the attention. Liked giving it too. Nothing serious or hurtful, just fun moments to fill the gaps of loneliness.

The rush of attraction and feeling of being admired dulled the senses to a loss he couldn't replace, and though his soul had begun to heal from Beth's death, none of the women reached into the empty space her absence left behind.

And he liked complimenting women. Blame it on growing up between two sisters, but he enjoyed making ladies smile, and he was good at it … except when it involved a certain, fiery blonde.

She stared at him, studied him, until the tension in her face relaxed. "This isn't a date, Dr. Murdock, but if it were, you'd show excellent taste in choosing Sarah." Rainey ran her palm over Sarah's golden hair. "She's a real catch."

"Without a doubt. I recognized that from the very start. She survived being stuck with me in my office without a single scratch. Right, princess?"

Sarah bobbed those blond curls around her adorable face. "And I got a picture too."

Alex tipped his head toward Rainey in an attempt to appeal to any soft part of her heart. "*And* she got a picture too."

Rainey cleared her throat and looked down at the table. "I thank you again. Those were unique circumstances."

"I get that I'm new here, and I'm not really sure it's the right place for me." He opened his palm toward her. "But all I'm offering is friendliness, Ms. Mitchell. Benign friendliness."

Rainey stared at him, caution bending. With a heavy sigh, she melted back into the booth and folded her hands together on the table, a sigh slumping her shoulders. "You're right. I think we both have some reevaluating to do." She tapped the table with her fingers as she talked, keeping her eyes down. "So … here's what I propose."

"I like proposals," he said with a teasing shift to his lips.

She groaned despite the faintest hint of a smile. Maybe. He could have been imagining the smile, but he held out hope. "Not only are we going to be working together, we're going to be neighbors … and my daughter likes you, which doesn't happen a whole lot with men. So, what do you say I tone down my overall cynicism toward you, and you tone down the whole"—she waved her palm toward his face, taking much too long for his liking to find a word—"Casanova-is-king thing you have going on here."

Alex blinked. "And who exactly do you think I need to be, then?"

"How about we start with whoever you are underneath all of those pickup lines?" She cringed. "Sorry, not the most generous thing to say. I'm tryin', okay? My past experience with flirts isn't the best." She captured his gaze again.

"I see."

"Yeah, so, how about you be authentic. It may be out of style in the city, but we country folk still appreciate authenticity. If this general flirting is authentic for you"—her expression appealed for him to deny it—"then, we'll sort it out. But in the meantime, we both could practice," she said and sighed before starting again, "*I* can practice being nicer."

His grin softened at her humble attempt. "And I'll try to stop being so friendly."

Her smile almost unhinged, and a tiny twinge of victory expanded his breath. Hurts ran deep in this one, and for some reason, with her adorable daughter at her side, Alex wanted to see them smile. More than anything.

But authenticity? It came at a higher price than just his possible failure. With the ghosts in his past, authenticity might lead to a much more dangerous outcome.

"And Alex, one more thing. Tone down the cologne."

"The cologne?"

Her small smile turned apologetic. "I don't know what you're used to in your former life, but you don't have to try so hard around here."

Chapter Three

Rainey checked her rearview mirror to see Alex Murdock following close behind. She'd rolled her eyes so much at the ridiculousness of that red Mercedes, her head ached. Not the most practical car for mountain roads, but Alex Murdock didn't strike her as the most practical guy.

"I like Dr. Alex." Sarah's voice pelted Rainey's solid annoyance like an axe into wet wood. "He has a happy smile, don't you think, Mama?"

She offered her sweet girl a tight grin reflected in the rearview mirror. Rainey wasn't quite so sure what she thought of the newest addition to Ransom, but one thing was certain—he left her feeling ... off-balance. "He does."

But genuine? Trustworthy? Rainey had a sneaky suspicion his "happy smile" left a lot unspoken. She shook her head at her internal monologue. *No, no, no!* She could be neighborly, but she didn't need to know any more about Alex Murdock than his class schedule and client caseload. Pure and simple.

That smile held all sorts of trouble. Unpredictable. Just in the little while she'd spent with him, her head waged some internal battle. Part of the time she wanted to relax into the easy conversation and charm he offered, and the other part she wanted to add a few years to his life in hopes he might mature.

Definitely too much emotional work for her.

She pulled the jeep up to her grandparents' old farmhouse, refurbished as a rental property. The place nudged her thoughts into a quiet appreciation for family, simple ways, and a golden era when the fog of loss and betrayal didn't hang over the past ... and interrupt perfectly calm presents.

Just the thought of Gray's e-mail made her want to beat her head against a wall. Why, oh why, had she opened this dialogue with him when she should have kept her mouth shut about the money like she had for the last two years? A sigh breezed from her lungs, relaxing her pinched shoulders back into the worn cloth seats.

Alex's cherry-red Mercedes pulled to a stop beside her, as out of place in front of the farmhouse as the man was in Ransom. She turned off her engine, crawled out of her Jimmy, and watched the guy unfold from the car like a slow-motion commercial for Benz. Her rebel eyes took him in as if she'd never seen a man before, and her annoyance needled deeper.

Lord, why couldn't she be distracted by the nice, new, predictable youth pastor instead of Mr. Flashy Car?

Rainey groaned at her own stupidity and turned to open the Jimmy door for Sarah to exit. *Maybe it was only her well-honed caution enhancing her senses. Yep. That was it.*

"Dr. Alex," Sarah called as soon as she jumped from the jeep. "Guess what I have?"

Rainey rounded the Mercedes, expecting Sarah to stay close behind.

He closed the door to his car and took a visual inventory of the house. Was he disappointed? Criticizing it in his high-bred mind? "What, princess?"

"I have a Pinkie Pie doll in my car."

He swung his attention to Sarah. "Do you? Is it one of the little ones or the big kind?"

How on earth did he even know these things?

"It's one of the biiig ones." Sarah exaggerated the word to emphasize the enormity of the shoe-sized horse. "I'll show you."

Without warning, she turned back to the Jimmy.

Sarah's seat was on the side of the dream car! "Sarah." Rainey took off at a run. "Be careful opening the do—"

A painful thud followed as Sarah slammed the jeep door into the sleek Mercedes' side, and a whimper crept from the man to her right.

Rainey turned to Alex, his green eyes wide in a terrifying mixture of horror and shock, and her stomach dropped down to her secondhand sneakers. He murmured something unintelligible, as if the truth hadn't sunk in.

"Listen, I know a great body shop in town, and I bet they can fix it right up. It's the tiniest mark, really."

He walked in horrified silence to the driver's side of the jeep.

Sarah climbed back out of the vehicle, totally unaware of the consequences of her behavior, and shot Alex a snaggle-toothed grin while holding up her Pinkie Pie doll. "See how big it is."

Alex didn't so much as look at her but knelt before the tiny dent like some desperate patron praying for favor from the car gods. Yep, this behavior fit her expectations. His gentleness with her daughter? No. The fact he even knew who

Pinkie Pie was? No. But this bowing prostrate before the mighty Mercedes? This matched all the shallow vibes he sent off.

His consolation prize…

She sighed and bent down next to him, his pungent cologne invading her air space. "It was an accident, Alex." She placed her hand on his shoulder. "You know she didn't mean to."

She waited for everything to click, for him to turn and release his anger on her, or worse, on Sarah. In quick preparation, she stood so her body hemmed between them.

"Dr. Alex?" Sarah's little voice melted into the conversation, not much louder than a whisper. "Did I hurt your pretty car?"

He stood and slowly turned, his hair kinking into tighter curls as a gentle mist fell upon them. Rainey braced herself. His chest pumped with his breaths for control.

"I'm really sorry I hurt your car," Sarah's voice wobbled her apology, but when Rainey turned to comfort her sweet little girl, Alex stopped her. He knelt by Sarah, Rainey close to her daughter's side in case things turned dangerous.

"I know you didn't mean to, Sarah." The words ground out, and he released a long, slow breath.

"And it can be fixed," Rainey said, snagging his attention.

He glanced at her, nodded, and turned back to Sarah. "And it can be fixed."

"So, you're not mad at me?"

Every ounce of frustration tensing those strong shoulders of his bent beneath the plea in Sarah's little voice. Rainey's thoughts fogged like the morning mountains, trying to piece together the anomaly known as Dr. Alexander Murdock.

"No, princess. I'm not mad at you."

His gentle voice smoothed over the words like butter on a biscuit, holding Rainey spellbound by their tenderness and erasing her misconceptions yet again. Authenticity.

Rainey cleared her throat. "It's good of you to be so quick to forgive, Dr. Alex." The name reminded her of the all-too-prevalent "popular psychologists" abundant on daytime TV. "People are more important than things."

His gaze flashed up to hers. "Yes." His words came slowly. "People *are* more important than things."

The concentration of his stare, the genuineness, sifted through her bitterness, leaving another slice of uncertainty tipping her off-balance. He stood, holding her gaze. The January day suddenly took on some balmy climate changes. Rainey hadn't felt the charge of attraction in … too long to remember. Her throat dried to dust.

Appreciating the way God made the man was one thing. Appreciating the man himself … definitely another.

Back away from the flirt.

His grin shifted into a sad angle. "My sister used to say that."

The meaning behind his statement told a heartbreaking story. "I'm sorry."

"Thanks," he murmured and turned back to the car with a sigh. "But some things are pretty important for a guy down on his luck."

Rainey released her stalled breath, shaking off her weird response to his mental touch. "We can check with Bob at the body shop about fixing up Marilyn next week, if you want?"

He switched his attention back to Sarah as he touched her head. "Hey, princess, how about you show me this new house of mine?"

Rainey blinked from the foggy sway of attraction and watched her little angel skip toward the house, hair bouncing around her in golden spirals.

Alex walked beside her, tossing his computer bag over his shoulder and sending an appreciative look to her family's homestead. "This place looks like something out of a movie." He caught Rainey's stare, shaking off the flicker of melancholy with his much-too-easy grin. "Hey, I watched *Little House on the Prairie* once or twice."

"*Little House on the Prairie*?" Rainey met him at the bottom of the porch steps, her laugh tempting to unravel like her unruly braid. Who was this guy? "Really?"

Just then a giant, black furry mass lumbered across the white-railed porch to the top of the stairs, directly in their path to the front door. Sarah bounded forward, arms wide to embrace the big dog.

Rainey gestured toward the dog with her chin. "That's Haus. He comes with the house."

Alex paused his forward movement up the stairs. "The dog comes with the house?"

"He's been here his whole life, so even after my grandparents died, he stayed." Rainey waved her hand, dismissing his concern. "He just does, okay? And he smiles."

"He smiles?" As if on cue, Haus unleashed his broadest grin.

Alex's eyes widened, all green and marbled. "That's not disturbing at all."

"He'll be your best defense against coyotes or unwelcome guests." Rainey passed him on the stairs, with Sarah leading the way. "You don't have to take care of him if you don't want to. Me or one of my siblings will stop by in the evenings to make sure he's fed."

Alex looked from Rainey to Haus and then shrugged his shoulders. "We all have our quirks, don't we, fella?" He scrubbed the dog's head. "Once I get used to that creepy smile of yours, we should be fine."

Haus leaned into Alex like they were long-lost family members. Despite her best attempts at being indifferent to the likely rascal of a man, the way he grinned into Haus' face reminded her of a little boy in need of a good friend.

Daggone, her soft heart! Her mama would be so proud.

She crossed her arms in front of her chest to ward off any further warming to the man. Alex caught her staring and offered a flirty wink.

Rainey squeezed her eyes closed and continued her determined steps forward, pushing the house door open and allowing Sarah to skip inside ahead of her. Rainey's assumptions received beating after beating, which upped her edginess level to the look-but-don't-touch zone with more certainty.

"Ah, Mama's left you some"—she peeked beneath the aluminum foil of the closest dish on the counter—"homemade lasagn—"

She turned to finish her statement, but Alex was right next to her, peering over her shoulder. She jumped back and nearly knocked some creamed broccoli off the counter. "Goodness gracious, Alex Murdock. Didn't your mama ever teach you about personal space?"

His expression wavered, tinted with a wound, before he cloaked it with a grin. "Of course she did, but there are times when personal space is all based on personal preference, and being close to you and that lasagna trumped etiquette."

Her face blasted with a new wave of warmth, and she pushed past him into the living area, its rich colors of reds and golds warming the previously bland exterior. Emma's favorite colors. Rainey would have gone with blues, but she couldn't deny how the dark autumn hues brought out the rich hardwoods with a perfect blend of homespun charm. "There's a list of important information on the counter by the refrigerator, along with a landline phone."

He raised his cell in response, but she shrugged. "Just a warning. Cell phones aren't highly reliable around here because of the mountains, so most folks still keep a landline."

"Didn't you say something about being my neighbor?" His grin crooked in a come-hither sort of way that sent her stomach lurching toward the door.

"We sure are," came Sarah's sweet voice, which stopped Rainey in her tracks. "We live right up there on the hill."

"Come on, Sarah." Rainey took her daughter by the shoulders before her little darling invited the man for dinner. "I'm sure Dr. Murdock wants to settle in."

"Is that your house up there? The one with the porch that wraps all the way around it?"

Rainey squeezed her eyes closed and released a stream of air through her nose. Super. Casanova knew exactly where she lived.

"Mmmhmm," came her little sweetheart's friendly reply. "That's my window on the tippy top. I can see right down onto your roof."

The two peered through the window toward Rainey's house like best buddies. "I bet you have a pretty view from way up there. A great spot for a princess."

Sarah giggled, and Rainey almost allowed the tiny sliver of warmth a temporary residence in her heart toward this *GQ* acquaintance. What a puzzle! Her natural caution, a byproduct of betrayal, brought a wariness to question every man's motives—especially the men that seemed to smile too much—but a gentleness peeked from beneath the pretty-boy persona she couldn't deny, causing a curiosity she wouldn't admit.

Didn't Alex deserve the benefit of the doubt? She shook away the whispered suspicion and cleared her throat. "Come on, sweet pea. We need to get on home."

Sarah tipped her face up to Alex, bestowing her sweetest smile. "Bye, Dr. Alex. You're gonna like Granny's lasagna."

"I'm sure I will."

He followed them to the door, where Rainey ushered Sarah outside first before turning toward him. "Can you remember your way back to the university from here?"

Alex stared down the road and then settled those pale green eyes back on her. "I think so."

"Well, you should have plenty of food to get you through the week, but if you did want to venture into town or maybe even up on the Blue Ridge Parkway, the signage is pretty clear from the end of Mitchell's Crossroads."

He rubbed the back of his neck and squinted at her. "With classes starting on Monday, I think I'll buckle down and prep the rest of this week and probably all weekend, but thanks."

"You ain't gonna work on Sunday, are you, Dr. Alex?"

His grin crooked and he bent down to Sarah's level. "Did you have something else in mind?"

"We go to church just down the road and then we get to eat up at Granny's. Granny invites everybody to come eat her good cookin'. I bet she'd love to have you—"

"Dr. Murdock probably has other plans for Sunday." Rainey kept nudging Sarah farther down the steps. It was plain as day Alex Murdock wasn't the churchgoing type, and the last thing Sarah needed was to have another one of her "heroes" fail. She might not remember much about her daddy, but she recalled enough to have quieted around almost every male outside the family. Except Alex. Weird. "Not everyone has the same Sunday schedule we do."

Sarah swung her head around and stared with wide blue eyes at Alex. "You go to church, don't you, Dr. Alex?"

His face paled, lips frozen crooked.

Rainey cringed and took Sarah's hand, making it to the jeep. "If you need something, remember Mama and my brother Trigg's numbers are by the phone." She opened the jeep door for Sarah, but the little girl kept her focus on Alex, who'd followed their exit to the bottom of the porch stairs. "Firewood is in the shed next to the garage."

"I'll be there."

His words stopped Rainey as she pulled Sarah's buckle around. Sarah popped up to stand on the edge of the seat so her face reached over the door, blond curls bouncing.

"What?"

"Church." He cleared his throat and lifted one shoulder into a shrug as if he were trying to get his muscles used to his confession as much as his mouth. "I'll be at church on Sunday. What time?"

Rainey blinked, looked at her little girl, whose face brightened, then back to Alex, processing this new information—and feeling a sudden sense of guilt at wishing he'd never agreed to go to her church. *Her* church. Her safe place.

"Um … ten forty-five."

"In the morning?"

She focused in on him with an "Are you an idiot?" stare, and one of his golden eyebrows slanted in playful challenge. Her stomach flipped like a pancake. Her best efforts at a disapproving frown failed. "I'm sure you'll figure it out, Sherlock."

Alex relaxed his position against the doorframe as he watched Rainey's jeep disappear into a cloud of dust. He'd never seen a place like this, at least not in real life. In black-and-white on the television screen, maybe. Trees with bare spindly branches couched the country cottage in a dip between rolling pastures on every side. Sure, he'd spent years in Charlottesville, Virginia as a professor at UVA, but he hadn't ventured out beyond the streetlamps and highways. He'd never needed to. This home and countryside were as relaxing and welcoming as Rainey Mitchell was reserved and suspicious.

But he'd glimpsed a few instances of softening. Maybe. A little.

She'd asked him to tone down the charm? Be authentic? He stared out along the empty road and stepped up to the porch railing, breathing in the wintry air. What did that even mean anyway?

And then there was Sarah. Breath whooshed from his lungs, and he jabbed his fingers through his hair. Everything about Sarah reminded him of his niece, all the way down to the dimples. His chest ached for one glimpse of a little face gone from his sight much too long.

He stuffed the fragile memories beneath all the other piled-up wounds and groaned. Church? How'd he get wrangled into attending church? He shook his head and sighed his breath into the cool afternoon air. He'd have agreed to anything to keep that look of admiration on Sarah's face. All starry-eyed and hopeful.

Haus stared back at him from his sunny spot on the other side of the long front porch, his big brown eyes thoughtful. "I'm pathetic, man."

Haus' head perked up, his right ear taking its lazy time to lift.

"I mean, dog." Alex waved a hand toward the large black canine and took a few steps across the porch. "Don't want to offend you. People aren't always the nicest sort, you know."

Haus stretched to a stand and ambled forward, his grin growing with each step. Alex stifled a grimace and shrugged away the eeriness of the bared teeth. The dog sat by Alex's legs for a pat to the head. "I can already tell you're a good listener. I like that in a housemate. It's a lot nicer than getting the evil eye from blondie back there." Haus' grin fell. "Right? What's the deal with her anyway?"

"She's a woman. That's the only answer there is."

Alex blinked down at the dog as if he'd achieved the ability to speak and then jerked his head toward a rustling of leaves to his right. An older gentleman emerged from around the side of the house, pipe clutched between his teeth, balding head uncovered, and one hand resting in his brown coat pocket. Visions of Alfred Hitchcock photos blazed a terrifying trail through Alex's brain.

Maybe that wasn't the best comparison for a stranger out in the middle of nowhere.

Alex stepped behind Haus. The dog's grin broadened. Yep, that wasn't helpful at all.

"You gotta be careful of that one too. She's the most dangerous kind." The stranger held to the step railing and climbed each one at a slow pace.

Curiosity overrode survival instincts. "What kind is that?"

"Memorable. Like her mama and grandmamma." He stopped in his climb, looked up at Alex, smiling enough to add crinkles to the permanent ones at the corners of his eyes. "And strong."

Alex studied the man as he finished his climb up the steps. "So … um … do you live around here?"

The man didn't answer until he'd reached the top step and righted himself. Haus, the not-so-guard-dog, moved to the man's side for a friendly greeting. The stranger then stood upright, an inch or two shorter than Alex.

He pulled the pipe from his mouth and blew out a large cloud before giving Alex a steady perusal with piercing blue eyes. "I do now."

Alex rested his hands on his hips and stiffened his smile. He already preferred Haus' creepy grin as a possible housemate feature to the pipe-smoking horror author.

The man pointed his pipe toward the hillside where Rainey's jeep had disappeared. "Got some of my grandnephews movin' me in as we speak."

Alex's suspicion relaxed along with his smile. "So you're a Mitchell."

"A Ross, actually. Jim Ross. Grace Mitchell's uncle." He shuffled past Alex and walked into the house, carrying the smell of pipe tobacco and menthol with him. "Heard there was lasagna down here."

Alex stared at the man's retreating back and looked down at Haus. The dog took the open-door opportunity to his advantage and waltzed right in behind the pipe-wielding stranger. Alex was pretty sure he could take Jim Randall if he turned psycho, so with a glance over his shoulder and a resigned shrug, he walked inside and closed the door behind him.

"You said you just moved in today? Like me?"

The stranger had already located a plate—two in fact—and was piling on lasagna, but he looked up at Alex's question. "That's right."

Alex placed the man's accent in Appalachia. "So, are you from around here originally?"

The man opened a few drawers and finally located a fork. "Down closer to North Carolina, but it's all part of the same mountains, if that's what you mean. My brother, Harvey Ross, bought land up this way and settled here, so the land's passed down to his young'uns and grandyoung'uns."

Alex took up a plate and gathered some dinner of his own. The savory scents swelled the room with warmth and welcome, something the entire house seemed to do.

Mrs. Mitchell, this landlady he'd only heard about through his former colleague, Dee, already presented a persona he didn't quite understand. Food? An entire banquet for her renter? As he scanned her note on the counter giving him information on the house, something beyond ink and paper reached out to him. Welcome. Kindness. Two attitudes as foreign to him as grinning dogs and country men with pipes.

A familiar *ding* broke the awkward silence, followed by a vibration. Both phones at once? Heat flushed Alex's face and he shot Mr. Ross a glance, making certain the man wasn't paying too close attention. With quick movements, Alex drew both phones out of his jacket pocket.

He sighed and read over a text from one of his colleagues in Charlottesville, carefully sliding the other phone, blue and special, into his pocket to check later. He shot back a reply and then continued to add more lasagna to his plate. The fewer people who knew about the blue phone, the better.

"You teach at the university?" Mr. Ross settled himself down in one of the four chairs around the round table in the kitchen.

"Sure do." Alex hoped so, anyway. He'd procrastinated about as long as a professor could before planning became a desperate act of survival—all in hopes that somehow fate might turn in his favor and he wouldn't have to move to the backwoods of Appalachia to continue his career.

Clearly, fate was not kind. "What's brought you back to these parts, Mr. Ross?"

"Jim," the man corrected and wiped his mouth with the back of his hand. "Or you can call me Uncle Jim, as most other folks do." He shoveled another bite into his mouth, then sat back in his chair. "Grace offered me a place near family, and since I ain't got no family anywhere else, I reckoned it the best choice. Ain't no place like bein' with family."

Alex took a drink of his water to cover his grimace. With his sister gone, the last thing he wanted to do was see his family. It rarely ended well. Alex took a bite of the lasagna and nearly melted into the chair. The combination of creaminess and spice created the perfect blend over his tongue. Mrs. Mitchell was already his hero ... and he hadn't even met her yet.

"You got family, boy?"

Alex nearly choked on the swallow. *All this family talk must be a country thing.* He loosened his grin. "Doesn't everyone?"

Jim narrowed his eyes as he took a drink of his water and slowly set the glass back on the table. "I've studied on it for a good many years now, and I don't reckon that's so, but I s'pose it's what you mean by family, ain't it?"

The direct, steely gaze nearly broke Alex into a sweat. "I reckon so." He tried to add levity by taking on the man's dialect and scooped in another mouthful of lasagna to deflect the man's stare.

Jim grunted. "You like fishin'?"

Alex paused the forkful of cheesy goodness halfway to his lips. "Fishing for what?"

Jim's mouth hinted at the slightest smile. "Fish, I reckon."

"Can't say I've ever been fishing for fish, Jim."

The older man finished his glass of water, allowing silence to pass between them as Alex took a few more bites. Alex squelched the urge to laugh at the current situation. Two months ago he'd been in a nice apartment in Charlottesville, Virginia planning a lifelong career in academia and now? The lasagna lodged in his tightening throat. Now he sat in a country cottage on the outskirts of the Appalachian town of Ransom, Virginia preparing to teach in an upstart program and talking to a stranger about family and fishing.

Maybe he was caught in a weird dream.

The quiet stretched to such an uncomfortable point, Alex pushed back his empty plate and nodded to his new acquaintance. "So ... um ... Jim, are lasagna and my fishing habits the only things that brought you for a visit today?"

"Nah, I got another reason for comin' down." The man pressed his palms against the table and leaned forward, his pale eyes pinning Alex to his seat. "I wanted to know what kind of loon would drive a car like that down a road like this."

Alex squinted, attempting to sort out Jim's accusation. "My car?"

"Yeah." The man pushed back his chair and stood. "Come on and take me for a ride to prove why you done such a fool thing. We can talk about fishin'."

The look on Jim Randall's face brooked no refusal, and for the life of him, Alex couldn't think of one reason to turn down the man's request. If anyone could win over an odd neighbor, it was Marilyn.

Chapter Four

Rainey needed a good sit-down with her mama to gain perspective on this Gray situation, but then her mom would offer her money, and that's not what Rainey wanted either. Her life had been decidedly better emotionally without any contact from Gray, apart from a Christmas card with some cash to buy Sarah a present.

And Alex Murdock at her school? His easy charm and overall sanguine disposition reminded her so much of Gray, distrust climbed up in her throat at the thought. She knew those judgments about Alex were wrong, but they ambushed her senses anyway, like flashing warning lights in the back of her mind every time he looked at her.

His smile was fine. Her lips almost quivered in response to the mental image. Too fine for her clear-headed thinking, evidently, but his smile held lots of secrets.

And secrets bothered her.

Gray's infidelity went on for a year before Rainey uncovered it. She'd spent months excavating lies, each new discovery hammering another nail of betrayal through the vows they'd taken.

She moaned and ran her palms over her face. To beat it all, while the entire family unloaded Uncle Jim's things into his newly refurbished cottage, her crazy uncle had gone on a joyride with Alex. Rainey could almost hear every male around her groan with appreciation of the gorgeous car when Alex had pulled up the driveway to her mama's house. Of course, her brothers held enough common sense to never entertain the idea of purchasing such an impractical vehicle, even if they appreciated its sleek curves from a distance. In all honesty, with such a car, a little ogling couldn't be helped.

And Alex with Uncle Jim?

Oh, what sort of mischief could those two conjure? Just the thought of Alex emerging from that car in all his suave masculinity twisted her stomach into a wrench hold, a contradiction.

She collapsed into her office chair and dropped her work bag on the floor. She did *not* want to be attracted to Alex Murdock. At all.

With a weighty groan, she made a mental note to call Dave Stevens for a possible follow-up date. The youth pastor had asked her for a second date weeks ago, and she'd stalled because, though he was a great guy with a predictably vanilla personality and a whole lot of safe stability, the attraction fizzled on low.

Her terror in making a big mistake again probably didn't help.

Mama's signature Thursday-morning-treat sat on Rainey's desk in a little Ziploc and Styrofoam cup. She smiled and opened the bag, taking in the delicious scent of raspberry scones and fresh-brewed coffee. With a tap of her laptop, the screen came to life, and she leaned back in her chair to enjoy her scone as her e-mails loaded. The sweet therapy of flour and sugar unwound her frenzied thoughts as only fresh-baked goodness and hot java could do.

Oh, when her mama retired from her position as cleaning staff for the university someday, Rainey would miss this carb-laden morning greeting. Mama probably left the same gift on Alex's desk, but as Rainey hadn't noticed Marilyn in the parking lot when she'd arrived, she doubted Alex had yet to experience the deliciousness of the breakfast treats. The tiniest twinge of guilt wiggled through her middle. Maybe she should've stopped to ask him if he needed directions from Mitchell's Crossroads to the university, but after his joyride with Uncle Jim, she assumed he could find his way out of their little cove.

An e-mail from her department chair pulled her back to her computer screen.

COME SEE ME AS SOON AS YOU GET INTO YOUR OFFICE THIS MORNING. WE NEED TO TALK ASAP.

Rainey leaned close and reread Dr. Shaye Russell's message. Something about the brevity and directness stole heat from Rainey's body and shoved her into motion. With the infantile Communication Disorders graduate program and the many complications of new hires, she could only imagine what exploded the weekend before their second semester of classes started. She pushed away from her desk and made her way up the stairs, her leg muscles, strong from her regular morning jogs, moving her at a quick speed.

The chair's office, nestled on the top floor, stood with the door slightly ajar. Rainey peeked in, always a little envious at the three large windows welcoming light into the bookshelf-lined room.

Shaye sat at her desk, head in her hands, and an unsettling number of boxes scattered across the floor. Was she changing offices again? She'd hinted at moving down to the main floor for a few months, but Rainey couldn't figure out why she'd ever want to leave the view from her top-floor space.

"Shaye?"

The woman, in her mid-fifties, raised her tired gray eyes, a frown pulling at her lips. Every warning flare in Rainey's body fired in unison. "Rainey, thank you for coming." She gestured toward a chair nearby. "Please close the door and have a seat."

Rainey scanned the boxes and the half-empty shelves as she pulled the door to a close and took a seat. "This looks ... interesting?"

Shaye rubbed a hand over her face and sighed back into her chair, eyes closed. "I suppose I should have shared with you the political banter before now, but I thought the dean and assistant dean would see the value of service over the limited funds. I was wrong." She shook her head and looked up. "I'm sorry, Rainey."

Rainey pinched the arms of the chair and leaned forward. "What do you mean?"

Shaye pushed a paper across her desk, and Rainey took it. "For the past year Dean Mercer and I have held several meetings regarding Tolliver Learning Center and its benefits to our college, and our department in particular. You know we've had to fight for that center since she became the dean."

Rainey ignored the message stabbing in between Shaye's sentences. The foreboding. "But we won her support every time."

Shaye nodded. "And each fight was met with more resistance." Shaye released another sigh and locked gazes with Rainey. "She's recently been pressured to reallocate the center's resources—to support a more lucrative option, and since the grant funding part of TLC's runs out this year, she's less inclined to see the full benefits of the clinic's existence."

Rainey's breath halted at the implication. *No.*

"You mean Dr. Mercer wants to close down TLC?" The question raked across her throat.

"She doesn't just want to. She is." Shaye pointed to the paper in Rainey's hands. "The decision has already been made. TLC will finish out its school year with funding gradually being redirected to a separate account and then…"

"What? Then what?" Rainey's mind spilled through possibilities. Part of the funding came from a combination of a grant, private sources, and insurance reimbursement for the patients they treated, but all of the tutoring and one of the salaries was provided free to children in the community and supported by funds from the university. Tens of thousands of dollars, easily. She scanned the paper. "They're going to create a university school? That's what they're doing with the funds from TLC?" Rainey slammed the paper back on the desk. "You know a school in the middle of town only helps the upper-middle-class families. What about the ones we see at TLC? They can't carpool to a school miles away from their homes."

"I'm sorry, Rainey. I tried everything."

Rainey stood, pacing the room like a tiger on the hunt. TLC had been a dream eight years ago that emerged into a reality to touch hundreds of families. What would happen to them? Where would they find the same kind of support they received now ... for free? "We have to do something. What can we do?"

Shaye lowered her head and then gestured to the boxes. "I'm afraid 'we' won't be doing anything. I've been encouraged to take an early retirement."

Rainey's legs lost strength and she dissolved into the chair. "What?"

"It was mutual." Shaye released a humorous laugh. "I told Dr. Mercer I didn't want to be affiliated with a group of individuals who thought the greater good only involved a small number of children. The committee basically told me to get behind their current plans or get out of the way."

"No, Shaye." Rainey's words barely made a sound.

She waved away Rainey's concern. "I'll be all right. I just hate that you and those families are in this position. I have plenty saved to take care of my needs, so you can plan on me showing up at TLC to help as I can. In fact, I'm planning to volunteer starting next month, because you'll need it."

Rainey gasped from another blow. "What do you mean?"

"They were going to pull part of their funds this month, but I convinced them that you needed time to speak with your employees at TLC. Dr. Mercer and her committee plan to begin reducing funds next month."

The implications bled through Rainey's foggy thoughts. She squeezed her eyes closed to fight back the building heat of angry tears. Jamie and Laura's jobs. Her blurry gaze dropped back to the paper and focused on the reduced support quote. There was no way she could keep both of them. The office manager was necessary, so Jamie would be the one staying, but with the financial cut, she couldn't keep a full-time tutor. Maybe Laura could work part time?

"I'll help tutor, Rainey," Shaye said, reading Rainey's thoughts. "And I bet Lizzie would be willing to offer sometimes too. She's worked with you for years. She knows your dedication and love for TLC."

Rainey pressed her fingers into her forehead and stood, pacing out her frustration. "There has to be something I can do. Anything to salvage this. If we keep the donors we have, then that covers some cost, right?"

Shaye's compassion stirred another bout of watery eyes. "Some, Rainey, but not enough."

"And I just can't ask them for more. They've given so much to TLC already."

"I've been working through options, so I printed out a list of possible grants for you to research, all with an emphasis on educating low socio-economic communities and a few focused on Appalachia. The funds wouldn't be available for this upcoming year, but they may be for the next or even the following year."

Rainey worried her bottom lip and slumped in the chair, the very thought of engaging the laborious task of grant writing stealing a little of the steam out of her fight. "I'm not the best grant writer out there."

Shaye tapped the paper and caught Rainey's gaze. "Maybe not, but do you realize 80 percent of the grants Alex Murdock has written have been funded? I reviewed his file, remember? It was one of his winning qualities. It seems he lathers on the charm in every aspect of his life, and in this case, it's been beneficial for a lot of folks."

So the guy wields winning and benevolent charm? That was new.

"And since you're going to be helping him in my stead, you'd have time to pick his brain and perhaps gain some insight for your own grant writing. Maybe even garner his help."

Rainey caught on to the weird glitch in Shaye's support. "Helping him? What are you talking about?" Her thoughts still snagged two sentences behind on the fact that she was losing her precious learning center ... and she'd have to write grants to possibly save it.

"Since I'm leaving, I'd like you to be his guide in the transition to Blue Ridge. Give him direction, offer support." Shaye waved toward her. "You know, your usual helpful, kind self."

Rainey stared at her friend. They'd known each other six years, and this was the first time she'd ever heard Shaye speak in a foreign language. "Me? Help Dr. Murdock?"

Shaye's previous frown took on a lighter tilt. "Yes, you."

"Why me?"

"Because Dr. Langley is going to be taking my place and, you know as well as I, she isn't the right choice for supporting one of *our* lecturers. The woman hardly knows what a speech-language pathologist does, and she certainly can't teach."

"Teach?" What did teaching have to do with Alex or this situation? "Then ask Lizzie. She already works with adults and, if I recall, Dr. Murdock's therapy is focused on the adult population, not child."

"He'll take whatever he can at this point to make his position work." Shaye lifted a stack of folders and turned to place them in one of the empty boxes behind her. "But from what I understand, he's quite good with both populations." She raised her gaze back to Rainey. "Perhaps he could help at TLC too?"

He didn't strike her as the volunteering sort, but with her biased view, she was still trying to digest any attributes to charm and flirting.

A flash of Alex with Sarah rocketed to the front of her mind. Sweet. Gentle. She wiped it away. Too distracting. "But he's teaching classes like Phonological Disorders and Motor Speech Disorders." Rainey grimaced at the memories of those courses. Not her favorites. "Both of which would align more to Lizzie's specialty areas than mine."

Shaye turned in her chair, fingers meeting in a teepee and a strange expression tinting the exhaustion on her face. "Lizzie is already supervising our other new faculty member, Geoffrey Percy, the one taking over Voice and Fluency. Besides, from what I understand, Dr. Murdock could use some support in teaching—a specialty in which you excel."

Rainey blew past the compliment. "Can't you think of anybody else? I'll need to focus on saving this clinic, not handholding Mr. GQ."

Handholding? That didn't come out quite right.

Shaye's smile spread wide with her chuckle. "Since Mr. GQ has a fabulous track record in grant writing, perhaps you two could teach each other a few things. One colleague helping another. That doesn't sound intimidating to me." Her manicured brow peaked. "What's wrong, Rainey? Are you afraid it's too much for you?"

Sour milk smelled better than this scheme. Rainey bit back every desire to run. "I'm not afraid. I just don't see how this is going to work. We're not exactly in the same book personality-wise, let alone on the same page."

"Oh, you work wonders with people." Shaye nodded, patting Rainey on the shoulder as she stood. "I have every faith you'll turn this to your advantage, and Dr. Murdock will be the better for it."

"Ugh," Rainey groaned. "Assuming I survive all of his flirting."

Shaye laughed. "Flirting can be fun now and again, Rainey. You could do with a dose of fun to lighten up your serious world a little."

Rainey groaned. "I'd prefer to be out of practice and in the shadows, thanks."

"He could help you save the clinic." Shaye's gaze sobered, a strange mixture of sadness and hope colliding in Rainey's chest.

"Oh, the irony that my hero would be someone like Alex Murdock." Rainey drew in a deep breath and bit back a long diatribe on the many reasons why it was sure to fail. "But to save the clinic?" She sighed in reluctant resignation. "I'll do whatever it takes."

Alex read over the class notes his colleague from Charlottesville had sent, eyes blurring from the massive amount of content. Motor Speech Disorders class information remained as interesting as it had been in college. Why did he get the least fun class to teach?

He took the last bite of his raspberry scone, still a little awed by Mrs. Mitchell's thoughtful surprise to him for the morning. A sudden rush of emotions constricted his swallow and he downed the last of his coffee. He'd barely met the woman for five minutes when he'd dropped Jim off at Mrs. Mitchell's, but she'd welcomed him with a kindness he didn't quite understand.

He blinked the computer screen back into view and groaned, swiveling away from the desk and hopping to his feet. The receptionist, Joy, had mentioned fresh coffee was available in the faculty lounge. Even if the brew tasted like Styrofoam, he needed a break from the monotony of study. At least the Phonological Disorders class showcased his expertise, but Motor Speech? He grimaced and shook his head. No, he couldn't fail. Not again.

He turned the corner of his office door and ran right into a forward-moving bullet of a person. A curiously familiar blonde with a tantalizing scent of citrus. He caught her by the waist to keep her from toppling, and her slim body pressed against him long enough for Alex to take inventory.

Her head came up, and Alex stared into Rainey Mitchell's aqua eyes. Her pupils widened and she pushed back from him, flushed cheeks deepening to rose. His breath strained to a stop. Those eyes, so close, swarming with a sheen of tears, paralyzed him. Alex knew attraction. Heck, he felt it often. But this? This sudden chink in Rainey Mitchell's armored expressions pinged on an emotion he hadn't experienced in a long time. Heart deep.

She wiped a hand across her face and cleared the look of vulnerability away. "What are you doing?"

"Keeping you from falling. Why the hurry?"

She opened her mouth as if she might say something, but then she clipped those pink lips closed and bypassed him without another word. So much for the glimmer of vulnerability.

Alex looked up in time to see a woman stick her head out of her office, her honey-colored hair falling over her shoulder as she peered into the hallway. He'd met her yesterday, if he recalled. One of the other professors and an adult language therapist. Lizzie, wasn't it?

He nodded in her direction and thumbed in Rainey's direction. "She's a real charmer."

Lizzie's smile lit with compassion. "She's had a rough week."

Alex glanced back the way Rainey disappeared, still feeling the pressure of her body against him. She was a great height for hugs. Just under his chin. Of course, her hugs would probably be more like wrestling.

And then his mind took a nosedive into how much fun those sorts of hugs might be, so he turned his attention back to Lizzie. "Well, that explains a little of her overwhelming friendliness, especially to guys."

Lizzie tilted her head, brow tipped. "Guys? What do you mean?"

"She has a real problem with men in general, it seems—and especially dads getting rights to their kids. She practically called the police on a man who showed up here last week looking for his kid. Then she acts like I'm carrying the plague every time she's around me." His palms came up in defense. "I'm healthy manhood here."

Lizzie examined him and added an eye roll that matched the one Rainey doused on an hourly basis. With a shake of her head and a pinched smile, she ushered him into her office a few doors down. By the time he entered her space, her smile carried more sadness than annoyance, and he nursed the too-familiar weight of guilt. "Listen, I didn't mean anything by what I said. I'm sure she's got a lot to deal with as a single mom, but it's pretty clear she has a chip on her shoulder the size of this building."

She waved away his words and slowly closed the office door behind him. He sat in one of her office chairs, awaiting his verbal beating. Girlfriends were a dangerous gaggle.

Lizzie perched on the corner of her desk, arms folded and hazel eyes fixed on him, but not in the "death by tongue-lashing" sort of way. "You walked into the middle of a lot of things, Dr. Murdock, and since you're going to be here for a while, someone needs to fill you in on all the missing pieces so you don't continue to look like a jerk or jump to the wrong conclusions."

"Thanks." His grin spread along with a sense of relief. "Where have you been all my life?"

She chuckled and unfolded her arms, planting her palms against the desk behind her. "Okay, a true-hearted jerk wouldn't be so quick to admit help, so I'm going to take a risk here and test that theory." She sighed, pushing her long hair off her shoulder and moving to sit in the chair beside him. "Rainey and I have been friends for almost ten years, so I know her pretty well. She's strong and determined, as you've probably already noticed."

"And then some."

"Right." Lizzie grinned, relaxing her posture a little more. "And she's needed both of those character traits all too often. Within the last five years, she's lost her dad to cancer and her oldest brother was diagnosed with it. Thankfully, her brother is now cancer-free and trying to step back into a normal life, but, needless to say, her emotions have been stretched thin."

Alex's stomach grabbled with tension. He hated the word "cancer." And losing someone to it? Oh, he knew the residual ache all too well.

"A few years ago she found out her husband was having an affair with her sister-in-law."

Alex bent forward from the blow. "What?"

"If she's leery of charming and charismatic men, she has her reasons." Lizzie sat back in the chair. "Gray moved out after everything came to a head, and they've kept communication to a minimum over the past two years since he left—that is, until last week, when she e-mailed him about support for Sarah."

"So here's another dad she won't allow to see his daughter?" The conversation he'd heard through the door seemed to paint a less-than-rosy picture of Rainey. "Seems to be the theme. I heard the same conversation from her last week in the office."

"I think the argument you overheard last week was of a very different and much more dangerous nature. Rainey and one of her undergraduate students had to report Mr. Edwards to Social Services because of abuse."

Alex winced.

"Exactly. Never a fun experience for anyone involved. She tried to be as discreet as possible, but some of the information came out. Mrs. Edwards and their children were placed in protective custody, and Mr. Edwards followed the trail back to Rainey. He's become more and more volatile."

Alex let out a long breath and pressed his palms into his knees. "Whoa."

"Yeah."

Silence permeated the moment as Alex digested the new information. The similarity between his sister's situation and Rainey's was uncanny, particularly with his fiery coworker's tumultuous relationship with Mr. Edwards. Rainey and his sister even resembled each other a little with their blond hair and stubborn personalities.

Poor Sarah, in the middle of all this. He'd jumped to the wrong conclusions too. "Does Rainey's ex want to see his daughter?"

"He hasn't seemed to show much of an interest so far."

Alex groaned. Regardless of what the parents had to work through, a dad should want to see his kid.

"Show her some grace, okay? There's an incredible woman underneath all of that hurt." Lizzie's smile returned. "Even if you don't always see it."

Grace? The word dug into him. He'd heard it before, but it never applied to him. The screwup? Yes—more times than he wished to count. One wrong choice, poor word, bad step after another. Even when his choices glowed with excellent intentions, the consequences blew up in his face, like the reason that had brought him to Ransom.

But grace? No. Most people didn't really give second chances, let alone hundreds.

He thought about the stubborn blonde and the misty vulnerability permeating through her aqua eyes.

"We all need grace, don't we?" Lizzie's marble gaze softened with her gentle smile.

"Yeah, we sure do."

Chapter Five

Sarah jumped out of the car as soon as it came to a stop in front of Mama's house, running to meet her cousin Lou on the tire swing. Oh, to be that carefree again. Rainey sighed and took the stairs to the porch of her mama's sprawling ranch overlooking the valley below. On the opposite hill, her own house faced her mama's, a testament to Rainey's hard work. Like TLC.

She'd designed that house, saved for the down payment, and watched while workers turned her paper dream into an adorable cottage on the hill. A tremor of pride heightened her stride. She could do this too. She could save TLC.

Her older brother's truck sat in the driveway, readied for his first weekend trip to Charlottesville for his new job as an agricultural consultant. Rainey grinned and continued her walk into the house. He'd probably visit Dee, his fiancée, too. With their flash-fast wedding in four months, they had tons to discuss.

Rainey pushed open her mama's front door, the scent of cinnamon and thick aroma of beef stew greeting her as she stepped over the threshold. Her stomach growled in appreciation. There was no place like home.

The room opened up from the dining room all the way into the kitchen where pots hung from the oak-beamed ceiling. Her mama loved this big room where everyone could "visit" and enjoy the company and noise of a big family. And somehow, her mama always managed to have a dish of cookies waiting for the next person to stumble through the door.

"Just in time to help peel some apples." Her mama's welcome pulled Rainey the rest of the way into the house.

"I knew I should've waited twenty more minutes before showing up." Rainey shot her mama a grin and bumped past her to wash her hands at the large-basined sink. "I never can get my timing right."

Mama's smile turned ruthless. "You could take some lessons from your uncle, then. He has the well-practiced ability to show up right when all the work is done."

Rainey chuckled and slipped the towel off the oven handle. "How's he doing? Been here four whole days and already causing mischief?"

Mama shook her head and smiled. "Manageable mischief at least." Her brow quirked. "For now."

Rainey slid beside her mom and snatched the apples away. "Where's Reese?"

"He's out back with Trigg unloading firewood. He plans to take some to Dr. Murdock later in the week. Says it's supposed to get real cold in the next few weeks."

Rainey flinched at the mention of Alex, the memory of his arms around her still playing havoc with her common sense. He'd toned down his cologne, replacing whatever pungent scent he had on when they first met with a more enticing mix of sandalwood and soap—a combination that made a woman want to linger … forever. Hmm … he'd taken her advice.

She ignored the prickly heat finger-tipping up her neck into her cheeks and delved into peeling apples with a vengeance.

"Is he settlin' in all right?"

Rainey looked up from her slaughtered apple. "Hmm? Dr. Murdock? I suppose so."

"Do you reckon he'd want to come join us for a meal on Sunday? He's bound to be lonesome at that house all the time."

"Oh, I wouldn't worry about Alex Murdock, Mama. He's the sort that finds company, I'm sure."

Her mama stopped slicing butter for the bread rolls she'd just pulled from the oven. "Ah, you've pegged him already, have you?"

"It's not that difficult." But even her statement raised doubt within her heart. "He has the charm down to princely proportions."

"Hey, lovelies," Emma called from the doorway, tossing her red purse into the rocking chair nearby. The youngest Mitchell still had her waitress apron on beneath her winter jacket but quickly removed them both to collect with her discarded purse. "Something smells scrumptious, Mama."

"All should be ready in about ten minutes, except the dessert. But we can eat while it's baking, so it will be nice and warm when the time comes to serve."

"Yum." Emma sashayed over to the counter and plopped herself onto the barstool, snatching up a piece of the apple peeling. "What's your topic of conversation that's leaving Rainey with a sour lemon look on her face?"

"I do not have a—"

"I was asking Rainey if our new renter is settlin' in well."

"Alex?" Emma popped the apple peel between her red-stained lips.

"Dr. Murdock."

Emma ignored Rainey. "Alex has been by the restaurant three times already this week. He seems to be doing well from that big ol' grin on his face. The other girls sure do like to see him walk in with his sweet talk and ready charm."

"Told ya he wouldn't be lonely for long," Rainey growled under her breath, taking out a whole side of the apple in her hand. "A little too free with his charm, if you ask me. It's unnerving."

"Oh, come on, Rainey, be nice." Emma pushed back a handful of her silky, caramel-colored hair and flashed a smile to her sister. "A little bit of flirting doesn't mean he's out to hurt anybody."

Rainey slapped the knife down on the table. "You have no idea. The man has enough ... woman power wafting off him to upend a convent."

"Woman power?" Mama raised a brow along with her lopsided grin.

Emma laughed and reached for another apple peeling. "Oh goodness, he's harmless. All that flirting is nothing but smoke. Well, I guess it's more like cologne." She sighed. "Sandalwood and such a smile."

"Don't even go there, Emma." Rainey pointed the small paring knife into the air. "Pretty is as pretty does, isn't that right, Mama? And we don't know much about him except for that pretty smile."

"Hush." Emma shook her head. "I'm only window-shopping. Alex is too old for me."

"Dr. Murdock," Rainey corrected again, making a poor attempt at keeping control of her inside voice. "And he's not that much older than your best friend, Jonathan."

"Jonathan's twenty-eight."

The way her baby sister exaggerated the age, a mere five years older than her, didn't help Rainey's attitude at all. "And I'd bet Alex is scraping by at thirty."

"Thirty? Really?" Emma's nose wrinkled in a grimace, then her smile flashed much too wide. "That makes him much closer to your age, sis."

"Oh no!" Rainey tossed the sliced apples into a prepared bowl of a sugary concoction of her mother's. "Don't you dare start your whole matchmaking voodoo on me, especially with someone like Alex Murdock."

"What's got your back up about poor Dr. Murdock, Rainey Mitchell?

He seems to take up a lot of space in that head of yours." Emma wiggled her manicured brows. "You're even grumpy about him."

"He is not taking up space in my head." Except the very mention of him and his sandalwood scent evoked visions Rainey refused to entertain. She pressed her fingers into her forehead and refused to look at her yenta-inspired little sister. "I just know his type."

"Right." Emma waved the apple peel at her. "Male."

Rainey shot Emma a wilting look, but it bounced off her ruby-red smile like a penny on JELL-O.

Mama came to the rescue. "Emma, Rainey's mature enough not to overgeneralize like that, right, honey?" She patted Rainey's shoulder in a sweet, comforting way, but "honey" really meant "straighten up and don't act stupid" in Grace Mitchell speech.

"Well, I can't really blame her being on edge with all this Gray mess." Emma waved an apple peeling and frowned. "That's the problem."

"No." Rainey sighed and shook her head. "Well, yes, the Gray mess has me on edge, but it's more than that." She sat down onto the barstool. "The university's pulled funding for TLC."

Emma dropped the apple peel in her hand, and Mama's head snapped. "What?"

Rainey explained the whole situation just as her two brothers entered from the back door, both donning their wood-chip-covered flannel.

"Mmmhmmm, something smells mighty good in here." Reese paused long enough to take off his boots and slip off his flannel overshirt. "Hardworking menfolk are surely appreciative." A call from the back room of the house grabbed his attention. "Well now, sounds like Brandon finished his nap just in time for supper."

Trigg lumbered forward and pressed a kiss to Mama's cheek, his signature greeting.

"Ya'll go wash up now, and we'll get the table set," Mama said, her grin still soft from Trigg's affection.

Both her brothers were softies, but Trigg had the gentlest heart, especially toward their mama. In fact, he brought her a rose from his bushes every morning when they were in bloom. Every morning. Rainey tried to work up a little nausea over the sickeningly sweet thought, but all that emerged was a distinct ache in the middle of her chest.

"Why the long face, Tails?" Trigg tugged on her braid as he passed.

"Get on and wash up, Trigg Mitchell." Mama waved her spoon at him and pointed toward the hallway. "We'll talk during supper, but right now this stew getting cold is going to make my face long."

"You mean to tell me that the university's removing funding for a facility that's helping hundreds of kids who can't help themselves and placing the money into a school for the elite?" Reese filled Brandon's plate with another helping of stew, and the adorable little blond rewarded the whole room with a cheesy smile, dimming some of the bite in Reese's words.

"I'm sure there are lots of benefits that I'm not privy to." Rainey took a drink of her tea and shook her head. "And the whole school has taken financial cuts in the last few years, so the fact that they approved TLC when they did is a miracle."

"Well, you're gonna fight for those kids, aren't you, Tails?" Trigg's electric blue eyes, so dark and intense, pinned her with the challenge.

"Of course I am. I've just got to figure out how."

"We'll all pitch in to help," Emma said. "Maybe we could have a big fundraising dinner at Daphne's."

"That's a start," Mama added.

"Shaye mentioned applying for some grants and even sending out a fundraising letter to untapped alumni, if possible."

"Both are good ideas," Reese said. "I'm working on a grant to help fund a position for me to teach at UVA once we move to Charlottesville this summer, but it's a big learning curve. Dee's been a real help in the process, but she's still new at it too."

Rainey perked straighter in her chair at the thought but then deflated. With Reese planning to move, working a couple weekends in Charlottesville, preparing for a wedding, *and* taking care of his two kids, he didn't have time to help her with grant writing.

"Do you know about grant writing?" Trigg asked.

"Not much."

"Will Shaye help you?"

"As much as she can." Rainey hesitated, an unwelcome taste of the anticipated words coating her mouth. "But she recommended I ask Dr. Murdock because his track record with grants is so good."

"Well that's plum perfect, ain't it?" Mama stood to pour Lou and Sarah some more tea. Both girls smiled their thanks, and Mama nudged Rainey as she walked back to her place. "He's just down the road, and you're both in the same department. He's a godsend."

Rainey choked on her tea.

"I think it's absolutely a godsend," Emma interjected, matchmaking fairy dust sparkling in her golden-green eyes. "It'll give you two a chance to get to know each other better, and you may even appreciate his certain brand of charm a little more, Rain."

"I'm certain his brand of charm is not for me," Rainey ground out through clenched teeth.

"Your Uncle Jim has a lot of faults, but he's a good judge of character, and he thinks Alex is a fine fella, just a lonely sort," Mama said. "Maybe you reachin' out to him will help him feel a part of somethin' bigger—part of a community."

Emma completely ignored Rainey's well-intentioned glare by diverting the whole matchmaking topic altogether and sending their mother a faux innocent look of sweet curiosity. "Where is Uncle Jim anyway? Wasn't he going to join us for supper?"

"He stopped by earlier and picked up something to take down to his cabin. Said he was turnin' in early tonight." Mama smiled. "I reckon he needs a bit of quiet after putting up with all of us this week. He's not used to a crowd."

Reese nudged Rainey with his elbow, his smile soft and not helping her watery vision at all. "I had the same conversation with Mama when Dee came to town last fall. I understand your reluctance, Rainey, but all Mama's saying is for you to show Alex some kindness, not sweep him off his feet."

"Knocking him off his feet might be more Rainey's cup of English Breakfast." Emma snickered.

Her little sis needed a good throttling. "Emma Mitchell—"

"Nobody's saying nothin' about datin' the man, Rainey-honey, but if he can help you with TLC?" Mama's voice gentled, pulling Rainey's gaze to hers. "You're a fighter. Don't let a little thing like a handsome face turn you off."

Why did that sound so wrong?

"I'm quite fond of handsome faces, myself." Emma grinned across the table as she took a bite of her stew, eyes alight with scheming.

Rainey cringed. "I just don't want to feel obligated to him in any way."

Because he could use it against her. And she really didn't want to look stupid in front of him. There were few things as demoralizing as constant criticism.

"That's pride right there." Mama's stare stripped away years until Rainey was left feeling like a reprimanded eight-year-old. "All of us need help from others. We ain't been put in this world alone. Asking Alex for help won't be a sign of failure. Maybe he's looking for a place to belong just as bad as you're looking for a place to save."

"And just maybe you can find something worth trading services for?" Trigg broke his silence.

What could Alex Murdock possibly need that she could provide? Just the thought deepened her cringe until her shoulders hurt.

"I bet if you really put your mind to it, you can find a way to make things work. You've always been good at that." Mama touched Rainey's hand, her grin tipping ever so slightly, the sweet comfort in her compassion soothing over some of the frayed edges of Rainey's emotions. "Swallowin' an ounce or two of that resentment and pride sounds like a really good way to start."

And the comforting sweetness vanished.

But they were all right. She had to do something … and all fingers seemed to point to Alex Murdock as the man to ask. Whether she liked it or not.

Alex pulled Marilyn up to the farmhouse as carefully as possible to keep the gravel on the driveway from dinging beneath her luxurious cover. He sighed back into the leathery seat. The weekend! He needed the weekend to figure out how he was going to teach his Motor Speech Disorder class without boring the entire room … or worse, looking like an idiot.

He grabbed his bags and slowly trekked to the front porch. Haus greeted him with the eerie smile, whip-like tail wagging in welcome.

"Hey, buddy." Alex scratched behind the dog's ear. "Hope your day was better than mine."

Haus seemed to catch the frustration in Alex's voice because he nudged Alex toward the door. Rest. Relaxation. A long nap. All of the above sounded like a good way to ignore every responsibility in his life at the moment.

A scrawled note on a bright yellow sticky stuck to the glass panes of the front door.

PICKIN' YOU UP AT 10:30 A.M. ON SUNDAY. BE READY. JIM

Alex jerked the sticky off and opened the front door. He didn't have a way to contact Jim to cancel—and didn't even know what he'd be canceling if he called. There was a good chance Jim was taking the downhill slide toward senility … or something. Sunday? Ten thirty? What on earth happened on Sundays at ten thirty?

A savory aroma teased Alex farther into the house. Mama Mitchell, as she signed her notes, was fast becoming one of his favorite people in the world. His mom had been reserved and quiet, a shadow to the boisterous, demanding personality of his father. Though her kindness complemented her father's more rash nature, it never seemed to penetrate the residual stings his father's harsh expectations left behind, and she always seemed to keep her children at a safe distance. A gentle, regal sort of woman.

Grace Mitchell shone with quiet kindness. His grin spread as he opened a half loaf of homemade bread and read over her note.

HOPE THIS KEEPS YOU FULL AND WARM ON THESE COLD DAYS. MAMA MITCHELL

An ache, an untapped yearning, slit open in his chest. Beth's mother had been thoughtful like Mama Mitchell, drawing him into a close-knit family he'd never experienced. He'd learned so much from Beth's family about how belonging could feel, the immense comfort of being included, flaws and all.

Alex peered into a pot filled with beef stew and cleared the emotions from his tense throat. He gave Haus a grin. "Okay, my day just improved considerably."

The dog followed him around the kitchen as he filled a bowl full of the steamy goodness, and then Haus settled at his feet as Alex sat on the couch, turning a CD on for some quiet music. He'd picked up a few disks of bluegrass music from a local shop in town because … well, that style took up the majority of the store.

Intricate strains of an acoustic guitar filled the silence with a melody Alex didn't recognize but liked. Calming and aching all at once. Something in him stirred to life, an unnamed emotion he'd felt before, which reached beyond the regular feelings to something he'd never been able to grasp.

A quiet ring broke into the music. Alex blinked from his stupor as a second ring followed. *The* ring. He stumbled to his feet so fast Haus jumped in response.

"Sorry, boy. Important call."

Alex rushed to his computer bag and ruffled through it until his hands grasped the vibrating phone, his hand shaking as much as the phone itself.

"Hello."

"Uncle Alex, I have to tell you something."

Alex's palm flew to his chest at the sweet sound of his niece's voice. She was alive, safe, and happy, and every phone call confirmed that uncertain truth. "Hey, peanut, you always have something to say."

"But this is *real* news."

He leaned back onto the couch, cradling the phone as a lifeline to this voice. "So, what is this *real* news?"

"I lost another tooth." Lily's words dripped with the exaggeration of a child. He loved every syllable.

"What? Another one? What does that make? Four?"

"Five."

"Five? I ought to talk to your mom about how careless you are to lose so many teeth at once."

Her giggle nailed him in the heart, and air barely seeped through his tightened throat. "Mama said that six-year-olds are supposed to lose their teeth."

Six. That's right. He hadn't seen her in a year.

"I guess so, but if you start losing your hair, we really should talk. Then you'll be like Great-Grandpa. No teeth and no hair."

Her giggle echoed again, belying the seriousness of the entire situation. Away. Anonymous.

It was a good thing Evie had shielded Lily from the danger in their situation. Her little voice wrung with untainted happiness.

"I love you, Uncle Alex. Mama needs to talk to you now."

"All right, peanut." His words rasped to a whisper. "Love you back."

"Go on to the living room, Lily, and put in that movie you wanted to watch, okay?" His sister spoke in the distance, drawing closer. "I'll be there in a minute."

"Hey, bro." Evelyn's familiar greeting almost sent him into tears. And his eyes were already burning.

She hadn't called in a month. Too long, when every second mattered and secrecy kept her alive. "Hey, sis. Sounds like you need to talk to Lily about her carelessness."

"She must get that particular personality trait from her adoring uncle."

Alex heard the smile in her words. "Blame it on the guy, as usual."

"If the Rockport fits."

"Ha," he said with an exaggerated laugh. "I see you're still working on that funny bone."

"You got all the humor, and I got all the responsibility, you know?"

Their age-old jeer somehow transformed the miles of distance and heartache into a next-door conversation. Oh, how he missed her.

A sliver of silence sobered the banter. "How are you?"

Compared to her? "Good. Lots to learn, but it's a pleasant place. Nice people."

"I know you're disappointed about Charlottesville."

"Don't worry about me, sis." The last thing his kid sister needed was another thing to worry about when every day she had to look over her shoulder. "My landlady makes supper for me every night. Great stuff. And you'd love the town. It's like something off *Andy Griffith*."

She chuckled. "Sounds like the perfect spot for your low-profile personality."

"You have no idea. I'm bringing all kinds of life to the place." He waited and then drew in a deep breath for the real questions. "How are things?"

"Well, I thought we were finally going to stay in one town for a while…"

Alex pressed his eyes closed, bracing himself for her explanation.

"John's been spotted in the US."

"No." After almost six months of quiet regarding his brother-in-law's whereabouts, now he turns up? Which meant the face-to-face meeting between Alex and his sister couldn't happen. Too dangerous.

"He must have run out of money in Europe, or wherever he's been, or he wouldn't risk returning to American soil."

Unless he wanted to end running from the police for good by finding Evie—the one person who could testify to her husband's crimes. Murder. Fraud. Embezzling.

"If the police know John's in America, why can't they catch him?"

"He has lots of friends in low places, Alex." Her voice quavered. "And they're willing to hide him until his money or luck runs out. His friends may not help him find us, but they won't stop him either."

Alex ran his hand through his hair, wishing he could reach through the phone and hold her, protect her, do anything to keep the fear from her voice. "Nobody knows where you are, Evie. Heck, they don't even think you're alive."

"But they know where Dad is, and they'll try to get information from him if they can."

"Dad doesn't know either."

There was silence for a moment before her breathless response. "What?"

"I couldn't tell him, not if it put either of you in jeopardy. I couldn't."

"Alex, you need to make amends with Dad, and silence only keeps you both apart longer. He thinks you … he thinks you…"

"Doesn't matter what he thinks. The important thing is keeping you safe." Alex shoved the memory of his father's blame far away. Blame for the car accident that "took" Evie and Lily from them, even though it had all been "planned" to send John off their trail.

And it had worked. So far.

"Alex—"

"We'll figure this out when John is caught."

"Stop sacrificing yourself for everyone else and live your life."

"I'll live my life when yours is safe."

Silence passed between them. Fifteen-minute conversations were all they had before the connection automatically shut off. A precaution.

"Inspector Carpenter said you're in a really remote part of the Blue Ridge Mountains."

"He got that right."

"There's a chance, since you are so far from everything, the police may still let Lily and I come see you. I'm not sure yet, but they haven't closed off the possibility."

"What?" He wiped a palm over his stinging eyes and sat up straighter on the couch. "Are you serious?"

"I'm going to keep asking. Even if it's only for an hour, at least it would be flesh and bone instead of static pictures and faceless voices. I *need* to see someone who knows me ... the real me."

He leaned his head back against the cushions of the couch. A warm tear slipped from one eye and trailed over his temple. He cleared his voice, refusing to let her share in his grief. He had to be strong. Had to pretend everything was fine. For her sake. "What's your name in this town?"

"Cassandra Beckett."

He grimaced at the moniker, about as ill-fitting as one could get. "You're nothing like a Cassandra."

"At least they allow Lily to keep her first name, so it's a little less confusing for her." A beep sounded on the phone, the only warning they'd receive. "We've gotta go, bro."

"I know."

"I've not prayed much, Alex. We weren't raised with that sort of thing, but, if you think about it, maybe ... maybe you could pray we get to see you."

The nameless emotion emerged again, deep and clinging to the idea of something ... someone willing to listen to them. And do something to help?

"I love you, Evie. No matter where you are."

"You too, Al—"

Alex waited a few more seconds, phone pressed to his ear, hoping for one more second, one more word, but the line silenced. He tossed the phone on the coffee table and crashed back into the cushions of the couch, switching off the music.

He stared up at the ceiling, replaying his sister's words through his mind. A visit? In person? After a year of only phone conversations, could that really be a possibility?

Pray?

He closed his eyes and mulled over the word again. Of all the people in the world, God didn't want to hear from him. He'd rebelled against his father, wounded women with his careless flirting early in his adulthood, stumbled about in careers like a fool. No, God wouldn't listen to him, but Evie? Yes. She'd always been the sweet one in their family. If God would hear anyone's prayers, it would be hers.

Beth used to talk about praying, about asking God to heal her. He never did, but she still prayed. It didn't seem to be something that worked, even for the good people like his deceased fiancée. Why would he think God would listen to some superficial failure from a broken family and a damaged present?

His gaze fixed on the ceiling, and he released a long sigh before closing his eyes. "But if You did," he spoke into the silence of the room, "please keep Evie and Lily safe."

Chapter Six

Rainey paused in front of the mirror before heading out the door for her morning jog. Her mass of hair fell around her shoulders in a blanket of wavy gold. She stared at her reflection—pale skin with the slightest hint of freckles across her nose, aqua eyes too big for her face, narrow lips.

Even now the flush of shame warmed her cheeks. Gray had something negative to say about almost every part of her.

She jerked her hair back into a ponytail and looked away from the mirror. She'd grown a lot on her own, become a more confident person. Why did the mere possibility of seeing him bring every insecurity back to the surface, just waiting to pull her under again?

It didn't matter. What he thought didn't matter.

Clearly, he had judgment issues of all sorts. Why on earth should his criticism hound her for years? Or even matter now? His words couldn't … shouldn't hurt her anymore.

She snatched a walkie-talkie off the counter by the door and hooked it on her jacket pocket.

"Do you have your walkie, sweet pea?"

"Sure do, Mama," came Sarah's quick reply from the den, along with the theme song from *My Little Pony*.

"Great. Be back in a little bit." Rainey locked the door behind her and stepped onto the porch, scoping her small running trail that followed the gravel road around the bottom of the hill below her house. Morning dawned over the rolling fields, painting the hills with a golden light that disappeared into the low-lying fog. Blue mountains peeked out from the mist in the distance, and the cool chill of morning pricked the skin on her face. She tugged the collar of her jacket close and ran down the porch steps, taking the driveway to the gravel road.

Cool mist sprinkled against her face, but the welcome, steady thrum of her elevating pulse pushed warmth through her limbs and energy into her pace. She took a quick glance to her house atop the hill, in sight of the road from any direction she traveled on her morning path, then started up the steepest portion toward the Old Spencer Place.

Her morning devotions accompanied her thoughts along her way and stung with enough conviction to increase her pace. She sucked a cold breath of air into her lungs and replayed the verses in her mind, their truths pelting her spirit in all the places she struggled most.

> So, chosen by God for this new life of love, dress in the wardrobe God picked out for you: compassion, kindness, humility, quiet strength, discipline. Be even-tempered, content with second place, quick to forgive an offense. Forgive as quickly and completely as the Master forgave you. And regardless of what else you put on, wear love. It's your basic, all-purpose garment. Never be without it.

Wear love? Forgive quickly? Compassion? It was too much. Too difficult. Didn't Jesus understand how difficult?

The words replayed in her head. *Forgive as quickly and completely as the Master forgave you.*

Her shoulders slumped as she capped the hill. Strength she needed—especially for her upcoming lunch with Gray—but compassion? The man picked her apart until he'd somehow removed all of her self-confidence and left behind a shell of uncertainty. The jerk then proceeded to have an affair with her sister-in-law, right under Rainey's nose, and then, like the coward he was, deserted his family. Compassion was the furthest thing from Rainey's mind for her good-for-nothing ex-husband. And forgiveness? She growled. She thought she'd forgiven him. When he stayed far away from her and her daughter, forgiveness seemed easier, but now?

Her gaze shot heavenward, toward the lightening azure sky. "Sometimes, it's too much, Lord."

A voice impressed a reply upon her heart. *That's why you need Me.*

She sighed against the call.

They need Me too.

They? Gray? He needed lots of things, a good dose of Jesus at the top of the list, but "they"? She made a U-turn just before she reached Old Man Spencer's place, his pack of dogs waiting to chase her as far away from "their" territory as possible. Halfway down the hill, another running figure met her.

Alex Murdock?

Oh, good grief. Had he followed her?

He wore navy sweats and a gray hoodie, his hair a tousled mess from his run, but his grin was in excellent working order. When his attention lifted to her, it started at one cheek and spread a slow flirty line over to the other cheek.

Funny, Lord. Really funny.

But she couldn't seem to look away from Alex fast enough. His relaxed morning look tempted her perusal in a way his professional persona failed to do, and her rebel eyes took their time appreciating each strong slice of his form.

Her brain needed a good throttling.

He tipped a finger to his forehead as they met, sending an appreciative glance down her body and back to her face. "Good morning, gorgeous."

The temptation to return his smile died on her lips. How could Gray have ruined that word for her? That teasing endearment?

Gorgeous? Gray had only used it when he craved intimacy, but any other time, she was more like a secondhand piece of the furniture than a treasured life partner, a wife.

"Mornin'." She fixed her gaze forward and passed him, ignoring the pull to peer over her shoulder.

Compassion, kindness…

"Okay, okay, Lord." She breathed out her words on frosted air. "I get it. Alex is not Gray."

But who was he?

A runner, clearly. She should have known from his physique. She pinched her eyes as another crash of heat lit her cheeks, then almost stumbled over a loose rock.

So … they had running in common, along with their profession, a love for hot chocolate, and an undeniable agreement Sarah was adorable. That was it. He had an easy way with people, which could help him build his client base, and if his writing abilities proved as persuasive as his charm, she might have a real possibility of getting some of these grants.

But she'd have to ask him for help.

Be in his debt.

Trust him.

She growled and slowed her run, glancing back the way she'd come. Oh no! Alex was headed directly toward Old Man Spencer's and the ferocious pack of dogs. She hesitated, a little fight-or-flight mamba dancing through her mind, then sprinted up the hill.

"Alex," she called to him, but he didn't turn. Against the burn in her legs, she pushed harder up the hill toward him.

Misty morning woods framed the road on both sides, and Rainey's attention honed in on her target. He had a nice stride in his run, solid and smooth, accentuating the tight shape of his backside in those sweats.

Oh, for heaven's sake! She groaned at her own mental plummet, and the image loosened in her mind. "Alex."

He turned his head, plucking one of his earbuds out as he slowed. "Miss me?"

"I'm being neighborly." She jogged to him, the two of them moving in place. "A pack of unfriendly dogs lives at the top of the hill, so unless you want to get a rough country greeting, you'll turn at the top of the hill and head back down."

"You warned me? I figured you'd rather feed me to the dogs."

Rainey opened her mouth to respond and then snapped her lips closed, the uneasy flicker of shame flaming to life in the warmth on her face. She tugged both of her earbuds out and worked up a smile, maybe. It didn't feel very friendly. "No one deserves that kind of fate."

"Wow, must be pretty bad."

"Midas is the worst. He's a boxer with jaws the size of … of…"

"Jaws?" His lips tilted with his stupid grin, and hers twitched in response.

"Something like that." She shook her head. "Anyway, just thought you ought to know." She turned back toward the hill, and within seconds he was beside her, his smile beaming too brightly for anyone pre-coffee.

"So … you run?" He fell in stride beside her.

Every fiber of her being wanted to bathe him with her most obvious "duh" look, but her devotions from the morning pricked at her annoyance like a seven-year-old with a scab. "I started in college. Mornings are my favorite time."

Oh great, why did she admit that to him?

"Mine too. You can watch the world wake up."

She turned to look for a sarcastic expression but found none. Why did she get the weirdest vibes around him? Half the time she wanted to slap the smile off his face, and the other half left her wondering if something much … more was going on behind those seafoam-colored eyes.

She cleared her throat, pushing herself to put her convictions into practice. Compassion. Kindness. "How is class prep going?"

He frowned. "Motor Speech is going to kill me, and none of my clients will call me back. I've had three hang up the phone on me as soon as I started talking."

"And you have a nice voice. Go figure." Rainey chuckled at Alex's glare. "Sorry, Alex. It's the culture. People around here are pretty insular and suspicious unless they know you, or at least someone you're related to."

"Then how am I supposed to make this work?"

She shrugged. "Keep trying. Leave a nice message on their voice mail and make it very clear. I imagine they have a harder time since you're a guy. Women make up 95 percent of our profession. They're not used to hearing from a guy."

"How about *you* call them for me?"

She stopped in the middle of the road, and he slid to a halt in front of her. "Me? Call them?"

"Small town, right?" He propped his palms on his hips and caught his breath. "Everybody knows you, and I don't always make the best first impression."

His admission paused her, drawing out a little more of that compassion she desperately needed to show. "Okay, Alex, I realize we haven't gotten off on the best foot, and that's mostly my fault, but you … you have the potential to make a great impression on people."

"Potential?" His messy hair and casual dress still threw off her thinking. Add in the quirked brow, and her thoughts actually stuttered for a second. Maybe she was dehydrated.

"Um … of course, if you wouldn't try so hard." She waved a hand toward him. "Right now, when you're not attempting to impersonate a Ken doll, you're actually pretty nice to talk to."

His lips split wide and he started to chuckle. "A Ken doll?" His laugh broke free. "That's exactly what I was going for. Plastic and perfect with a vacant expression."

She desperately tried to bite her lips into submission, but they flared into a full smile despite her best attempts.

"Do I run like my body is stiff and pieced together with hinges too?" He imitated a robotic-style walk, and Rainey caught her chuckle with her hand.

"Oh goodness, stop." She touched his shoulder, laughing. "That makes you look like you need to visit the gastroenterologist."

His laugh burst out again, low, deep, and infectious. "I did *not* need that mental image."

"Neither did I." She squelched the chuckle but failed to keep her lips from continuing to spread.

His entire face brightened with humor, so much so Rainey's doubt took a gut punch. Their gazes locked. And held.

For the first time in two years, the swell of attraction peeled through the distance and captured her scattered breaths. Air caught in her lungs, and tantalizing warmth spilled from her cheeks, down her neck, and into her chest. Her smile fell. His softened. Her pulse zoomed into her eardrums with a deafening note. *No!*

"Well, um … I've gotta go. Sarah's waiting."

He blinked and seemed to reorient himself from the same sort of shock radiating inside of her. "Sarah? Where is Sarah?" His eyes widened. "Did you leave her alone without any contact with you?"

Those lovely tingles dispersed into the morning mist. All she needed was someone else criticizing her. "Yep, I'm that kind of mom." She nodded toward her house on the hill. "I can see my house at every point of the run and…" She held up the walkie-talkie, pressing the little button on the side. "Hey, sweet pea?"

Silence followed and then the walkie-talkie came to life. "Hey, Mama."

She stared at Alex as she talked, drilling her point home. "Whatcha doin'?"

"Watching *Ponies*, like you said," her sweet voice replied. Rainey raised a brow to her doubting Alex. "Pinkie Pie just ate too much cake and she's going crazy."

"Pinkie Pie is a crazy pony, that's for sure."

"Are you running with Dr. Alex?"

Rainey shielded her eyes from the morning sun and peered up the hill. The top of Sarah's golden head bobbed in the window.

She shifted her gaze back to Alex, whose grin hinged with a flirty tilt. This guy was relentless. "Umm … yes, sort of."

"That's good, Mama. You don't have to run all by yourself now."

Rainey backed away from the Ken doll as if Sarah's declaration stung as much as Alex's smolder. "Sweet pea, I'm on my way up. Would you unlock the door for me?"

"Sure, Mama."

She replaced the walkie on her sleeve and forced her gaze back to his. "See ya later, Alex."

"Bye, Rainey."

She whipped her body toward the house and refused to abate her curiosity about whether he watched her run away or not. Even the thought had her mentally slapping herself. Her breath puffed a pattern of frozen air into the morning, and a chill inspired her feet to make greater distance between her and Alex Murdock. She sprinted, running as if her past nipped at her heels like Old Man Spencer's wild dogs. For some reason, she was afraid it did.

A loud bang at the door shot Alex straight up in bed. He rubbed his eyes, weary from staring too long at the computer screen trying to figure out his lecture notes for the week. Haus whimpered and stood from his place on the floor. The banging continued.

Alex ran a hand through his hair and slipped from the bed, padding down the hall to the kitchen with Haus by his side. Sunlight spilled in through the windows, showing the lateness of the morning. Since he hadn't crawled into bed until after 3:00 a.m., he'd taken his time meeting the morning. What on earth brought the cavalry to his front door?

Donned in a navy polo and khaki slacks, thinning hair slicked back on his head, Jim greeted him, a frown lining familiar grooves on his face. Alex barely recognized the old codger.

"You ain't ready a'tall."

Alex looked down at his athletic shorts and crumbled T-shirt. "Ready for what?"

"I heard tell you promised one of my great-grandnieces you was goin' to church today, so I come to catch a ride with ya."

"Church?" Alex ran a hand through his hair and released a long stream of air through his nose. Right. He'd promised Sarah. "I forgot, Jim."

"I reckoned as much." The man walked into the house and reclined onto the couch, pulling a pipe from his jacket pocket. He looked up, brow raised as if he were surprised to still see Alex standing there. "Well, go on and get ready then. We ain't got all day."

Alex quirked a brow at Haus, who had the gall to sit down at Jim's feet as if nothing out of the ordinary were happening, but Alex knew better. He hadn't entered a church since he said goodbye to his fiancée and watched the pallbearers carry her white casket away.

He turned toward his room and rifled through the clothes in his closet, a nervous energy propelling him into motion.

Before Beth, church was something his family attended for weddings, funerals, and Christmas, but Alex had learned of a deeper relationship behind all the Jesus talk when Beth's gentle personality entered his brash world. She'd drawn him in, introduced him to something that stirred his spirit but he'd never really grasped, and then … the God she loved so much took her away. A gentle and expected goodbye, but no less painful.

Her faith remained steady to the end, calling to his heart for one small sliver of whatever held her heart together in those last days of fighting an unseen enemy. Now another female tugged him away from his typical routine into the realm of faith. He hadn't seemed to get away from it since Beth died, the thought lingering in the back of his mind like an unfinished story.

Alex adjusted the collar of his green polo, made quick work of his shaving and teeth brushing, then met Jim in the living room. His sister had asked him to pray—maybe this was a place to start.

"Ready, Jim."

The older man looked up and stood, sending a nod of approval. "Let's get in that fancy car of yours and git on down the road. We're gonna be a bit late anyhow."

The church stood as an exact image of what Alex had expected. White, box shaped, a steeple peering over the grassy meadows on either side, much like an inspirational greeting card. Alex looked around, taking in the picturesque surroundings. Maybe he was dreaming. The countryside? The view? Jim? The whole scene breathed of a time and place he'd only seen in movies. Even a hint of Christmas vibes lingered in the ice-tinged air. How was that possible?

"Git a move on, boy, or we'll miss the singin'."

Alex jerked out of his stupor and followed Jim up the steps and into a pine-scented sanctuary. The size and space of the room surprised him, much larger than the unassuming exterior presented. Alex followed Jim to a seat in the back, a familiar spot. His parents always sat in the back during their rare church appearances. A younger man, perhaps in his late forties, whom Alex presumed was the preacher, wore a calm smile and stood behind a podium at the front of the church.

"Our choir director is currently at the hospital welcoming his first baby with his dear wife, so the choir won't be singing for us today." He grinned at the people coming forward to the stage. Alex's attention landed on a blonde in a long brown skirt, her pale blue sweater highlighting the gold streaks in her hair. Rainey. She moved forward with her brothers, Emma stepped to the piano, and a dark-haired woman Alex didn't know took one of the microphones.

"It's a rare treat that the Mitchell family will sing for us, but today I asked them to lead our congregation in a song to help us get our hearts and minds in place for the sermon." His gaze seemed to zoom in on Alex. "Remember, God takes us just as we are."

Rainey's oldest brother, Tigg or Trigg or something like that, stood with a bass in hand and nodded for the group to start. Alex's attention pulled to Rainey, a violin tucked beneath her chin and her eyes forward as her bow moved gracefully across the strings to add a beautiful melody over the other instruments.

The tough exterior she'd shown him fell away as her long fingers glided from one string to the next, creating a beckoning "voice" of melody reaching beyond the pews to his seat. His breath squeezed through his throat, and he could only stare and listen.

Words from the song, resonating from Trigg's deep voice, filtered into Alex's fascination.

JUST AS YOU ARE, BROKEN AND SCARRED
HE'LL PICK UP ALL YOUR PIECES AND MAKE YOU WHOLE AGAIN.
NO PAST TOO DARK, NO PATH TOO LOST.
HIS GRACE WILL STILL THE LONGING YOU FEEL WITHIN YOUR SOUL.
HE LOVES YOU SO
JUST AS YOU ARE.

Just as he was? Alex looked over at Jim, but the man didn't seem to react to the words. No past too dark? No path too lost? His attention landed back on Rainey, her eyes closed as the soprano strains pierced his heart like a cry.

His grace has washed away the bitter stains.
His love will heal the ragged wounds that remain.
He'll never let go or loosen his hold.
His grace will keep your heart even if it tends to stray.
Rest in his love. It is enough.
Just as you are.

The words seized him, spoke to him, almost as if someone eavesdropped on his heart and saw all the ways he'd messed up his life, all the backfired good intentions. Could this God, this Christ Beth spoke of be powerful enough and compassionate enough to change the past? To … redirect the future? To rescue his sister and salvage his relationships?

The pastor's sermon kept the same theme. Taking hearts and making them new. Love covering over past mistakes. God's strength to make wrongs right and change the wayward soul.

Broken? Wayward? Mistakes? Alex lived them all. Could this one thing … this sweet, unfathomable truth be what Beth had tried to tell him all along? Despite his horrible past and stupid actions, God loved him? As he was?

His mind couldn't wrap around it. He stood for the final hymn, oblivious to the song, and followed Jim's nudging to the back door at the conclusion of the service.

"We'll see ya at the house, Alex."

Alex looked up to see the woman he'd only caught a glimpse of earlier in the week. Mama Mitchell. She stepped forward to the end of his pew and swept him into a hug as if she'd always known him. For that brief embrace, Alex was surrounded by the scent of spearmint and ginger and a sudden sense of … belonging.

"Um … I don't want to intrude, Mrs. Mitchell."

Her smile softened and Alex's eyes stung. What on earth was wrong with him? "No intrusion. You *have* to come. I made enough food for a herd, and I'll need your help getting rid of it."

She winked and Alex smiled, glossing over the ragged ache in his chest with his usual shield. "I'm pretty good at getting rid of food." He patted his stomach. "And I never refuse free stuff."

She tapped his shoulder. "Smart boy. Then you are in the right place at the right time." She turned to Jim with a grin. "Make sure he finds his way, will you?"

"'Course," came Jim's gruff reply as he stepped out the church doors.

Mrs. Mitchell shook her head and raised a golden brow to Alex. "Actually, I was talkin' to you, Alex." She winked and walked past him to the door. "Make sure Jim finds his way to the house, will you?"

Grace Mitchell offered a kinship Alex didn't hesitate to snatch up. Something in the teasing glint, the unfettered welcome in time with the words of the sermon, nudged awake a longing in him. A need. He'd felt lost for years, wandering from job to job, potential success to the next potential success, but in her gentle gestures—from the meals to ushering him into her family—Grace Mitchell brought the evasive scent of home.

He cleared his throat and gripped the back of the pew where he'd sat, flashing his grin to cover the unsteadiness of his lips. "Of course. You can count on me, ma'am."

Her gray gaze settled on him before she slipped out the door. "I'm planning on it."

Count on him? No one counted on him except his sister. Few people took him seriously enough to try. Her simple statement, spoken with such certainty, burned through him. Yes. He wanted to be that man.

He glanced back to the front of the church, where Rainey gathered her violin and purse. Sunlight bathed her in a golden glow from the nearby window, and her head was back in full laughter, Emma nearby with the same expression. Alex's breath closed off, taking in the beauty and unfettered happiness. She'd laughed like that during the jog, and an unexpected connection pinged to life between them. Or so he thought.

Superficial flirting was safe, temporary, but the feelings bleeding through him filtered from their typical monochrome into a rainbow of color, surging beyond his pain from the past to his soul. It had been years since he'd entertained the notion of pursuing a deep relationship. Doing so seemed impossible after Beth died, but knowing the wounds that hid behind Rainey's eyes—seeing the strength and kindness she tried so hard to hide—awakened an attraction, a curiosity, he'd quelled for years.

What would it be like to bask in the glow of such a smile again? To live in a world where a woman like her loved a man like him? Where he belonged?

She looked in his direction then, their eyes catching. Her smile faltered, her large aqua eyes holding his attention. The same connection zinged to life.

The same pull to know her ... to make her laugh again, to open that closed, wounded spot in his heart.

He released his hold on the pew and marched to the church door, severing the inexplicable connection. What was he thinking? He had too many secrets. Too many broken relationships. He didn't belong with a family like theirs, with a woman like her.

He hesitated before pushing the door wide and then sighed. People didn't get another chance at something they never deserved in the first place. Without a look back, he left the church and the idea of any future with Rainey and the Mitchell family.

Chapter Seven

The table rumbled with its usual chatter, at least three conversations at once. Some of the children's voices rose above the adults to ask for second helpings, but most of the rabble came from the grown-ups. Football talk, Reese sharing about his new job, Trigg discussing cattle, Emma and her most recent matchmaking exploits, and, of course, church talk.

The latter tipped her attention back to Alex, who sat across the table from her. He slipped right into the crazy conversation, as if following three different topics at once wasn't confusing at all. Even his simple polo gave him a less starched look, or maybe it was his expression she'd noticed during church as she'd played the violin. The pasted smile, the boyish devil-may-care look in his eyes, slipped away to reveal a very different Alex Murdock—much like the glimpses she'd seen over the past week.

An uncomfortable pinch wound her stomach in a knot, turning the chicken-n-dumplings to lead. She didn't have time to investigate the deeper layers of Alex Murdock, even if they existed. She had a daughter to protect and a clinic to save, but his voice brought her attention back to him.

"You have lunch like this every Sunday?"

Mama chuckled. "It's a lot to take in all at once."

"Are we scaring you, Murdock?" This from Reese as he wiped off his two-year-old son's mashed-potato-covered fingers, his grin ruthless.

"Are you kidding me?" Alex leaned forward, palms on the table. "This is amazing. I've never had a lunch like this before."

Emma's laugh filtered in with their mother's. "They don't have loud and crazy lunches with a herd of people where you're from?"

Alex's grin tipped and his green gaze landed on Rainey, sending a little quiver through her chest. "Loud and crazy? Sure, but not like this. This … this is…"

Rainey rested her chin on her palm and narrowed her eyes at him. "Yes?"

A fiery glint lit his expression, then gentled to a rosy glow, intensifying her quiver into a full flutter. "Just as a family should be, I think." A glimmer of sadness marked his words before he covered it with another smile and turned to her mother. "And the food is fantastic."

Mama's gaze flitted from Alex to Rainey and back again. "You're welcome any time, Alex. To church and to lunch. We're used to a big gang around here."

His attention faltered with his grin. He reached for his napkin and wiped his mouth, as a distraction, if Rainey guessed right. "Thank you."

The conversation continued, but Rainey couldn't shake the notion that Alex hid something behind his megawatt smile. Away from the university, in the intimate and unguarded surroundings of church and home, glimpses of another man attuned her senses to the smallest details. The way he flirted with Emma turned into helping her clear the table. A joke deflected a personal question. A light of unveiled tenderness transformed his plastic expression as he knelt to talk to Sarah about her cute braids.

Was it all as much a façade as Gray's had been? Short-sighted and wayward-hearted? She'd always been a sucker for wounded souls, despite her best attempts at turning off the inner savior. The rescuer in her zeroed in on Alex with a coon dog's scent.

"Well, I was expectin' him to be a different sort than he was," Mama whispered as Rainey placed dishes besides the sink and started drying the clean ones. "He's still fancy but his gleam isn't too shiny for country folk."

"He's different here." Rainey snuck a look over her shoulder. Alex stood chatting by the fireplace with Uncle Jim and Trigg, his Adonis appearance in contrast to her darkly handsome brother.

"Good food brings out the best in people."

Rainey shook her head and grinned into her mother's sparkling eyes. "If anybody's food could, Mama…"

"Good food, good company, and Jesus? I reckon that's the best combination there is." Mama chuckled and went back to her work, her face sobering. "He's a lonely sort, Rainey. I don't know if he recognizes it or not, but he is."

Rainey dried another plate, refusing to study Alex again. The fact that she had to fight the urge just made her mad.

"He's come to the right place then, hasn't he? Between you and Emma, I imagine he'll get his fill of welcome."

Her mother's intense stare drew Rainey's attention like a paperclip to a magnet. "I'm not askin' you to court him, Rainey, but he's in our lives right now for a reason. The least you can do is be nice to him."

"Mama, I'm plenty nice to him." The look in her mama's eyes wilted Rainey's thinly veiled lie. Her shoulders dropped in defeat. "Fine, I could be nicer. It's just... I can't get... He's so much like..."

"No, he's not." Mama touched Rainey's arms with her warm, sudsy hand. "Not if you look hard."

Rainey drew in a breath and put a few more plates away, her heart wrestling against the request.

"God's placed him right here in my life and in yours for such a time as this. Don't waste His time with a stubborn heart."

Rainey paused in her reach for another plate, placed her palms down on the counter, and lowered her head. "That stubborn heart thing?" She turned her head to her mama. "It's a good defense against jerks, idiots, and pain."

"Hmm..." Mama nodded, lips pursed as she piped up a solid rebuttal. "I think you're confusing stubbornness and wisdom."

Rainey rolled her eyes and lost a bit of control of her smile. Leave it to Mama to put her in her place with sugar on top. "Is that it?"

Mama's eyes lit with a hidden smile, gentling her reprimand. "Pain is a lifelong fixture in a broken world, girl. All of us need strength from God to face hurts from inside." She placed a palm against her chest. "And outside." She raised a brow. "A stubborn heart closes off possibilities—and in this case, kindness. A wise heart is brave enough to offer kindness, smart enough to bypass jerks, and faithful enough to believe in possibilities. Ain't no tellin' what our family can offer Alex Murdock. God used us to make a difference in Dee's life. Maybe He's given us another opportunity to make a difference in someone else's."

Rainey nodded, tempering her fear with her mother's truth. She'd watched Dee change and soften under the care of Mama and Reese, seen her lostness fade with the acceptance of family.

"He's not Gray, honey. The only thing I'm askin' you to give away is your kindness." Mama handed Rainey another plate. "Not your heart."

Rainey eyed her mother. "Oh, you don't have to worry about that." She placed the plate in the cabinet and released a sigh. "But I will try some kindness."

73

Rainey stepped into the house after checking on the children playing outside. Kids seemed immune to cold. Even a forty-degree day in January sent her in search of a nice warm fire, oversized sweatshirt, and good book. She turned the corner of the doorway toward her mama's toasty rock fireplace and nearly bumped into Alex, who peered at the photos on the mantel.

"Oh, sorry, Alex."

He looked over, eyes glistening like a mischievous child's. "You have a habit of running into me, Miss Mitchell. I'm starting to think you're trying to get my attention."

She pinched the bridge of her nose and shook her head. *Kindness. Kindness.* She tensed her smile. "Or perhaps it's a personality trait for me—I'm either not paying attention, or I'm on a mission unstoppable."

All Casanova fled from his expression, and his grin widened with a somewhat contagious boyish delight. "Mission unstoppable, eh?"

"I'm giving you fair warning." She placed her palms on her hips, her smile slipping from her hold. "Once I set my mind to something, I'm scary."

A rush of warmth flushed her cheeks as he examined her from shoes to head, pausing on her eyes. "Yeah, you're really scary." But his soft voice didn't sound one bit afraid, and her body tensed all over.

"Well, I'm gonna get my jacket and head home."

He snatched her arm, halting her escape. "Wait a minute. Could you tell me about these photos? Is that your whole family?"

He pointed to an eight-by-ten of the family from nine years ago, Rainey's more rounded days. Mama, Daddy, Trigg, Reese, Emma, and she—even Haus had made it into the picture. It certainly wasn't a staged photo. Emma was the only one looking at the camera, a definite personality trait. Everyone else was looking at each other, some laughing, but all smiling … even Haus.

"Is that your dad?"

Rainey focused in on the face missing from the family table. Trigg and Reese looked the most like him, with their tall, dark good looks. And that smile? She could almost hear him laughing through the photo, reaching out beyond the ache grief leaves behind and igniting her memory with a thousand little touches.

"Yeah." She blinked her attention back to Alex. "Great guy. Definitely not smooth talking or classy." Her gaze returned to her dad's face. "But he was certainly a big-hearted, fun-loving mountain man."

"Who's to say that's not classy, right?" He turned back to the photos, his grin growing. "Whoa, is that you?"

She cleared her throat and looked into the fire, avoiding the plastered memory of her lifelong struggles with weight. "Yeah … um … college was the beginning of a self-discovery for me."

His gaze shimmied down her again, reigniting the deepening warmth. "Well, I think you found whatever you were looking for." He shrugged and peered closer at the photo. "From the look in your eyes in that picture, the only thing that shrank was your outside. You still have a whole lot of personality in you." His eyes widened. "In fact, you *are* a little scary."

She couldn't contain her laugh in the light of his faux terror. What was it about this crazy man and laughter? How on earth could ridiculousness be so … so … sweetly funny? "Then my evil plan is working."

Their gazes held for what felt like minutes before he turned back to the photos.

She steadied her hand on the rustic mantel, her legs suddenly a little unbalanced. Alex's comment, without a hint of disgust at her former self, shook her. Only one photo lining the mantel displayed her after-college look. The rest portrayed the round, freckle-faced little girl with glasses too small for her face.

"There are a lot of worse things you could be in high school, you know?" He picked up one of the frames and studied the photo before peering over the top to her.

She shifted her attention away from his gaze and pushed a rebel strand of hair behind her ear. "What? Were you some scrawny nerd in high school who everyone wanted to beat up?"

He placed the photo back and leaned close to her, wrinkling his nose with a playful grimace. "No, I was something much worse than that. I was a mean, arrogant rich kid."

His stare challenged her before it fleeted back to the mantel. That one sentence unveiled a lot more about Alex Murdock than she would have guessed. The self-admittance alone plunging her into insatiable curiosity. It didn't help that his sandalwood scent drew her to him like her mama's lasagna brought her entire family to the kitchen table.

She cleared her throat. "And all that meanness and riches scared people away, huh?"

"Oh no." He shook his head and rested his hand on the mantel next to hers, their fingers almost touching. "No, I had lots of friends." His chuckle deflected the seriousness of the question, attempting to throw her off the subject, but she knew better than to take his humor at face value. "None of those friends stayed with me when I chose speech-language pathology instead of the family enterprise. None showed up when my mom passed away during my senior year." He shrugged. "Heck, my dad didn't even seem to notice she was gone." He narrowed his eyes and fisted the next photo. "He just kept working, like always."

Silence enfolded his words, deepening their truth and sting. Rainey stared at his serious profile, grappling for something to say in the wake of such a confession ... by such a man. He put her out of her misery with a counterfeit smile. "But I had it all together on the outside."

Against every warning buzzer in her head, she covered his hand resting on the mantel, studying him with fresh eyes. "Like now?"

His gaze shot to hers, flashing with surprise before he shrugged away from her touch with his palms raised. "What do you mean? Of course like now. I have Marilyn."

She curled her fingers against the mantel and offered an obligatory smile but continued to study him. Lost? Alone? Oh, he wore it like the plastic smile on his face. She didn't know what was worse—that her mother had been right all along or that Alex Murdock desperately needed rescuing.

The fixer in her rose to the challenge. The betrayed woman cowered in defense.

Kindness. Just offer kindness. "And I thought having a stunning beauty for a baby sister was a problem. Sounds like you win the teenage angst contest."

His smile shifted as he leaned closely to look again at the family photo, probably noting every rounded part of her pimpled face. "Stunning beauty?" He switched his gaze to where Emma stood in the kitchen, shoving Reese's shoulder and fussing about something or other. She watched his green eyes make their way back to her. "Emma's cute."

Rainey curbed the tiny pang of disappointment with a dry laugh. "She sure is."

He snatched back her attention by covering her hand with his against the mantel. "But you're the one who's beautiful." His stare held hers for the briefest moment too long, pulling her broken heart toward the sweet sliver of tenderness into another glimpse of a man she didn't know ... but wanted to.

A chill splashed through her at the attraction. She wasn't the one to rescue Alex Murdock. That was God's job.

She drew in a breath, shaking the interest off the chill and drawing her back a step. *Stop this, Rainey. You can't do this.* "Beautiful, huh?" She crossed her arms, guarding her shaking heart. "Are you still trying to get me to call your clients for you?"

His grin deflated but he recovered like a well-seasoned charmer … or a man who appreciated the lifeline she'd thrown him in the deep conversation. "Oh, come on, Rainey. People know you. All the names on my list? They're from Ransom. They won't return some unknown guy's call."

Which could certainly be true for her insular Appalachian natives. "Try again. Tell them you work with me." She placed a hand on her hip and scanned him from toe tip to wavy hair, hesitating just a moment on those changeful eyes. "Charm them. Aren't you good at that?"

His lips curled into a frown, and he placed both hands on the mantel, drawing her attention to his lean, strong frame. "Right. Charming." He growled, pushed off from the wall, and met her stance head on. "I know what you think of me."

Her chin stiffened, taking on the challenge. Confrontation? Arguing? She could handle that. The unexpected peek into Alex's vulnerability and wounds, igniting a deep desire to just hug him and feed him some of Mama's chocolate cake? She pinched her hand into a fist. *That* she wasn't ready for.

"Oh, yeah? What do I think of you?"

"You think I'm a superficial, arrogant, noncommittal joke." A brutal grin unfurled from his grimace. "And mostly you'd be right."

"So you're not some handsome, arrogant, noncommittal joke?"

His brow crooked and a light glimmered to life in his expression. "Handsome?"

The reality of her slip of the tongue dawned like an explosion of heat on her face. She fished for a ready reply but nothing came.

"The handsome part is true … and the arrogant part too, sometimes." He leaned so closely, sandalwood invaded her senses like a drug. "But if you really knew me, you may be surprised by what you'd find."

She stared him down, refusing to give way to the tug of his scent or the pulse of retreat. Know him better? Her pulse hammered into a stampede. "I'd probably find enough charm, innovation, and confidence to contact those clients without any help from me."

He groaned his reply, and she turned toward the kitchen. "You should get dessert before you leave. You don't want to miss Mama's caramel apple cake."

She could feel his eyes on her as she walked away, and against every piece of common sense within her, she looked over her shoulder to confirm. Sure enough, the rascal's attention zeroed in, increasing her internal temperature until her throat went dry. He wasn't what he seemed, but she couldn't risk lowering her defenses just because of his backstory ... or his wounded heart. Alex Murdock needed to stay exactly who she thought he was.

The air, wet with hints of snow, froze Rainey's face as she stepped from her jeep into the university parking lot. The time on her clock flashed with the possibility of being late on the first day of classes. Sarah's sniffly nose took a downward turn overnight with an added low-grade fever, but thanks be to Emma, who came to the babysitting rescue this morning! Rainey couldn't miss the first day of the semester.

She reached into the back seat of her Jimmy and pulled her computer bag up onto her shoulder before closing the door and starting for her office. The winter wind added another dose of cold to the already freezing temperature, and she tugged her scarf over her mouth, keeping her java safe and sound in her other gloved hand. Only a few steps toward the communication disorders building, she stopped and shot a look over her shoulder.

The hair on the back of her neck stood to attention beneath her scarf, sending off the undeniable twinge of being watched. She half expected to see Alex driving up in Marilyn, but her gaze settled on a red small-bed pickup truck at the end of the lot instead.

Ice clung to the frame of the front windshield but not enough to block the driver's identity. Dan Edwards. A new chill crept up her spine as Mr. Edwards continued to stare directly at her, unmoving, smoke from his truck's exhaust swirling upward.

Was he following her? Trying to scare her?

She raised her head and pushed her bag farther up her shoulder. Well, she wouldn't give him the satisfaction. Without another glance his way, she marched toward her building, her rapid breaths creating puffs in the wintry air. The weight of his stare followed her until she turned the corner of the building out of view. She pressed a palm against the brick wall and released a long sigh, her stomach still clenched at the man's creepiness.

Could he be dangerous? She dismissed the thought, even though the entire scene lingered in the back of her mind like the remnants of a scary movie. She switched off the worry and smiled as she entered the previously quiet office area, now abuzz with students and activity. The energy always proved contagious. One of Rainey's favorite things about working at the university was teaching. She thrived on watching the students learn and catch the passionate fire of their profession.

Her steps took a lighter turn. She glanced to Alex's office as she passed, but his door was closed. One look at her watch told her why. He had the early class—phonetics. She cringed at the thought of teaching a class filled with the nuances of speech sounds, dialect differences, and every intricate production in between. With her Appalachian background, the class had been hard enough for her to survive as a student. Her ears just couldn't hear the differences between pin and pen. It took years of careful training for Rainey to make even a B in the class. Thank the good Lord people could have specialties.

She placed her bag down at her desk and turned on her computer for a quick e-mail check before heading to the classrooms. Gray's name popped into the inbox, weakening her into her chair. She'd hoped his interest in Sarah was a fleeting one, something that if she agreed to without a fight, he wouldn't really follow through on. In his e-mail, though, he offered a few dinner dates when they could meet.

SUBJECT: TO DISCUSS A TIME WHEN I CAN SEE MY DAUGHTER.

His daughter? The one he'd abandoned when his sin caught up with his two-timing hide.

She sighed back into the chair and reread the e-mail. Short. To the point. But nonconfrontational. Maybe he was behaving himself for Sarah's sake, because that's the only way she'd let him see the little girl who didn't even remember his face.

She shot back a reply, choosing the latest day he listed as an option. Saturday at Daphne's. At least she'd be on familiar turf. That's the least Gray could have done after ripping out her heart, deserting his family, and disappearing without so much as a child support payment. She should've fought for more, but at the time, all she wanted was to be rid of the cheating scoundrel forever.

She lowered her face into her palms, reality digging the guilt deeper. She'd brought this calamity on herself by asking him to help pay for Sarah's private school. What was she thinking? Just another quick decision that had backfired.

She climbed the stairwell to the second floor, where classrooms lined the long hallway from one side of the building to the other. Rainey heard his voice through the open door of the classroom before she reached the doorway. Somewhat monotone and too much professional jargon for the class level, but maybe … maybe he was just getting warmed up. She always had the jitters the first day of a lecture, but as she stood listening, and the minutes turned into a half hour, the rumors melded into truth.

He lectured like a board, talking at the students instead of engaging them. She knew he was smart enough to handle this, clever and creative. If he had such a great reputation with grant writing…

Her head popped up and a smile pinched into her cheeks. She didn't need to feel indebted to Dr. Murdock. She could strike up a deal with him. Kindness and business all wrapped into one, and then she could save her pride … and her heart.

Chapter Eight

A lex had forgotten how much he hated teaching. Okay, perhaps "hate" was too strong a word. Highly disliked? Especially knowing from the vacant expressions in the room that everyone else in the room enjoyed his lectures as little as he enjoyed the task. He shrugged off his work bag and let it drop to the floor by the couch, the grating sound of his father's voice shouting "failure" in the back of his mind.

Would he ever get something right? Beth had been the only good thing in his life, besides his younger sister and niece, but his father had turned his nose up at Beth's humble upbringing. Now here Alex was, at this tiny university in some nowhere-town and failing at teaching, as adrift in his life as ever.

He tossed his keys toward the coffee table, and they landed in a jingly heap on the church bulletin from yesterday's service. A line on the front read:

> "You're no longer wandering exiles. This kingdom of faith is now your home country. You're no longer strangers or outsiders. You belong here, with as much right to the name Christian as anyone."
>
> Ephesians 2:19-20

He tugged off his gloves and lay down on the couch, taking up the bulletin and rereading the words. Stranger? Outsider? *You belong here.* He couldn't deny the pull in the words spoken and sung on Sunday. Memories of Beth's small, gentle family melded with new experiences with Rainey's. Could he belong here? His gaze dropped back to the bulletin. With God?

A motor rumbled outside, drawing Alex's attention from the couch to the front window. A massive, well-used truck with a bed full of wood slices backed up to the side of the detached garage and stopped. Trigg stepped from the driver's door and Reese from the other, both with nothing more than jean jackets over their clothes and ball caps over their heads to brace them from the cold. Were farmers cold resistant? The low-thirty-degree weather didn't seem to faze Trigg one step, even though his breath spotted the air with white clouds.

The unintelligible conversation between the brothers from the vantage point of the front window beamed with good-natured comradery, from the playful punch in the arm Trigg gave to Reese, to Reese's haphazard toss of work gloves into Trigg's face. A double-edged sting shot through Alex's chest, one side piercing a longing for such friendship and the other corner pricking at a long-standing fear of failing ... yet again. He'd always been able to connect with girls, probably from solid experience as the lone son squished between two sisters, but solid comradery with guys? His father's domineering personality along with the superficial bent on the world his dad created left Alex craving something he wasn't quite sure how to develop. A bond between men.

But ... but something seemed different here in this small part of the world. His attention pulled back to the coffee table and the bulletin with such powerful words etched on the page. Could it be true? A place to belong?

Well, he wouldn't let those guys unload *his* firewood on their own, even if he wasn't the best at making fires. With a longing look at the fridge housing Ma Mitchell's leftover meatloaf, he zipped his coat up to his chin, snatched his gloves, and headed out the front door.

The evening air stung against his cheeks, bringing his senses to life after a day languishing over research papers and lecture notes. He hadn't talked with the Mitchell boys much, but from the bits of conversations, the eldest seemed the quietest of the clan, with an almost unnerving penchant for observation. The younger son gave off more relaxed vibes, but Alex wasn't too sure of where he stood with Reese after trying to move in on the man's future bride. Well, she wasn't his future bride when Alex had asked her out, but the truth still blurred the expectation of Reese's reaction to him.

They'd both been nice to him at Sunday lunch ... but their mother's watchful gaze on them during the meal made all the difference.

"Need some help?"

Trigg's head came up and he wiped the back of his dirty-gloved hand over his forehead. "A smart man never refuses help." He unleashed the faintest smile. "And my dad didn't raise no fool."

Alex's dad would disagree on the same assessment of his own son.

"Well, unless we're talkin' about his love life or movie choices." Reese climbed into the bed of the truck and tossed a log into his brother's chest. "Then I might just disagree."

"You're one to talk." Trigg turned to stack the log in place and then shook his head as if in consolation. "A garden wedding? Flowers and candlelight?"

"Hey." Reese shoved another log at his brother. "I'd wear a pink tux"— he frowned—"okay, I'd do almost anything to make that woman my wife, so flowers? Candlelight? Gardens? Count me in."

Alex slowed his approach, taking in the brother-banter with a resigned ache. He didn't know that sort of friendship, brother or not. The same tug toward belonging nudged him closer to the massive pile of hacked wood and the unlikely comradery.

"Sounds like you have your priorities right."

"Somebody has to in this family, Alex." Reese gestured toward his brother with his shoulder since his arms were laden with another two logs. "That one takes too long to do anything. Sloooow."

"Just because I'm not impulsive like you, don't mean I'm slow." Trigg grabbed the logs from Reese and plunged them onto the growing pile. "I'm careful."

"Is that what Mama told you?"

Trigg shot his brother a glare, and Alex's grin widened as he delved further into the conversation and waited for Reese to add him to the work. Alex grunted as the two large logs struck his chest with more force than he'd expected. He covered the surprise with a quick turn, following Trigg's lead by stacking the logs onto the growing pile just inside the oversized garage.

"I've always wondered about this," Alex said, turning back to Reese for another load.

"What exactly? Troublesome brothers or garden weddings?" Reese's grin twitched as he added two more logs to Alex's waiting arms.

"Well, I don't have a brother, so that's certainly a curiosity." He turned to the pile, passing Trigg. "But I was talking about unloading wood. I read about it once but wasn't quite sure how it worked."

Silence greeted his words and he turned. Both men stared at him, but Trigg was the first to speak. "You ain't never unloaded firewood before?"

"My family wasn't exactly the country-loving sort, and my dad was no hands-on man. He liked to…" Dictate. "Delegate work."

Trigg's grin softened the previous shock on his face. "Well, if you're willing, we can teach you a whole bunch about country livin'."

"I'd like that." Reese's expression turned doubtful, but Alex quickly followed. "I haven't been here long, but I can already tell there's something about the country I want to learn more about." He gestured to the wood in his hands. "Like loading firewood, chopping firewood. In fact, I've never really learned how to light a fire either."

Trigg snickered and tossed another set of logs onto the pile.

"Don't you even, brother," Reese warned as he handed another set of logs to Alex, his attention on his snickering brother.

"Hey, Alex, if you need any help learning to light a fire—"

"Trigg Mitchell."

"Reese's an expert, I hear."

"Shut up."

"He lit Dee's fire in no time a'tall." Trigg's words disappeared into a chortle.

A ball cap went flying through the air, hitting Trigg on the shoulder. "You're never going to let me live that down, are you?" Reese growled. "Just wait, Trigg, your time's comin', and we'll see what you do with garden weddings, candlelight, and fire lightin'. Yes, sirree. I'll gladly sit back for a good laugh when it happens to you."

Trigg shook his head and laughed. "Don't plan on it for a while yet, but I'm sure I won't be moonin' around like you. It's embarrassin'."

Alex's grin kept growing until it sprouted a chuckle. He picked up Reese's cap and returned it to him. "If that's the most embarrassing thing that ever happens to you, Reese, then you're in good shape. I have a whole backstory filled with plenty worse."

Reese crammed the cap back on his head and sent Alex a thoughtful appraisal. "Well, I have the highest respect for you, Alex. I'd say you had a big hand in getting Dee the job in Charlottesville, even if losing your spot wasn't in the plan."

Alex didn't move. Couldn't. His blunders usually upended his life, with his good intentions going far from noticed. A response, if he could think of one, clogged somewhere in the middle of his shock and lack of practice in hearing a genuine compliment.

"Ain't that the way God works most of the time." Trigg patted his back, including him in the brotherly comradery. Alex's chest expanded with another breath of belonging. "U-turns and unexpected stops. He always ends up putting

His kids into the right place at the right time though, even if we go along kickin' and screamin'."

Alex shot a look to each man, but they'd started the wood-unloading routine again, oblivious to his hesitation. He'd never been around guys like them. Easygoing, good natured, adding God talk into conversation as if it were the most natural thing to do. Beth's father had been very reserved about his faith. Kind and generous in his behavior, but not open. Alex reached for another set of logs, testing his theory about the brothers.

"I feel the kicking and screaming part right now." Alex ducked his head and set two more logs on the stack. "Ransom certainly wasn't in my plans."

Reese ran a hand over the bill of his cap and settled his attention back on Alex. "Well, if you're here, then I reckon you're right where God wants you." His grin widened with humor. "And I bet you've never had a schoolin' like the one you'll get here."

"You know what, Reese." Trigg nodded toward Alex, his cobalt stare holding a lot more confidence in Alex than it ought. "I think Murdock is up for the challenge." Trigg took a log and pressed it into Alex's arms. "First, unloadin' wood. Next, getting acquainted with the cows."

"Cows?" How did he go from firewood to cows?

Reese's laugh pulled Alex's attention back to the truck. "And I imagine Trigg will have some fence mending come spring."

Trigg placed a hand on Alex's shoulder. "I think I like God's plan for your life, Alex. 'Specially if it involves help with mending fences."

Rainey turned the corner of the hallway at TLC, each familiar room fueling her determination to save the place she'd envisioned for years—a place to touch the lives of the children in the hills and hollows. The forgotten ones. Children she'd grown up beside who still lived in dirt-floor houses and existed on meager gardens hidden away on the mountainsides.

Despite the changes in the world all around them, parts of Appalachia remained decades behind in so many ways. Whether the children grew to stay in the mountains, like she'd done, or leave for other places, at least TLC could help provide them with opportunities.

"Ms. Mitchell."

From the other end of the hall came Dean Mercer, the woman whose power and position secured the reallocation of funds for TLC. As she marched forward, Rainey could almost hear the Wicked Witch of the West's theme playing in time with the click of the woman's heels against the floor. Dr. Mercer kept to her ivory tower of administration on most occasions, painfully disconnected from the regular working folks in the trenches, so her unilateral decisions weren't a surprise.

Infuriating, especially in this case, but not a surprise.

Rainey painted on a smile and walked toward her current enemy. "Dr. Mercer, what brings you to TLC?"

The dean had the unnerving ability to keep her face placid, without hinting at any real emotion, whereas Rainey was pretty sure her face blared every ugly thought she had. She pushed her smile wider, complete with gritted teeth.

Dean Mercer stopped a few feet away, her dark-purple suit a perfect match to her shoes and nail polish. "I was hoping to have a word with you. The secretary told me I may find you here."

Dr. Mercer folded her hands and glanced around the simple but professional building. Rooms faced each other on either side of the hallway. Next week, they'd be filled with tutoring and therapy sessions. The sweet hum of learning.

Rainey's smile stilled on her face. But how long could the learning continue?

"Would you like a tour? We serve over one hundred children a week from preschool to high school. And we've even created a cool game room upstairs—"

"I'm certain it is all quite impressive, but I would prefer speaking to you in a more private location. Your office, perhaps?"

Oh, Rainey would save TLC just to spite the awful woman. "I share my office with the front desk staff, who are currently making phone calls to schedule appointments for next week, but we could meet in one of the treatment rooms? Kid chairs in most, but they're empty until next week."

Dr. Mercer opened her red-lined lips as if to protest and then turned them up for a tense smile. "Of course. It shouldn't take long."

Rainey matched her stare for stare, then led her into the nearest treatment room—a bright purple color with cream-colored wobbly chairs. Her lips twitched into a smile on one side. *Perfect.*

With the smallest bit of guilt, Rainey sat on the wobblier of the two chairs. Dr. Mercer hesitantly took the other. After a wiggly moment of orientation, she attempted to fold her hands in front of her and maintain her composure, but her unmovable expression actually balked a little. Rainey did everything in her power to hold her smile in check. *Lord, if you don't mind too much, can we not mention this one moment to Mama? Please?*

"I know Dr. Russell made you privy to the college's most recent decision about funding for TLC."

"Yes."

Dean Mercer examined Rainey before continuing. "Many times we must make choices that appear unthoughtful, but as the head of a growing college, adjustments must be made for the greater good."

"The greater good? By a university school that will play to the wealthy minority of our community?"

"There will be a raffle for all children," Dr. Mercer countered. She attempted to fold her arms across her chest but proceeded to almost lose her balance on the wobbly chair. "With each child having equal opportunity."

"And what sort of transportation would the school provide for these kids to have equal opportunity?"

"Carpool for the first few years, but the plan is, of course, to build in public transportation so more children can be reached." She wobbled again and immediately stood. "I recognize your investment in TLC and all the hard work you've put into it, Rainey, but this is a bigger decision than TLC. It isn't personal."

Rainey shot to her feet. "Not personal? That's where you're wrong, Dr. Mercer. This decision is very personal. It impacts dozens of families right here in our community." She sighed, releasing a little of her frustration in an attempt to appeal to Dr. Mercer's softer side, assuming she had one. "Can't you reconsider? At least to give us enough time to raise money through grants? The department's choice impacts a lot of lives. Surely they're worth some extra consideration."

The slightest flicker waved in the dean's expression, then disappeared. "The decision has already been made. I've extended funding for one employee until the end of the semester, but apart from that, there is nothing I can do."

She turned and left the treatment room, but Rainey walked to the door after her. "This is a service worth fighting for, Dr. Mercer, and I plan to save it."

The woman paused and turned. "Then I wish you luck." With that, she disappeared down the hall.

Rainey pinched her fist and pressed it into the doorframe. Time to swallow her pride and ask Alex Murdock for help.

Despite Alex's wish for a different outcome, his second week of teaching emulated his first. Disinterested students, a lackluster instructor. *Boring.*

What was he doing wrong, besides drowning in self-doubt and studying material that made his eyes droop? If he hated reading the stuff, how could he make the students enjoy it?

And it couldn't be all their fault.

He'd peeked into Rainey's Language Disorders class. The very same students sat on the edge of their seats, commenting, asking questions, and actively participating in a way that burned a jealous bulb to life in his chest.

He reached into his to-go bag from Daphne's and snatched one of the chocolate chip cookies. Sure, a big container of chicken and dumplings waited at the bottom of the bag, but cookies? A day like today justified dessert first.

Alex shrugged. Well, having dessert first always sounded like a good idea. He moaned through a big, gooey bite of the heaven-made baked good. Living the country life was growing on him—or creating an addiction to butter and sugar.

A phone rang. *The* phone rang. Alex crammed the rest of his cookie into his mouth and tried not to get the sticky chocolate on the pristine steering wheel as he dug into his computer bag for his phone.

Marilyn swerved on the damp road as Alex wrestled with the phone, his sticky fingers, and the steering wheel. At least he was passing through the less curvy part of the backroads in Ransom. Despite the muddy embankment from the recent rains, the scene still stretched over wintry fields and forests to the rising mountains, which framed every side of his view.

He slowed the car and lifted his phone, but the reception dropped the call. *No!* What if it was an emergency? What if Evie had figured out a time to visit? He knew she'd try to call back immediately, so he waved the phone around in an attempt to find reception. A little bar flashed to life as he moved the phone by the window. He quickly pushed the button that brought down the window and stuck the phone out as the bar remained solid.

Okay, so … he'd have to drive the next five minutes to the farmhouse with his arm out the window. At least the unseasonably warm January weather meant a short windy ride wasn't so bad.

A bump in the country road sent his loose hold on the steering wheel into chaos. As Alex scrambled to main control of his car, the phone flew from him into the air.

Through the rearview mirror he watched the phone soar behind the car and disappear out of sight. His stomach ground to a halt along with Marilyn's wheels. With quick movements, he pulled Marilyn over to the muddy side of the country road and jumped from the car. His loafers hit a patch of sloshy mud, turning the suede into a much darker shade of brown.

With a groan, he trudged around to the back of his car and checked the road. Nothing. Could the phone really have bounced off the gravel stretch? The embankment took a steep turn downward into a muddy field. Alex studied the area, but not one hint of bright blue marked the position of his phone. Then, just out of reach, on the edge of the embankment, he spotted it half buried in the mud.

A squelch of sludge squished beneath him, seeping through to his socks, as he bent forward and reached. His fingers came within two inches of the corner, and a closer look proved his ninety-dollar phone case's boasts true. Safe and sound. He grinned and moved a step closer, fingers brushing the edge before … he lost his footing. One foot moved against his will over the edge of the embankment, bringing the rest of his body along for a muddy ride, face first, down the steep edge.

The recent rain left nothing dry enough for a saving foothold, and down he half rolled, half slid until he reached the bottom of the embankment. His palm pressed an inch into the mud as he pushed himself onto his knees and took inventory. The slimy, thick sludge covered every inch of him from the chest down, with sticky patches splattered across his face. Muck oozed a cold chill through the front of his dress shirt, around his buttons, and directly to his skin.

"You've got to be kidding me!" He struggled to a stand and shook the mud from his hands, wiping them on his trousers. With a groan at the steep but small embankment, he snatched the precious phone and began a long and messy battle to the roadside.

The day waned to dusk before he topped the edge and stood on flattened gravel again. Shadows fell long over him, darkening his muddy form into something that resembled the *Creature from the Black Lagoon*. This gave a whole new definition to "black sheep of the family." He took the somewhat-clean underside of his suit jacket and wiped at his face and phone as he rounded Marilyn's driver side.

Unbelievable.

Just when he was beginning to like the countryside, this happened, and left a scathing reminder of why he preferred street lamps, sidewalks, and nearly glitch-free cell phone reception. And these were his favorite shoes too.

He jerked open the car door and started to climb in, then froze. What was he doing? Enough mud clung to his trousers to add a few pounds onto him, sludge crusted into the creases of his dress shirt buttons, and his filthy shoes held enough clods to add an inch to Alex's height. There was no way he'd mess up the interior of a brand-new Mercedes with the grimy mire dripping from his body.

He looked up the road. It was only a couple of miles to the farmhouse. He could walk. His gaze dropped back to his precious car. But then, he'd have to leave Marilyn on the side of a country road unattended. He shuddered from the cold sinking deeper into his body as the sun lowered further behind the mountains' silhouette.

Casting another glance around the quiet countryside and seeing only a few cows for an audience, Alex shrugged off his hesitancy, stripped away his heavy jacket, and removed his soaking shoes and socks. With slow, stiff fingers he unbuttoned his shirt.

A cow mooed and Alex looked over the car to the field. "You'd do the same thing if it happened to you, buddy."

He scanned the vacant road behind him before pulling off his trousers and taking the muddy bundle to the back of the car. Even when he opened the trunk, he couldn't justify placing the clothes into the pristine interior.

Unbelievable. How could things possibly get any worse?

He rubbed his chin, forgetting about his muddy fingers until he felt the slippery substance on his face ... and hair. *Ugh.* A cow mooed again, mocking him. With another groan, he quickly placed the bundle on the side of the road and ran back to the driver door, the cold leather seats touching him on almost every part of his bare skin.

His reflection in the mirror, muddy hair erratic, face smudged with brown, nudged a laugh. He almost gave in to the prodding. Evie would be hysterical by this point. He grinned. Well, that was something.

The Mercedes hummed to life at his turn of the key, the sound a happy purr to his wounded ego. He cranked the heat up to full power, then shifted into drive. The tires spun but the car didn't move, and the cookie in Alex's stomach took a sour turn. He placed the car in reverse. The tires spun with a sound of splattering mud under the body of the car.

No, no, no!

Alex tried drive again, but the car only began to slide toward the embankment, so he jerked his foot off the gas pedal, placed the car in park, and pulled the emergency brake. With a half moan, half laugh he lowered his head to the steering wheel. What on earth was he going to do?

"God, if You're up there and watching this whole thing, would You mind telling me what You're trying to teach me, because I've had plenty of humiliation in my life, but this may be the tops."

A rumble surged behind him. Alex froze and looked into his rearview mirror to see a blue Jimmy. Rainey's blue Jimmy.

Of all the people in the world…

His mouth dropped wide and something like the sound of a whimper squeaked out. A car door slammed shut. He glanced heavenward. "I appreciate Your poignant sense of humor."

Alex looked down at his bare chest and legs, his striped boxers, and his muddy hands. Without another thought, he pulled his computer bag onto his lap to cover what little he could, crossed his arms over his chest, and greeted Rainey with a smile much too bright for the circumstances.

Chapter Nine

How did Alex get Marilyn stuck so deeply in the mud? Rainey examined the car's tires in the fading daylight as she walked toward the driver's side. That car wasn't going anywhere tonight. Once the mud dried, perhaps. In the morning. She pulled her jacket closer around her shoulders, the evening chill fingertipping over the thin cloth.

The tinted driver window obscured Rainey's view of the car's interior, but she could make out Alex's silhouette, so she tapped on the window. With a pregnant pause, the window descended and Alex's signature grin emerged.

"Hey Alex, are you ok…" Her eyes widened as the lowering window revealed his bare shoulders and chest. "What?" The window glass graciously stopped lowering as she realized Alex's computer bag probably blocked a lot more than his belly button. "What on earth…"

His grin brightened, too much. "It's a funny story, actually."

She blinked, still trying to form her thoughts into words. From her standing position, even in the fading light, she caught a clear glimpse of a broad chest and muscular arms. Her brain just couldn't figure any excuse as to why Alex Murdock would be sitting on the side of this country road in nothing but his underoos. "Funny?"

"I ran off the road and dropped my phone."

She studied him, trying to find the logical connection between dropping his phone and dropping his drawers. "Which automatically meant you stripped down to your skivvies in forty-degree weather on the side of the road?"

He laughed. *Laughed.* Which immediately caused a responsive crash of two thoughts in her head. One, she wanted to chuckle too—at the sheer ridiculousness of the entire scene. In fact, a tickle waited for release in her throat as she wrestled with thought number two—Alex Murdock was crazy.

But she did like his laugh. And his boyish smile. Which might mean *she* was the crazy one.

"My phone flew out the window."

"Your cell flew out the window?" Yep, he was crazy.

"Yes."

She tilted her head, playing along with the obvious delusion. "Did the fairies take it?"

His smile dropped and he forced a humorless laugh. "No, I couldn't get reception, so I stuck my phone out the window, then hit a bump in the road—"

"You were checking your phone while you were driving?"

He looked away, caught, and shrugged his strong shoulders. She flipped her gaze from his chest to his guilty expression. A sudden warmth in her cheeks dispersed the growing chill of evening. What did she expect? Someone this crazy had to be contagious.

"I was going slowly, and no one was on the road."

"Slowly or not, Alex, it's not the safest or brightest thing to do." She placed her palms on the window sill and leaned in, staring him down. "Stupid number one, you think?"

"Obviously."

His expression took such a penitent turn, Rainey's fight fled on a sigh. "You're an experiential learner, aren't you?"

His lips quirked up on one side. "In a bad way."

She nodded and pressed her fingers into her forehead. "Okay, so you lost your phone." She waved toward his legs and bare feet. "Is this some sort of northern form of meditation to get it back?"

He laughed again, louder. "Do you think we're from different planets or something?"

She made a pointed effort to scan his naked chest. "From where I'm standing, I'm beginning to wonder."

He rubbed at his arms, drawing her attention to the biceps he hid beneath those dress shirts. Okay, city boy had a build. She inwardly groaned. "Never mind, you can tell me on the way home. We need to get some clothes on you before you freeze."

His brow quirked. "We?"

Rainey's finger shot out at him. "Don't even, Dr. Murdock. I have you at a distinct advantage right now, so unless you'd like me to call my brothers, or even better, my cousin on the police force, so they can witness your current state of undress, you're going to behave yourself. Understood?"

"You need to smile more."

Her reprimand didn't even make a dent. Alex Murdock introduced a unique breed, that was for sure. One that sat half naked in a Mercedes at nightfall. She fought the growing grin, the tickle to laugh producing a cough. "Wait right here."

She jogged to her Jimmy and reached behind the seat, tugging out an old camouflage hunting jacket passed down from Trigg. At least covering his chest would help *her* mental clarity. "Put this on." She shoved it through his open window. "And then join me in the Jimmy. I'll drive you home, and you can regale me with the reason losing your cell phone meant you had to lose your clothes too."

"You don't happen to have some matching pants in that Jimmy of yours, do you?"

"No," she said and turned toward her SUV. "And even if I did, if you could fit into my pants, I'd probably kill myself."

Rainey texted her mama she was running a few minutes late to pick up Sarah. She looked up from her finished text in time to see Alex ambling forward, the hunting jacket hitting him at the hips, and his bare legs shone white in her headlights. She coughed through a laugh. He did have nice legs. She coughed again and her eyes burned.

Ridiculous man.

He sat in the Jimmy's passenger seat and placed his computer bag over his lap. "Oh man, it's so cold out there."

That was it. She couldn't take any more. Him, sitting in her brother's hunting jacket, hair tinted with mud, laptop bag covering his underoos, and then … his irrepressible grin? The laugh she'd grappled with for the last ten minutes started with a snicker and then erupted into a full-blown cackle. She leaned her forehead onto her hands against the steering wheel and tried to repress the urge, but every attempt ushered another convulsion of laughter until tears rolled down her cheeks, and her stomach ached. Everything from the time she'd peeked into his car to the image of this city boy sitting in her Jimmy in almost nothing but his smile sent her into hysterics.

She couldn't remember the last time she'd laughed so hard. Years?

"I don't usually resort to such drastic measures to make just anyone smile."

She shook her head and waved a hand toward him, unable to respond or even catch her breath.

"But you're special, so I pulled out all the stops."

Her head came back up, opening the volume of her laugh, and she pressed her arm against her sore stomach. "Oh my goodness, I think you gave a whole new definition to impressing a woman." She lost control of her laugh again, but not before catching the sweetness in his widening grin. Alex Murdock looked utterly delighted with her Joker-like laughter.

She swiped at the tears raining down her face and put her Jimmy into gear. "Dr. Murdock, you desperately need rescuing."

"Are you volunteering for the job?"

She chuckled and wiped at a few more tears. "I'm not certain I have enough stamina for a job like that."

He grew quiet, so she sent him a look in her periphery. His smile had gentled, catching her attention for a moment longer than she'd planned. "What?"

"You have a great laugh—like you mean it—and your whole face lights up when you smile."

Butterflies flittered to life around her heart, and she turned her attention back to the road. "You leave me little choice, Alex. And if you go around doing things like this…" She waved toward him and lost control of her laugh again.

"I'd rather make you laugh than cry, so I'll take up the challenge."

She allowed his admission to dissolve into silence, mainly because she didn't know what to say in return. His antics tonight paired with what she'd learned on Sunday left her emotions a little lopsided in an annoying kind of way. She should see Alex as a man-child from some of his reactions, but then he'd say something incredibly sweet and play it off with humor. For protection? Out of insecurity?

What really hid beneath that carefree smile?

She'd respond in kind. Teasing ran deeply in her family, so she put the Jimmy into gear and shot Alex a grin. "Is this what living next to you is going to be like? An adventure of mud-slinging proportions?"

He shrugged a shoulder, and the rascally grin returned. "Oh no, it will probably be much worse. I'm just warming up with this one."

Her chuckle escaped, his unique brand of charm catching her off guard again. "I'll warn Mama."

"That's probably wise."

She caught his look, playful with a hint of something she couldn't define, but whatever it was, her pulse shimmied into a canter. She drew in a deep breath and turned her attention back to the road, the farmhouse coming into view ahead. "So, this phone?"

"Right. It landed in the mud on the side of the road, and when I went to retrieve it—"

"You took a nosedive down the hill?" Rainey envisioned the whole scenario and, despite her best efforts, started laughing again. "Oh, Alex. And your clothes?"

"I couldn't get back into my car like that."

She snorted. "That must be one important phone."

"It is."

"Too many girlfriends' numbers in there to lose?" What? Why had she asked that stupid question? Like she even cared.

He hesitated and then the grin flickered again. "What can I say? Every woman is looking for her Prince Charming."

Every ounce of humor fled. "I think I just threw up in my mouth."

He shook his head. "Rainey, if I desperately need rescuing, you desperately need a date."

"As a matter of fact, Dr. Love, I've been on a date recently."

"Must have been a really bad one, then."

Her face warmed at the thought of her coffee date with Dave. Sweet guy. Easy conversation. "Actually, it was fine."

"Fine?" Clearly, Dr. Murdock was unimpressed. "That's definitely not good."

"What is that supposed to mean?"

"When a woman finishes a date, she should have a clear understanding. Yes or no." He shook his head, and a clop of mud hit the seat. She almost snickered again. "Fine is bad, like drinking lukewarm coffee or eating fat-free ice cream."

And the conversation turned into territory Rainey had no intention of discussing with Dr. Too-Many-Girlfriends-Murdock, but she did have a perfect topic on her mind. Besides, she didn't like the way his definition of dates hit her in the chest. She'd been on a dozen dates with half a dozen guys in the last year and most of them were ... fine. She almost cringed. Some of them, she could barely remember. None of them zinged with a clear yes or even left her thinking much about the guy afterward.

Maybe she was meant to remain single. She shook away that thought and sent Alex a look, grinning again at the sight of him.

She pulled the Jimmy to a stop in front of the farmhouse. "So, Alex, besides practicing as a half nudist and rescuing phones in distress, I've heard you have a skill for which I could use your help." His brows took an interested slant, and she continued an explanation to clarify. "I hear you're particularly good at grant writing."

"That wasn't the skill I was hoping you needed, but yes, I've had some success with grant writing. Why?"

Rainey turned to face him and drew in a breath for strength, accepting the partnership with a simple offer. "I'll teach you how to be a better teacher, if you'll help me save a clinic."

Rainey lost her place in class preparation for the third time. For some reason, reading an article about the newest research on autism failed to keep her mind from drifting to a certain scantily clad coworker. She sighed into her office chair and made another futile attempt to tame the smile pinching from one cheek to the other. The grin quickly transformed into a reluctant chuckle. It was impossible not to smile at the image of Alex Murdock half naked in her brother's hunting jacket. That man left a mark on her psyche, but she wasn't sure exactly what kind yet.

With a shake of her head, she tapped her computer to check e-mail. Gray's address popped into view. Well, if that wasn't a way to kill a smile...

Her entire body tensed, a habit forged from a six-year marriage to a critical man. She battled the residual sting with an inward prayer and breathed out her pent-up breath with the relief she didn't have to worry about what Gray Randall thought anymore. She was free from never measuring up to his inflated expectations.

With a click, she opened his message. He was canceling their meeting tomorrow with a request to reschedule for two Fridays away. Rainey nodded, checked her calendar, and shot back a reply. Well, it was probably for the best. She needed to focus on TLC and getting classes off to a good start this week instead of worrying about a meeting with Gray. She'd survived this long without his help, but dipping into her savings every month was taking a severe toll. Whether she wanted to or not, they needed to meet.

Her phone buzzed on the desk, and she smiled at the name displayed. Dee Roseland ... soon-to-be Mitchell. She touched the phone to her ear.

"Well, how is Dr. Roseland doing in her new position in Charlottesville?"

Dee laughed, a rarity becoming more frequent the longer the reserved professor stayed around the crazy Mitchell clan. Mama always said the best kind of crazy rubbed off like a sweet scent instead of a stinky one, so Rainey could only hope theirs was the best kind.

"I have a lot to learn and some pretty impressive expectations, but I get to teach some of my favorite courses."

Dee's excitement stood in direct contrast to Alex's reaction to teaching when he and Rainey had discussed their agreement last night. Rainey saw the struggle, the desire to make learning interesting to the students, but poor Alex lacked the tools. Fortunately, her college experience was littered with amazing professionals who instilled in her a solid understanding of good teaching—and she didn't deny some God-given talent there too.

"How are the wedding plans going?"

"They've been pretty simple so far. Since we both want something small and quiet, I've planned on spending my money on the dress and food, and Reese is spending his money on the honeymoon."

Her brother, the unlikely romantic, although Trigg was the real surprise. Her quiet, oldest brother, a notorious procrastinator, felt things deeply. What sort of girl might turn his head? "Sounds like a great plan to me. I'm just glad you're having it here in town, so we can help out more."

"With your mom and Emma on the prowl, I don't know that I'll have to lift a finger."

Rainey rolled her eyes with her burgeoning smile. Emma and her happily-ever-after-brain inspired romance enough for a Disney princess movie. Of course, Emma would offer to take over ... um ... help.

"How is Alex doing?"

Visions of the poor man in a camo jacket nearly undid her laughter again. "He's learning a lot too."

"Really?" Dee's response came slowly. "I hope so, Rainey. I'd always thought of him as an arrogant player, but the more I consider what he did for me to get recognized, the more I realize he's not exactly what he appears."

The book cover didn't seem to match the innards. Rainey was tempted to agree with her Mama's wise words. "I think he needs this place, Dee."

"I think he needs your family too, like I did."

Rainey drew in a breath, not quite ready to accept Alex with such open arms just yet. "Well, you're probably right. He does remind me of a lost puppy in a way."

Dee chuckled. "That's a good way of describing him." Silence paused the conversation. "I heard about TLC. Will you let me know how I can help?"

"I will, but right now I'm just trying to look up some grants and organize a plan."

"Grants? That's a great idea. You know, Alex is really good at writing grants. I worked with him on one or two when I was his graduate assistant. It's pretty impressive how well he can shine a proposal."

"So I've heard." Rainey tapped a pen against her desk, releasing a reluctant admission. "He's agreed to help me, and I've agreed to give him teaching lessons."

"A wager?" Humor laced Dee's words. "You made a wager with Alex Murdock?"

Rainey pinched her eyes closed. No way was Rainey going into that conversation. Dee and Reese's "wager" turned into a full-fledged romance. Rainey was staying plumb clear of fairy dust and moonlit nights. "Well, more of a friendly agreement between two colleagues. Definitely not your kind of wager, Dee."

Laughter greeted her from the other side of the phone. "Oh my goodness, Rainey. You'd better watch out! From my experience, a little wager … um … agreement can be life altering."

Alex adjusted his new tie in the rearview mirror of his car, adding a self-satisfied smile to his expression. It had taken him two hours to find the perfect tie yesterday. He'd visited every store in the little town of Ransom before finally coming upon it in some sort of hunting shop called Game Season. With a quick slide from his car, he searched the parking lot for a certain feisty blonde, fairly certain he could resurrect that smile of hers.

He walked past her Jimmy on the way to the sidewalk from the university parking lot and ground his feet to a halt. The icy chill of wind whipped over his skin directly to his heart. Two of the tires on the side were slashed, flat to the ground. He walked around to the other side to find the same results.

Evie! Alex's breath pulsed in puffs against the frigid air as he barreled toward the communication disorders building. His brother-in-law gave warnings before Alex and Evie were forced to fake his sister's and niece's deaths. A broken window with family pictures missing from their apartment, even as a policeman guarded the front of the house. A token of roses left on the sidewalk Evie used for work every day. Slashed tires. A gunshot that barely missed Evie's head.

Alex pushed through the glass doors and made a direct line to Rainey's office. Her door stood ajar, so he burst into the room without knocking and released his clenched breath when the vision of her, safe and sound at her desk, greeted him.

"You're here."

She made a slow turn in her swivel chair, eyes wide. "Good morning to you too?" And then she stood, palm to the back of her chair, studying his face. "I didn't know your face could look so serious, Dr. Murdock."

"You don't know."

Her expression sobered. "What's wrong?"

"Come with me." He grabbed her hand and pulled her down the hallway. About halfway to the door, she managed to wiggle her fingers free from his, even though he attempted to snatch them back.

"Where are we going? Alex?"

"Someone's slashed the tires of your car."

"What? My tires?" She took off at a faster pace, long strides in full swing, toward the parking lot. "People don't do things like that around here." She tossed the statement over her shoulder.

A revelation that gripped his chest even tighter. This wasn't random.

She rounded the Jimmy with Alex on her heels, his gaze sweeping the parking lot for any hint of the mastermind behind the act.

"Who would do something like this?" Rainey murmured more to herself, but Alex had been entertaining the question since the moment he discovered the vandalism. Who? The slashes ran long and deep, from a strong hand. A man. Heat slithered up Alex's neck and into his face, a raging fury waiting under his skin to propel him into protective action. This hit too close to home. Too familiar.

"You need to call the authorities right now. I think you're in danger, Rainey."

Her gaze slowly pulled from the tires to his face. "Danger? Why would I be in danger?"

"It doesn't matter why, but this is a serious offense. A warning." He marched to her side and pulled his cell from his pocket. "If you don't notify the police, I will."

"Whoa there, trigger." She covered his hand that held the phone, a weak smile playing across the lines around her mouth. "Let's not jump to conclusions too quickly. Maybe it's something simple like one of my TLC teens taking their hatred of geometry out on my tires?"

"You don't believe that any more than I do."

She crossed her arms and examined the car, worrying that bottom lip of hers with her teeth. Her breath puffed into the misty morning. She had to be cold. "Well, whatever the reason, I guess I'll need to call Mama for a ride home."

"Call the police." He walked to her side, removing his jacket and sweeping it around her shoulders. "*I'll* take you home, but we're not going anywhere until I know you've let the authorities know about this."

Those aqua eyes stared up at him, studying his face in silence until his neck grew warm beneath his collar. "This is really important to you."

He made a weak attempt at a shrug. "Safety is important, and if this incident has to do with that Edwards fellow, you may be facing a lot worse than an angry teen." His smile crooked in an attempt to curb his own concern, the practice becoming almost second nature. "Though geometry always brought out the worst in me too."

A hint of a smile smoothed away a few of the worry lines in her brow, and her gaze dropped to his chest. "Nice tie, by the way."

"I bought it special."

She fought the grin. He could see the struggle as the corners of her lips tugged upward, and somehow that glimpse, his effect on her, caught him right around the heart and held on tightly. Her smile mattered. To him. In a way a smile hadn't mattered in a really long time.

Her attention went back to the SUV, but her lips continued their teasing tilt. "I'm glad you found clothes to go with that tie."

"Like I said before. Special moments for special people."

And she lowered her head to hide her chuckle, but he heard it. Felt it, actually, reigning him toward her like a wild stallion toward home.

His gaze flitted back to the tires, and he touched her shoulder, gaining another peek of her aqua eyes. "Call the police, okay?"

"Okay, Alex. I will."

"I've seen these kind of signs before, Rainey." His palm dropped from her arm. There was no way he'd let her go home tonight alone. This was the perfect excuse to keep her safe, to not relive the past. "When you're ready to leave school, I'll get you home."

Chapter Ten

Rainey stared at her computer screen, unseeing. Despite her attempt to appear nonchalant in front of Alex, the instance with the slashed tires opened an uneasy Pandora's Box of possibilities. John Edwards beat his wife and children, so what would stop him from lashing out at anyone threatening his world?

Her cousin, Derek, a sergeant for the local police department, investigated her Jimmy, then had it towed to Clive's for new tires. She rested her face into her palms and sighed until her elbows hit her desk. She didn't need any more distractions from this catastrophe with TLC. *God, what are you doing right now?*

"Are you okay?"

She jumped at the sound of Alex's voice and turned to see him standing in her doorway, arms folded across his chest and those marble-like eyes of his taking inventory of her in the same focused way he'd done outside. She could ignore his playboy attitude, but something about the intensity in his concern, his appeal of racing toward her to ensure her safety, rocked her to her core.

The lost dreamer inside of her craved the protection, the care, but the sensible part of her, especially every scar, screamed for a fast retreat from a pull toward her weaknesses. Her heart.

"Besides being carless for the day and a little distracted, I'm okay."

"Well, I am going to take you home in style."

"Are you sure Marilyn won't get jealous?"

His eyebrows wiggled. "Should she be?"

Rainey snapped her laptop closed and stood. "I think Marilyn is safe."

"You say that with such conviction, Rainey." He stepped into the office and brought the warm scent of sandalwood with him. "But just so you know, Marilyn doesn't mind sharing."

She tried to ignore him as she packed up her things. "Slow down there, Romeo. I'm much more interested in starting our little chats about grant writing and teaching. Would you have time tonight? I have some roast in the crock pot, and after we pick up Sarah from Mama's we could head over to the house to work and eat."

His palms came up with his much too bright smile. "Wait a minute. Is this a date?"

"A date?" She slung her bag over her shoulder and laughed. "It's two colleagues discussing work over food. That's it."

He turned toward the door with a shrug. "Still sounds like a date to me. I'm going to call it a date."

She rolled her eyes heavenward and prayed for strength as he held the door for her to step into the hallway. Why did she suddenly feel this whole wag ... er ... agreement was a bad idea?

"What a great house." Alex followed Sarah into a house brightened with oak floors and pale blue walls. The mouth-watering scent of roast welcomed him as much as the surroundings. He turned the corner of the hallway into a large room with a rock fireplace on one side and an archway into the kitchen on the other, with windows lining the entire wall to showcase a view of the expanding countryside bathed in golden sunset.

"Look where I put your picture." Sarah led Alex through the archway to the refrigerator, where his Pinkie Pie drawing waited with a cluttered display of child artwork and photos. Alex scanned the pictures of Rainey and Sarah—one at Christmas, one on a tractor, another with her cousins.

He'd never seen such a messy and heartwarming display, like watching a Hallmark movie come to life in front of him. A beautiful house styled with country charm, the smells of home cooking wafting around him enough to make his stomach growl, a little girl pulling him through warm and welcoming rooms in soft colors, and a sassy blonde who was starting to nudge at his heart in distracting ways. He certainly didn't fit into something as wholesome and sweet as this, but, boy, he wanted to.

"Look at that." Alex leaned down and tapped Sarah's adorable nose. "My picture right in the middle of all your beautiful artwork."

Sarah's smile brightened and she pointed to the top of the display. "Up there is the picture of you riding Pinkie Pie, Dr. Alex."

His grin spread to the laughing point. He swooped Sarah up in his arms. "You're going to have to show me which one so I can appreciate what I look like on Pinkie Pie."

He glimpsed Rainey's grin and a sweet softening around her eyes as she tossed her keys on the table and shed her jacket. A connection zinged to life, then simmered beneath his skin into a warmth of rightness. Yep, he was happily distracted by two beautiful blondes. Man, life was good.

Rainey looked away first, hooking her jacket on the back of one of the chairs in the breakfast nook, a place she obviously enjoyed because the little round table sitting perfectly in the curve of the bay window was covered with papers and books, like a makeshift desk. The view alone—a tree-framed look toward Mama Mitchell's house on the hillside—would inspire anyone to pause and appreciate the wonders of nature.

"That one right there." Sarah pulled his attention back to the direction of her petite finger. "See how fast you're going."

He tilted his head and tried to make out the colorful blots on the paper. "Wow, I've always wondered what I'd look like riding a pink pony. Who's that up in the clouds?"

"Can't you tell? That's me."

"Of course, you're on Twilight Sparkle."

"Mmhmm." Sarah nodded and bestowed her dimpled grin on him. "And Mama's riding Apple Jack."

Alex cut Rainey a look. "I'd expect no less from your mama." The sassy, independent, country-style pony fit Rainey Mitchell down to the mischievous glint.

Rainey rested a palm on her hip. "And what is that supposed to mean, Dr. Alex?"

He lowered Sarah back to the floor. "That the hoof fits pretty well, is all."

"I reckon I could say the same thing about you on Pinkie Pie then."

"I do look pretty good in pink."

She narrowed her eyes at him as she squeezed between him and the refrigerator, her body grazing his. Alex's gaze plummeted the length of her, appreciating how her khaki slacks fit her curves to perfection.

As if her body read his every wish, she paused in front of him, almost against him, her golden brow tipping with doubt. "You wear pink?"

He leaned in, drinking in a deep breath of her citrusy aroma. "Real men do, you know."

Her stare glistened and then she continued her slide out of reach to the other side of the kitchen. "By the way, there's a coat rack by the door, if you'd like to get a little more comfortable." She lifted the lid to the crockpot, ignoring him, but the hint of pink in her cheeks let him know she felt the impact of that accidental touch too.

"Sure thing." He shrugged out of his jacket, his steps lighter as he rounded the corner and deposited the outerwear on the rack. A homemade rack from the looks of it, beautifully carved into a ... tree?

"This is amazing." He returned to the kitchen, pointing behind him. "That coat ... tree. Wow."

Rainey rewarded him with a sad smile. "My dad made it. He was always piddlin' around with wood and craft ideas."

"Can you buy things like that?"

She turned toward him and placed her palms against the counter behind her. "Sure. There are at least two shops in town that sell well-made Appalachian crafts. My cousin Casper apprenticed under Daddy for years, so I'd recommend his shop first. It's called Mountain Memories and is a few blocks down from the courthouse on Main Street, but I'm not sure there'd be a lot of his items that would fit in a fancy, upscale city spot, if you're looking to move on from Ransom."

He caught Sarah as she ran past and swung her around, her giggle filling the room and his heart. "Oh well. I think country charm is growing on me." He held Rainey's stare, his grin slowly widening. "As a matter of fact, I'm sure it is."

Believing him felt like a mental tug-of-war. He'd toned down Mr. Flirty Face a little, but why did she still feel pulled toward him. The ready smile, the teasing tones, the easy stride that drew her attention in ways that brought heat to her face? Somehow his very presence uncontrollably loosened her smile. And then his way with Sarah? If Alex played a part, his tenderness and interest appeared so genuine, she was beginning to doubt her own senses. In fact, her heart beat down every argument her mind conjured against the devilishly handsome man sitting across the table from her.

And that terrified her much more than winks and smiles and warm fuzzies in the pit of her stomach. Trusting her heart again?

"Here's another link for grants. Wait, I think." He reached into his shirt pocket and pulled out a pair of glasses, slipping them onto his nose. Something about this dashing man wearing glasses kept Rainey staring like a dazed teen.

"You have glasses, like me?" Sarah asked from the other side of the table where she sat in her pony PJs, coloring another picture for Alex's barren refrigerator.

Alex tapped the frames. "Yes, ma'am. My eyes get tired after reading a lot if I don't wear them."

"I fink you need to get green ones like your eyes."

"Do you?" He pulled his glasses off and stared at them, as if her suggestion held weight. "I suppose silver isn't as interesting as another color. Yours are much cuter than mine."

Sarah's grin spread wide again, and she went back to her coloring. They'd been buddies all evening, and Alex moved right into their after-dinner cleanup routine as if he'd always belonged, chipping in to help with the dishes and straighten up the kitchen.

He turned his laptop toward Rainey, who finally blinked out of her stare. "This link is focused a little more on educational development for low socioeconomic populations."

She forced her gaze from his face to the screen. "That sounds promising."

"It won't be active for the upcoming year, but the next. And it's renewable."

"Which is definitely something we need for continuity of care." Rainey leaned back in her chair and rubbed a hand against her forehead. "We're planning to begin filing insurance more regularly. That should bring in extra revenue."

"Right, that should help a little, but grants like this will save the clinic."

"If I can get them."

Alex shrugged and relaxed in the chair. "I don't see why you can't. What you've told me about TLC sets it up as a prime candidate for these grants we've chosen to research. We'll need to use our elbow grease to fill out all the paperwork, but I don't see any reason why we can't get TLC funded for the future."

She sighed. "But not this upcoming year or the remainder of our current year." Her shoulders deflated from the weight. "I've got to figure out something to do in the meantime."

"Didn't your family mention something about a fundraiser? Maybe you could raise awareness by writing an article for the local newspaper or trying to get a television spot for an interview?"

Rainey's mouth dropped wide. "Oh, no, I'm not a television spot kind of person."

"You're the best spokesperson for TLC there can be. You're passionate. You know it the best, and you're really easy on the eyes."

And reality hit. She tried not to smile at his obvious flirting, but one corner of her lips tilted against her will. "That may be my only redeeming quality when I stare at the camera, too nervous to speak."

"It'd be enough for me." Alex shook his head and chuckled. "But I doubt you're at a loss of words much, Rainey Mitchell."

He hadn't seen her in front of a camera. "Mama mentioned maybe we could do something at the Founder's Day Festival at the end of next month. I'm not sure what, but loads of people show up for it every year, with a parade and vendors all down Main Street."

"That's a great idea. My father once used a similar situation to draw attention to a new venture he'd created." Alex relaxed back in the chair, braiding his fingers behind his head and stretching out his legs to cross at the ankles.

She appreciated his form way too much, like she hadn't noticed a man in two years or something. Heaven help her, she was noticing now. "Your dad is a businessman, right? A pretty successful one."

His gaze came up, sadness lingering around his eyes despite the upturn on his lips. A strange mixture of curiosity and interest battled every caution within her rising to defense.

"He's good at what he does."

There was a whole backstory behind that sentence. "Why do I get the sense you don't meet his expectations?"

He folded his arms across his chest, his fake smile wavering. "I don't. Never have." He sighed. "Don't get me wrong. I could sell water to a fish, but a world of constant meetings, business deals, late-night conferences?" He shrugged. "I saw it my whole life and wanted something more. *With* more."

"Like what?"

He chuckled and looked down at the table. "As old-fashioned as it may sound, I wanted a family. The whole Mayberry experience. Soccer games, packed lunches, meals around a table."

Rainey leaned her chin on her palm, closer to him. It was easy to forget how blessed her life was when normal wasn't normal for everyone and riches didn't purchase peace. "I wouldn't call that old-fashioned. I'd call that classic."

His grin brimmed with authenticity, and he searched her face with an intense perusal that dried out her throat. "I like classic."

She should move back, display complete indifference, but the gentle tug of his stare encouraged her to tarry in the romantic haze. "Well, there's something we can agree on."

He moved closer, an almost-wonder dawning in his eyes. "That's a start."

Her breathing dwindled to a weak strain of air through her parted lips. He looked at her as if he liked what he saw, a craving battered by her ex-husband's incessant criticism and ultimate betrayal. How long had it been since a man "saw" her? Had anyone ever looked at her like this?

"Is it?" A warm touch blushed from her chest to her cheeks. It couldn't be true. He barely knew her, and she certainly didn't know him. Rainey cleared her throat and lowered her eyes to her watch. "Time for bed, sweet pea."

Sarah's head popped up from her work. "Can I finish Dr. Alex's last picture first? I just have to color his boots."

"All right, but then it's off to bed." Rainey stood and stretched, tossing Alex a look. "Want some coffee?"

"You mean, I get to stay longer?"

She turned toward the Keurig, avoiding his teasing expression. "We've talked about grant writing and researched grants for the past hour and a half. I still have to give you some teaching tips." She turned and waved a coffee cup at him. "It's part of the deal."

"By all means, keep your end of the bargain. This beats hanging out at the farmhouse by myself and watching *Andy Griffith* reruns."

She laughed. "You spend your evenings watching *Andy Griffith* reruns?"

"Sure." He winked, and her face flooded with another wave of warmth at the unexpected responsive flutter in her stomach. Ugh, what was she? Thirteen? "How else can I learn about the natives?"

"Ha-ha."

"I'm finished with your boots, Dr. Alex." Sarah hopped down from the table and gave him a fourth picture. "You're wearing shiny silver boots because they're magical."

He drew Sarah up onto his lap, bending forward to peer at the paper. "That's some hat I have on my head. And it's silver too?"

"Yep." She looked up at him, and Rainey's heart squeezed at the adoration on Sarah's sweet face. "It's a magic hat. Helps you think big thoughts."

"I've needed that hat my whole life, princess."

Rainey caught her laugh in her hand and turned back to the Keurig. Who was this guy? So arrogant and yet quick to beat up himself? Such a sweetheart to her little daughter? She was beginning to find this anomaly much too intriguing for her own good.

"Now you have one *and* your refrigerator will have lots of color."

"Say goodnight to Alex, sweetie, and head up to bed. I'll be right up to pray with you."

"Okay, Mama." Without provocation, Sarah leaned over and gave Alex a kiss on the cheek. "Goodnight, Dr. Alex. I like your glasses."

"Night, princess." Alex's voice barely made a noise, a gravelly whisper. The tender, glassy-eyed look he gave Sarah shifted another piece of caution away from Rainey's heart.

A buzzing noise interrupted the scene, but Alex didn't notice. He just sat there, his dumbfounded expression following Sarah as she skipped from the room toward the stairs. A phone buzzed again.

"Hey, Alex, you're buzzing."

His green gaze settled onto Rainey's. "What?"

Another buzz broke into the silence. Alex jumped as if the vibrations stung and jerked the phone from his pocket. "Oh, I need to go take this."

"Is everything okay?"

"Yeah." He avoided meeting her gaze and shifted toward the door. "I've been waiting for this call, though, so I need to answer."

"I hope everything's all right." She followed him down the hallway to the coat tree.

"Um, yeah, it's good. Just something I need to work out, you know?" His grin emerged too quickly, his eyes too brightly. Secrets hid within his smile—and she hated secrets.

"Sure." She shoved her hands in her pockets and waited by the door as he slid into his jacket. "Thanks for all the help."

"I expect turnaround to be fair play, Rainey." His eyes glimmered with playful mischief, but her smile failed to respond with its former enthusiasm. She reined in the pull to enjoy the banter, to fall just a little more into liking him too much. "You're supposed to make me a fantastic teacher, right?"

"I'll certainly do my best." She opened the door for him, fighting the sudden swell of disappointment. She had a half gallon of dark-chocolate ice cream in the freezer designed for this very moment.

He paused in the doorway, the hall light playing a game with the color of his eyes. Were they emerald? Seafoam green? She pinched her eyes closed. What did it matter?

"Thanks for tonight."

She shrugged off the gratitude. "Thanks for the ride home."

His hand covered hers on the doorknob, drawing her gaze to his. "I mean it. It was the best date I've had in a long time."

"Alex Murdock!" Rainey yelled as he closed the door on his chuckle. She flung the door wide and watched him disappear toward Marilyn. "This was not a date."

He didn't so much as turn around.

Insufferable, arrogant man! She gripped the doorframe and hoped he looked back as he pulled out of the driveway. She had her evil glare ready and pointed directly at him. Her fight died as his car disappeared into the night, and she closed the door.

What was she doing? Rainey needed attraction to someone faithful, dependable, and honest, not someone with a phone full of secrets … and yet there was no denying how her pulse raced with their fun repartee or how she wanted to lean closer to him for a deeper sniff of sandalwood or how something inside her came to life when he looked at her. She rested her head back against the door and shut her eyes, desperately trying to close off her emotions.

Help me, Lord. Please take away this attraction for Alex Murdock. Please. He can't be good for me or Sarah.

Silence responded along with Alex's lingering scent. Secrets brought pain. The last one a man kept from her ended in a child who wasn't hers. Despite what Alex said, and even what he might feel, he was dangerous to her heart.

Chapter Eleven

Alex had never *not* wanted to answer his sister's call before ... until this evening with Rainey. Memories played like a movie, reeling through scene after scene of fun and sweet moments. From Sarah's complete adorableness and big-hearted welcome to Rainey's teasing and tantalizing presence all the way to the atmosphere of her cozy home, everything fit in place inside him like a missing puzzle piece. Then he watched the puzzle shatter with one single phone call.

He usually responded with a more believable excuse for the call, but he'd been lost in the tenderness of Sarah's kiss and Rainey's nearness, too distracted to gather himself for his usual protection of his sister's existence.

With a heavy heart, he stepped from the porch and started his morning jog ... and maybe held the slightest hope Rainey's timing fit his. He took the gravel road and breathed in the cold morning air. A myriad of red, pink, and orange hues lit the morning sky with stunning beauty, stirring his thoughts away from Rainey or his sister and toward something ... Someone who boasted an understanding and care for them both.

A sweet familiarity accompanied Alex's observations of Rainey's interactions with Sarah. The vocabulary of her faith—"show grace, Sarah" and "God's blessed us, hasn't he?"—even with the pain of Rainey's past never failed to surprise Alex. It all reminded him of Beth and the draw he felt to her faith, the reality of it lived out.

Rainey had prayed before their meal last evening, linking hands with him on one side and Sarah on the other. As soon as his fingers wrapped around hers, his world clicked together. Not only did he want the moment to last, but ... he craved a peace with this intangible faith he didn't understand. His gaze flipped to the fiery sky, burning brightly with rising dawn, and his mind, his heart reached out to the unseen within the seen.

Did He take failures? People who derail their own lives? The screw-ups? The message from the Mitchells' church, directly from the pastor's mouth, told him "yes," and the promise of belonging to Someone who accepted him despite his stumbling and mistakes grabbed him soul deep. A switch flipped inside him, a convergence of the past whispers of Beth's faith and this current understanding … call.

His feet skidded to a stop, and he faced the rising sun, the first rays warming his face like a touch from heaven ushering his trust.

"Okay," he breathed. "I know You've been pursuing me a long time, and I can't understand why You'd want me." His throat tightened with the foreign collection of emotions. "You know I'm messed up, but if You'll take me as I am, Lord, I'm yours."

The glow of sunlight somehow took on enough warmth to press all the way through him. A beginning right in the middle of his life. He laughed and shook his head, taking in the wonder. He belonged somewhere, at his core, at last. Why had it taken him so long?

"Okay then." His words emerged in rasped awe. "Thank you."

Crunching gravel drew his attention away from the horizon, toward a princess riding a pink bicycle and a feisty blonde in a pair of sweats that did nothing to hide her curves. Alex chuckled. Despite his heavenly experience, his mind returned to earthly thoughts easily enough. He studied their approach, his grin untamable. Though, just maybe, there was something angelic about the two blondes coming toward him that might have more heavenly hints than earthly.

"Dr. Alex." Sarah's sweet voice rose with a lilt that played across his heartstrings. "Mama, look. He's not still asleep." She brought her bike to a stop in front of him. "Mama said it was too early for you."

Alex looked to Rainey, who avoided his gaze. Aha, she'd hoped to beat him on her run and miss him altogether. Well, who could blame her?

"I didn't want to miss the sunrise." Alex bent down to Sarah's level and gestured toward the sky. "Isn't it pretty?"

Her grin dimpled as she looked up at him from beneath her purple helmet. "It has lots of pink."

The afterglow from his prayer still poured through his chest with newness. "Sure does."

Rainey came closer, and he tipped his head to her. "Mind if I jog with you?"

She shrugged and waved her hand toward the gravel lane. "It's a free road."

She jogged past him at a slower pace, allowing Sarah to lead the way on her bike. Alex fell into rhythm beside her.

"I want to apologize for last night."

She kept her face forward. "What do you mean?"

Stubborn woman. "The phone call. I don't know why I didn't just tell you about it, but it caught me off guard. You see, it's a private family matter and ... I can't really go into it."

"Of course." She tilted her head in his direction but kept her eyes ahead. "Is ... is everyone okay?"

Family. Just from the short time he'd spent with the Mitchells, the bond and love of family beat as the pulse of who they were.

But how to answer? "For the most part." He'd thought through what to tell Rainey and exactly how to tell it safely. "Since we lost my sister and niece after a car accident last year, my dad and I haven't really been on the best terms. We weren't on the best terms before, especially after Mom died, but things became worse after the accident."

He was rewarded with a flash of aqua and a pace that slowed to a complete stop. "Oh Alex, I'm so sorry. I can't even imagine that kind of loss."

His conscience twinged. He'd used the same sentence for a year, but for some reason, as he stared into her upturned face, the story bled with deception in a way it hadn't before. He wanted her trust.

Her shoulders relaxed with a sigh, and she reached out to touch his arm, inviting back the closeness he'd experienced with her last night. "I'm too quick to jump to conclusions, and I'm sorry." She studied him with such a tender look, his defensive wit failed him, and he had no response to buffer her apology.

"What do you say we meet this afternoon so I can give you some teaching tips for this upcoming week? I'm helping Trigg on the farm this morning, but maybe after lunch?"

"Another date, then?"

She shook her head, and her ponytail flapped back and forth. "Sarah will be with me."

"The best kind of date."

She fastened him with a stare and then finally released a long sigh. "Okay, Alex. Sure." Her tone turned consolatory, and she took off jogging.

Score. Oh man, he liked her a lot. A whole lot. An ache-down-deep kind of like. He caught up to Rainey, her pace a little faster to catch up with Sarah, who'd ridden ahead while the two of them talked. "Do you need a computer and papers to teach me?"

She glanced up at him again, her brow in wrinkles. "Um ... no, not to start. I can e-mail you some references and videos to watch."

"Oh, good. Then maybe you could teach me while we could go for a hike."

"A hike?"

"Yeah. Now that we're dating and all, I thought we could enjoy the scenery while you're teaching me."

She smiled and rolled her eyes at him, a signature expression of hers he was beginning to understand. "You're ridiculous, but okay."

"There's a mountain trail I've read about online. Sunset Spot, I think is what it's called, on Calver's Ridge. We could hike and you could talk." He shot her a grin. "And I could try really hard to listen."

"If you haven't been to Calver's Ridge, then you definitely need to go. There's no better view around."

"Then it's the perfect place to expand my creative mind, right?"

"Alex, I'm not sure your mind needs any more creative expansion. You seem to have a heap of it without any help."

"Oh, my dear Miss Mitchell, my brain is filled with useless information and way too much motor speech terminology to be much good. I'm hoping you can provide some useful enlightenment to make me a better man."

She laughed, a sound as inviting as the comradery in their jog. "Well, I don't know about making you a better man, but it's my plan to make you a better teacher."

Rainey gathered her lunch and headed toward the teacher's lounge, trying to temper her curiosity about how Alex's morning class went. Their trip to Calver's Ridge proved to be one of her weirdest teaching experiences yet—but not so much because Alex was a difficult student. On the contrary, he took in the information she shared as they walked the tree-lined path to the mountain's summit like a student hungry for knowledge. The conversations flowed easily, and he made certain to sprinkle lots of fun along the way, teasing her caution down more and more.

She liked him.

Surely all the sweetness couldn't be a façade. The way he scooped Sarah onto his shoulders when her little legs became tired. The moments he took Rainey's hand to help her bridge a gap in the unpredictable rocks. The gentle way he'd wiped a smudge of dirt from her cheek and stared into her eyes with wonder, as if … as if she dazzled him in some way.

She'd never dazzled anyone. Not like that.

Being tough, fencing off the daydream-y part of her spirit, came from a life with two older brothers and expectations for the oldest girl on a farm. When romance became smothered beneath Gray's criticism and betrayal, she'd resorted to snuffing out the tempting draw of daydreams, but something in that one look from Alex rekindled a quieted longing. A hope.

Her pulse stuttered in retreat, her thoughts reeled from the shock, but her heart failed to flee. She wanted a fairytale. And her crazy brain believed Alex Murdock might be the hero to give her one. Maybe she was still lightheaded from the altitude change up on Calver's Ridge. She couldn't wrap her head around how it could work, but her heart seemed to understand.

She flipped her gaze heavenward and breathed out the fear. God knew what He was doing, even if her emotions flipped like an upside-down kaleidoscope. She trusted Him to guide her heart, mind, and soul—even if two of the three wavered in the spin.

Time would tell whether Alex proved true or not, and maybe—her smile inched wide as she pushed open the faculty lounge door—it would be worth the great unveiling.

The small lounge held a few café-style tables and chairs, plus a corner kitchen. Despite the demanding schedules at BRU, the lounge stayed remarkably busy throughout the week while faculty rotated in and out as their schedules fit and took opportunities to socialize. Lizzie waited at their usual table by the lone narrow window, and two of the other tables were also occupied. Dr. Ramsey at one table, with her ready smile, sat across from the debonair and dashing Dr. Khatri, whose tall, dark, and handsome Indian looks wooed many a student into a dreamy-faced state. Luckily for him, he was a happily married man with two gorgeous, dark-haired boys who'd probably grow up to break a dozen hearts each.

But the people at the other table snagged her attention—actually, only one of the people at the other table. Alex looked up from his conversation with Dr. Teddy Ryken, and his grin unwound her own and tipped the temperature of the room into the red zone. *Stop the crazy, Rainey.*

She hoped her expression returned a subdued response instead of the heart-eyed emoji running wild in her mind's eye, the thought only magnifying the heat of her cheeks. She refused to succumb to the ridiculousness of her own thoughts and drew her gaze from Alex's with a lifted chin of purpose. Foggy-headed thinking never helped a woman make a clear decision, and she'd step into any romantic relationship with as pristine a vision as she could this time around, especially for Sarah's sake.

She sat into the chair across from Lizzie and offered her brightest smile. "Hey, friend, how's your day been?"

Lizzie raised a carrot. "Exciting stuff. I got two new referrals, both post-stroke patients and perfect for my new research project, which means…"

"Therapy is free for them." Rainey opened her *Star Wars* bag and drew out her sandwich of roast beef leftovers. Perfect winter lunch. "I love it when we can help people like that. All the more reason for TLC."

"And how is that going?"

Rainey's gaze slipped to Alex, who had Teddy laughing so hard his face was red. "I have some help with grant writing, and we've been brainstorming some fundraising strategies, so that's a start."

Lizzie's attention shifted from Rainey to Alex as she took a bite of her carrot. "Um … that sounds like an interesting endeavor."

Rainey stopped her movements with her sandwich halfway to her mouth. "What is that supposed to mean?"

Lizzie shrugged. "Nothing at all, just that I'm sure Alex makes the research interesting."

Rainey narrowed her eyes at her friend, attempting to mine the underlying meaning. "Let's talk about something else besides TLC and Alex Murdock because your expression is making me nervous."

Lizzie chuckled and chewed her carrot. "I could always talk about my most recent research on my new swallowing client."

"Oh, no way. Last week you talked almost the entire break about him, and I still haven't gotten over it." Rainey shook her head and took an extra-large bite of her sandwich in case the nausea from last week returned, so she'd at least get a taste of the delicious meat.

Lizzie snorted. "Wimp." She leaned forward, sobering. "Is the meeting with Gray still on for Friday?"

The delicious food suddenly lost some of its flavor. "So far so good."

"You know it's all going to be okay, don't you?"

"I know." She set the coveted sandwich down and opened the canned soda she'd snatched from the drink machine. "And it's not that I want him back or anything. It's just been so long since I've seen him, and something feels ... weird and a little uncertain about the whole scenario." She took a drink and sighed. "I've thought a lot about it and, I think, I want him to be sorry—sorry for what he lost. Does that sound stupid?"

Lizzie touched Rainey's hand on the table, comforting her with a smile. "Not at all, but you need to prepare yourself that if he was stupid enough to leave you and Sarah, there's a good chance he's stupid enough not to realize, or maybe even care, about the mess he made or the hurt he caused."

Rainey grinned, the looming sadness a little lighter when shared with a friend. "What is it that Daddy used to say? Ignorance can be cured, stupidity lasts forever?"

Lizzie laughed. "Oh my goodness, your dad and his quips."

Rainey rolled the tension off her shoulders and grabbed the sandwich for another try. "Okay, you got any distracting news to talk about?"

Lizzie tossed the rest of another carrot in her mouth and unfurled a mischievous grin. "Well, I know how you love to hear romantic office tales."

"Right." Rainey took a bite of her sandwich, savoring the roast beef while she had the chance. "As much as I like to have a twelve-hundred pound cow step on my foot."

"Whatever will serve to distract."

"This is true."

"Amy went out with one of the new history professors last night."

"Amy Randall? Isn't this her third guy in as many weeks? Do we need an intervention?"

"I don't know." Lizzie leaned closer. "She told me this guy was the *one.* Apparently she felt his kiss all the way from her toes to her future."

Rainey laughed. "She said that?" She shook her head. "Oh, what am I saying? Of course Amy said that. Her diet consists of vegetarian burgers and romance novels. She definitely needs an intervention."

"We could probably plan one at lunch tomorrow."

Rainey groaned and took a sip of her soda. "Kisses are overrated." She munched another bite while the thought spiraled through her head. Two mouths on each other? She'd never felt a kiss to her toes and didn't plan on it.

Definitely novel material, but not real life.

"I never minded a good kiss." Lizzie swirled her straw in her sweet tea. "When Tom took the time to kiss me, it was nice ... just short."

Rainey laughed. "That'd be Tom for you. To the point."

"Now, Rainey, when you and Gray were first together, it looked like there was plenty of heat between the two of you."

"Heat?" Rainey nodded. "That's all it was. No substance. Besides, Gray always kissed me like he was hungry."

A choking noise sounded from nearby. Rainey had forgotten about the other people in the room. The poor men, in particular. If she thought the conversation was stupid, they must have been completely tortured by it. Kissing talk? Just the notion sent her longing for a run.

"Sorry, guys, I forgot you were over there."

Teddy's look pleaded not to be added to the conversation. Alex's grin said quite the opposite.

"Sounds to me like you need to broaden your experiences, Rainey."

That good long run was sounding better and better all the time, but there was no way she'd let him see her discomfort. She stood, gathering her trash and bag. "I'm suddenly feeling nauseous, and Lizzie didn't even talk about her recent swallowing patient's therapy."

"Hey," Lizzie said, coming to a stand as she collected her own items.

"I'd say it's time to study something *really* important." She passed Alex's table.

"It's a shame your priorities are so out of sync, Miss Mitchell."

She didn't even turn at his comment but headed directly for the door, her face aflame. There was one thing worse than the overt flirting of Alex Murdock—the way her body and mind responded to him.

Run, Rainey, run.

Alex almost had Rainey's schedule memorized. Tuesdays and Thursdays were probably his favorite of her days because she stayed at the university late instead of working at TLC. His fascination with her kept growing, and although he didn't really need an excuse to walk her to her car after work, he had a list of about five reasons to do so—starting with a request to borrow a book and ending with teaching her the finer points of mouth-to-mouth invigoration.

He grabbed his bag and closed his office door in time to see Rainey do the same two doors down. She glanced over at him. "Walk you out?"

"I suppose you're going to anyway." Her pinched-lipped response did little to encourage him, but a softening humor in her eyes brought him toward her.

"I suppose you're right."

She walked down the hall, keeping her stride with his. "I wanted to see how teaching went today anyway."

He couldn't contain his grin. "Different, in a great way. Just those few changes—a video clip here and discussion question there? It was like magic."

"See, you have it in you."

The praise warmed him through, and he nudged her shoulder with his. "I only needed the right teacher. I can think of a great way to reward you."

"You don't break for a second, do you?"

"You inspire me." He held the door open for her to walk out into the frigid January afternoon. "I'm certain I could leave a better impression on your mind than 'hungry.'"

Her gaze flipped to his, catching his allusion to her earlier conversation. A beautiful flush of rose added color to her cheeks. Yep, he had another goal to add to his "great teacher" plans. Right in front of him.

"With all that confidence, you shouldn't need much more of my help with teaching techniques, Casanova."

Oh man, she diverted the embarrassment like a pro, but he wouldn't let her off the adorable blushing-beauty moment without a fight. "I'm sure there's a lot more you could teach me."

She stopped at the top of the parking lot, where the cars diverted to their various spots, and turned to laser those beautiful peepers on him. "I have a long list, but I'm afraid they all start with lessons in humility."

"Your grumpiness makes me like you more and more. Keep it up and we'll be married by the summer."

She laughed. Loudly and freely. He'd only heard it once before, but he wanted to hear the sound again and again.

"You're so weird."

"You say that to all the guys, don't you?"

She shook her head and continued to chuckle. "You're the first."

He stepped closer, staring down into her smiling face like a man in shadows drawn to sunshine—fiery, a little dangerous, and definitely hot … all the way down to her sensible shoes. "So, when's our next date?"

"We're not—" She lowered her head, her ponytail swishing back and forth. Her eyes squinted back up at him. "I'd like to talk more about fundraising ideas and…" She winced. "I've filled out the first grant application. If you have time, I'd love your input."

"Do you have any more of that chocolate cake you brought to your mom's house on Sunday? I will work for food."

"Come on up to the house around six? I'll feed you, give you cake, let you charm my daughter, and then we can talk grants and teaching."

His palms turned up in surrender. "What man could ever say no to that?"

Her smile slipped from its place. "I can name a few."

He matched her serious tone with a step closer. "Not this one. Ever."

Chapter Twelve

Y ou've made some great contacts in a short time, Rainey." Alex tossed the dishtowel over his shoulder and handed Sarah a dinner plate to stash in the cabinet. "And the one grant application you've completed is fantastic. With the few tweaks I've suggested, it should be good to go."

"I couldn't have done it without your help." She pulled her gaze from the man who was way too comfortable in her house. And oddly distracting, especially with a dishcloth tossed over his shoulder. A tickle of laughter threatened to emerge. The shoulder she'd seen quite bare last week ... along with a lot of other skin. She swallowed and turned back to the sink to finish the last dish.

"We do make a pretty good match." He nudged her with his shoulder, which brought her attention back to his face. He wiggled his brows and leaned close. "And in only two dates."

Her smile snuck out but Sarah turned Alex's attention. "I'm almost as tall as you, Dr. Alex." Her daughter's grin shone with unabashed admiration as she perched on the step stool to reach the cabinet.

Alex hunched down to Sarah's height so they were almost nose to nose. "I can make you even taller." He swooped her up in the air until she giggled, and the sound hit Rainey in all the wounded spots Gray's absence left behind.

He should have been here, caring for his little girl, making her a priority.

Instead, Rainey had to force him to meet with her just to get financial support without involving the law.

And Alex was here, stepping into a place she'd never imagined he'd fit, almost seamlessly.

She loosened her grip on her reserve and did something she hadn't done in a very long time. She imagined what life would be like with another man. What would it feel like to come home to a man like Alex Murdock? Safe? Sweet? Would he resort to criticism as a weapon?

Something in her hitched at the thought of Alex repeating Gray's betrayal, especially since getting to know him a little better over the past week. A peace had fallen over him, somehow bringing out the gentleness she suspected had always hid beneath the playboy veneer.

"I'd be careful of doing too much of that after supper, Dr. Alex, or else you may wear a little of it."

His eyes widened and he slowly set her daughter on the ground. "Point made." He chuckled as Sarah took off into the living room. "It's been a while since I've been around little kids."

Rainey folded her arms and leaned against the counter. "How old was your niece?"

His smile froze and he looked away from her. "Five at the time of the accident."

Rainey groaned. "Sarah's age."

He tipped his head, eyes sad despite his teasing expression. "She'll be six next month."

Rainey grinned and stepped closer to him, wishing to resurrect his smile. "Which I'm sure she's repeated to you at least ten times."

He rubbed the back of his neck, a glimmer returning to his eyes. "Or a little more."

"Well, you know women. We like to repeat ourselves until we're heard." Her thoughts slipped back to his weird behavior over his phone and his innuendo about the many possible ladies' numbers in it. Time for a topic change. "Do you have any other siblings?"

Alex shoved his hands into his pockets and joined her against the counter. "An older sister. My father's protégé."

"Ah, the golden child." And probably another reason he put up a careless persona. Maybe he'd built a wall around his heart just like Rainey had—one to guard against the hurt and failures—but his was made of fake smiles and sly topic twists instead of distance and caution.

"Indeed." He nodded, sending a whiff of sandalwood her way. "The perfect fit for my father's dynasty." His sigh almost confirmed Rainey's guess. He'd been wounded too. "Angelica was born to lead. She's smart, energetic, and totally devoted to Dad. I challenged him too much, couldn't seem to think inside the box. Shocking, I know."

"We work in a profession of broken people who need our help. You have to be able to think outside the box."

"We're all broken in some way, aren't we, Rainey? All searching for another chance?" He held her gaze, all humor leaving his expression.

"Of course." She couldn't ignore the subtle message in his words or the sweet warmth pulling her deeper into this attraction. Was she ready for a second chance? Willing to have her heart broken again?

She attempted to bypass his unspoken question. "But that's why we need Jesus, you know?"

His smile softened with his eyes and an unexpected kinship bloomed. "I know."

The tenderness in his gaze disarmed her and attracted her in a whole new way—a terrifying way she hadn't expected so soon. She drew in a quick breath and looked away, snatching her coffee mug between her hands as a barrier between him and her sudden fascination.

If Alex noticed her mental stumble, he didn't show it. He slid the towel from his shoulder and draped it over the oven handle, so near to Rainey his hand brushed her arm. "Any favorites in your family?"

Her sigh thanked him for his topic change. "I can't think of any, although we all tease Emma about getting special treatment because she's the youngest." Rainey unleashed her pointer finger. "And the only one who didn't grow up doing as much of the farm work, but overall, we're a really happy bunch."

"Yeah, it seems that way. And you don't mind adding a few more to your 'gang,' as your mom calls them."

His childhood sounded like an odd mixture of privilege and neglect rolled into this handsome anomaly before her. Despite the frantic thrumming of her hesitant heart, her head propelled her into motion. Forward. Toward knowing him better.

"She loves a crowd. All shapes and sizes." She gave his shoulder a gentle slap. "You've unloaded firewood and been to two after-church lunches? There's no going back now."

"I don't want to go back. It's been amazing to feel so welcomed."

"You like Ransom, do you?"

His attention zeroed back on her, along with enough sparks in those green eyes to warm Rainey's face to her hairline. "I like it a lot."

Her throat tightened, but she dove into the teasing conversation like she knew what she was doing. "Even the natives?"

"They're my favorite part."

Oh heavens, he was good at this. She was not. "Really?"

"Especially blondes." He slid a step closer. "I have a thing for blondes."

Rainey pinched the cabinet behind her to keep herself from swaying toward him. She'd stepped way outside her comfort zone now. Flirting? Gray had always told her she was too direct to flirt. "That's funny. You strike me more as a brunette kind of guy."

He tipped his head and examined her a minute. "I plan to keep messing with your assumptions, Rainey Mitchell, because I really want to be a whole lot more than who you think I am."

"And why is that?"

With the slightest movement, his fingers grazed her cheek, his gaze searching hers, his touch stealing her breath. "Because I've had more fun doing dishes with you and Sarah than I've had doing anything else in a really long time, and if there's a way to keep this little taste of Hallmark in my life, I'll prove I'm worth it."

Alex winced for the twentieth time since leaving Rainey's house a few nights ago. She'd made it pretty clear she wasn't interested in him for much more than help for TLC, but in one mindless moment he'd blurted out exactly what was on his mind without stopping for reflection.

He couldn't help it. Everything about being with her—from sitting side by side at the table while working, to holding hands to pray before the meal, to cleaning up, playing with Sarah, and teasing Rainey— wound around his heart in a perfect fit.

He wanted that life. All of it.

He groaned and shook his head. What was he thinking? He'd barely been in Ransom one month, and he'd already set the course for the rest of his life?

He pinched the bridge of his nose and paused before looking out his office window. A pale ream of clouds hung low in the late afternoon sky, almost nestling on the distant mountains like a halo. Despite the barren trees near the school, the evergreens enriched the horizon with layers of dark green. A reluctant smile formed as Alex's heart responded to the beauty in a new way. The beauty, precision, and majesty weren't haphazard marks on a global map, but a beautifully designed masterpiece from the caring fingertips of God. His appreciation no longer disappeared into a thought or paused moment, but swelled into an internal thanksgiving to the One who made the scene. He sighed. And even made him, with all his flaws.

For the first time, Alex knew he lived for a purpose bigger than his father's approval and his success in academia. He'd never thought about how a simple life, far from the towering expectations of his father's world, could grow to be more endearing than a future with gilded halls and fancy cars.

A future with two adorable blondes?

"I'd be okay with that, Lord. I'd even be okay if you wanted to add an entire houseful of adorable blondes along with those two."

Something had shifted between him and Rainey. A softening around the edges of her suspicion—or at least, he hoped that's what he saw. She'd leaned near him as they prepped for his next class together, her citrusy smell blended with orange and mango emerging at such close proximity and somehow making motor speech disorders something worth reading about for another five hours. She held a rabid intelligence and, underneath all that caution, beat a generous heart.

His grin etched as he scrolled through his notes. It didn't hurt that she wrapped all her fierce personality in a gorgeous covering. What would all the blond hair look like in curls around her shoulders? His palm crashed against his chest. Angelic.

His attention flicked to the clock on his computer screen. 6:00 p.m.

Rainey was meeting with her ex right now.

His smile fell. He didn't even know Gray Randall but had a deep desire to have a serious conversation with the stupid man … with his fists. What kind of man would leave his wife and daughter, then refuse to take care of them? It was deplorable.

"You've not left yet?"

Lizzie stood in his doorway, red coat buttoned to her chin and falling to the tops of her stylish black boots.

"Just trying to get everything ready for the next week so I can enjoy the weekend."

She nodded and pushed her bag onto her shoulder. "Very adult of you, Dr. Murdock."

He swiveled around in his chair, crossed his feet at the ankles, and braided his fingers behind his head. "Don't tell anybody, okay? You'll ruin my image."

She lowered her shaking head, smile growing. "Your secret is safe with me." She looked up, eyebrow peaked. "Along with your other secret."

Heat siphoned from his face. There's no way Lizzie could know about his sister. Impossible. "My other secret?"

"Mmmhmm." She nodded, crossing her arms over her chest, eyes narrowing. "About a certain blonde who's had an unfortunate history with men."

Alex sat up straight, breath straining through his tightening throat. How did she know about Evie? "Lizzie, I—"

"Don't even try to deny it, Alex. The whole attraction sticks out as much as Marilyn does in this parking lot."

Attraction? Blonde? He released his closed-off air. "If what you're accusing me of is true, I'm sorry to say, Lizzie, it's a lost cause. I don't think the recipient of my coveted affections reciprocates." He raised a brow. "*If* I were interested, that is."

"Oh, really? From what I understand, you've been on two dates?"

Alex wrestled with a grin. "Dates? I was told it was only two single colleagues chatting over dinner."

Lizzie chuckled. "That sounds suspiciously like a Rainey Mitchell definition."

Alex stood and closed his laptop. "You know her well, then."

"I do." The certainty in Lizzie's tone pulled Alex's attention to her face. "And I wouldn't be too sure about the lack of reciprocity, Dr. Murdock."

He paused as he placed the computer into his bag. "What do you mean?"

"I'd wondered about it before, from the way she'd talk about you, but when I saw the two of you in the faculty lounge … well, then I knew."

Alex shrugged into his coat and grabbed his bag, approaching her to hear every word. "Knew what?"

"She may not want to like you, but she does."

"Yes." Alex pumped both fists in the air.

"And she's meeting a rather nasty fellow tonight."

"I know." Alex growled.

"And if you like her as much as I think you do, I'm pretty sure that stubborn blonde could use your help tonight more than she'd ever admit."

Every ounce of him propelled forward. "What does she need?"

Lizzie's grin took on a mischievous lilt. Alex had the sudden feeling he'd just passed some test. "A little bit of rescuing, I'd wager."

"And from the looks of it, some mischief-making too?" The glint in Lizzie's hazel eyes gave him his answer. "Rainey Mitchell and mischief-making?" He grinned. "Count me in."

Gray looked good. Really good. Relaxed, dark jeans hugged his hips, and a red button-up brought out the light hints of russet in his brown hair. Rainey squeezed her tea glass and forced a smile as he approached. She hated to admit it, but she had been hoping he looked as miserable over his stupidity as he'd made everyone in her family. Maybe even shown some balding out of pure shame, but nope. He walked toward her through Daphne's with the same easy stride that attracted her years ago. If he harbored any regret from his past choices, he wore it brilliantly.

She slid to the edge of the booth bench and stood as he reached her. "Gray."

His gazed traveled down her and back. "Good to see you, Rainey."

Her fingers fisted into a ball. *Jerk.* "I'm glad you could make it."

"Yeah, sorry I had to reschedule. Work has been crazy." He sat down in the booth and she followed.

"You look like you're doing well." His word tinted with enough surprise to flint her annoyance.

"It's been two years. Besides, I'd learned to take care of myself long before you ever left."

His smile stilled on his face. "Yeah, you didn't need anybody, did you? Not even a husband, really. You always had everything figured out without me."

Rainey flattened her palms against the table, loosening the tension in her muscles with a breath. "I certainly didn't have you figured out. I overestimated you." She stared at him and released a long sigh. "But showing up here tonight has the potential of vastly improving my opinion of you, so I'm hopeful."

He paused his prepared rebuttal in the wake of her softening remarks and fumbled around in silence a moment.

"I don't want us to argue. I want us to come to an agreement for Sarah's sake, and that's it." Rainey released her anger out on a sigh. "Arguing doesn't solve anything for us. I'm sorry I started it."

"Well, that much hasn't changed."

The edge of her tongue sharpened for a reply, but she sheathed it with a clear picture of sweet Sarah in her head. "You've read over the reasons for my asking to meet you and gain your financial support, yes?"

"I did." He lowered his eyes to the table. "But there's no way I can afford that amount, Rainey. It's not like I'm made of money or something."

She stifled the inner tigress. "I'm sorry if this makes finances tough for you, but it's not easy raising a little girl on my own either."

"Listen, it's not easy showing up here and being reminded of what I did wrong, okay? I feel the weight of what I did."

"Do you? Well, there's nothing wrong with that."

"And despite what you think, I've moved on. I *can't* pay what you want, Rainey." The hardened edges around his expression softened a little. "But I want to try to do something more than give Christmas and birthday presents."

"I'm glad to hear that, at least."

"Well, look what the rain brought in." Emma sidled up to the table and speared Gray with a glare. "I heard it was raining cats and dogs, but no one told me the storm had turned so nasty."

Gray leaned his back into the booth and looked up. "Good to see you too, Emma."

She twirled her pen in her hand. "Coffee? Tea? A conscience?"

"Emma," Rainey warned, even though Emma's brand of defensiveness tickled Rainey's funny bone. This idea was quickly proving to be a bad one. What had she been thinking to bring him back into the picture now, after her heart had healed and she'd finally gotten settled into a life without him? Had she really believed he'd want to help? *Stupid, Rainey.*

Emma's attention settled on her sister and probed deeply—too deeply. Rainey branded a smile. "Two coffees, okay?"

Emma raised a brow at Rainey, then turned and narrowed her eyes at Gray before walking behind the counter to get their drinks.

"She's changed," Gray whispered. "She used to be so sweet."

"Lots has changed, Gray." Rainey reached into her purse and retrieved a photo. "Here's a prime example." She pushed the photo across the table of Sarah's most recent picture, double-dimpled grin in full gleam. "I thought you may want to see this."

Gray had the good sense to look shocked. "She's so big."

"Almost six."

His attention flashed up to Rainey and then back to the photo, gently fingering the edges. "She has glasses."

"Last year."

He nodded. "When can she get contacts?"

Rainey blinked and leaned forward. "What?"

"Contacts. You'd be able to see her eyes much better without those big glasses."

Rainey's goodwill teetered on the brink of her jumping across the table and plucking out each and every bit of his manicured five o'clock shadow stubble. "She's five."

Gray shrugged a shoulder. "Kayla says children as young as five or six can learn to wear contacts. Don't you want to show off Sarah's eyes instead of hiding them behind those ridiculous glasses?"

"Kayla? Who is Kayla?"

His eyes widened and he tucked the photo into his shirt pocket. "That's right, you probably don't know."

Warning flared in her chest but failed to fully prepare her.

"Kayla's my wife." He glanced up from his folded hands. "We've been married about seven months."

He'd married Kayla a little over a year after he'd left Rainey? The ache clenched her chest, pressing her breaths into a miniscule strain of air. The old wound seeped with new pain. "I see." Stupid man. Stupid emotions. She bridled the sympathy with a clear memory. "I'm sorry this makes your finances tough, Gray, truly. Most months I can scrape by with my salary, but as she gets older, costs become higher. Glasses or *contacts* being prime examples of additional costs."

His countenance softened a little, loosening the pinched crimp of his brow. "What if I could give this?"

He named a price that was half of what she'd asked. Rainey stared in silence, working through a reply. At least it was something. More than anything he'd given before.

"Come on, Rainey. I'm trying to start over." He ran a hand through his dark hair. "We have twins coming in the summer, and I need to save all the money I can."

Another sucker punch took her breath. Her voice and fight whooshed from her like a shock of cold air hitting her face in the morning. She turned to her purse, fumbling for her phone in a veiled attempt to gain some composure, but nothing cloaked the barren truth. What was wrong with her? She didn't want Gray back, but the sudden awareness that he'd moved on ... that he had a family and somehow replaced not only Rainey, but Sarah, crippled her confidence. Every dark lie she'd overcome through prayer, time, and family love resurrected. *You are not good enough. You are easily replaced. You'll never be enough.*

Oh God, help me face this fear. Face this past.

Chapter Thirteen

The butter-cinnamon warmth of Daphne's enveloped Alex from the evening chill in the sudden burst of 'wind snow,' as the natives called the flurries swirling in the night. At least the rain had stopped. He preferred the snow. He breathed deeply of the baked aroma as he unwound his scarf from his neck and unbuttoned his jacket, taking in the room with a swift glance. His beautiful target sat in a corner booth looking very un-Rainey-like. She stared at the man across the table, her face noticeably pale, even from Alex's distance. A protective fire blazed in Alex's chest.

Alex changed his focus to the man talking to her, shook his head, and pulled off his coat. Unimpressive. Rainey could do so much better.

"Well, well, Dr. Murdock. You look like you came here on a mission."

Emma Mitchell walked toward him, coffees in hand, and quirked grin tipping her pink lips with challenge.

Alex matched her grin for grin. "A secret search and rescue mission."

"No matter what anyone else says, I think you fit right in." Emma raised on tiptoe and gave him a kiss on the cheek. "And I do believe your *date* could use some help."

It happened again—one of those Mitchells making him feel like he'd finally come home. Now all he had to do was spend however long it took convincing the stubborn blonde in front of him of it too.

He sent Emma a wink, tossed his coat over his arm, and strode directly for the corner booth. Without hesitation, he slid into the booth beside Rainey and draped his arm over her shoulders, basking in the shock lacing those beautiful eyes. "Hey, gorgeous, sorry I'm late." He waved his hand back toward the door. "Traffic and all."

"Traffic?" The guy across the table shifted his attention between Rainey and Alex.

Alex tipped his head and offered his free hand. "Alex Murdock. Nice to meet you, Gray."

Alex turned back to Rainey, who stared up at him, adorably confused. "Did I miss anything important?"

Rainey narrowed her eyes, words forming slowly. "I'm not sure."

"Alex Murdock?" Gray's dark gaze rose, void of welcome.

Alex's grin broadened and he hugged Rainey a little closer to his side. Yep, felt just as nice as he thought it would. "I was meeting Rainey here for supper after work. I'm sorry, were you guys about finished?"

Gray examined Alex, crinkles deepening to doubt-filled chasms on his much-too-big forehead. "You're meeting Rainey?"

"Sure. We're dating." Alex leaned in, adding another wink. "And I'm playing for keeps, if you know what I mean. When you meet someone like Rainey, you'd be an idiot to let her go."

A choking sound came from the beauty to his left.

"I'm sorry, sweetie. Do you want me to leave? Or maybe I could order while you two finish your conversation? I didn't mean to interrupt."

She stared up at him for a long moment, her face so close he had the overwhelming urge to snatch a kiss. The thought spiraled his attention into taking inventory of those lips. Would she let him? Maybe they could arm wrestle for a kiss? He grimaced. What if she won?

A fascinating glimmer twinkled to life in her eyes, and her lips softened into a gentle, somewhat resigned smile—almost as if she read his derailed thoughts. "No, I think we're done." She looked over at Gray. "We have an agreement."

"That's it? You're going to take my offer without an argument?"

She sighed and relaxed against Alex, giving his fingers freedom to smooth over the strands of her hair dangling against his hand. "Yep. Besides, I've found somebody else who's a lot more fun to argue with—and behind all of this, I just want to make sure Sarah has what she needs. I hope down deep you want that too."

Regret had never looked better on anybody than it did on Gray Randall. From the slow and somewhat pained transformation on his face, Alex bet the man didn't wear that emotion half as often as he ought to.

Gray cleared his throat and moved to the edge of the bench. "Yeah, I want that too." He looked between the two of them and then stood, patting his shirt pocket. "Thanks for the photo. She looks happy."

Emotions warred across Rainey's face, a fleeting sting of pain giving way to strength. "She *is* happy, and I hope you and your family will be too."

He shrugged into his coat, nodded at Rainey, and turned to walk away, then pivoted back to face them. His frown carved deep lines into his brow, and he fixed his attention on his ex-wife. "I'm sorry, Rainey."

Rainey stiffened, so Alex slid his palm back around her shoulders, easing a caress down her arm.

"I'm sorry for everything, and I hope ... I hope you can be happy again." Gray tipped his chin to Alex, then walked away.

Rainey kept her face down, her back tense, so with the gentlest of movement, Alex touched her chin and raised her gaze to his. Nothing prepared him for the well of tears swimming among the aqua and golden hues of her eyes, nor for the way his heart rushed to the rescue to banish all the hurt colliding for release in her expression.

"What do you need me to do?"

He shouldn't have said a thing because somehow his questions burst the floodgates and the tears spilled over their boundaries to course down her cheeks. Alex looked up to find Emma already on her way to their table, bag in hand.

"I saw that coming."

Did she? Because Alex was still trying to figure out what went wrong.

Emma pushed the bags into his chest. "Dinner. Take her home. I'll call Mama to let her know to bring Sarah over to the house in an hour or so."

"My car?" Rainey whispered.

"You can get it tomorrow." Emma dismissed the concern with a wave of her hand. "Right now, I don't even think you could see to drive." She nailed Alex with a grown-up warning stare. "This cry has been a long time coming. I packed two double-chocolate-chip brownies for the occasion." Her finger jabbed at him. "Neither piece is for you."

"For a little sister, you sure are bossy."

Her sassy grin emerged. "As a little sister, it was a learned skill. Now git goin'."

Alex helped Rainey with her coat, shielding her from any onlookers who might have overheard part of the conversation, and guided her toward the door.

"You don't have to do—"

"Do you really think I'm going to defy that little sister of yours?" He pulled her close as the cool wind almost took his breath. "Besides, I know you've wanted another ride in Marilyn ever since the last time."

She rolled those watery eyes of hers, almost donning a full smile. "I'm weeping like a junior-high girl over my jerk ex-husband. I think you should be questioning my intelligence right now."

He opened the car door and stared down at her as she took a seat. "I think the reason you're crying has a lot less to do with your intelligence and a whole lot more to do with the tender heart you keep trying to hide."

She stared up at him, her bottom lip quivering in such a way his heart flipped over about fifty times. "Rats," she whispered and wiped away another tear. "My secret's out."

"Don't worry, Rainey." He leaned in as he brought the door closer, hoping she read much deeper into his words … all the way to his intentions. "It's safe with me."

He snapped the door closed and drew in a deep breath as he rounded to the other side of Marilyn. The strangest concoction of feelings struggled through him—like the first time he ever took a girl out on a date, except … this moment, this experience, speared deeper. More than sweaty palms and stupid conversations ending in a first kiss, this instance pulled from life's hardest lessons and most fragile hopes. He wanted much more than a first kiss with Rainey, even if his hands were starting to get a little sweaty. He swallowed before opening his door. He wanted her trust. And her future.

They rode in silence for a few minutes with nothing but the sound of Rainey's sniffles and the healthy hum of his beautiful car. Rainey had been quiet and shocked, but not near tears, when Alex took his seat. As he replayed the scene, the pinpoint break came when Gray apologized.

Did he place two years of wounds into that apology?

Air whooshed from Alex's lungs. Had Rainey been waiting two years to hear it, or was she still in love with her ex?

"I'm sorry, Alex." She wiped at her face with her hand. "I … I don't do this."

He paused the car in front of one of the three traffic lights in Ransom and reached in the glove compartment for a pack of tissues. "Why are you sorry? You faced a monster from your past and stood your ground with grace." He paused to stare at her, infusing every ounce of sincerity in his gaze. "That's called bravery."

"Brave?" She laughed. "I'm leaking like Sarah's Baby Alive doll. I … never—"

"You miss him."

Her laughter turned harsh. "Heavens, no. I don't miss him. Not even a little."

Alex really shouldn't smile at a time like this. It was a good thing the shadows in the car hid part of his face.

"He never apologized, you know? After the awful story came out of how he'd secretly cheated on me with my sister-in-law for a year and then fathered a child by her, he never once looked sorry—except in being caught. It's like … like a part of my heart had been on hold until that instance. The onus is on me to forgive, to let go."

Alex kept his gaze forward on the road. "Can you?"

"Yes." Her voice caught, as if the answer came as a surprise. "Gladly. I've wanted to for so long and didn't quite know how."

His connection to her knotted, moving deeply into his chest and filling every space. Love? He should have known. The first time he'd met her months ago, her witty responses and feisty personality fascinated him, but now, in this soul-baring exchange, she branded a place in his heart. He reached over with his free hand and covered hers. "It takes a lot of strength to forgive somebody who has hurt you so much."

She didn't move for a second, but then, with the caution of thawing snow, she turned over her palm and braided her fingers through his, an intentional acceptance. "Maybe Gray will be happy now, because I certainly didn't make him happy. I was never classy enough, or funny enough, or sexy enough, or pretty enough. I seemed to fail at everything."

"You've gotta be kidding me? He said you weren't sexy enough? Pretty? Man, your ex needs glasses *and* a brain."

Her other hand moved to sandwich his between both of hers. "He criticized everything about me, to the point I started listening and believing it, so even when the signs of his adultery showed, I didn't really see them because I second-guessed everything about myself."

"You know he was wrong, don't you?"

"My head knows it." She shrugged. "My heart is catching up."

Alex squeezed her fingers "Well, he was wrong and stupid. Seriously, he reached a whole new level of idiot by letting you go. I can't even imagine how he could look back at his life and not regret what he's lost. You *and* Sarah?" He groaned. "His loss, Rainey." He shook his head. "And you are totally sexy, especially in sweats."

"In sweats?"

"You think I'm kidding? A woman who is comfortable enough to wear sweats in front of a guy *and* rock them like you do?" He released a low whistle. "Mmmhmm. Sexy."

Her full laugh welcomed him. "You keep doing that, you know?"

"Doing what? Checking out your sexy self in sweats? Guilty."

She leaned her head back, her full smile almost distracting him from the road. "Making me laugh."

He shrugged and gave her another appreciative glance. "So you've seen past the debonair façade into my utter ridiculousness."

"Oh, I've seen past the façade all right." She chuckled. "All bare chested and phoneless."

"I like to leave an unforgettable impression."

Her laugh loosed again and warmed him all the way to his toes. "Well, you've succeeded." Her voice softened. "I was wrong about you, Alex."

"What? You thought I was an arrogant, superficial Casanova?" He pulled the car up her driveway.

"Pretty much."

"And you were right." He killed the engine and turned to her. "I was all those things at various points in my life, but ... I hope I'm changing for the better."

He exited the car and rounded to her side in time to close the door behind her. With his hands in his pockets, he walked her to her front door. Flurries swirled around them in the light of her front porch, dusting the world with a fairy white. Magical. And the queen of the land stood before him wrapped in her white coat, loose strands of gold falling from beneath her cap to frame her beautiful face.

"I think you're growing on me, Casanova and all."

"You mean like a fungus?"

She chuckled. "I was thinking more like the smell of a new house— uncomfortable at first, but time blends the familiar and unfamiliar into home."

He edged a step closer, her gaze welcoming a new intimacy. "That sounds much better than a fungus."

"You like that, huh?" One golden brow poked north.

"Yes, ma'am. There's pretty much nothing I don't like about you, Rainey."

She hesitated, then stepped toward him, their bodies almost touching. Tears still swirled in her eyes, beckoning him to caress the hurt away with a lip-to-lip distraction. He'd fallen short with Beth in so many ways, chosen his interests over hers or talked her into doing the things he wanted when he knew down deep he should have given more. She gave generously, something he appreciated more in painful hindsight than in real time.

That same generosity lived inside Rainey, the same selflessness. Alex touched her cheek, cool against his fingers. Her breath puffed in a pillow-like cloud toward him, shallow but soft. Her fingers inched around his back, urging him to complete the distance between them.

He breathed in the cold air mingled with the scent of mango. It was amazing what lengths a guy could go to in search of fresh mangos in a grocery store just because of a woman's shampoo. His thumb trailed her chin and paused at the little dip in the middle, slowly tilting her face nearer.

"You're hands-down the best non-date I've ever had in my life."

"Thank you for showing up, Alex." Those aqua orbs searched his face, completely vulnerable to him. "I don't know how I can repay your perfect timing."

Her words stilled his forward momentum. He wanted to kiss her, to abate his curiosity, to revel in being consumed in citrus and Rainey, but something in her confession paused his inner predator. If he kissed her in this weakness, would she regret it in the morning?

What she *needed* suddenly became decidedly more important than what he *wanted*. Their first kiss shouldn't be a payment for services rendered or her response in a moment of weakness. Nope, he wanted her to be perfectly cognizant of her actions. From the wounds he'd witnessed tonight, she already harbored too many regrets.

He released a long sigh, wrestling the animal-instinct in submission to honor … or maybe even something deeper than honor. With gentle movements, he leaned forward and placed a chaste kiss to her cheek, breathing in her scent as a consolation prize to a kiss.

"If you need me, you know where I live."

Her dazed expression blinked into focus. She stepped back to the door. "Yes … um … thanks again, Alex."

Alex shot a look heavenward as he marched back to his car. *I wouldn't have minded a kiss, Lord, but I'm going to trust You have an even better one in mind, right?*

The flurries blew in tandem but held no answer. Well, one thing was for certain—if God gave him the desires of his heart, a kiss was definitely in his future.

Rainey pulled up her mama's driveway, a double dose of groceries in the back of her jeep. The scent of snow bathed the air as warning, and from the looks of the sky *and* the size of the halo around the moon earlier in the week, they were in for more than a dusting.

She'd called Trigg first thing to ask him for a ride to Daphne's, keeping her attention as far from her grandparents' farmhouse as she could, but her mind wandered in that direction anyway.

Sarah sat in the back with her plush Pinkie Pie in tow, singing some *My Little Pony* song about the weather. Apropos. Rainey caught sight of her grandparents' farmhouse in her rearview mirror, and a wave of warmth blasted up her neck into her face. She touched her cheek where Alex's lips left a tingle and an unexpected reaction in the pit of her stomach. Why hadn't he kissed her? From the way his gaze kept dropping to her lips, he'd wanted to.

Had she done something wrong?

Her chest tightened with her breaths, and a small smile slid into place. Unless he'd stopped because he didn't want to hurt her? Would he do that? She'd not had a lot of experience with that sort of self-control from a man, but Alex Murdock kept surprising her.

His car smelled like sandalwood, and the scent lingered on her coat, teasing her with a kiss that should have been.

She pulled the jeep to a stop and Sarah hopped out, leaving Rainey to load up each arm with enough groceries to get Mama through a storm. Of course, with a basement full of canned goods from a summer garden, Mama could probably survive an apocalypse.

She walked into the vast kitchen and dining area to the distinctive aromas of baked apples and ham. Her mama's house had its own scent—a settled, welcoming one of home, family, and childhood haunts. Alex's childhood painted a pale story in comparison—sad and lonely.

"Aren't you the best girl?" Mama walked from the kitchen to retrieve a few of Rainey's grocery bags. "Taking care of your mama so well."

"Oh, funny. As if you ever need someone to take care of you." Rainey placed her bags on the countertop. "You're the toughest person I know."

"But I don't mind letting people take care of me." She held up a package of Oreos. "Especially when they bring sweets. I hope you bought your own stash."

"I can't imagine being trapped inside for a few days without chocolate, Mama."

"I raised smart young'uns." She offered her sneaky grin and opened the package enough to snatch two cookies. With a wink, she offered one to Rainey. "Your hair looks nice today. Tryin' somethin' new?"

Rainey ran a palm over the back of her hair. She'd foregone the ponytail, deciding to clip back the sides and leave the back loose. "Are those ham hocks I smell?"

"Yes, ma'am, and some apple pie."

Rainey joined her mother in putting away the groceries. "I would have helped you cook for tomorrow if you'd told me your menu."

Mama shook her head. "Ain't no use in botherin' you when I have plenty of time to do it. Besides, you've got enough keeping you busy. How is the grant writing going?"

"Alex and I have sent two in already, and we're working on three more."

"And what other ideas have you two conjured up to save TLC?"

Rainey handed a large carton of eggs to Mama. "Alex helped me write a piece for the paper, and he's even sending a letter off to some of his father's associates to see if they'd be willing to make some charitable donations." Rainey's smile pulled wide at Alex's animated discussion on ways to woo with letter writing. He certainly excelled in the art of influencing people with words. She'd rather just have people see her hard work and reward it. Charm made everything so much harder.

Mama placed the extra milk carton in the refrigerator and looked over her shoulder. "He's been a real help to you."

Rainey looked away and turned her attention back to placing a bag of potatoes in the bin. "He's been a good surprise."

Silence permeated the conversation, gnawing at the back of Rainey's head until she pressed her palm against the counter and turned. "Emma's talked to you, hasn't she?"

"She has the tendency to now and again."

"And she mentioned last night."

Mama took another Oreo and pointed at her. "Somebody knew I'd be worried and needed to know you were all right."

Rainey folded her arms across her chest and stared at Mama. "Rose petals and fairy dust usually accompany Emma's reports. I don't know if I'd trust them."

"Alex didn't show up at Daphne's last night?"

"He did."

"But he didn't come to your rescue with Gray."

"I don't know that I'd call it a rescue." Rainey's chin stiffened. Although, she wasn't quite sure what else to call it.

"And you didn't ride home with him?"

"He *drove* me home," Rainey corrected. "That was all."

Mama poured two glasses of milk and handed one to Rainey. "That was all?" She clicked her tongue, and her grin hinted at all sorts of unvoiced ideas. "I reckon that was enough."

Rainey felt the simple implication all the way down her spine. "He was very kind to intervene like he did."

"Indeed. Ain't no harm in being rescued, Rainey. In fact, the best men are willing."

Rainey pinched her lips closed, struggling with her own internal argument between her head and her heart. She didn't *need* to be rescued. She could make it on her own—she'd done it for years now.

Her thoughts slipped back to the laughter Alex brought with him, the tenderness in his gaze, the touch of his hand to her face. He'd made her feel … beautiful. Cherished.

"Stronger and wiser is the heart that's learned from pain and softened from experience," Mama said in an afterthought. "How about another Oreo?"

Rainey took the proffered cookie and read between the lines in her mama's smile. Maybe beneath the fear of failing, she *wanted* to be rescued—and that's what scared her the most.

Chapter Fourteen

A lex grinned at his reflection as he shaved. Evie's call last night gave him even more hope for a face-to-face meeting. For an entire year, they'd only spoken on the phone—and those calls were sporadic and short-lived. But the possibility to see her smile? Hug her? Play *Mario Kart* with Lily?

His eyes burned with a sudden rush of emotions he usually kept pinned down. Alex lowered his razor and leaned against the sink, staring at his reflection. Evie had their mother's golden hair, like him, but she'd gotten their father's brown eyes—so had Lily.

He wiped his face and sighed. Evie had been a great help with brainstorming ways to raise money for TLC, even recommending some deep-pocketed friends of their families who held even deeper loves for education ... and tax deductions. Plus, she'd resurrected the idea of a television interview to gain more visibility. Rainey would be great on television, especially when she talked about TLC with her infectious passion.

Haus sat with a curious tilt to his head at the bathroom door, watching Alex. "Yeah, I'm up early on a Sunday. You're shocked, aren't you?" The great black mutt turned his head the other way as if examining the situation, one ear flopping downward. "See? People can be trained too." Alex scrubbed Haus' head and stepped around the dog in the doorway.

A sudden sound from the porch sent Haus scurrying out of the room just before a thundering knock came from the door. Alex glanced at the clock on his nightstand. *What? He still had three hours before church started. What was Jim thinking?*

Alex pulled on a pair of jeans to go along with his T-shirt and marched to the door. Trigg Mitchell greeted him, ball cap in place, some sort of yellow jumper covering his flannel shirt, and an entire world of white creating a backdrop behind him.

"It snowed."

"Told ya." Trigg grinned, alluding to an earlier discussion the two had when Rainey's oldest brother showed up to check on Haus. "You could taste it in the air."

Alex laughed and then sobered, covering his palm over his chest. "I will never doubt your Appalachian wisdom again."

Trigg tapped his hat. "If that ain't the smartest thing you've ever said, I don't know what is."

"Come in out of the cold, Trigg, and tell me what brings you by so early on Sunday."

"Actually, I came for your help." Trigg didn't budge. "Reese is out of town this weekend, or I'd have asked him. He usually helps me shovel the snow off the church parking lots and steps when it's needed."

It took five seconds for Trigg's words to connect with Alex's understanding. "I can help. Sure." He reached into the closet by the door and pulled out his coat. "Do I need to bring anything?"

"A good attitude and strong arms is all you need." Trigg gestured toward Alex's overcoat. "And something a lot less fancy and whole lot warmer than the coat you got right there."

Alex looked down at his overcoat and back to Trigg's patchwork ensemble.

Trigg laughed. "From that look on your face, I'm guessing you ain't got nothin' less fancy, so come on. You can wear one of my jackets." He patted Alex's shoulder. "Don't worry. When I'm done with ya, Alex, people'll think you were born a redneck like the rest of us."

Alex grabbed his hat and followed Trigg out the door, chuckling. "Exactly what I've wanted my whole life."

It hadn't taken too long, especially with Trigg's tractor's help. After about an hour of shoveling, Alex forgot all about feeling cold. In fact, he'd pretty much grown numb from his fingers to his jawline. But as soon as the first car drove into the parking lot and Trigg offered to help an elderly woman to the church's door, the mild annoyance in the work fell victim to a new emotion. Pride. The good kind.

The simple act of service, no strings attached, pooled a pleasant warmth through every fiber of Alex's frozen core. As he joined Trigg in assisting the few parishioners inside the church, each smile, every thank you swelled the sense of belonging deeper.

Service. He'd never really thought much about it before, even though his profession dubbed him a service provider. He'd always been good with people and smart at solving people problems, but this dipped deeper.

To the soul.

Serving others could be something more than praise and a salary. It brought a reward all its own, and Alex wanted more. Wanted to *be* more. Was this just another byproduct of belonging to Christ? Results of his floundering prayers and inconsistent attempts at Bible reading?

"You're gonna be sore tomorrow," Trigg offered over the sounds of the church bells.

"Tomorrow?" Alex rubbed his arm, the low ache inciting a groan. "Why wait until tomorrow?"

Trigg laughed and gave Alex's aching arm a firm squeeze, nearly buckling Alex to the ground. "Don't worry, we'll get you toughened up in no time." Trigg's smile turned lethal. "Mama's driveway is next."

Alex shook the ache from his arm and offered Trigg a well-fought grin. "I asked for it, didn't I?"

"I know a willing victim when I see one." Trigg loosened his collar and gestured toward the church doors. "You coming in for the service?"

"Wouldn't miss it." He started walking toward the doors, stretching out his sore back. "Even if I won't be able to get up after I sit down."

Trigg patted his back. "God's strength is made perfect in weakness."

"Then I'm going to be pretty near perfect for the rest of the week." Rainey's Jimmy pulled into the parking lot. Alex stood up a little straighter. "Think you can convince Rainey how perfect God's making me? I may win some brownie points."

She stepped from the Jimmy and found his gaze. Something was different about her today. He paused in his walk. Her hair spilled like spun gold from beneath her gray woolen cap, falling over her shoulders with an angelic shine.

"Looks to me like you're already on the right track." Trigg moved a few steps ahead.

"I'm a pretty rotten choice for her, you know." Alex shoved his hands in his pockets and shrugged, unable to take his gaze from her as she helped Sarah out of the car while Lou jumped from the other side. "I have good intentions most of the time, but good intentions aren't always good enough to make up for my mistakes."

"One of the great things about God is He makes up for our mistakes. He knows we're lost without Him, but..." Trigg shook his head, his smile growing with a look of wonder. "He loves us more ... and gives us better than we deserve."

"I'm beginning to understand." Alex grinned over at Trigg, still amazed at the lightness in his chest when he stopped to consider such a love. "And I wouldn't complain if He wanted to give me better than I deserve."

His gaze fastened on Rainey as she walked toward him, Sarah at her side.

"You may be stronger than you think, then." Trigg chuckled and opened the church door. "Because that one?" He gestured with his chin toward his sister, glint lighting his dark blue eyes. "You'll need to be strong and a little crazy to handle her."

Alex ignored the ache in his shoulders and closed in on the lovely pair, pretty sure he met one of Trigg's requirements—and it wasn't strong.

"I see you wore your winter best to church this morning, Dr. Murdock."

Alex tugged at the collar of the well-worn yellow jacket. "Your brother helped me out."

Her gaze shot down him and left a trail of fire behind. "Yep, that's definitely more his style than yours."

He pulled his attention from the softening expression on Rainey's face and grinned at Lou. "It looks like you have an added beauty with you this morning."

Lou's grin broadened enough to boast a missing canine. "Sarah said you talked sweet."

"Did she?" Alex knelt down and tugged on one of Sarah's braids. "All of your sweetness must rub off on me."

Lou giggled and grabbed Sarah's hand, leading her into the church, with Alex and Rainey following.

Rainey slowed her pace to match him, her shoulder nudging his as they walked through the church doors. "Your sweet talkin' *is* pretty impressive."

He kept his face forward but leaned in her direction with a whisper. "Don't distract me with compliments, Ms. Mitchell. I'm saving my sweet talking for the Lord this morning."

"So you two are talking now?"

"I think a more accurate description is I'm *listening* now."

Her smile softened, inviting him to linger in her attention for a second longer before she broke contact to rush ahead and maneuver the girls into a pew between him and her. The pastor welcomed everyone as usual, his energetic greeting bouncing off the wood-hewn rafters and colorful stained-glass windows—a style reminiscent of an older generation, Alex guessed.

The rustic architecture mixed with more modern instruments near the front of the church fitted the authentic feel of the church without stilting the charm. Beth's church had been a large, modern style, with chairs instead of pews and screens that showed song lyrics. No hymnals.

Alex appreciated the more acoustic flow of the music. Guitar and piano suited this setting and culture, curbing the bucolic atmosphere with relaxing strums and strings. Despite his appreciation of the musical choices at today's service, Alex's lack of "churching" showed every time as he struggled to locate the song the pastor announced and then attempted to follow along with unfamiliar words and music.

Lou looked over at him, her lips twisted into a critical pucker. "You ain't done this much, have ya?"

Alex ruffled the pages to the right spot. "Nope. My parents didn't think church was that important."

Lou's eyes popped wide. "Well, that's plum crazy. How on earth do you manage without Jesus?"

How indeed? His family was a prime example of how external success did not lead to happiness. "Not very well, Lou."

"I'd say not." She looked straight ahead and started singing the first verse with the gusto of any good Scots-Irish descendent. Wholeheartedly.

Alex followed along, waiting to hear the melody a few times before attempting the words.

"Sometimes I don't understand the songs either," Lou whispered to him.

He leaned down to hear her better. "You don't?"

"Nope, like what we just sung. I ain't never understood why God needed a bullhorn with him being God and all. I reckon He can make himself loud enough if He wants."

Bullhorn? Alex skimmed over the first verse and almost lost control of his laugh.

A mighty fortress is our God. A bulwark never failing. Bulwark, not bullhorn—but since Alex didn't know what a bulwark was any more than Lou did, he shrugged to his hymn-buddy and stifled his inner chuckle. No wonder she sang bullhorn instead.

He looked up and caught Rainey staring at him, a mesmerizing vision with the morning sunlight gleaming against her loose, golden hair. The same tender invitation she'd worn a few nights before, when he'd refrained from kissing her silly, beckoned him to try again … and complete the task. Evidently, she'd made up her mind. He was pretty sure it was the stupidest thing she could have decided, and if he were a selfless man, he'd leave her alone.

His train of thought, in church no less, proved God still had a lot of work to do on his heart.

What had Rainey told him before he left her mama's the day before? Don't try to drive Marilyn in the snow. And what did the brilliant Alex Murdock do?

Slid out of his driveway directly in front of her oncoming Jimmy.

She'd jerked the wheel to miss him, sending the Jimmy into a snow-covered ditch, cushioning the impact a little. The silly man needed a solid slap of sense.

Marilyn didn't fare as well as the Jimmy. The Mercedes had slid across the road, almost clipping the front of her jeep, then continued her backward momentum directly into a tree. Rainey winced. Well, if he learned through experience, this was the hard way.

Rainey breathed out her pinched breath, relaxing the muscles in her tensed shoulders before turning in her seat to check on Sarah, whose big blue eyes widened behind her glasses. "That was a really big bump, Mama."

"It sure was, sweet pea."

"Snow is a slippery mess," she said, quoting Rainey from earlier in the morning when Rainey had almost skated off the back-porch steps. Overconfidence and misstep did not mix.

Her driver's side door suddenly jerked wide, revealing Alex's pale face. "Are you okay?" His words burst out on shallow breaths. "Is Sarah okay?"

Rainey's aggravation dwindled a little in the light of his concern. A thin trail of blood sliced a red line on his forehead, and those green eyes zipped from her face to Sarah's as if his life depended on her answer.

"She's fine. I'm mad, but I'll get over it."

He lowered his head with a sigh. "Praise God."

His response shook her a moment. Praise God? Plus his comments at church earlier in the day? What was going on with this guy? "I told you not to drive your car until the roads were cleared. Marilyn is not the type of car for snow."

"Trigg asked if I could come help shovel Jim's walkway and driveway, and since it's just up the road, I thought it couldn't be so bad." He groaned and looked back up at her, pleading. "I'm sorry, Rainey. If anything had happened to you or Sarah…" He ran a gloved hand through his hair and sent a tense smile to the back seat. "I'm sorry if I scared you, Sarah."

"We hit a really big bump, Dr. Alex."

His smile wavered, emotions warring across his strong face, and Rainey realized even more the depths beneath his smile. As stubborn and stupid as he appeared sometimes, he cared deeply.

"Were you scared, princess?"

She nodded, eyes still wide. "But then I thought it was like riding one of Uncle Trigg's horses."

"I'm sorry you were scared, Sarah." Alex turned his attention back to Rainey. "I can't believe I almost hurt you. Is there something I can do to help get your Jimmy out?"

"I'm going to try to put it in four-wheel drive and see if I can get myself out, but if not, we'll have to ask Trigg to bring his tractor out here."

"Of course." Alex stepped back. "Just let me know what I need to do to make this up to you. I'll do anything."

She touched his hand still poised on her door. "Alex, we're okay. Yeah, you shouldn't have been out in your car today. Yes, it was stupid. But apart from a little scare and delay, plus a cut on your head"—she gestured with her hand—"we're all fine, and that's what counts."

Alex raised his fingers to his head and nodded. "I'll call a tow."

"I think I can get out of here without a tow."

"But I don't think I can."

Rainey followed his gaze to the Mercedes, its trunk bent from the impact against the tree.

"Okay, you call a tow and I'll try to get on the road."

After a few tries, the Jimmy settled back on the snow-covered road, so she pulled next to Alex's car. He leaned against the hood, still on the phone. She took a closer look. Hadn't his cell phone been blue? The current phone was black. Did he get a new one?

She shook off the questions and examined the car. A snowflake-like crack highlighted the driver's side of the windshield. Did the impact of Alex's head against the glass cause that? She examined him with more scrutiny. The cut over his right eyebrow proved only one wound. A large purplish-green knot formed in the center of his forehead all the way to the bridge of his nose. Poor guy.

"Sit right here, Sarah. I'm going to talk with Dr. Alex, okay?"

"Okay," Sarah's sweet voice responded.

Rainey climbed from the Jimmy just as Alex ended his call. "The truck's on the way."

"Good. Now let's get you inside the house and put some ice on your head." She reached up to brush her fingers over his bruise. "It will help with the swelling."

He grabbed Rainey's fingers in his hand. "What if I'd ... what if..."

"Stop. You didn't."

"But you told me—"

"Which goes to show that you should listen to me in the future, Doc." She shoved her free hand on her hip and sent him a playful glare, trying to add some levity to the grief in his eyes. "Show me you've learned how smart I am by getting into that house right now."

She opened the back door of the Jimmy. "Come on, Sarah. Let's go play with Haus a little while so I can take care of Dr. Alex's boo-boo."

Alex's pulse still hammered in his chest as the near-collision flashed through his mind again. Rainey made him sit at the kitchen table, Sarah keeping watch with Haus by her side, as she filled a Ziploc with ice, wrapped it in a dishtowel, and placed it against his head.

"Stop looking at me like I'm dying. We're fine." Rainey scooted closer to peer at his head. "Do you feel okay?"

"My head hurts and my heart aches, but otherwise the only other wound is my pride."

Her lips slanted. "Well, that needed a little beating I think."

He wanted to respond to the humor, but the fear that he'd hurt her or Sarah placed a stranglehold over his funny bone. What if he *had* hurt them? He'd never forgive himself.

"I'll pay for the damages on your car and anything else you need. What can I do?"

She shook her head. "You're desperate, aren't you?

"I am. I'll do anything to make up for this."

A glimmer lit her eyes, and his hope soared. "Well, there is one thing."

"Name it. Fix dinner every night for a month?" He shook his head. "No, that would backfire. I'm a terrible cook. Babysit Sarah while you go"—he waved his hand toward her—"have a manicure?"

She raised a brow, stamping him as idiotic as he felt.

"Right, not exactly your cup of tea."

Her lips tilted into a lethal smile, and a foreboding tingle shot down the back of his sore neck. "I think I have a perfect ... opportunity for you."

His nausea took another turn in his stomach for a whole new reason. Warning lights blared in the back of his mind.

"I need a tutor at TLC. Due to budget cuts, mine left at the end of January, so I'm a person short. You can come two days a week after school and tutor teens."

"What?" He snatched the ice compress from her and stood. "You can't be serious."

"You said *anything*, Alex," she replied, folding her arms across her chest. "Are you a man of your word?"

He groaned and slumped back down in the chair. *She* was the desperate one. "Come on! I'm not good for messed up kids. I *was* one."

She chuckled. Chuckled! "All the more reason for you to get involved with them, then. You understand what it's like."

"But ... but I haven't had a load of experience with teens, and by that I mean pretty much none." He leaned forward, his head throbbing with more force. "Most of the kids I worked with were young elementary and preschool ages. Bring candy or toys and they're your friend for life."

"I figure it may be a new skill for you, but you're an experiential learner, remember?" She winked and almost distracted him from his argument. "I have every faith you'll catch on quickly."

She held a whole lot more faith in him than he did, but he mustered up a smile. "Well, that's progress at any rate. When we first met, I'm pretty sure you thought my best quality may have been my car."

She winced and removed the ice pack from his hand, then those aqua eyes flickered to his. "I'm sorry about that, Alex. You hit on every jerk nerve in my system. I was afraid you'd be like—"

"Your ex?"

She stared a moment, her gaze rounding to vulnerable before she flipped on her smile again, staring him down like Mrs. Riley from his fifth grade science class had so long ago. He shuddered.

"So, speaking of teaching teens, what can you do?"

He took the ice pack from her control and grimaced. "What can I do?"

"Sure." She leaned back in the chair and folded her arms. "What are your talents? Gifts? Skills?" Her golden brows rose with challenge. "I assume you have some."

His grin stretched up on one side. "I'm afraid you haven't tapped into all of them yet."

"Come on, pretty boy; impress me with your smarts, not your charm. I know you much too well now to fall for ignorance."

His face fell and he groaned. "I don't know what you mean. I'm a better teacher because of you. I can write grants, but I don't see how that helps troubled teens." He wracked his brain, the black hold of uselessness looming before him like always. "I played baseball in college."

"You did?" Her eyes sparkled with interest, fueling a fresh wave of warmth through his chest. "That's great."

A sliver of self-confidence strung his world together. "Pitcher and occasional outfielder. And I enjoy tennis. Oh, and I can play the guitar."

That statement paused her. "You can?"

"Yeah." His soft response somehow gentled her entire expression. The sudden urge to run his fingers across the smooth skin of her cheek almost had him dropping the ice pack and distracting her from this crazy notion that he could help troubled teens.

"Well, that's a neat surprise." She blinked and sat up straight. "But the guys will love that you played baseball. We have a few serious players at TLC. How were you at math?"

He shrugged. "Straight As, except in trig."

She clapped her hands together and stood. "Dr. Murdock, I believe this is going to be a beautiful arrangement. I'm so glad you offered."

"Offered? I think the word Lou would use is bamboozled."

Rainey's grin lit her entire face. "Whatever it takes."

He lost his response somewhere between the soft tilt of her lips and her citrusy scent. His fingers itched to get trapped in the massive folds of her hair, to kiss her until she whispered his name. Sauna-like heat moved into his face, thickening the air, drawing him closer. "You're beautiful, Rainey Mitchell."

Her smile wavered with an exhalation of air. "Don't try to change the subject, Alex. I'm serious."

"So am I."

Sarah's little chatter to Haus from the next room stopped his forward momentum to her lips. "But … um … this tutoring thing? You actually think I'm going to be more of a help than a liability?"

She snagged his jacket and jerked it a little, eyes narrowed in scrutiny as if measuring his worth. "I think all you need to do is find that hero inside, Alex, and show it to these guys. I know he's in there."

"Really? You believe that?" He attempted to keep his voice light but held his breath for her response.

"Yeah, I do." She pressed her finger into his shoulder. "So prove me right."

His breath seeped out on a slow sigh as the sound of a truck rumbled from outside.

"Mama, Dr. Alex, the tow truck's right outside." Sarah bounced to their side, Haus at her heels.

Alex stretched to a stand and placed the ice pack on the table. "I guess it's time to learn about the damage."

"I know what will cheer you up." Rainey leaned down and whispered something to Sarah, whose eyes brightened like sparkling sapphires.

"Dr. Alex, do you want to come to our sleigh ridin' party tonight?"

Alex knelt down in front of the little girl who claimed a tight hold on his heart. "What's a sleigh riding party?"

Rainey stepped toward the door, tossing a grin over her shoulder. "Oh, it's where a bunch of Mitchell lunatics get together for a near-death experience on sleds at night."

"And there's lots of hot chocolate and cookies," Sarah added, dancing around Haus.

Alex didn't take his eyes off Rainey. "Well, when you describe it that way, how can I refuse?"

Chapter Fifteen

Alex stared out the window at the dirty-brown Chevy truck in the driveway. The monster of a vehicle was the only option Rusty from the garage gave him as the mechanic worked to fix Marilyn.

Alex shrugged into his jacket and walked out onto the porch, Haus at his heels. "You like Marilyn better too, don't ya, boy?" Haus sat at his feet, staring up at Alex without one hint of his creepy grin. "Come on," he said and waved toward the truck. "That can't be cooler than Marilyn." The dog's expression didn't change. "I know it's more practical, but ... brown? King cab?" Haus' grin crept full. "Well, I guess it's go big or go home, right?" His phone buzzed in his pocket, and he pulled it to his ear. "Hey, sis."

"Hi, Alex. I thought of a few more names to share with you for fundraising, and I have great news. After some investigation of your new place, the detectives think they can plan a face-to-face meeting for us within the next two months."

Alex sent a fist pump into the air and yelled so loudly, Haus jumped up on all fours. "That's the best news I've heard in months. So, the police are sure Ransom is a safe enough place for you to stay with me?"

"They'll know for certain after they do a few more checks, but it's the most promising option since this whole situation began."

Alex sighed against the porch railing, taking in the vast view of white over the rolling hills. A fairyland. "You'll love it here, Evie. The people are great, and the setting is like something out of a movie."

"You've changed your mind a lot since you moved there." Her statement was tinged with humor.

"I'm teachable."

"Mmhmm," came his sister's quick reply. "And rather fascinated with a local, I think."

"You'd like her, Evie. She's strong and smart and funny."

"And beautiful?"

"Well, there is that." Alex grinned.

"You seem to like her family too. A bit less dysfunctional than ours?"

"I've never met a family like them. They have their quirks, but … well, they all just love each other and accept others in this weirdly wonderful way."

"Weirdly wonderful way, eh?" She chuckled. It was good to hear. "You're almost poetic, so I know you're falling hard."

He scrubbed Haus' head, restoring the dog's grin. With a deep breath of the crisp air, he allowed the serenity and beauty of the landscape to seep into him, calling him to linger. To belong.

"You'd like it here, Evie. Once John is caught and prosecuted, and we can go back to a normal life, I want to bring you here to start over. It's a good place for new beginnings and finding home."

"Sounds nice." Her voice pearled with longing, an ache he understood all too well.

"And I'll introduce you to Rainey, Sarah, and the whole Mitchell clan. Sarah and Lily could play *My Little Pony* for months."

Evie laughed, and they ended the conversation with a few more business contacts for Alex. He shot a prayer of gratitude to heaven and patted Haus' head. "I guess that truck isn't so bad."

Valentine's Day reeked of broken promises.

Or at least that's what Rainey told Emma two years ago when her happily-ever-after turned into a nightmare-come-true. The holiday dripped with a sickening sweetness that those who were less fortunate hated to taste, especially in its confectionery saccharinity.

But this year, the hues of pink and red failed to turn her stomach into a knotted lump of stay-at-home. She stared into the mirror and brushed out her hair, its glossy length nearly reaching her waistline. Life pretzeled in unexpected directions—a total three-sixty. Six months ago, she'd have laughed if someone told her she'd be distracted with the thought of kissing Alex Murdock, but those musings took permanent residence during her unoccupied moments.

She was caught.

His notorious flirting covered a tenderness that thawed through years of Rainey's resentment like hot chocolate on the snow. Yes, she grinned. That's exactly what had happened. A consistent mixture of hundreds of little conversations and moments with her and her family, glimpses of the kindness rustling beneath the humor and the sweet protectiveness, melted the walled-up fears in her heart.

She liked him a lot. Too much for such a short amount of time, but his magnetizing combination of playful, tender, and easygoing broke down her defenses. *Heaven help her, she loved the combination.*

It certainly didn't hurt that he was sexy and smart too.

And the way he looked at her? He *saw* her—and from the grin on that handsome face of his, he liked what he saw. She'd never been one to go easy and this thing with Alex? Well, her heart was ready to jump all into the future—kissing, Casanova, and all.

She closed her eyes and relived the way his arms wrapped around her and Sarah on the sled at her mama's house. And yes, he'd screamed like a girl the entire way down the hill, but he'd never let go. By the third trip down the hill, she leaned into him, wrapped as tightly in his sandalwood scent as his arms, and she knew she was ready to leap.

She swept through a brief application of makeup then hesitated with another look in the mirror, barely recognizing the reflection. She hadn't worn her hair all the way down in a long time. Its lengths cascaded over her shoulders, softening the sharper edges of her face. Her fingers itched to pull back the locks, somehow protecting a softer, more vulnerable part of herself. Even when she'd struggled with her weight in school, her hair had been her shining glory. The one beautiful thing about her. After Gray... Rainey paused, staring in the mirror at her image. She'd stopped wearing her hair down when he left.

A surge of certainty, almost in rebellion against her fear, stiffened her spine, infusing determination into her reflection.

It was past time to allow Gray to control any more of her future.

With a lighter step, she went through her morning routine, helping Sarah get ready for school, cooking breakfast, and taking a few moments to sip her coffee and stare out the window toward her grandparents' farmhouse.

"Mama, do you like Dr. Alex's new truck?"

Rainey looked down at her cutie pie, who'd requested braids for the day. With a pink bow above each braid and her favorite frilly matching dress, Rainey had a hard time figuring out how such a girly-girl landed in her life. For Emma, yes? For the tomboy of the family? No. Oh, but she loved her princess. Pink, dimples, ponies, and all.

"It's certainly a better choice in the snow."

"I liked Marilyn better. She was shiny like a piece of candy."

She? Rainey caught her smile in her mug. *And about as useful as one.*

"Who is your valentine today, Mama?"

Rainey grinned down at her little cherub. "Why you, of course."

Being almost six must have wisened Sarah up because she shook her head, her baby-doll lips pursed tight. "I can't be your valentine. I'm your daughter. You need a boy valentine."

Rainey turned from the window and placed her mug and Sarah's dishes into the sink. "Do I?"

"Mmhmm." Sarah followed behind with a little bounce in her step, her dress fluttering around her. "I think Dr. Alex is your valentine."

The heat from Rainey's coffee lingered in her cheeks as she ushered Sarah toward the bathroom. "And why do you think that?"

"Because he thinks we're pretty. And he's nice and funny and smells good."

Does he ever! Rainey fixed Sarah's toothbrush and then her own.

"And he acts like a prince, like Emma said."

Rainey halted the brush to her lips. "What else did Emma say?"

Sarah's words blurred around the bubbles in her mouth. "He finks your pwetty, and he wescues you from twouble like wif the car cwash." She spit and smiled, totally oblivious that the car crash was Alex's fault. "And he holds your hand even when he doesn't have to, like he did at the sledding party. Because you could walk just fine in the snow, but he held your hand anyway."

Rainey wiped Sarah's face with the towel and placed a kiss on her forehead, smiling at the memory of Alex's hand around hers. "And what does Emma say the princess does during all this time? Just wait around for the rescue?"

Sarah kept talking as they pulled on their coats. "Lou says a real princess rescues the prince right back."

Rainey zipped Sarah's coat up to her chin. "I like Lou's way of thinking. It's all well and good for a handsome prince to come to the rescue, but it doesn't hurt if the princess rescues the prince right back." She took her daughter by the shoulders. "You don't *need* a prince, Sarah. You're going to be strong and smart enough to make it without one." Rainey swallowed down the tinge of fear lining the inside of her throat and forged ahead in faith. "But if God brings one into your life, you can also be strong and smart enough to let him rescue you."

With an armful of valentine's cupcakes for Sarah's school, Rainey made her rounds of dropping off Sarah and the dessert, teaching class, and running her early morning clinic at the university without seeing her "prince" once. When she pulled into TLC and saw Rusty's truck parked in the lot, a shimmy of excitement flooded through her. Anticipation. Hope.

Slow down, Rainey. Alex probably doesn't even know its Valentine's Day.

And they weren't ... together. Really. She raised her chin and headed inside. *Yet.*

He looked up from his phone as she walked through the doors, and he froze, jaw dropping.

She really tried not to smile, but she'd never caused a man's jaw to drop before. Ever. "I'm glad to see you found your way here, Dr. Murdock." She redirected her tickle of delight and gestured down the hallway. "What do you think of TLC?"

He blinked out of his stupor, leaving her to bask a little longer in the sweet power of this attraction. Watching Casanova stumble a little propelled her shaking heart forward with more certainty. No, he wasn't like Gray.

"Um ... it's nice." He stepped closer, his gaze raking over her face and hair. "Sturdy and ... um ... cube-like."

Her brow inched upward with her smile. "Cube-like?"

He rolled a shoulder and shoved his hands in his pockets. "What can I say? I appreciate symmetrical buildings." His grin took on a roguish tilt. "You've done something new with your hair. It's nice."

"Nice?"

"Really nice."

"Thank you." Her grin almost brimmed into a laugh. "Are you ready for the tour?"

"You mean you're not going to put me straight to work?"

"That will come, but I think I'll break you in slowly."

He nodded, following her down the hallway, his look of appreciation almost intoxicating. "That's wise. I should only be allowed to ruin one child at a time in slow succession."

She shook her head and continued forward. "From what I know of you and these kids, I have a funny feeling you're going to be the perfect fit."

She led the way, moving from one room to the next. "We have kids from all over the county. A few are high-end kids who struggle with school because of developmental delays, learning disabilities—you know, things like dyslexia and such." She waved toward a treatment room to her right, then one to her left. "But most of our kids are from the lower end of the economic scale."

"And you think I'm a perfect fit for them … why?"

She stopped in front of the materials closet, hands on her hips. "Because you care and despite your deflective charm, you know what it's like to be misjudged or undervalued. You can talk to these kids on a level others can't."

He grew quiet as she pressed in the key code to the closet. "I hope you're right."

She tossed a grin over her shoulder. "Me too."

The tease in his smile pushed a warm rush through her that landed solidly in her cheeks as she clicked open the door. His grin really was too distracting for her clear-headed intentions. She focused her attention forward. "Some basics to remember. No taking the kids off site—we don't have the liability coverage for it. Also, only parents can provide snacks because of possible food allergies. And, of course, no weapons.'"

His expression sobered. "Oh, well that's a problem. I always carry one with me."

She spun around.

His brows wiggled. "My smile."

She rolled her gaze away from his handsome face and turned so he couldn't see her own grin responding despite her best efforts. "I'll make sure to keep any of my dreamy junior-high girls away from you for their own good."

Rainey waved a hand to the room. "This is our materials closet. Any assessments or treatment materials you may need you can find in here." She slid past him to an electronic box on the wall. "This is the check-in and check-out system. Each item has a number, and you'll be assigned one too. All you have to do is scan your item, key in your number, and the item is checked out or in."

"Sounds easy enough." He edged closer, his gaze locked with hers. "I saw your therapy session today, the one with the ten-year-old with autism."

Rainey leaned back against the shelf. "Jake."

"I've never been able to work with kids who can't talk, but you were amazing. You just kept repeating the expectations, offering him the pictures to communicate over and over and over. It was remarkable."

The walls of the closet closed in, and Alex's warming scent hooked around her with magnetic powers. "You can handle this, Alex. Not only are you becoming a great teacher, but you're a smart student, and despite all your pretense, you have a big heart."

All arrogance fled his expression, and the look in his eyes stilled the pitter-patter of her heart. So vulnerable and real. "Thank you, Rainey. That means a lot coming from you."

"From me, huh?" She made a weak attempt to resurrect a little sass, but her words caught in her dry throat. "I've been that hard on you?"

His grin twitched but his eyes held hers, *seeing* her. "Because you challenge me to be better. I'm amazed by you. You're smart, generous, a great mom, and a remarkable teacher." His whispered words tugged her nearer. "I've never known anyone like you."

Rainey wasn't sure what force took control of her. The warm admiration in his stare? The gentleness in his smile? The longing for a perfect opportunity to finish what they'd almost started a few days ago? But somehow the magical combination intercepted her senses and thrust her body into motion.

She breached the short distance between them and grabbed Alex's collar on either side, tugging him against her. His eyes shot wide, confirming her own surprise at her behavior, just before her impatient lips found his. Despite her constant musings on the topic for the past few days, nothing prepared her for the actual contact of his surprised mouth on hers.

A schism of warmth shot from the heat of his lips to her quickening pulse, inciting a gasp. She couldn't remember the last time she'd kissed a man. Well over two years, but this reintroduction to the activity proved more memorable than any kiss she'd had with Gray.

The sizzling intensity shook her with a jolt of certainty. Home and hope suddenly smelled a whole lot like sandalwood and tasted like the best hot chocolate on the planet. She quivered as his arms encased her, pulling her into his warmth and somehow stirring her back to her senses. Good heavens, she was in the materials closet at *work*! What had she been thinking?

She jerked back, hand to her mouth to savor the last memory of those wild feelings. An apology waited on her tingling lips, but she dared not look at him. She'd never initiated a first kiss in her whole life. Ever.

Not that she'd had a whole host of *first* kisses. Her face warmed for a whole new reason.

"Alex, I ... I'm—"

His finger touched her lips, silencing her and drawing her gaze up to his. The look in his eyes held her breath and stilled her barrage of weak excuses. If she trusted the reflection of herself in his eyes, the way he stared at her with such unadulterated tenderness, she couldn't help but feel beautiful.

He didn't say a word but ran his hand along her cheek until he caught the back of her neck. Slowly, with painstaking gentleness, he drew her back to him, holding her attention until her vision blurred, and she closed her eyes. Her breath held, waiting for release. The finger touching her lips moved down to her chin and tipped her face up, closer. With the sweetest of meetings, he glided his mouth over hers, teasing hers to respond.

A quiet moan slipped from her moistened lips, and her fingers found their way to his shoulders, holding him in place in case he decided this insane decision proved too crazy for either of them. Crazy was quickly becoming a preferred status quo—and flaming inside of her like a welcome wildfire.

He took his time. His mouth seemed in no hurry to leave hers, almost like he savored the touch as much as she did. His palms trailed her cheeks with feather-light caresses, sending tingles skittering over her skin. At some point, she probably needed to breathe, but how could she risk breaking this spell?

His touch, his careful control, cradled her wounded heart like a precious possession. Cherishing her from his lips to hers. Every word she'd spoken about "a kiss just being a kiss" melted away with this magical and surprising intoxication. Sweet mercy, she was in so much trouble.

Glorious trouble.

He pulled back from the kiss and leaned his forehead against hers, his palms stroking her face.

"Rainey?"

She touched her nose to his, inching her fingers up to graze his cheek. "Mmhmm."

His smile slanted like the flirt he was. "Will you be my valentine?"

Alex glanced over at the single red rose in the passenger's seat of the truck. He might be a day late on the Valentine's roses, but in his defense, Rainey just became his official valentine yesterday.

Valentine's Day had moved up in ranking as one of his all-time favorite holidays. He'd never be able to enter the materials closet without grinning like a starstruck idiot and feeling the sudden urge to instant replay his introduction to the place.

Of course, if being kissed crazy by Rainey meant he walked around dazed all the time, bring on the idiocy. *She'd* kissed *him* first, a truth he'd never let her live down but also a boost to the old confidence. From what he knew of Rainey Mitchell, she didn't make decisions lightly or impulsively, despite her claims otherwise. No, she'd thought about that kiss long before it took hold of her, and the very idea of her struggle encouraged his grin to brim a little wider.

To prove beyond a shadow of a doubt what a lovesick dope he was, he'd arrived early to the university parking lot so he could greet her with a rose in hand and, possibly, get another kiss or two as a reward.

It was her fault, really. A woman didn't spring a kiss-attack on a man without consequences.

And boy, oh boy, he liked the possibility of those consequences.

He leaned his head back against the seat of the oil-smelling truck and offered thanksgiving to God. Life was good, and he wanted to keep it that way.

For years he'd danced around relationships, his heart bending and mending from the loss of Beth. He'd kept his emotions at a safe distance. But not anymore. Nope, he'd grabbed tightly and wasn't letting go.

His grin lit. Well, actually *Rainey* had been the one to grab *him* tightly and pull him right into a whopper of a kiss.

If things went as Evie expected, John would soon be behind bars, she could step back into her life, and Alex would be free to tell Rainey the whole truth, with no secrets to muddy up this sweet start.

The rumble of a motor drew his attention ahead. Rainey saw him from across the cars and offered him a beautiful morning smile as she pulled into a parking space a row below his. He hoisted his computer bag onto his shoulder and tucked the rose behind his back as he set out on a mission to begin their morning with a kiss.

Just beyond Rainey's Jimmy, a movement caught his attention. A man walked toward her, his face hardened with the same purpose in his approach. He weaved between the cars, each step drawing him closer to her.

A chill of warning shot up Alex's spine. *No!*

"Rainey," Alex yelled, taking off at a run as she stepped from her jeep. "Watch out."

Chapter Sixteen

Rainey teetered dangerously close to swooning. Just one look from her Casanova in his beaten-up truck and her mind dipped back into the glorious memory of their only kiss ... or several kisses during one rather extended material's room tour.

How on earth would she be able to check out another assessment without thinking of sandalwood and swooning ... and knee-weakening kisses?

She squeezed her eyes closed before rounding her car to meet her handsome rogue's approach. Surely she could exert a little self-control instead of stumbling all over herself like a rabid fangirl.

She sighed as an onslaught of sandalwood and closet kisses poured through her memory in complete rebellion against her frail attempts at self-control. Come on! She was an intelligent, grown-up single mom for goodness sakes. But she also really liked kissing Alex Murdock.

Tugging her bag farther up on her shoulder, she slipped from the Jimmy and walked toward the back of the jeep just as Alex's shout materialized into recognition.

"Watch out!"

Why was he running toward her with his phone to his ear? She turned in the direction of his focus, and all heat drained down through her fingertips. Dan Edwards closed in, the shiny tip of a blade in one hand. He lunged at her, his dark eyes wild and bloodshot.

With a quick turn of her body, she grabbed her computer bag and blocked Dan's attack. His blade ripped through the cloth, shocking him enough that Rainey swung the bag toward him and knocked him backward. Between the misfire and his stumble, Dan lost his hold on the knife, but he was quick to recover, spinning toward Rainey and grabbing a fistful of her hair as she attempted to sidestep him.

Jagged pain ripped down her neck, weakening her to her knees. She bit back a scream and stared into her assailant's unshaven face.

He lowered his face to hers, his rancid breath curling her stomach. "Nobody takes my family from me." Spit sprinkled over Rainey's face, and she tried to turn her face away, but he held her head in place with a jerk of her hair. "I don't need no knife to kill you. I can do it with my bare hands."

His fingers gripped her exposed throat, but she pinched her nails into his hand, attempting to loosen his tightening hold. He growled and squeezed her neck tighter, closing off her airway. Just when she started to lose focus, Alex flew into her blurry periphery and slammed into Dan.

The impact loosened Dan's chokehold, and both men stumbled to the ground. Rainey fell to her palms and knees, coughing as air seeped into her burning lungs. Alex and Dan wrestled across the gravel, the latter man thrashing like one possessed. Rainey swiped the tears from her bleary vision and reached for her computer bag, which was just out of reach, as Dan brought his knee into Alex's body, crippling him into a fetal position.

"No," Rainey cried, catching the madman's attention.

He kicked Alex in the stomach and then sprang for her again.

She struggled to a stand, raking a handful of gravel as she stood, and then tossed the dirt and rocks at Dan's face. It distracted him long enough for her to grab her computer bag and deflect his onslaught for a second time, hitting him in the chin.

His fury proved her downfall. With the power of his anger, he took control of the computer bag and slammed it into her chest, knocking her backwards into her jeep. Knives of pain shot up her back and neck.

Alex stumbled from the ground and grabbed Dan by the shoulder. "Rainey—" Alex's words ended as Dan's fist connected with his face, sending him back a few feet. Dan spun toward Rainey, only to grunt when Alex threw himself against Dan's back. When his assailant retaliated with an elbow to his stomach and a punch to his face, Alex dropped to the ground with a muffled moan.

"Alex!" Rainey pushed away from the jeep and grabbed one of Dan's flailing arms. With practiced movements, she twisted Dan's arm behind him like she'd learned in self-defense class, disabling him long enough for Alex to secure Dan's other arm and push the man's face to the ground.

Campus police ran forward, taking control of the situation. Rainey straightened from her hunched position, the pause in defense awakening her senses to a throbbing ache down her jaw and throat. "His name is Dan Edwards.

He already has a record." She gestured to the knife on the ground by her car. "He came at us with that."

One of the policemen cuffed Dan as the wild man spurted threats and curses. "Your cousin told us to keep a watch out for him. We can already get him on trespassing."

"And you'll find lots more in his file." Rainey stepped to Alex, who was bent over with his hands on his knees. She ran a palm up his shoulder. "Are you okay?"

He turned toward her, and she winced from the sight. His nose and lip both bled, and one eye was already beginning to swell. "I've been better."

"Alex," she whispered, taking his face between her palms with a light touch.

"The paramedics should be here in a few minutes," one of the policemen offered.

"I'll be fine." Alex groaned and gestured with his chin toward Dan. "Just get him out of here."

The police wrestled Dan away, and with the increased distance between them, her stomach released the pinched tension in a quiver. He'd tried to kill her.

Alex stumbled against Rainey's jeep, drawing her attention back to him. She slipped her arms around his waist to keep him from sliding to the ground. "You need to see a doctor."

He grimaced and kept his eyes closed. "Are *you* okay?"

Her throat burned, her chest hurt, and her insides shivered in a way she wasn't ready to acknowledge yet. "I'll be all right."

He gave her a narrow-eyed look, mostly because one eye had almost swollen shut. "I think we need to go back to your house, make hot chocolate, and snuggle by the fire. That would make me feel loads better. How about you?"

She smoothed her hand over his bruised forehead. Not being alone sounded really good. "Okay." Her fingers moved down to inspect his nose. She squinted as he winced from her touch. "You'll be wearing quite the face tomorrow. The kids at TLC will be so proud."

He grinned. "Yeah, the cool guys are the ones with the dented noses, right?" He started to laugh, then moaned from the pain. "Why didn't I feel cooler in middle school?"

She paused at this admission, tapping it to the back of her mind for later. "You could have been killed."

His one unharmed eye widened. "You could have too."

"But this was *my* problem. You didn't have to get involved."

"You can't believe that. Not after we've gotten to know each other a little better." He lifted his head from its rest against the car and reached into his jacket to remove a crumpled rose. He focused the full power of those seafoam green eyes on her, searching her face but tagging on a grin for levity, she guessed. "Maybe I'm trying to find the hero inside."

Her hands stilled against his cheek, the vulnerability in those eyes opening of emotion, unfamiliar, yet terrifyingly familiar, at her core. "Oh, I think you definitely found him." She swallowed the sudden lump in her throat, tears on the brink of falling. "And I'm really thankful you did." She focused on his bloodied face. "After the paramedics check you out, let's cancel classes and get that hot chocolate."

"And the snuggles?"

His plea, like a little boy's, revived her smile. "Yeah, I think some snuggles would be nice too." She pressed her face into his shoulder so he couldn't see the tears or the fear. "Really nice."

Maybe having a hero around wasn't such a bad idea after all.

"What happened to your face?" Blake, one of the kids in Alex's new tutoring class, marched forward with a mile-deep grimace on his face.

He'd been with the guys for a week, mostly focused on the five high school boys, with some other tutoring sessions for a handful of middle schoolers. Rainey had been right. He connected with the boys at a real level. Misfits. Smart, but prone to mind-wander or mischief-make. From his conversations with some of them, he read between the lines about broken homes and absent parents.

He knew that life all too well.

"My face?" Alex shoved a baseball bat into his bag and shrugged, one eye still swollen enough to blur his vision. "Giant snowball."

Blake's stone-like expression almost broke, but his friend, Mike, released a full laugh. "They got you good, didn't they, Doc? They put rocks in that snowball."

"No kidding." Alex pulled the bag up on his shoulder and headed for the door. "You guys ready to practice some geometry?"

"Geometry?" Suspicion remained a permanent fixture on the boy's face. "Are you trying to trick us, man?"

"You said we were going for batting practice," Joe, the youngest of the group, argued. He tossed his coat on the chair and crossed his arms. "I ain't doin' geometry. I can't."

Alex raised his palms and kept his voice calm, hoping the bits of conversation he'd pulled out of the boys might encourage their trust. "Come on, guys. Didn't you know you can learn geometry in baseball?"

After enough grumbling to match a Disney dwarf, the guys caught the learning bug—at least a little. Blake proved the hardest to soften. The kid's dad left when Blake was young, and his mother was in jail for using meth. His elderly grandmother housed him and his little sister, but Blake was the real caretaker of the family. Coming to TLC provided him with the help he needed to make it through school. The kid knew he'd have to get a job to support his sister.

Alex understood the protective streak. His elder sister, Angelica, proved too independent and prickly for Alex's care, but Evie, the younger and sweeter one, brought out his protective instinct with life-changing force. After their mother left and their father won full custody—more from Alex's father's financial powers and Alex's mother's lack of stamina than either parents' virtues—Alex took on the role of caregiver to Evie. Any maternal influence died with their mom a year later. Angelica, four years older than him, disappeared into college, leaving Alex and Evie to adjust to life without their mother and within their father's demands.

They'd moved from one new city to another, and Alex had learned how to act and please people without indebting his heart. Until Beth—she drew him in with her sweetness, her love. Alex smiled. A sweetness and love he'd never expected to find again.

Alex took his place at the rough-made home plate and positioned the boys throughout the outfield, where they stood with the enthusiasm of going to the dentist. He rolled his shoulder, picked up a bat and ball, and hit his first ball as a flimsy line-drive down to third base.

"If that's all you got, Doc, we're going to need to move closer," Mike shouted, his toothy grin spreading wide as he shot a laugh to Blake.

Alex narrowed his eyes and turned his body, readied for another try. It had been years since he'd felt the smooth metal of the bat against his palm or moved in the rhythm of the swing.

"Watch it, Mike, or I'll have you doing algebra next."

The boy's smile faded into a frown. "Y'ain't playin' fair with those kind of threats, Doc."

Alex drew in a deep breath, tossed the ball with one hand, and brought up the bat with the other. The crack of contact echoed through the field, and the ball popped high into the air over second base.

Mike's eyes shot wide and he readied for the catch. Despite the awkward angle of his glove, he caught the ball.

"Nice catch, Mike."

The boy's smile bloomed into a look of unconstrained pride. It was the simple things that made all the difference. Encouragement—something Alex had seen in other dads at times but rarely experienced from his father. Faith in the person—another untapped opportunity in his family.

But it didn't take much. A kind word here. A listening ear there.

"Okay, do you see Joe?"

Mike nodded toward the younger boy, who stood in the outfield behind first base. "Yeah."

"What angle would you, me, and Joe make? Acute or Obtuse?"

All three boys exchanged looks and then from the outfield behind third base, Blake shouted, "Acute. It ain't wide enough to be the other one."

Alex pointed the bat in his direction and tamed his smile. "You got it, Blake. Let's try another."

On they went, discussing various elements of geometry through the game until Alex had two of the three boys laughing and even Blake sharing a smile ... not to mention some pretty solid understanding of angles.

Rainey had been right again. Despite his doubts, working with these boys—reading their insecurities and need for a man's influence—fed an untouched calling he didn't even know he had. He wanted to do more for them.

He packed his bag and started for home a few hours later, his head down as the realization of the blessings Ransom brought pressed deeper inside him. How could God have orchestrated so many things to fit Alex's life like this? A place and people he'd never imagined making such a difference to him, changing him, showing him who he could be in this vast, unpredictable world.

Even the boys at TLC. The entire experience from day one in Ransom left him humbled to the tip of his faded Rockports. Maybe Ransom had started as a demotion, but somehow God turned it into the best promotion of his life—not so much by changing the circumstances, but by changing him.

He rubbed the back of his sore neck, still feeling the effects of the attack from Dan Edwards, and slowly made his trek through the dimly lit halls to the exit of TLC. The receptionist had long gone, leaving the emergency lights glowing in the waiting area.

"Hey, handsome, wait up."

He turned to see Rainey approaching from the other hallway, her smile another item to add on his gratitude list. Safe and sound. After filing the police report on Dan, they'd spent the day watching old movies on her couch and talking of childhood memories. Hers, mostly. His weren't very interesting.

He'd found his way up to her house the next afternoon too. Welcomed into the cozy aroma of apple pie and southern sweetness. Yep, he could do with both for the rest of his life.

"I thought you'd already left."

She shrugged a shoulder and met him at the door. "I had to finish up some paperwork." A crooked grin played upon her lips, lighting her eyes. She had great lips. "Are you hungry?"

He dragged his gaze from her mouth and reoriented to her question. Hungry took on a whole new meaning.

"What did you have in mind?"

"Well, I could pick up Sarah and meet you at Daphne's. Emma's taking a pastry class, so I bet she'll have some tasty treats to try."

He sidled up next to her and wisped a stray hair from her cheek, narrowing his eyes as he closed in. "Miss Mitchell, are you asking me on a date?"

She swayed forward on her tiptoes and gave him a surprise kiss. She'd been doing surprisingly sweet stuff like that since the things with Dan—lowering her guard and suspicions. If he'd known this hero gig had such heart-stopping perks, he'd have invested more time in it long before now.

"You can bet on it." She swung to the door and turned her head to him. "Besides, I have some grant news to talk over with you."

Alex exaggerated his sigh, appreciating her walking in front of him. She still limped a little from the twist in her ankle during Dan's attack, so Alex slipped her free arm through his for more support. "As I recall, you said two people discussing work over food isn't a date."

She shook her head and squeezed his arm close to her side. "Kissing changes things."

"It sure does," he whispered loudly enough to flare her grin ... and add a slight rosy glow in her cheeks.

Alex's future walked through the door of Daphne's about fifteen minutes after him. Sarah skipped at Rainey's side, her blond hair in pigtails bouncing along with her steps. *Don't screw this up, Alex.* He wanted to seize this future with both hands, but he was a clumsy dreamer, and the last thing he'd ever want to do was hurt either of them ... or their family.

He stood as they approached, certainty clicking with each step that drew them nearer.

"Hi there, princess." Alex helped Sarah remove her jacket.

Sarah's grin rewarded him all the way to his heart. "Mama said we're on a date."

Alex flipped his gaze to Rainey. "Did she now?"

Sarah nodded, eyes wide. "She said you might hold our hands."

"Hmm." Alex knelt and picked up Sarah's tiny hand, examining it. "I *might* just do that." Sarah giggled, and Alex tucked the sound away in his memory for safe keeping.

He stood, reached for Rainey's hand, and gave it a squeeze. She squeezed it back. Yep, this felt right. "I think I like this dating idea. What do you think, Sarah?"

"Well, you can't hold my hand when I'm drinking my hot chocolate, Dr. Alex, because I need both hands." She slid into the booth.

"Important dating rules to follow, Dr. Alex." Rainey raised a playful brow to him as she sat next to Sarah.

His chest expanded to Marvel Comic proportions. Dating was much nicer when the lady liked the notion too.

"So, tell me about this news."

"Well…" She focused on her hand as she tugged off her gloves. "We've had three responses from committees about whether TLC has a chance with the particular grants we're researching. One already stated we weren't a good fit for their foundation, so no need to apply."

"Stupid group," Alex murmured and Rainey shot him a warning glare, gesturing toward Sarah. "I … um … mean, not stupid." He stared back at Rainey. "Inane."

Her lips twitched. "Another asked for more information to give better clarity on whether filling out all the paperwork is worth our time."

"And the third?" he asked, leaning forward, hands folded before him.

"Great fit … and it's on their list to be reviewed in April."

"Yes!" His fists shot into the air. "Which one?" She shared the name and the amount of funding offered. "That's the big one we tried."

"I know." Rainey's aqua eyes danced. "And if some of these regular donors come through, and we can get a few other grants, we have a real chance of saving TLC and gaining grant renewal for upcoming years."

"So we just need to focus our fundraising on getting us through the next school year."

"Right."

"That's huge news." He covered her fingers on the table with his. "I didn't understand your love for TLC before, but I'm starting to."

"You're holding her hand." Sarah giggled and crawled onto her knees in the booth to smack her hand on the table. With those big blue eyes locked to his, she waited for him to respond.

Alex covered her tiny fingers, and Sarah's giggles erupted again. "We're all on a hand-holding date." He gazed from Sarah to Rainey and found her eyes focused on him. He wound his fingers through hers. "My favorite kind."

"Hey, I need your help." Emma placed herself beside Alex on the restaurant bench, phone at the ready. "What words can I possibly spell with these letters?"

Her caramel-colored eyes flipped from Rainey to Alex with glowing expectation and fell to their hands on the table. "Whoa, whoa." Her mouth dropped wide, then spread into a smile. "I knew it. I knew this would happen."

"You knew we'd date?" Rainey drew her hand away from Alex's and shook her head.

"Of course I did." Emma pressed her fingers into her chest. "I felt it when I first saw you guys together." Emma patted Alex's shoulder. "I have a feeling about these things. Three for three."

"Three for three?" Adorableness ran in the Mitchell family, that was for sure.

"In matchmaking." Emma tossed her hair, her pearly whites gleaming. "It's a gift."

"I like to call it meddling, busybody, intrusi—"

"Hey." Emma held up her palm to her sister. "Point made." She flipped her smile back to Alex. "Hater gonna hate."

Emma jumped when her phone buzzed in her hand. "Oh, right, letters."

"Scrabble." Rainey sighed and looked to Alex. "Emma's best friend, Jonathan, is working at a law firm near New York, but the two of them have this ongoing Scrabble game that's lasted ... how long has he been gone?"

Emma grimaced. "Three years. *Three whole years.*" She shook her phone at Alex. "I love the idea of traveling, but moving away for three whole years? Not cool."

Alex peered down at her phone. "So, you guys have this ongoing game of Scrabble on your phones?"

"Yep." She grimaced at the screen. "But he's gonna beat me this round unless I can get a few extra points from these letters."

Long-distance relationships had never been Alex's forte until Evie ended up "dead." Now he understood distance was worth the trouble if it meant keeping a relationship alive. "And what are the letters?"

"CSRAABS," she read them off. "I've already thought of 'crabs,' but that won't give me enough points."

"What about 'scarabs'? That would use all your letters."

Emma's nose wrinkled and took off about ten years on her age. "Scarabs? We have to use real words, Alex."

"Hey now, short stuff, I'm smarter than I look." He nudged her with his shoulder. "I first learned about the Scarab brand when my dad bought one of their boats, but later I learned it was a type of beetle, so the word should work for your game ... *and* impress your lawyer buddy."

She shrugged. "It's just Jonathan. I don't care about impressing him as much as beating him."

She typed in the word and set the phone down. "So, you guys know I'm catering for the wedding right?" Her body nearly trembled against Alex's arm as her hands waved in the air. "My first real catering job using the recipes I've learned in school."

"Hey, that's great! Rainey said you had some new things to offer tonight?"

Emma popped to her feet, pad in hand. "You betcha. I made an all new chicken pot pie, *and* tonight I'm introducing beef bourguignon pot pie, which is perfect with spinach puffs or creamed broccoli."

"Sounds great to me." Alex turned to Rainey, who hesitated. Aha, the country girl took some time to sort out new food, he bet.

"What exactly is it?"

Emma bit her bottom lip and looked skyward in thought. "Well, it's kind of like chicken pot pie, only with beef and a little added"—her fingers flared out for effect—"pizzazz."

"Come on, Rainey, give it a try." Alex winked and enjoyed the beautiful rush of pink infusing her cheeks. "Adventure. Danger. It's like dating me."

"How cute is that?" Emma sighed. "Yep, you guys are MFEO." She pointed her pencil at Rainey. "Focused, reliable, bossy, prone to too much seriousness." And then the pencil pointed to Alex. "Flirty, relaxed, a little dangerous, and easy on the eyes. Made for each other."

"Your tip just doubled," Alex said.

"Fine," Rainey growled. "I'll try the beef … whatever, and bring Sarah her usual grilled cheese, pretty please." After Emma moved out of sight, Rainey snatched back Alex's hand, drawing his attention. "You realize she will die for you now, right?"

"I see my plan is working." Alex released a mock-evil laugh, and Rainey's smile bloomed.

"You are such a big kid. I bet you still play video games."

"Who doesn't?" He squeezed her fingers. "But I can be a grown up when I need to." Her raised brow challenged his statement. "Okay, most of the time."

"Well, you're certainly making an impression on the boys at TLC. I overheard them talking about you, and they actually said 'he's cool.'" She lowered her voice and swung one of her hands down in a "cool" gesture the boys used.

He brought up his free palm in mock offense. "You say that as if you're surprised by my coolness."

"You're surprising in a lot of ways. Good ways." Something new flickered to life in those eyes, a fiery sort of light, heating up the attraction to dangerous territory. Whew, he'd take it.

"I like the way you say that, gorgeous."

She pinched her lips together but failed to rein in the struggling smile. "You know what? I just realized I need to take my own advice. The kind I gave to Dee several months ago."

"What kind of advice was that?" He narrowed his eyes. "Farmers make great husbands?"

Rainey laughed and Sarah looked up from her coloring with a matching grin. "You want a farmer husband?"

Rainey touched her daughter's golden hair. "No, sweet pea. Dr. Alex was joking with me."

Sarah's nose scrunched with her grin. "He does that a lot."

Rainey's gaze swung back to him, eyes aglow. "He sure does."

And Emma's observation settled deeper in his heart. Sure, he was easygoing and sometimes immature, but somehow he brought a smile where maybe, just maybe, smiles had been scarce. "So what was this brilliant advice?"

Emma interrupted just then to drop off their drinks and send both of them her victorious-matchmaking smirk.

Rainey took a sip of her iced tea. "Assumptions can be dangerous and misleading things."

His thumb trailed over her fingers. "Some of your assumptions were right. I still have a lot of growing up to do."

"We all do." She pulled his fingers into her palm. "But there's a tenderness about you I refused to see—that a lot of people don't see in you." She punctuated her words with a squeeze to his fingers. "I'm glad I see it now."

The sweetness pinged on emotions he kept safe from the impact of others, except his sister and niece, until now. He let Rainey in, took the intensity of her confession, and rallied with humor. "Well, you've been a little surprising too."

"Oh really?" She released his hand and took another sip of her tea.

"Mmhmm. I think you may be a better"—he glanced from Sarah to Rainey, lowering his voice—"k-i-s-s-e-r than me." He thought she might look away, maybe blush a little more, but she stared him down, the fiery light glowing in her eyes with fascinating attraction. Yep, she was a keeper.

"Hmm, that's a pretty high-quality comparison in my opinion, Dr. Murdock." Her brows raised. "I suppose you've had lots of practice?"

He shook his head. "Lots of daydreams, but I'm all for practicing, especially when I have such a partner."

The corner of her lips tilted in acceptance, spiking his pulse into glorious victory territory. "I'm up for the practice. I like a good challenge."

The temperature in Daphne's, not to mention in his chest, rose to the boiling point. Warning! Warning! Time to deflect some of the kissing talk for a later, and much more private, conversation. "So…" He cleared his throat, taking a drink of his unsweetened tea. "Speaking of challenges. I have a really good idea to get some visibility for fundraising for TLC, especially with the festival coming up soon."

Rainey's smile drooped. "I'm still not sure I like this plan of giving a presentation at the festival, Alex. I'm not really an upfront sort of person."

"It wouldn't be long. The television spots are less than five minutes."

Her eyes widened and she dropped her straw into her tea. "Television spot?" Her head went the way of her disapproval. "Oh no, no, no."

"Just an interview. The local news loves personal interest stories, and when I pitched TLC, they couldn't wait to learn more."

"You already pitched it?" Rainey's palm came up. "No, Alex. There is no way I'm going on TV."

"Oh, come on, Rainey. It's a great way to share your passion for TLC so others will see the need too."

The fire in those eyes took on a different glint … and not the "kissing" kind. "Alex, I won't have you deciding what I'll do. I can make decisions for myself."

What in the world? "Of course you can."

"And I'm not comfortable doing a television spot."

"I can prepare you, Rainey. You're perfect for this. I know you can—"

"No." She slid from the booth and turned to Sarah. "Come on, sweetie. Momma forgot that she has something she needs to do at home."

She was leaving? Over a television spot? "Rainey, I don't know what—"

"I can't talk about this right now, Alex, and I'd appreciate if you'd respect my opinion."

He stood, fumbling through helping her with her coat. He knew full well that he was the master of disaster, but how had he managed to ruin a perfectly wonderful evening with the blonde of his dreams?

"Rainey—" His phone rumbled to life, and he reached into his pocket without thinking.

Her attention followed his movements, and she pulled back from him, taking Sarah's arm as she turned. "I'm sure you have an important call to take, Alex, and I need to go."

Chapter Seventeen

She couldn't really say they'd had their first argument because, in all honesty, they'd argued on and off since the first day he moved to Ransom. But she'd left things unfinished between them. Well, he'd left the conversation in Daphne's before she did, to take another mysterious "family" phone call, but she still didn't like the way the evening ended.

She'd returned home to retreat to her little haven of solitude, but solitude failed to soothe now that she knew how comfy and sweet a strong pair of sandalwood-scented arms felt around her.

But ... but what was she supposed to do?

First, Alex dropped the "television interview" idea, shocked she wasn't excited about the opportunity to make a fool of herself in front of a few thousand people, and then, in the middle of the "discussion" he left to take a phone call? Had he come back inside the restaurant to look for her?

She hadn't waited to find out.

Her jerk radar blinked back to life with a long list of red flags she should have noticed with Gray but ignored. Her stomach groaned from the tension. The very idea of screwing up in front of Alex combined with his mysterious phone calls unsettled her. The combination churned a backstory into a three-dimensional maelstrom at the forefront of her thoughts.

She couldn't make the same mistake again. For her heart and for Sarah's.

She turned the car from its previous course and crested the drive toward her mama's house. The sweet scene of home welcomed her, with Sarah jumping from the jeep to lead the way.

"Mama, can I go see Mustard?"

Rainey nodded to her adorable daughter with her ever-loving adoration of her mama's crazy mutt. "Only for a bit, sweetie. I'm stopping in to give Granny some of my leftover dessert, but then we need to get you home and ready for bed."

The evening brought a mild wind after the snowy days, allowing the snow to melt into the moist ground. Rainey watched Sarah run toward the back of the house, the gentle light of the lamppost in her mama's front yard casting a glow over the yard in tune with the growing moonlight.

"Mustard! Where are you?" Sarah's call disappeared around the side of the house, and Rainey took the porch steps to the front door.

The house carried a certain scent of peanut butter and chocolate, which could only mean Mama conjured up some preacher cookies. Emma's newest concoction was good, but Rainey had an unhealthy addiction to those chocolaty no-bakes "doctored up" with her mama's secret touch of cinnamon.

"Yoo-hoo," Rainey called into the empty entry, her usual greeting to warn Mama of a visitor.

"Yoo-hoo," came the reply from one of the back rooms.

Rainey slipped to the counter and snuck one of the preacher cookies from the plate. A small one. Enough to fit into her mouth without leaving any evidence. She shrugged out of her coat and sat on a barstool, her mind rushing back to her dilemma.

What had she been thinking? Could those calls really be some private family matter or was she playing directly into the hands of another schmoozer with a wandering heart? His past, his personality, the unnerving existence of his phone, which pulled him away from conversations at unexpected times with no real explanation from him afterward. All the suspicions rose to life anew after he'd thrown this idea of a television interview on her, reigniting her insecurities like a flint.

She knew her weaknesses—his charismatic charm hit on each and every one of them.

The fall of love, the sweet warmth of attention, the powerful flame of attraction. She'd loved them all—and loved them still, but they weren't enough to create a lifelong romance.

Not enough to stand the test of time and hardship.

She used to be the girl who laughed without shackles and loved without shadows, the woman fiercely daring and unfettered by fear. Did that woman still exist beneath the rubble of a broken dream and heart?

And Alex? She'd witnessed an honorable core beneath the flirty sheen. Or so she hoped. Her fingers moved to her lips, the touch reminding her of their closet kiss.

Could she learn how to freefall again?

"Hey, Granny." Sarah entered from the side door at the same time Mama rounded the corner from the hallway, both sporting rosy cheeks. One from the cold and another from working in one of the back rooms, if Rainey knew her mama.

"Well, what a nice visit." Her mama dusted her hands on her pants and reached out to give Sarah a squeeze. "You been out with Mustard?"

"Sure was. I ain't seen him in a long time."

Mama patted Sarah on the head and grinned at Rainey.

A few hours was a long time to a five-year-old.

"And what have you been doin' today?"

Sarah danced from her granny's hold and walked over to a bottomless toy box. "We went on a date with Dr. Alex."

Mama's gaze took a curious turn, but she merely stepped to the counter and started up the coffeemaker. Questions buzzed through the kitchen with the potency of peanut butter and chocolate.

"Any news on the fundraising?"

Just like her mama to take the scenic route to the point. "It looks like we may have about sixty percent of next year funded through donations and expected revenue, but we're still a stretch away from having the upcoming years covered."

The coffee machine gurgled and spewed as the thin brown liquid coursed a trail into the coffee pot. "Well, that's hopeful. With the festival comin' up and all Alex's bigwig contacts from northern Virginia, plus our local fundraisin', we can't go wrong."

For the future, TLC's existence looked promising, but the present? Through the upcoming school year? She studied her mama as she set some French vanilla creamer onto the counter beside the sugar bowl. Stalling. Well, Rainey could wait her out.

"Want some chocolate shavings on top of your coffee today? Try somethin' new? A little sweetness to offset the bitter?"

Her mama's smile held messages within the happy creases. Rainey narrowed her eyes. "I don't know if it's a good idea to try something new."

Mama's gaze flipped up with a raised brow. "Well, if you're not ready, then you shouldn't. But if you're ready for somethin' new, it'll taste all the sweeter."

Rainey placed her palms on the table and groaned. "Okay, Mama. Just spit it out. It's not like I haven't dated once or twice in the past two years."

Gentle as ever, Mama took her time gathering some mugs from the cabinet and a couple of spoons from the drawer before making her way back to the counter.

"That's exactly right." Her noncommittal response fired up Rainey's defenses. "And I'm perfectly capable of dating now and again if I want."

"It's good and healthy for you too." She returned to the coffeemaker and carried the brimming pot back to their mugs, complete with chocolate on top.

"It doesn't have to mean anything, you know?"

Those gray, fathomless eyes shot to Rainey's. "But does it?"

Rainey avoided the piercing gaze by adding a heaping helping of both sugar and creamer. "Dave Stevens and I have been out several times. Great guy. I don't see why dating Alex should be any different."

"It shouldn't, unless it is."

And the Cheshire cat puzzle-talk emerged. "Mama."

"It ain't bad to open your heart again, Rainey. The two of you have enough sparks flying between you to light a Christmas tree. If you was smart, I expected this to take its turn."

Rainey put her face in her hands. "Smart? You think this is smart? I feel like I'm in some sort of video game where the walls are closing in. I'm so afraid of making the same mistake twice."

"You've grown since then, honey." She patted Rainey's hand, the sweet comfort of her love moving up Rainey's arm and hugging her heart. "You were young when you were with Gray. And God's done a lot to soften that head of yours. And you listen a whole lot better now."

Rainey squeezed her eyes closed, the painful truth dawning. "You always knew there was something about Gray, didn't you?"

Her mama nodded and added some cream to her coffee. "He liked himself a whole lot. I was hopin' it was just from him being young."

"And I imagine I was just too stubborn to listen."

Mama chuckled. "You've always been one to set your mind pretty hard on somethin'. Once set, it was like bending an iron bar to get you to see otherwise."

Rainey ran a hand through her hair and whimpered. "And look where all my hardheadedness brought me."

"You're a smart woman who's learned a lot from her past."

She searched her mother's eyes, absorbing some of the faith mingling with gray and gold. "And Alex? What do you think of him?"

"It's not so much what I think about him as what you think about him. I just told you that you were smart."

"Mama, you'd better take this golden opportunity of me listening to you." Rainey attempted to keep her smile trimmed. "And of my hardheadedness being a bit softer than usual."

Mama chuckled again. "You're right. I may never see a moment like this again. I better git to talkin'."

Rainey squeezed her mom's hand and took a sip of her sugar-laced coffee. Mmm, really good addition.

"Honey, a wise person recognizes when something good comes into her life. She takes the sweetness with gratitude. Life's full of bitterness and hardship, and that's why we cherish the sweet things all the more."

Rainey's heart longed for the answer. "And how did you know it was the *right* sweet thing?"

Mama took a sip of coffee and settled down on a stool. "Well, back in the deep woods of Appalachia in my day, there were some who still believed in courtin'. As you know, courtin' was a much more serious affair than datin' because you didn't say yes to the man unless you thought he was marriage material. There were six questions I needed answered before I agreed to court your daddy."

Rainey leaned forward, trying to resurrect this conversation from her memory. "And those were?"

"Let's see. One was whether he had a teachable spirit or already knew everything about everything." Rainey mentally measured Alex by the first standard and knew the answer. He'd humbly and gratefully allowed her to instruct him on how to become a better teacher.

"Another one"—her pointer finger rose from her mug—"and this one's important. How does he respond to gettin' riled or bein' embarrassed?"

The roadside phone incident popped into Rainey's mind and brought a ridiculous smile with it.

"I see the notion doesn't hit on a sour note."

Rainey shook her head, pinching her grin tightly. "I think he may be two for two so far."

"Does he have a tender heart? A gentleness when gentleness is needed?"

Every moment spent with Sarah confirmed this one. Alex had shown nothing but the sweetest care to her little girl.

"How about his steady mind?"

Rainey looked up to the ceiling. "We may have to revisit that one. He's certainly unpredictable and a little crazy."

"But in a good way, I'd say."

Rainey nodded, her smile softening. "In a good way, *if* I was even thinking of something as serious as courting."

"Of course." Mama slid her a look that sent Rainey back to the sulking six-year-old age. Talk about somebody knowing everything about everything! But even as Rainey inwardly grumbled, she thanked God for her mama's comfort ... and the surprising confirmation of her wisdom.

Her pulse steadied out a little.

"And the last two?"

"Well, this one is the most important, in my opinion, and the next a pretty close second." Mama tapped the side of her mug. "Are your souls seeking the same thing?"

A definite shift had taken place in Alex since he'd moved to Ransom—an almost indefinable change, like he'd been waiting to walk right into faith and finally stepped into it. Was that even possible? His prayer before their meal at Daphne's had been simple but so sweet and heartfelt. To answer this question, she'd need more time.

"And the last one?"

"I already know the answer to this one. He wears it as clear as day."

Rainey squinted. "What?"

"Life is so hard sometimes, and some of the steadiest people I know are the ones with the best senses of humor. Laughin' often and bringing laughter to the ones you love? It can get you through a heap of hardship."

"And it's just plain fun." Rainey's vision blurred from the tenderness wrapped up within her mama and her sweet words.

"Ain't that the truth? Laughter has a wonderful way of softening the edges of life."

Rainey touched her mama's hand again and studied her, afraid of the answer. "Did we have this conversation before I married Gray?"

Mama looked up, not saying a word, and Rainey released a long sigh. "To be the daughter of such a wise woman, how could I have been so stupid?"

"Wisdom has a tendency to follow experience and age. I didn't always make the right choices either, Rainey. You've been through a lot of hurt and heartache, but God doesn't leave us in that season. The gospel is all about second, third, and one hundredth chances. His love not only covers our mistakes, but also strengthens our hearts to choose with more wisdom the next time."

Her mother's words marinated deep within Rainey's uncertainty, touching her wavering heart with hope.

With a rough hand, she twisted her hair back into a haphazard knot and stepped through the quiet house. Sarah had gone to bed at least an hour ago, and the rooms nestled in their evening slumber, but her heart trembled with anything but rest. No, it played an unhappy waltz between falling into this attraction to Alex, or staying back, safe from disappointment, conflict, and more heartache.

The possibility seemed less frightening in the light of her conversation with Mama and a little bit of prayerful introspection. With a slight tremor at her rising courage, she took her granny's frayed patchwork quilt from the chair by the fireplace and wrapped it around her shoulders. Its weight hugged her frame, stilling her apprehension. As if from a whispered memory from her sweet granny, the words from Psalm 46 cascaded warmth through Rainey.

GOD IS WITHIN HER, SHE WILL NOT FALL.

The entire chapter celebrated the strength and power of the Lord, including another verse that pricked at her conscience.

BE STILL AND KNOW THAT I AM GOD.

Life was busy and her mind straggled to keep up, but out of the midst of the maelstrom in her heart, God called her to be still. A realization she'd contemplated in the quiet of the evening.

A wintry chill sent a reminder of the February days as Rainey stepped onto the moonlit back porch into the quiet night. The haloed glow basked the countryside in a frosty scene of angelic hues, and she pulled the quilt tighter around her shoulders to take in the quiet beauty. Cool air caressed her cheeks with its mild touch, drawing her to the porch railing. With a slight hesitation, she peered down the hill toward her grandparents' house, half hoping and half fearing she'd see Alex.

A silhouette stood on the front porch, waiting as if for her to beckon him. The moment hung on an eternal second.

She gripped the railing and waited, suspended in a choice—to return to her nice, predictable world of safe singleness or to trust Alex, not only with her heart but with her insecurities. With a release of her clenched air into a long stream of frosty night, she offered her trembling heart this second chance. The silhouette moved... In the pale night, he marched forward, his steps determined as if he knew much more certainly what he wanted.

She pinched the blanket at her neck and turned to the sound of his footfall on the porch steps. He emerged from the shadows of the house into the light of her porch like a knight to the rescue, his gaze focused on hers with dazzling resolution. Rainey caught her breath as he came into view, his jacket hanging open and his breaths puffing thick clouds of frozen air around him.

"I'm sorry about earlier … at Daphne's." Her confession tumbled forward.

"I'm sorry about the phone call. I promise, this family situation should be resolved soon."

She released her doubt and closed her eyes, believing him. "I'm not doing the interview, Alex, and I need you to respect my decision."

He matched her step for step, head tilted as he examined her. "Rainey, I'd never force you into doing anything." His grin slanted. "Even if I could. I think you'd be great at an interview, just like you're great at about everything else you do, but if you don't want to do it," he said and shrugged, "don't."

His faith in her spiked her certainty and acceptance. "Teaching students is different than sitting in front of thousands of viewers to answer questions."

"Okay. Then we'll focus on the festival. No big deal, right?"

She studied him, trying to figure him out. "Right."

He bridged the gap between them, cupping her shoulders. "And by the way, I plan on you making up for leaving me at Daphne's without any defense. I had to listen to Emma talk about what food she's making for Dee and Reese's wedding for about a half hour. Half of the stuff sounded foreign."

The humor sweetened his acceptance all the more, and she fell. Hard. He'd come back for her. "You're not going to push the issue about the interview?"

"No." An adorably confused expression wrinkled his face as he rubbed warm palms over her shoulders. "I know you would be great at it, but I care about *you* more than some idea."

A sudden rush of tears blurred her vision. She lowered her gaze to his chest and settled her palm against the soft lapel of his coat. "I'm sorry I left you … and with chatty Emma of all people."

His fingers moved to brush a hand over her cheek, bringing her attention up, awareness dawning in his eyes. "He really made you second-guess yourself, didn't he? The jerk ex-husband. Now I wish I hadn't been so nice to him."

Her frown pricked up at one corner. "I don't think I'll ever understand you."

"It's quite the feat to plumb the fathomless depths of my personality."

Her smile grew and she tightened her hold on his jacket. "Watch out, buddy. I'm starting to suffocate from all the awesomeness wafting off you right now."

Alex coaxed her forward, a gentle tug that brought her body and heart toward him in perfect synchrony. "I love it when you sweet-talk me."

She chuckled and breathed in a wonderful breath of sandalwood. A moonlit spotlight shone down on them as if God orchestrated this heavenly stage for Rainey's decision.

Alex stared down at her with a smile playing across his lips like a dizzying melody, drawing her into his embrace.

"I want to trust you, to trust this"—she waved her hand between them— "but I may be a little slower on the uptake than you."

He shrugged one shoulder. "That's okay. I'm kind of like Haus. I plan on sticking around until you just can't get rid of me."

Her body swayed toward him, asking to be cherished in his arms the same way his gaze touched her soul. Those strong arms wrapped her against his warmth, drowning her doubt in sweet protection. A cacophony of emotions snagged in her throat.

"Well." She closed her eyes, pressing her cheek against his shoulder. "You are kind of warm and cuddly like Haus, but you smell a whole lot better."

She could picture his grin slitting crooked. With a gentle movement, he pulled back from her and put his fingers beneath her chin, tilting her face close. Slowly, time blurring with their mingled breaths, he pressed his warm lips against one corner of her mouth. She froze, waiting. What was he doing?

He repeated the tender touch on the other corner of her mouth, a feather-light trace. With ever so light touches of skin on skin, his mouth moved until it hovered against hers just enough for Rainey to trace the faint ridges of his lips. Her fingers fisted the cloth of his shirt, requesting he finish what he'd started.

"I've never been much of a hero." His grin inched up on one side. "But I want to be your hero, and I'll do whatever it takes to help you understand how amazing you are. From the heart out." His whispered words vibrated against her mouth, pouring through her with a sweetness that brought tears to her eyes and ignited a tendril of tingles down her neck.

Without another hesitation, as if to seal his statement, his lips covered hers, as warm and wonderful as the swirl of heat firing through her. His hand moved to the back of her head, twisting his fingers into her bun until he worked it loose. The full weight of her hair fell around her shoulders, encasing both of them in a citrus-scented cocoon.

Oh, heart!

Alex drew back only far enough to murmur against her lips. "You taste like peanut butter and chocolate." His grin tilted against her smile. "The perfect match. I'm the nut and you're definitely the chocolate." He nuzzled his nose against her cheek, his voice rumbling tingles down her neck. "I think we have a happily ever after right here."

She lost her smile in another kiss, slipping her palms inside the warmth of his jacket. The seconds moved from one kiss to another, each more intimate and breathtaking than the previous.

Practice or not, Alex Murdock knew how to kiss a woman, and Rainey was a wonderfully dazed recipient. She clung to him, inviting their further exploration of each other, enjoying the cool air steaming to hot between them.

Before she knew it, they'd moved across the porch. She reached for the handle of the sliding-glass kitchen door and pulled, tugging him to the entrance. "Let's continue this conversation by the fire. What do you say?"

His hands tightened against her back, and he made to follow her, then stopped, bouncing her against him with his sudden halt. "Don't tempt me, gorgeous."

Her palms smoothed down his back, teasing his steps into the kitchen. "It's been a long time since I've been kissed like that—maybe never—so I would really like more practice with you."

He groaned and took her face in his hands, an explosion of passion nearly buckling her to the floor. *Sweet mercy.*

He drew back, hands moving to her shoulders and eyes lit with a fascinating fire, drugging her with the sweet power she wielded. Had she ever known such influence over a man's heart before? Certainly not with Gray, but Alex? His attention mingled with a mesmerizing combination of tenderness and passion that poured over her wounds.

"Oh, Rainey, you flatter me." His palms slid up her neck to her face. "And I want to pin you to the wall with enough kisses to blur your thoughts."

She pressed up against him, begging him to fulfill his promise.

He swept back her hair from her face, his touch flitting her heart. "After your kisses tonight, my thoughts have plummeted in a dastardly direction." His gaze glittered with devilish humor. "And I think yours have too." His moonlit gaze caressed her face. "I won't be careless with your heart, Rainey. You need to know I want your trust... even more than kissing practice by the fire until we question our morals."

She paused, searching his face, a flush of awareness stilling her movements. What was she doing? Argh! Her all-or-nothing heart! "I ... I'm sorry, Alex."

"Don't be sorry. Not about your kisses." He seized her mouth in a quick kiss and moaned. "Nope, never by those." His fingers trailed down her cheeks. "The past few years of my life have changed me. It's been a slow process, and I didn't realize it was leading me here to God and I think ... to you." His lips took a humorous curl. "And despite my roguish good looks and tempting persona, I've kept my heart at a distance from deep relationships."

Her brow rose despite her best attempts.

"Ah, you doubt me, but it's true." His expression sobered, an unfamiliar side of Alex rising to the surface. "Painful circumstances have taught me to cherish moments and people—something I never used to do. If you pull me into that house after branding me with your kisses, I'm pretty sure cherishing isn't going to be on either of our minds. I don't want you to have any reason to doubt that I'm in this for the long run—and I'm wearing great tennis shoes."

Her eyes misted at Alex's words. When he pulled away, she caught him by the arm. "Just so you know, I'm wearing great tennis shoes too."

"To run away? Because I'm pretty sure I'm faster than you."

"No." She shook her head, smile weak. "To run with you, because that's where I want to be."

Chapter Eighteen

Every curveball thrown the next day at Alex bounced off his ridiculous optimism. He was sure of it. Even the teen boys at TLC, their moods particularly trying, failed to douse his grin. One replay of the previous night's events had him ready for a repeat with a prolonged ending.

His plan to start the weekend with a run dwindled with an early morning wake-up call. Alex jerked on some jeans and a T-shirt and lumbered to the door to find Trigg on his front porch, a crooked grin in place.

"You still in bed?"

Alex scrubbed his head and yawned. "Do I look like I'm still in bed?"

"You got plans this morning?"

"Maybe a jog." And a bit more kissing practice with the blonde up the street.

Trigg nodded. "Remember offering to help me mend some fences?"

Alex squinted.

"I have a section that's down, and the cows are getting out of the field. I've got to get on it fast, but I could use the help to get it done lots quicker. You in?"

Alex's gaze slipped to Rainey's house in hesitation. Well, it couldn't take too long to mend a hole in a fence, and besides, today he could leap tall buildings with a single bound. "Sure. Be ready in five minutes."

"I really appreciate it, Alex. It'll make the job faster." Trigg thumbed behind him. "I'll wait for you in the truck."

Trigg carried a subtle friendliness Alex found easy to appreciate. As they worked and Alex fumbled learning a new skill and trying not to end up clawed by the barbed wire, a quiet comradery formed.

Through the little bits of information Alex had gleaned from the family and his conversations with Trigg, the last few years had been rough on the guy. Cancer. Alex cringed. He hated the word. And in the middle of the cancer treatments and associated sickness, Trigg's fiancée left him for a job in Charlotte.

The story stung close to Alex's heart. He'd been the fiancé ... and he'd stayed until the end. Leaving might have been easier, but the thought of abandoning

Beth as she fought her losing battle ripped him to pieces on the inside. He'd been the last person she'd seen before her eyes closed forever.

He drew in a breath, twisting the wiring around the wooden pole as Trigg had taught him. "Are there any ladies on the horizon in Ransom for you?"

Trigg took off his cap and scratched his head. "I ain't really in the market at the moment, even if there was." His gaze moved to the horizon and he stood, resting his hands on his hips. "The cancer, well, it changed things for me. It's gonna take some time before I sort out my future plans."

Layers of story waited between the pauses in that sentence. Time might help Trigg share with him because Alex was pretty sure he could understand in some ways others couldn't.

They worked in a gentle mix of amicable silence and easy conversation until the afternoon brightened with winter sunlight.

"Why don't you go to Mama's and let her know we're finishin' here?" Trigg tied the last wire. "I'll clean up."

Alex's expression must have showcased his confusion.

"Mama knows we've been workin' all mornin'. You can be sure as shootin' she's got a mess of lunch ready for us."

Alex looked up the hill toward Mama Mitchell's house, the concept still such a revelation. A mother who'd cook something for them because they'd been working hard all morning? What a sweet thought.

"Are you sure she's expecting *me*?"

Trigg's grin slanted. "She always cooks for a herd of people, but she knows you're with me. I saw her peekin' out her curtains about two hours ago."

Alex trekked up the hillside and opened the kitchen door at Mama Mitchell's welcome. The mouth-watering hints of bacon and some buttery bake brought Alex forward like a cartoon character floating in the air.

"Well, what a nice surprise." Mama Mitchell moved from the laptop at a small desk built into the wall in the adjoining sitting room, her golden hair, with streaks of white, pulled back in a soft bun. "You've been busy this morning."

Alex rubbed his shoulder and unzipped his coat. "No kidding. I didn't realize how much work went into mending a fence. I was thinking a 'flat tire' time period."

She chuckled and walked to the kitchen, slipping a mitt on each hand and opening the oven to release another warm waft of buttery-bacon goodness. The granola bar from breakfast lost its potency hours ago.

"Mama Mitchell, I'm pretty sure I'm in love with you."

Her chuckle turned to a solid laugh. "I'm pretty sure that's a sign you're famished. Sit yourself down at the counter, and I'll get those lovesick thoughts right out of your head and into your stomach."

"How can I help?"

She turned a keen gaze to him, her hand paused on a drawer handle. "Well now, I reckon you could fix up a cup of coffee for yourself and Trigg. I've cooked up some Breakfast Bake—a good mix of eggs, cheese, veggies—and cathead biscuits with homemade apple butter, so coffee should set you right up."

Alex felt both of his brows lifting. "Um ... it all sounds fabulous, Mama Mitchell, but what exactly do you mean by cathead biscuits?" The visual popping into his head produced anything but a tantalizing image.

She placed a plate of biscuits as big as his hands directly in front of him. "Catheads."

"Aha." He grabbed one and grinned. "I can't tell you how glad I am that you removed the eyes and whiskers before serving."

He put the biscuit on his plate and crossed the kitchen to the coffeemaker, filling the two mugs she'd set out for him. Waiting for Mama Mitchell to settle, Alex offered a quick prayer of thanksgiving, then went straight for the apple butter. He'd heard at Daphne's about the caramel-colored delicacy but hadn't tried it before.

"Thanks so much for this feast, Mama Mitchell. You're amazing."

"Didn't your mama fix you meals?"

Alex lathered the apple butter over the steaming bread. "Dad had a chef on staff, but he didn't made food like this." He took a bite and groaned as the sweet flavor mixed with the buttery bread and poured over his tongue. "And my parents never ate with us."

She paused her cup to her lips and peered at him over the rim, her gaze taking a steely look. "I imagine that could be real lonesome."

Alex busied himself with some more apple butter. "I had my little sister, Evie. We've always been best friends."

"The sister you lost?"

He froze with the biscuit to his mouth, his last swallow lodging in his throat. He'd used present tense when describing Evie. "Um ... yes. We were very close." He pushed down an exaggerated swallow and took a drink of coffee. Time for a redirection. "How do you find the time to make these amazing meals, take care

195

of grandkids, and work around your university cleaning schedule?" Her raised brow hinted that she'd caught on to his deflection, but she took a sip of her coffee instead of calling him on it. Alex stifled a sigh.

"I like keepin' busy, and I've always had a love for cookin'."

"Well, you're a pro. Is that where Emma gets the passion?"

"She's a lot like her daddy."

Alex's eyebrows shot north. "Your husband was a matchmaking cook?"

Mama Mitchell grinned. "Well, he was always the romantic one, but Emma has his joy. He was a really happy man."

Rainey knew a world and a family he'd only seen on television. The warmth and welcome surrounding them, bringing him in, carried its own healing properties, all the way down to the food. Comfort food? Yeah, he got it now. The comfort might start with butter and sugar, but it ended with sweet fellowship. He took a bite of the breakfast bake while the silence encouraged introspection he fought—of his father, his mother, and the broken relationships among them all.

The Mitchells meshed like adhesive, their tight-knit love pouring over the people they gathered into their fold. The awareness not only swelled his gratitude but ripped open the breach in his own family.

"From what I can figure, there's been a lot of hardship between you and your daddy."

Alex was sure he'd given off plenty of those vibes. "He's not the warm and fuzzy sort like you, Mama Mitchell. He's pretty prickly."

She stood and walked to the coffeemaker, bringing back the pot to top off their mugs. "Those prickly sorts can be demanding, have high expectations, may even lather on some criticism?"

"All of the above." Alex nodded his thanks for the coffee. "But he's brilliant at business. He knows how to talk to people, which businesses to buy and which ones to pass. He manages hundreds of people, gives inspiring speeches, stays as fit as a man half his age, and loves dating. He's a real success."

"Is that right?"

"It's like he can't fail. Everything he touches turns to gold." Alex waved a piece of biscuit at her. "I didn't get that trait from him."

Those gray eyes took him in, and he replayed his confession. It was the truth. His dad had it all and knew how to use it. Alex fell short, and if he was honest with himself, he'd been trying to catch up ever since birth. He knew how to act, how to play the social game. He'd learned it from the best, but somehow the Midas touch never reached his fingers.

Ransom had provided a new start for him—a place where, just maybe, the rules of the world tilted in a direction he could follow and flourish under.

Mama Mitchell examined him a moment longer, then walked over to a basket filled with assorted paraphernalia by the phone. She picked a small, round ornament from the disheveled conglomeration of "things" and returned to the counter. "I thought I'd packed all my Christmas decorations in January, but I found this little ornament stuck behind the couch this morning. Must've fallen off the tree."

The blown-glass golden ball glistened in the afternoon sunlight through the window, its textured markings, faded in red and silver, swirling like technicolor snowflakes among the shimmering gold.

"Pretty, ain't it?"

"It's beautiful." He set down his coffee and reached to touch the exterior with a careful hand. "It is a family heirloom?"

Her smile softened and she placed the globe in his hand. "I have a whole gang of grand-young'uns who'd as soon climb the Christmas tree as decorate it, so I don't hang any fancy decorations on my tree."

Alex laughed and studied the ornament, surprised by its light weight. Upon closer inspection, the sparkling exterior proved nothing more than cheap glitter and paint on plastic. "It's a good imitation."

"From a distance." She took the ornament back. "Despite its fancy outside, it's still hollow on the inside."

Alex's gaze met hers, and the biscuit thickened in his mouth. He pushed down a swallow, her implications tapping against his buried wounds. "You think he's empty inside?" How could that be true? His dad had everything. An expansive job and reputation, any woman he wanted, a prestigious place at the club ... and then the realization dawned.

His months in Ransom had scraped away some of his faulty logic. What did all of it matter without love and peace? If there was no one to come home to? If nights passed in restless and troubling dreams? If the only face to greet you in the morning was the one you saw in the mirror?

Alex had read something about this very idea earlier in the week, about how menial everything was without love. Love made the smallest task meaningful, transformed the humblest person into someone beautiful, and changed the hardest work into a service instead of a chore.

Love held power. And without it, life became a clanging cymbal … a hollow, cheap imitation.

"You have a tender spirit, Alex, deep with caring."

One of his brows darted high. "Now, Mama Mitchell, don't go ruining my reputation."

She touched his hand. "A tender heart is the best because it's ready to be used, shared, touched."

Her gaze held his, reading deeply into him at all the ways his world had shifted in the past two months. But somehow, through his childhood and even his time with Beth, God *had* been working out the stiffness, the selfishness, to massage his heart into one ready for Him. Maybe even ready for Rainey.

"It's who you are—and I think you're startin' to recognize the scale of success looks mighty altered through a different lens. Ain't nothin' wrong with wealth and achievements, but the greatest success is found here." She pointed to his chest. "It's priceless, with the potential of touching people forever."

The words burrowed deeply, burning with truth he'd felt for weeks, but somehow hearing it defined in such a way added purpose to his choices. He snatched another biscuit, his grin spreading wide enough to pinch his cheeks. Home smelled like biscuits and sweet tea, like citrus scents and moonlit kisses, like Sarah's giggles and Jim's pipe tobacco … like hope.

The emotions rose into his throat, so he countered with his usual defense. "So I could end up as a penniless success?"

She softened his deflection with a gentle quiet before adding, "God's changed you in lots a ways since you got here, but He's also using you just the way you are. That's what He does. He takes the basics of how He first made us—with you, your humor, joy, and kindness—and grows them into something even more fit for His plans because you belong to Him."

Belong. The word percolated with a sweet comfort and fragrant assurance. "What do you think He wants to do with me?"

She looked down at the ornament, then back to him. "Maybe He wants you to find a way to help others belong too."

"How's retirement going?" Rainey walked with Shaye Russell down the hallway of TLC, her former colleague tutoring for the third time that week. "Bored after only two months?"

Shaye rolled her eyes, her salt-n-pepper hair newly trimmed to its pixie style. "I can only sit and write for so long before I need to actually do something active."

"Which book did you decide to start with? The adolescent language disorders book or the parenting troubled teens one?"

Shaye sighed, her ingenuity and energy more like a woman half her age. "Well, I started both of them, but the one sticking with me *today* is the language disorders one. Those kids?" She gestured toward the "teen" room up the hall. "They're misunderstood and brushed over so often."

Rainey folded her arms and leaned back against the wall. "I can see that."

"It's not an easy population to serve, but"—she pressed her palm to her chest—"they have my heart."

Rainey tilted her chin with a grin. "Well, kudos to you. Give me the preschool droolers anytime over the sassy teens."

A door opened farther up the hallway—in fact, to the very place Shaye had referred to earlier. The teen room.

A redheaded girl, Laura, burst from the room. "I never want to talk to you again, jerk." She ran in the opposite direction from Shaye and Rainey. A blonde, Myra, followed.

"Laura, wait. He was joking."

Rainey looked from the distraught teens back to Shaye. "Yep, give me the droolers *any* day."

"I'll go after Laura." Shaye started up the hallway and tossed the rest of her words over her shoulder. "Perhaps you should uncover what happened to Dr. Murdock's group dynamics."

Oh, good grief! He'd worked so well with the boys, she'd encouraged some of the girls to join his math group and now... She squeezed her eyes closed.

Instead of rushing into the therapy room and undermining Alex's authority, Rainey slipped into the observation room first. The one-way mirror framed the therapy space where Alex sat with three of the guys, two wide-eyed and another grimacing like he'd swallowed a prune ... whole.

Alex's palms pressed onto the table, and he looked at Ross. "That didn't go so well for you, did it?"

Rainey leaned forward and turned the volume up on the wall speaker.

"How was I supposed to know she'd get so riled up?"

Alex pressed his fingers to his head and groaned. "Because any time you imply that a girl looks ugly, you're going to hurt her feelings. It's the way the world works."

"Hey, she looks better with makeup. That's all I was sayin'."

Yep, Rainey was sticking with therapy for little kids who didn't talk. Much less drama.

"Mike, Jason." Alex gestured toward the other boys. "Will you guys head on out for the night? I need to chat with Ross alone."

"Sure, Doc."

They almost stumbled over each other in their haste to leave Alex and Ross to the uncomfortable conversation to come. Rainey leaned closely to the mirror, curious how Mr. Suave might work his wonders with this troubled kid.

"How long have you been into Laura?"

"Into her?" Ross shifted his gaze to the door. "I don't like her at all."

Yep, and the clouds were made of ketchup.

"Listen, it's never cool to make a girl feel ugly. Never. Even if you don't have a crush on her."

"I don't."

Whatever.

"Yeah, whatever, Ross. I'm a guy. I get it. We're stupid around the girls we like most." Alex shrugged. "Keeps us humble."

Rainey caught her smile in her hand, his exploits bringing a tickle of laughter to her throat.

"Have you tried just hanging out with her? Talking about regular stuff?"

Ross folded his arms over his chest and frowned. "I ain't talkin' about girl stuff, Doc. I'd be laughed off the basketball team."

"Well, that's too bad." Alex leaned back in his chair, fingers to his chin. "I heard Laura was a master at that role-playing game you like. She talked about it with me yesterday."

Ross shot forward. "You're joshin' me."

"Nope, and she plays basketball too. She may even be a better shot than you. I saw her game last weekend."

Air seeped from Rainey's lips. Alex went to Laura's basketball game in Casper, at one of the most backwoods schools in the county? She stared at him, surprised once again by his stark contrast to her only real comparison. Gray.

His tenderness and care pooled through her insecurities and encouraged her to become who he thought she was. Brave. Strong. Willing to take on an interview.

"A better shot than me?" A light of interest pulled Ross's posture straight.

"I think you have a lot you could talk about, if you wanted." Alex shrugged as if the statement didn't matter all that much. "But listen, when you *do* find a girl you like, take my advice. Be real. The smart girls see straight through fake. And sometimes she may look prettier than other times, but as you really get to know her better and she becomes the person you want to hang out with most in the world? Well, then she kind of always looks beautiful, no matter if she's wearing makeup or not. But if you go around talking to her like you just did on a regular basis, you're never going to get to find out what that kind of romance is like, man."

"I don't see no ring on your finger. Heck, I ain't even seen you with anybody else but Miss Rainey." Ross hesitated before narrowing his eyes. "How do you know so much about girls?"

A soberness fell over Alex's expression, a look which pulled her closer to the two-way mirror. Grief? Regret? "I'm a guy, right?"

"That don't make you no expert."

Alex chuckled. "Well, I was only an expert on one girl, actually, but I was a knucklehead first. Said and did stupid stuff around her, but she saw something in me anyway."

Ross nodded toward Alex's hand, interest sparking in his dark eyes. "She leave you?"

"Yeah, in a way." Alex sighed and folded his hands on the table. "She died a few weeks before our wedding."

Rainey's breath caught in her throat—all the assumptions she'd made about this man suddenly tasting sour upon reconsideration. How could she be so wrong about everything?

"Man, that's bad."

"It was horrible." But a gentle smile touched his face in such a fascinating way, Rainey couldn't look away. A glow of a love remembered softened the pain in his eyes and almost inspired her own smile. "But she taught me more about love and kindness and friendship than I'd ever known." Alex cleared his throat again and sat back in his chair. "So, I'm just sayin', don't be an idiot like I was. You're smarter than me. Get things right earlier." He shrugged. "You know …

if you like Laura."

Ross grumbled something under his breath and sent a glance toward the door. Oh man, Alex's plan had worked. He'd placed enough doubt in Ross' head to set the boy's mind spinning. Ross pushed himself up from the table, attempting to look nonchalant, but from the continued redirection of the boy's gaze toward the door, Rainey knew exactly where the young hothead was going.

"Well, I need to get on home, Doc."

Alex's grin grew and he crossed his arms over his chest. "Well, if you decide to take any detours by the basketball court, shoot a few three-pointers for me, okay?"

As Rainey stared through the two-way mirror at this anomaly of a man, she realized the name of the emotion stirring to recognition in her chest. Love. She was in love with Alex Murdock.

Chapter Nineteen

S o what was her name?"

Alex turned from a therapy table full of math sheets and grinned. In three strides, his warm palm settled at her waist. "Hey, gorgeous."

She looked over his features, a bit mesmerized by the new information she'd learned. The charmer's gloss took on a very different gleam. He fronted his broken heart, his loss, with a carefree flirtation and polished off the Casanova façade to hide who he'd always been—and who he was becoming. Everything began to fall into place, and her heart gave way to not just care about him but to trust him.

"What was her name?"

He placed a chaste kiss on her cheek. "Who?"

She rested her palm against his chest, smoothing the wound beneath his grin. "Your fiancée?"

She would have missed the catch in his gaze if she didn't know him better. "You've been eavesdropping, Miss Mitchell."

"A skill of the best country girls, Dr. Murdock."

His smile turned sad, his gaze softening into hers and pulling at her, unraveling heartstrings. "Beth. Short for Bethany."

"Beautiful name." Rainey's words pressed to barely above a whisper.

"She was a beautiful person." He wrapped a strand of her hair around his finger, smoothing it between his fingers. "She challenged me. Made me think differently, urged me to be different." His voice softened. "She fought hard too."

She gave a playful tug to his shirt. "I think you could bring out the fight in anybody."

Her comment upturned his smile into the crooked tilt. "Another one of my many charms."

She tempted the conversation into uncharted territory. "What happened?"

"Cancer."

The one word brought a moan from her. "Oh, Alex."

He watched her, the intensity of his search forcing her watery gaze downward. "We tried to have the wedding before she became so sick, but she took a fast turn near the end."

"You knew she was sick all along?"

He shrugged a shoulder, returning his focus to her hair. "She told me after we'd been dating six months. Tried to talk me out of staying with her." His gaze came back up to hers. "But ... but I just wanted her for as long as I could have her, no matter how short the time."

Rainey slid her hand into his free one and squeezed, encouraging him to continue.

"She was everything I didn't think I wanted, but somebody I desperately needed." He chuckled, despite the crinkle in his forehead. "If you think I'm arrogant now, you should've seen me then. I was arrogant *and* angry. Lived life exactly the way I wanted. I started going to this popular coffee shop where Beth was a waitress." His expression softened with memory. "She was a gentle sort of person, an old soul. I'm not really sure what she saw in me—probably the messed-up guy that I was—but she swooped in like a guardian angel, breaking from her work to sit, talk, and listen." He grinned. "Mostly listen. I've always had a lot to say."

Rainey smiled, braiding her fingers through his for a tighter hold.

"I talked about my parents, school, goals I could never meet, and over the course of a couple of months, she went from being invisible to becoming the most beautiful person I'd ever seen in my whole life." His focus came back to Rainey's. "Her family was a lot like yours—maybe a little quieter—but they had the same kind of warm welcome. It blew all my misconceptions about love and family out of the water. They saw me in a way I'd never seen myself, and it made me wonder how I could become that person."

His face blurred in her teary vision, but she refused to look away. She wanted to know the layers buried beneath Alex Murdock's ready laugh and embrace him wholly. "How did you heal?"

"Time." He released her hair and touched her cheek. "You."

Her breath tangled in the tenderness.

"After her death, I went through a dark time for a while. Made some stupid mistakes with life and work. Got angry and blamed God. Then one day, when I was cleaning out my apartment, I discovered the letters Beth had written me. Her words, her faith, helped me find some acceptance, but more than that, they sparked a curiosity about what she believed and this confidence of belonging she exemplified, even to her last breath."

"You wear your wounds well."

He lowered his forehead to touch hers, his fingers making their way down her cheek to her chin. "We all have backstories. We just don't wear them the same way." He closed his eyes and tugged her against him. "Besides, I hadn't healed. Not really. Not until I came to Ransom. I think God had been working in me, cultivating this gnawing curiosity about Beth's faith, which He answered here. With your family. With you."

She rested her head on his shoulder and held him closely, burying her face in his neck, breathing in his scent and this new story defining him. Her emotions warred for words to say, comfort to impart.

"Alex," she whispered, searching for some way to show him how he was taking up residence in her heart.

"Rainey?" he teased back, his voice swooping low and spilling warmth through her.

"If you'll help me, I'd like to do the TV interview."

Alex followed Rainey up the driveway to her house, still a little surprised at her change of heart. The news reporter hadn't filled the spot yet, so Alex was able to secure the interview, but Rainey only had two days to prepare.

When a smidge of uncertainty darkened her eyes, Alex almost tried to talk Rainey out of the interview. But she was determined to make good on her decision and had even asked him to help her figure out what to wear.

He brought Marilyn to a stop and hopped out. Being raised in a high-class socializing family had its perks, if it meant helping a beautiful woman feel more comfortable in a new situation. Rainey would shine.

Afternoon sunlight bathed Rainey's house in an orange spotlight, casting fading hues against the covered front porch.

Alex swooped down and tossed Sarah on his back. She giggled and wrapped those little hands around his neck, burrowing closely with the smell of citrus like her mama.

"You know, Sarah, your house is pretty perfect, I think."

"Mama says my room has so much pink it smells like peppermint."

Alex gave Rainey a look, and she took a step closer to him in their walk up the steps, weaving her arm through his. Perfect fit. Right in his heart.

"Your house reminds me of something out of a Hallmark movie."

Rainey released her hold on his arm and unlocked the front door. "What do you know about those sappy-sweet Hallmark movies?"

Alex slid Sarah off his back and ushered her into the house. "As a matter of fact, I love those sappy-sweet movies."

She shot a look of unadulterated skepticism over her shoulder on her way to the kitchen. "Are you kidding me?"

He leaned a hip against the counter and crossed his arms, watching her long hair swish against her back as she pulled open the refrigerator to retrieve two bottled waters.

"There's a lot you don't know about me. I actually love Hallmark movies and costume dramas."

She cringed as she twisted open her bottle. "I think you might be dating the wrong Mitchell."

He snatched his bottle off the counter and moved a step closer to her. "Nope, I have the right one. Somebody has to keep their cool during the final scenes of *Jane Eyre*."

She nearly spit out her water. "You're crazy." She laughed and wiped her mouth with the back of her hand. "I'm a little afraid to ask what other insights you have to share about your likes and dislikes."

"I'm partial to blondes, but I think you knew that." He winked and enjoyed the rush of pink blooming in her cheeks.

"I figured that one out on my own." She sidestepped him and reached into the pantry to retrieve a juice box for Sarah.

"I have blond hair," Sarah said, tugging at one of her braids. Alex scooped her up in his arms.

"That's right. My favorite. It's all thick and shiny like your mama's."

Sarah giggled and squeezed out of his hold to take her juice box. She skittered off to the table with a bag of crackers as Rainey pulled sandwich meat from the fridge.

Alex took his cue and went for the bread. "I am a diehard *Mario Kart* junkie. You should see me playing as Luigi. I look hot on a motorcycle."

"I can only imagine, with his Italian moustache waving in the breeze."

"That's the only way to ride on a *Mario Kart* bike, my dear." He looked up at the ceiling before adding another bit of information. "And I hate oatmeal. I was tricked into eating something made from oatmeal when I was little, and from that point on, oatmeal was a no-go."

She placed the condiments beside him on the counter, then handed him a knife, her smile lighting her eyes. "You know those preacher cookies you ate over at Mama's last week?"

He took the knife. "Those great chocolate ones?"

Rainey raised a brow.

"No way! Oatmeal? Man, I've been hoodwinked again."

"By my mama, no less."

He nodded. "It's always the sweet ones you have to look out for."

She grinned and shook her head as he turned to slice open the hoagie rolls for sandwiches.

"If I'm going to watch a movie, I like it to have action in it." Rainey sidled up beside him, and they moved in an assembly-line fashion to complete the sandwiches. "I really enjoy superhero movies, but if a romantic movie has a thoughtful premise and some good humor or intrigue, I can handle that too."

Alex nudged her with his shoulder, then tilted his chin up. "And of course, a dashing hero."

She sighed. "I do have an unhealthy crush on Chris Evans."

"Chris Evans?"

"And definitely Chris Hemsworth."

Alex conceded with a shoulder shrug. "Well, who doesn't?"

She slit him a sneaky grin that inspired all sorts of unheroic thoughts. "And I could totally take you at *Mario Kart.*"

He placed his palm down on the counter, his body blocking hers, keeping her close. "Okay, Miss Smarty-pants, I challenge you to a game of *Mario Kart.* Tonight."

She poked her finger into his chest, aiming for confidence but with a rivulet of uncertainty in her eyes. "After we figure out what I'm supposed to wear to this interview."

"Right."

"And after you feed me mock questions."

"Got it."

Her lips took on a sassy tilt. "Then I might let you win at *Mario Kart* as your reward for helping me."

"Oh no, no, Miss Mitchell." He snagged her pointy finger and pulled her arm to wrap around his waist. "You're going to lose fair and square."

Alex gave Haus a scrub under his furry chin as he stood from tying his tennis shoes. Life was good. His late night up at Rainey's ended in a nail-biting *Mario Kart* challenge, of which Rainey was victor, but she'd consoled him with a rockin' goodnight kiss. He'd gladly lose every time for that sort of reward. And as far as the interview? It took a full half hour just to find something classy-professional inside her tomboy closet. She favored dark, bland colors and Plain Jane styles. As the only boy between two daughters of a socialite businessman, Alex knew a few things about dress. Bland and plain were forgettable, but classy, even if simple, with a bold complementary color, made the difference.

Evidently, his knowledge of sophisticated dressing impressed his lovely lady because she asked, with some hesitation, if he'd help her find something to wear to Reese and Dee's wedding ... and if he'd be her date. Huzzah! First, a date to a wedding and then… His thoughts took a sugar-coated spin into happily ever after. Yep, he needed to watch a Hallmark movie soon.

He snagged his jacket and walked to fill up Haus' food bowl, only to stop at the sound of his phone. With a few easy strides, he pulled the cell phone to his ear.

"Good morning."

"Hey, Alex." Evie's voice settled into his heart, a comforting reminder of her safety. "Do you have a few minutes to chat?"

"Sure." He finished up feeding Haus. "Any news?"

"Well, that's why I called. I have a few things. One good news and one…"

"Let's go with the not-so-good and get it over with."

"The police tracked John to Fairfax yesterday. Surveillance cameras caught him snooping around Dad's firm and house."

Alex deflated into a kitchen chair. "Why would he come back to the scene of the crime?"

"I don't know." Evie's voice quivered, and his stomach pinched with a helpless ache. "One of the agents wonders if he's been tipped off that … that…"

"You're not dead." The declaration groaned from his lips, an unearthly chill prickling his skin.

"They're tracing him now, though, since they have some good footage of his appearance to share with other agencies. I … I need to believe this is almost over."

"Me too, sis. Me too."

"You have to tell Dad, Alex. He needs to know." Her words pierced him with their painful truth. "It would heal your relationship with him. I know it. And if the worst happens…"

"Don't even think thoughts like that, Evie. They're going to catch John and then we can go back to having a normal life."

"I don't even know what that looks like anymore."

He ran a hand over his face, inwardly praying for guidance. "I've learned that healing can't come from my strength. I have to seek help from someone greater than me."

"Yes, I'm learning that too," she whispered. "I miss you."

His voice closed off, clenched with millions of bundled up griefs. "You too."

Silence blanketed the powerlessness with awareness. God had this. Alex didn't know a lot about the Bible or this new faith, but from what he'd been learning so far, God held it all in His hands. Even the grief.

"I think now is a good time for that better news."

She released a stream of air like a quiet laugh. "You're right. The investigators have approved our meeting. I'll only have one night, but we'll be dropped off after dark and picked up a little after dawn. It's short."

"But it's something."

"Right."

"When?"

"I think it will be within the next month. I'll only be able to give you a few hours' notice."

He nodded, the sweet hope pushing back the fear for a moment. "I'll be here."

Rainey pulled her hair clips out for the fifth time, allowing her hair to fall around her shoulders. The simple brown dress Alex suggested she wear to the television interview, paired with the teal and golden scarf, really did look much nicer than anything she'd chosen. The wrap-around style enhanced her figure in all the right places, and the teal in the scarf brightened her face and eyes.

He'd been right. Again. Another nail to her prejudice and pride. She stilled her grin with the tiny hint of doubt. He'd missed their morning jog because of another mysterious family phone call.

Or at least that's what he claimed they were.

She wrangled the doubt underneath every scene of him over the past month and stared at her reflection in the mirror. She could trust him. She *would* trust him. With a quick ruffle of her hair, leaving it loose and long, she sprayed a quick shot of Mango Twist and stepped from the bathroom.

Sarah sat in the middle of the living room floor, the full ensemble of every My Little Pony known to mankind surrounding her—along with the castle, the stable, and other paraphernalia. She looked up as Rainey entered the room, and her snaggle-tooth grin bloomed.

"You look pretty, Mama."

"Thanks, sweet pea." Rainey tugged at her scarf a little, searching for her confidence while wrapped in a girly dress. Hiding behind ponytails, jeans, and T-shirts was so much easier. She slid her feet into some strappy heels waiting for her by the couch and checked her watch.

Mr. Babysitter should arrive any time.

She took her cheat sheet off the counter, a quick reference of things Alex had recommended she jot down and replay in her mind, but her thoughts shimmied to their last few evenings together. Sweet and spicy, like some of her favorite foods. Mmm, and boy, oh boy, could the man kiss. Her lips might never recover—and she didn't want them to.

A knock pulled her wayward thoughts to the door.

"He's here! He's here!" Sarah jumped up from the floor and raced to the door.

"Hey there, princess. You're really rockin' those pigtails today." His voice melted down the hallway and warmed Rainey's skin with its mellow tones. Yep, she loved trouble. Heaps of it, wrapped in sandalwood and... Alex rounded the corner. Dark jeans and a long-sleeved green T-shirt. She took her time appreciating every inch of him. Whew, heaven help her.

"Thanks for staying with her, Alex."

He took his own time giving her the once-over, his eyes darkening as he approached. "Ponies and pizza. Sounds like one amazing lunch break to me."

"Teacher workdays don't always hit at the best time. Mama's out with Emma shopping for wedding stuff, or I wouldn't have asked you." That's what her words said, but her gaze said something totally different. "But I figured since you're off work today like me…"

He slipped the pizza box onto the counter, his eyes speaking the same nonverbal language as hers. Were her cheeks on fire? "Ask me any time you want, Rainey. I love spending time with you guys."

Speaking of cheeks, Alex sported a strange black smudge on his right one. She reached up to wipe it away, snagging the full-attention of those seafoam green eyes.

"And with Pinkie Pie," Sarah added, dancing the pink pony across the counter toward the pizza box.

"And, of course, with Pinkie Pie." He zoomed his gaze back to Rainey and put his hand around her waist. "You look amazing, by the way. I mean heart-stopping kind of amazing."

"I had some help."

His gaze took another journey down her body and back. "My help was nothing. You already had the goods."

"Alex." Rainey shot him a warning glare despite fighting a grin. "What have you been doing today anyway?" Rainey reached a second time to swipe at the black smudge. Without any warning, he dipped his head and seized her lips for a much-too-swift welcome she felt all the way to her toes.

"I was helping Jim tinker with a lawn mower."

Her brows skidded high. "You know how to fix lawn mowers?"

"Nope, but I don't think Jim does either, so we just experimented."

She laughed, reluctant to move from his touch. "You two have really hit it off, haven't you?"

Alex kept in step with her. "He doesn't give me much choice."

"That's Jim for you." She reached for her cheat sheet and tucked it into her purse. Her throat tightened at the reminder of what she was getting ready to do. In front of thousands of people on live television.

"Hey, you're going to do great." His palm covered her shoulder and then traced her back. "You love those kids." His smile softened. "That's all you need to remember."

She breathed in his confidence, kissed him for good measure, and headed out the door.

Alex sighed back into the couch, the most content man on the planet. Rainey snuggled to one side, and on the other Sarah slept curled beneath his arm while the movie credits rolled to a stop. Lunch turned into dinner and a movie, Disney style.

Darkness hung heavily out the windows, and despite his current joy in being a man-sandwich, he needed to get home. He smiled at Rainey, her head resting on his shoulder. She'd performed beautifully during the interview, just as he'd known she would. It had been a live interview, but once she'd gotten over her initial jitters, when the questions turned toward TLC, her natural passion and intelligence shone on the screen.

He looked heavenward and prayed people with deep pockets heard the clarion call for help. Despite the interest from a few foundations, it would still be a while before anyone made decisions about who would be funded, and TLC still needed enough funds to make it through the upcoming school year.

He brushed a kiss to her head, breathing in Rainey's citrus scent. "I better get going, gorgeous."

She yawned and nodded her head against his shoulder, murmuring something unintelligible. Oh man, this was torture. Who would ever want to leave something this sweet? Alex glanced back to the window. How bad would it look if his car stayed outside her house all night long?

He cringed. Not ideal. Despite his mostly good intentions, he didn't want to mar Rainey's reputation at all. He pushed back an errant strand of hair from her face, his chest tightening with a familiar and not-so-familiar love. No, he wanted to protect her at all costs.

With a careful twist of his body, he maneuvered himself from between his girls, reluctant to lose his spot. Sarah's little head tilted in an uncomfortable direction, so he lifted her into his arms, tucking her close to his expanding heart.

"Rainey," he whispered.

Her aqua eyes flickered open like a sleeping beauty, and her smile nearly had him joining her on the couch.

"I'm going to take Sarah up to her bed, then head home, okay?"

Rainey drew in a deep breath, her eyes widening. "Yes, thank you." She slowly stretched to a stand, bringing attention to all her curvy grace.

Whew, it was a good thing he was leaving—otherwise all of his excellent intentions might tilt strongly toward the dark side. She caught his look and kept staring, her grin growing as she closed in to claim a quick kiss. "I know I should encourage you to leave, but I really want you to stay."

He released a low growl and took a stiff turn toward the stairs. "You and me both."

She followed close behind as he made his way up the steps and gently placed Sarah in her bed. Rainey's palm slid across his back as he tugged the frilly pink blanket around Sarah's shoulders.

"You're good at this, you know," she whispered.

"At what?" he whispered, walking back to the hallway.

"At taking care of people." She tugged him close. "You hid it pretty well at first, but it's certainly a part of who you are."

He settled his palms on her hips and eased her a step closer. "Come on, say it. I know you want to."

A smile lit her eyes and made a gracious descent to her lips. "Say what?"

He lowered his lips to hers until they nearly touched, her quick intake of breath her dizzying response. "Tell me I'm your hero."

"You're my hero?"

"See, was that so hard?" He rewarded her with a kiss, and her body melded into his.

Her arms wrapped beneath his to bring her palms against his back, moving in slow, tantalizing strokes. Despite the inner radar blaring into the red zone, his mouth took a pleasant journey down her jawbone to her neck, her moan encouraging his expedition.

She was warm and soft and perfect against him, and she smelled like mangos. His body surged to alert, to need. It had been so long since he'd felt anything like this for someone, and to have Rainey respond with the same passion blinded every reasonable argument. Her hold begged for more. His body ached to comply. Every growing affection within him crashed into this unabated need to *be* with her.

Do you love her?

The question surfaced from deep inside him, above the mad pounding of his pulse in his ears.

Do you love her?

Yes, his heart responded. More than this.

He brought his mouth back to hers, easing the pace of their kisses until he pulled back, staring down into her passion-glazed eyes. *He did love her.*

"I'm gonna go before I do something we'll both regret."

She tightened her hold on him. "I'd rather you stay."

"Rainey…"

Her mouth took possession of his, and he stumbled back against the wall. Sweet mercy, even in his wildest dreams he hadn't imagined this. Her palms captured his face, holding him in place as her lips played havoc with his good intentions. Her teeth seized his bottom lip with the slightest nibble, and he almost threw her to the ground in response.

With every bit of willpower he could muster, Alex broke the kiss and touched her face. "Rainey, I have big plans for our first sleepover, but … but this isn't that time." He ran his fingers down her cheek. "And as hard as it is to leave you right now, I'd never want you to regret what's happening between us."

She blinked up at him, her gaze clearing with a remnant of the disappointment pinging in his chest. "I warned you about my driven personality. I'm sorry."

"Don't worry, gorgeous. I have a feeling we'll make up for lost time."

Chapter Twenty

"A lex Murdock?"

Alex turned from his position beside Sarah at the Rock the Boat carnival game and searched the crowd. His gaze finally landed on Dr. Adelina Roseland.

A fashionable close-cropped hat topped her dark hair and matched her red coat, but her smile was the real showstopper. The only other time Alex could remember seeing such an expression on his former colleague's face was when she'd danced with Reese Mitchell at the Autumn Leaves Ball. Dee had finally found where she belonged—or with whom she belonged, to be exact.

After spending a few months with the Mitchell clan, he understood how easily that could happen.

"I wondered when you'd make your way back down to these parts of Virginia."

She scanned the crowd and placed her hands in her pockets. "There's been so much to do with the transition to Charlottesville and now getting ready for the wedding."

"Look, Dr. Alex, my ring caught a boat." Sarah jumped up and down, clapping her hands and bringing his attention to a toddling boat in the middle of the pool with a plastic ring around it.

"Oh boy, princess. Great job. Let's hope that boat has a red dot on the bottom. Then you can pick out the largest, most obnoxious stuffed animal in the pen, and your mama will just love it."

Dee caught her laugh in her hand. "I'd heard you'd acclimated well to Ransom, but some things never change."

He raised his palms in defense. "What's that supposed to mean?"

"You're still a bit of a troublemaker."

"What does oboshus mean?" Sarah asked, looking at him as the vendor reached for the boat she'd caught.

Alex grinned at Dee and gave his brows a playful wiggle. "Something to surprise your mom."

Sarah's smile widened. "She loves surprises."

He stared at the adorable little girl, thinking Sarah spoke more for herself than her mother.

"It's a red one," the festival worker said, showing off the red dot on the bottom of the boat. "Take your pick, sweetheart."

Sarah's wide eyes met Alex's. "It's a red one."

"Well then, if your Mama loves surprises, I think you ought to get…" He scanned the stuffed animals, then nodded toward a giant pink and yellow polka-dotted giraffe. "The giraffe?"

Sarah's mouth dropped and she nodded, clapping her hands again. "The giraffe. She'll love the giraffe."

The festival worker took the giant toy from its hinges and lowered it to Sarah's level. The stuffed animal stood taller than her, but she hugged it to her little body as if the obnoxious animal was the best toy on the planet.

"I see Ransom really has grown on you." Dee stepped forward, touching the giraffe's giant nose and smiling at him again. "And it looks good. Peaceful."

He raised a brow, acknowledging the truth. "It's a good place to settle, I think."

"The people have a way of grabbing hold of your heart, don't they?"

He took hold of the giraffe with one hand and Sarah's hand with the other. "Definitely."

Dee walked in step alongside him through the crowd. "Rainey's presentation this morning was fabulous. Reese is still waiting back there to congratulate her. From the crowd of people standing in line to speak with her, the community response to TLC's needs looks positive."

"For the upcoming year, there's really no other way to keep TLC going except generosity and hard work. She certainly has the hard work covered."

"And a good helper at her side, from what I hear."

He shot her a grin. "That's exactly where I like to be."

Dee's expression softened, and the hard edges she'd so frequently shown him gentled into a beautiful smile. "I'm really happy for you, Alex. I think we were both so lost in our own heads, we never saw each other clearly."

"Things are looking up for us, aren't they?" He waved a hand toward her. "You're getting married in … how many weeks?"

"Two." Her eyes widened like Sarah's. "Only two."

"April seems a crazy time for a wedding. In the middle of the school year? Are you on spring break that week?"

"Exactly." She looked ahead as they walked. There was no mistaking the glow in her face. He knew bits and pieces of her broken past, enough to acknowledge the preciousness of finding happiness after all her loss. It had been a hard fall for him to lose his position at Charlottesville for the one in Ransom, to trade the "prestige" and "connections" for this backwater farmland, but in hindsight, God knew exactly what Alex's heart needed.

And Ransom had captured his heart with two beautiful blondes and one amazing family.

"You're coming to the wedding, aren't you?"

"You bet." Alex weaved toward the concession stands and tossed a wink to Dee. "I'm going with my date."

She laughed. "I'm glad, Alex." Her expression sobered, a mutual understanding settling between them. "It's a good feeling to belong, isn't it?"

He nodded, giving Sarah's hand a little squeeze. "It sure is."

"Oh, come on, Rainey. There's a whole lot to be happy about, even if we still need to raise more money."

The man's optimism grated on her deep need to pump pessimism for a little while. "Over thirty thousand dollars, Alex. How on earth will we find that much money by the time the school pulls their funding at the end of April?"

He threaded her arm in his as they walked through the mall. They'd driven several hours to spend the day together in search of a dress for Rainey to wear to Dee and Reese's wedding, but her heart wasn't in the expedition. Of course, she rarely enjoyed clothes shopping, but Alex provided extra incentive and turned the entire journey into something fun. Clothes shopping, fun? What a thought!

And Dee had made it easy on her matron of honor. Choose a teal dress. Any kind.

But the truth hit deeply. Even after a successful presentation that raised over twenty-five thousand dollars of additional pledge money, nights of prayers, *and* a Saturday date with the man who left her swooning like a lovestruck princess, she couldn't find peace over the impending loss of such a resource.

TLC's mission, its growth, helped her resurface after the whole fiasco with Gray. And all those children the clinic benefited? She couldn't let them down.

"Hey." Alex's gentle voice pulled her attention to him. "We're going to win this. You still have several possible donors from my dad's contacts, right? Besides, I kind of want to see Dean Mercer get a good dose of homespun shock when TLC succeeds. I'm not above rubbing it into her face, you know."

His humor shook off her gloom, a pattern she appreciated more each passing day. She covered his arm with her hand and leaned into him. "I love it when you get all sweetly vengeful like that."

He chuckled. "I gotta fight for my girl. What hero would do less?"

"I really started something with the hero-talk, didn't I?" The bustle of people through Valley View Mall created a quick hum behind them as they took their leisurely stroll.

Even though she found the physical aspect of their relationship incredibly enjoyable—and in all honesty, rather daydream-y—as they walked arm-in-arm through the mall, their camaraderie settled over her with profound certainty. His compassion, friendship, and laughter touched a deeper place in her heart that his kisses didn't quite reach.

"I still have those possible donors you referred to me from Fairfax."

"Right." He grinned. "Now you're thinking strategically. And those are some of the most generous names from my dad's list. Deep pockets. Big hearts. I'm expecting great support from them." He steered them between some groups of teenagers toward the larger department stores, his expression falling. "That reminds me, I need to head up to Fairfax to see my dad next weekend."

"Looks serious—an unusual expression for you."

His smile widened but didn't reach his eyes. "What can I say? He brings out the best in me."

Her protective instincts jumped in with both feet. "I have an idea. What are you doing next week?"

"Well, I have a killer basketball game with the guys at TLC on Thursday, and I'm giving a review session on Tuesday for the Thursday exam. You know, bog the poor kids down before spring break so they're really happy to leave."

Her mind spun with unspoken plans. "My graduate assistant can do the review session on Monday for my Wednesday exam. Do you think you could move your clients around to later in the week?"

"Sure." He slowed their pace, studying her. "What do you have in mind?"

"If I could set up appointments with those possible donors on Monday morning, we could travel together Sunday."

"We?" He pulled them to a stop in the middle of the mall and turned her to him.

"Sure. You can tell me your whole distorted backstory during the seven-hour drive." He stared at her with a look of such unadulterated tenderness, she squeezed his fingers. "Hey, I love convoluted backstories, and I have a certain fondness for this speech-language pathology professor I met."

He blinked from his stare, tugging her arm back through his. "That's a long ride. Are you sure you want to spend it with *me* to visit my grumpy dad?"

The joy lighting his eyes confirmed her decision. "One hundred percent sure."

His smile wavered then spread to an almost uncontainable place. A sweet hum of pleasure at being the one to bring him such happiness internally lit her body. She was in love with Alex Murdock.

Clearly, she was crazy.

"This may be the first time I've ever looked forward to a road trip." He released a long sigh. "Well, I'm definitely going to have to embellish my backstory to hold your interest. Don't want you getting bored with me or anything."

She nudged his shoulder with hers. "Alex, I may get annoyed with you, possibly even angry, but bored? I think that's impossible."

"Whoa, whoa." His free hand shot up like a stop sign, halting their forward motion. "I don't see how this trip can work."

"What are you talking about?"

"If we're going from Sunday to Monday, that means we spend the night." His gaze darkened with his smile. "I cannot be trusted with that kind of responsibility."

She chuckled and squeezed his arm again. "That does pose a problem because I'm pretty out of control when I'm alone with you too."

His palm slammed against his chest. "Those are the best words you've ever spoken to me."

"But like a very wise man recently told me, I care more about you than the need for this." She waved her hand toward his very attractive physique. "And with God's help, I'll remember that."

"Good, because it's your turn anyway." He winked. "This time I can keep my mind in the gutter."

Her laugh loosened fully, echoing off the high ceilings. "What am I going to do with you?"

"You can keep me forever, and I'll be content with that."

"I kind of like that idea."

They walked on, their silent agreement humming a pleasant bond between them. Minutes passed as they window-shopped and then, Alex suddenly halted. "That's the one."

She followed his gaze to a massive display window. A flowing strapless confection of aqua fell to the knee and reminded her of the gown Julie Andrews wore while dancing with Captain von Trapp in *The Sound of Music*. "Are you kidding?"

He moved his attention from the dress to Rainey and back, allowing his gaze to measure her from the chin down. "You're right. You'd better not wear that one. Too much temptation for your date."

She rewarded his appraisal with a crooked smile. "Well, maybe we should take a quick look."

"Thanks for watching Sarah during our trip, Mama." Rainey walked out of the early service at church at her mother's side. "I'll pick her up from your house Tuesday morning if you wouldn't mind having her ready for school."

"It will be a treat. I have Lou and Brandon this weekend too, so the girls can have another good sleepover before the wedding."

Rainey nodded, taking in the gravity of change. Lou and Sarah weren't only cousins, but almost inseparable. Once Reese and Dee returned from their honeymoon, Lou and Brandon would move with them to Charlottesville. "I'm glad they'll get this time together."

"Sarah will be fine, Rainey. She's weathered a lot for a little one." Mama touched Rainey's shoulder. "Besides, she's got a whole gang of people who love her, and I wouldn't be surprised if there ain't a few good changes in her future."

Rainey followed Mama's gaze to where Alex exited with Sarah at his side, her smile as big as his. The sight touched Rainey in all the sweet spots in her heart.

"Well, I think that kind of talk is a little too soon, don't you?"

Mama's eyes took on their mischievous sparkle. "Not if it's the right person at the right time."

Rainey dragged her gaze from his and neutralized her expression before returning her attention to her much-too-perceptive mother. "Well, it's better not to rush into anything. I have Sarah to consider, of course."

"Yep, looks like you courtin' Alex has really hurt her."

The sarcasm broke Rainey's failed attempt at disinterest into a smile. "Okay, Mama. I'm head-over-heels and may very well be stupid enough to say yes to a proposal from the guy faster than a Disney princess to her prince, but he has a lot of undisclosed family stuff he's dealing with. Maybe this trip will alleviate some of my curiosity about it."

"And if it doesn't?"

Rainey sent another look to the cutest pair on the church steps and sighed. "I'd still say yes."

"How does he measure up to those questions?"

Rainey rolled her eyes despite her broadening grin, undeniably confirming the answer her brilliant mother already knew. "For me? I think he may be a perfect fit, Mama," she whispered as the pair closed in.

"Y'all have a safe trip." Mama focused her words at Alex. "And I hope things go well with your daddy."

"Me too." He ran a hand through his hair. "I'd appreciate those expert prayers, if you don't mind."

"You got 'em." Rainey covered her smile. Her mama looked about as smitten with Alex as Rainey was. "Speak from your heart, boy. It's done a lot of changing over the past few months. You got a strength now you didn't have before."

"Right as usual, Mama Mitchell. Thank you for that reminder." Alex leaned in and kissed her cheek. She batted him away with an embarrassed chuckle. "You git on your way now. Don't y'all have a dinner date with your dad?"

Alex groaned. "Yep. His secretary was nice enough to set it up since he didn't have time to talk with me in person."

"Keep your head, boy. God's got this." Mama wagged her finger at his chest. "And keep your heart too."

He glanced at Rainey and leaned close to Mama, as if what he had to say was some great secret. "Too late. My heart's already taken, but I'll work really hard to keep my head."

Rainey pulled Sarah up in her arms, snuggling her close. "Be good for Granny, okay? And have loads of fun with Lou."

"'Kay, Mama." She wiggled out of Rainey's arms and grabbed Alex's leg. "Bye, Dr. Alex."

He swooped her into the air, then pulled her close, nuzzling her neck until she squealed. Rainey nearly melted into the paved parking lot. "Bye, princess. Don't let Lou boss you around too much."

"We better get on the road, Dr. Alex," Rainey interrupted. "I hear your dad is a stickler for punctuality."

His grin slanted. "Then we have all the time in the world."

Sensibilities, one of the most impressive and high-end restaurants in northern Virginia, displayed the same sleek monochrome style Alex remembered from his father's office. The red-carpeted entry breathed the rich world of Alex's childhood all the way to the scent in the air. At least he had the right kind of car for such a place.

Alex handed his keys over to the valet and met Rainey on the other side of the car. They'd changed from their relaxed travel clothes at the last rest area before reaching Fairfax, and if Alex had the smallest worry of Rainey's ability to meet the challenge, when she'd emerged from the ladies' room, his worries died a sudden death.

She rocked the little black dress like a dream, with her hair swept back into some sort of messy bun that highlighted her slender neckline. She even risked heels, placing her at the perfect kissing level with almost no need to bend his neck to reach those lips.

He offered his arm to her, her hand slipping through for a perfect fit. "After that long backstory and a seven-hour drive with me singing karaoke on occasion, you still sure about this?"

Her palm went to her stomach, and she stared up at the restaurant as they took the stairs to the door. "About you? Yes. About this..."

"If you can handle me, you can handle anything." He drew her hand up to his lips. "Just be yourself. You're the most beautiful person I know."

The hostess showed them to a table at the window overlooking the lights of the city, and his father stood to greet them.

"Alex." His father's smile formed a plastic greeting. The undercurrent of their last argument hung between them as thick as the savory scent of steak in the room. The blame, the hateful words … the memories pricked the grip of his hand with a renewed sting.

"Dad."

His father's attention shifted to Rainey and back. "Newest conquest, son?"

"Actually, I'm a willing victim." Rainey held out her hand, her smile challenging his father's assumptions head-on. Alex almost dropped to his knee and asked her to marry him on the spot. "Rainey Mitchell."

An unveiled look of interest replaced his father's surprise. "I see you have a mind of your own. That's a nice change from his previous dates."

"The country life has been good for me." Alex held Rainey's gaze, hoping she read the gratitude on his face. "Really good to me."

"I'm glad to see that a demotion can turn in your favor." His father gestured toward the chairs.

The tenderness in Rainey's eyes pushed calm through Alex, seizing his fight. He didn't have to prove anything to his father. God accepted him as he was, flaws and all, and Alex held the hand of the best prize on the planet.

Don't fall into Dad's trap or play his game.

Alex pulled out Rainey's chair, then took his own seat. "Best thing that's ever happened to me, Dad."

"You've always been the simpler of the three children. Your sisters were born for the complexities and status of this life, but not you." Sarcasm underscored each word, sarcasm and … pain. "You've never been one to work when you can play."

He saw it then, in the dim lighting, age catching up to this giant of a man. Grief at the loss of a child, at the destruction of a marriage, at countless meaningless and hollow relationships. The hollow ornament.

"Maybe I picked a profession where I could do both."

His father scoffed and waved for the waiter. "Is that what you believe?"

Alex's hand fisted on the table, the old fight rising to the surface against his newfound peace. He scraped for slips of Bible verses he'd read to prepare him for this meeting.

A SOFT ANSWER TURNS AWAY WRATH.
LOVE ONE ANOTHER AS I HAVE LOVED YOU.
LOVE YOUR ENEMIES AND PRAY FOR THOSE WHO SPITEFULLY ABUSE YOU...

Rainey's hand covered his, drawing his attention away from his inner battle and to her smile. As his father rattled off drink orders to their waiter, Rainey's gentle touch reminded Alex that he had two things with him in this encounter with his father that he'd never possessed with any of the others. His faith and Rainey.

"The business seems to be going well." Alex squeezed Rainey's fingers and turned to his father. "From the last conversation I had with Veronica, she seems comfortable at the helm of your New York company."

His father hesitated as he unfolded his napkin, blinking as if he'd expected a different response. "She was made for the position."

"And how does Peter like New York?"

His father averted Alex's gaze and adjusted the napkin in his lap instead. Uh oh. What was going on with Alex's brother-in-law?

"Peter chose to remain here and start over."

Alex's shoulders slumped forward from the news' impact. College sweethearts, best friends... The expectations of the high-profile job shattered their happily ever after just like they had done to his father and mother.

An incomprehensible compassion softened Alex's response. All the screwed-up priorities and the constant scramble for the next achievement to be greater than the last, only to end up in a half-a-million-dollar house alone with a string of broken people in your wake?

"Do you know what you would like to eat? The squid is a particular delicacy of Sensibilities."

Rainey hid her distaste like a pro but for the slightest grimace. Alex's smile nudged for release. Country girl tastes.

"We checked out the menu on our way up here." Alex listed off their orders, then turned the conversation to much more pleasant topics. "Rainey works with me at Blue Ridge University. She's an excellent teacher and a true advocate for the kids in the community."

His father took a drink of his wine and turned his attention to Rainey. "And if you're such a sensible young woman, why are you associated with my son?"

"Well, it's pretty clear he took his good looks from his dad." Rainey's eyes shimmered in the candlelight from the table. "And he couldn't have turned out to be such a thoughtful gentleman without a strong role model."

His father paused the wine glass to his lips and lowered it back to the table, studying Rainey with renewed interest. Alex's chest almost burst with enough pride to roar like a lion. Oh, this woman was smart!

"And what exactly do you and my son do at this Blue Ridge University?"

Rainey barely held her anger under control for the duration of the meal. At almost every opportunity, Eli Murdock found a way to berate Alex. She'd been warned on the ride to Fairfax. Not only had Alex refused to take his place in his father's business, which had started the rift between them, but Eli blamed Alex for the car accident that took his daughter's and granddaughter's lives. Alex and the accompanying policeman were lone survivors.

Instead of garnering his father's compassion after the tragic accident, Alex reaped his father's disdain and blame. All the false arrogance and constant flirtation, the need to purchase Marilyn and the overwhelming gratitude Alex harbored for her family, made more sense.

As crazy and loud as they were, her family loved big.

And Alex's thirsty heart needed some big love.

Rainey crossed the hallway from her hotel room to Alex's, happy to be out of the fancy clothes and back into the comfort of sweats and a T-shirt. She tapped on his door. After a few moments, the door opened and his tired gaze met hers. He'd slipped into his sweats too. "Hey," he said, opening the door a little wider, the sadness in his smile undeniable.

Without another word, she stepped forward and wrapped him in her arms, pressing her face into his shoulder and holding him close. He stiffened, then encased her in his embrace, his face resting in her hair. They stood in silence. She breathed in sandalwood and soap. He ran his fingers through her hair, his breath ragged. Seconds turned into minutes and then he drew back, his palms framing her face.

Unshed tears glistened in the green depths of his eyes, squeezing Rainey's heart in a vise. How had he borne all the criticism? The biting sarcasm? For how long?

"Thank you," he whispered.

"I didn't do much but try to deflect some of the bullets from you." She shook her head. "I'm so sorry. I can't even imagine how much his words must have hurt you for so long."

"They didn't seem to sting as badly since you were here. Now, tomorrow morning when I meet with him alone? I'll have to pretend you're sitting nearby with that beautiful smile on your face, helping me keep my cool."

She rose on tiptoe and kissed him. "I think the sooner we get back to Ransom, the better. You have a whole crew of people down there who are pleased as punch to have you."

He caressed her cheeks, the intensity of his stare locking her gaze to his, stripping her breath.

"Rainey Mitchell, I love you."

He didn't give her a chance to respond before sealing his declaration with a kiss so gentle, her body melted into him with complete acceptance of his promise.

She loved him—and sometime soon, she'd work up the courage to voice that truth too.

Chapter Twenty-one

Alex followed the secretary down the familiar corridor to his father's office. A few of the paintings on the walls had changed, and his father had modernized several furnishings, but everything else remained the same since the last time Alex had walked this hall. A year ago, after Evie...

The door opened to a vast office space complete with a wall of windows behind his father's sleek desk. Eli Murdock failed to stand and instead gestured toward one of the chairs in front of his desk.

"As I'm certain my secretary told you, I've worked you in between meetings, so I don't have a lot of time for this conversation you deemed so important last night." He shuffled some papers on his desk without looking up.

Alex released a breath through his nose to calm his galloping pulse. He'd prayed before coming. Rainey had even stopped by on her way to meet with donors and offered a few prayers. If he was honest with himself, though, there was no easy way to break the news.

"Dad, I've spent the last few months learning about what a healthy family looks like. How they act. How they love each other." He braided his hands in front of him and leaned forward, trying to keep a nonconfrontational status. "I'm sorry I've not acted or responded in a way that showed you respect or love."

His father's hands paused on the desk. He looked up, eyes narrowed. "What have you done? How much will it cost me?"

Alex shook his head. "I don't want any money from you, Dad. I..." Alex forced the words forward. "I'm asking for your forgiveness, first and foremost."

"My forgiveness?" His father's brusque response mirrored the confusion on his face.

"I've said a lot of things in the past that were hurtful, and I'm sorry for them." Alex pressed his palms against his knees and straightened. "And ... and I've done something else."

"Ah." His father's palm came up. "Now we get to the real issue. Is this Rainey girl pregnant or something? I knew there had to be much more to her visit than just trying to raise money for her little tutoring clinic."

Alex split through his annoyance with the sentence he'd practiced all the way to the office. "Evie isn't dead."

His father shot to his feet. "Get out! That isn't funny."

Alex kept his voice calm. "The accident was planned by the police to fake her death because they knew John was trying to silence her."

"I said get out!"

"I've been communicating with her via a phone the Witness Protection Program provided to me." Alex slid his hand into his pocket and drew out the blue cell phone. "And I requested they send one for you too. So you could talk to Evie, hear her voice … know the truth."

His father pushed a button on his phone. "Security, come escort my guest from the building at once."

"The phone should ring in five minutes." Alex placed the phone on his father's desk and backed toward the door. "I didn't tell you about her because I was afraid the more people who knew she was alive, the more dangerous it would be for her."

"Are you telling me she's alive? This moment? Lily too?"

Alex nodded, his smile warbling for assurance. "I was trying to protect them … and you by keeping it a secret, but I should have told you a long time ago." Emotions frayed his voice as he stared into his father's wide-eyed gaze. "I was afraid John may use his goons to—"

"You're lying. We buried them."

"You know how dangerous it was. The investigators came up with this plan to save them from John doing much worse than he'd already shown himself capable of. I think, at first, I didn't tell you because I was angry at the way you'd demeaned me as subpar for not being the son you wanted, but then I kept it from you for your sake and Evie's."

"You knew all along, and you let me think she was…" His father's voice broke, and he snatched the phone in a white-knuckled grasp. "I can't…"

"I'm sorry, Dad. You've been hurting a long time—years before Evie's accident. All I saw was an angry, driven man who cared more about the next big deal than about me, but you've been hurting too."

"If this ridiculous story is true, how can you possibly believe I'll forgive you?"

Alex shrugged. "I've learned how to believe in a lot of things I didn't used to, so maybe I'll be surprised with this too."

The office doors burst open, and two security guards marched forward. Alex backed toward them, palms in the air, still facing his father. "When the phone rings, answer it. You won't be sorry."

Alex stared at the same midterm exam he'd attempted to grade for the past ten minutes, but his mind kept wandering back to the weekend. The pain that had laced his father's expression during their morning meeting seared through Alex's conscience. He should have told his dad the truth months ago, but that sliver of doubt that his father would choose money over his family if the price came high enough kept him silent. He'd remained silent when the investigators informed his dad that Evie's and Lily's bodies hadn't been recovered from the river in which their car had crashed. Kept silent as he mourned the loss of a daughter and granddaughter. Alex had allowed him to believe the worst.

In his defense, the investigators had told Alex it would be best if his father didn't know the truth. The fewer people who knew Evie and Lily survived, the better chance his sister and niece had of staying safe.

But the memory of the pain on his father's face etched a knife of grief through Alex, an open wound since this whole horrible mess began. Once again, his best intentions went wrong. Even with his sister's urging, he shouldn't have told his father Evie and Lily were alive.

And only giving Rainey snippets of information on their ride to Fairfax ate at his conscience too. She was a smart woman. She knew he hid something, especially in his vague excuse for his father's hatred and less-than-detailed recap of the car accident. He'd left out that Evie and Lily were being chased by some of John's cohorts—a chase that ended in a gunfight that left the two thugs and secured Evie and Lily's admittance under the Police Protection Program.

Lord, please help me do the right thing.

"Hey."

Alex looked up from his page to find Rainey standing in the doorway, looking as lovely as ever in a pale-blue blouse and black slacks. "Hey."

She stepped into his office and pulled the door closed behind her. Without hesitation, she crossed the room and knelt in front of him, taking his face in her warm hands and delivering a lingering kiss.

"Are you okay?" she whispered, her gaze searching his, her sweet affection pouring over his parched heart.

"I'm loads better now."

She pulled back ever so slightly. "I can't get you out of my thoughts, Alex."

He pushed her hair behind her ear. "Then I'm right where I want to be, gorgeous."

Her hand dropped to the collar of his shirt, and she gave it a tug. "I'm serious." She slipped into a nearby chair, and he rolled his closer to her. "I've grown up in such a healthy, supportive family, and I can't imagine dealing with everything you've endured." She growled. "Your father?"

Alex looked down at her hands and captured her fingers. "Yeah, he leaves an impression, doesn't he?"

"You grew up playing some kind of game, didn't you? Pretending so you could fit into his world?"

"It was the only way to please him or get what I wanted."

"And your charm became your defense mechanism and coping strategy, I think."

"Oh, come on. I can't just be charming without an ulterior motive?"

"You *are* charming." Her grin bloomed, then sobered. "But I see how you've used it for more than just charm, like you're doing right now to avoid getting too serious. It's okay to trust the right people with your wounds, Alex. They won't laugh or judge you. They'll help you heal."

He brought her fingers to his lips, keeping his gaze fixed on hers. "In so many ways, they already have."

Rainey had shown up early to Reese and Dee's rehearsal to help Emma with her preparation, but with Mama, Lizzie, Maggie, and half a dozen other women from church, Rainey's attempt seemed futile at best. Especially since she was much better at direct therapy and much more comfortable in jeans than this wispy gown and heels.

Emma had secured childcare, so Rainey couldn't even use Sarah as an escape plan to take a trip back home for a little while until the party started. She joined in where she could, even taking in the plethora of compliments the women kept pouring on her about her attire— a foreign experience for Rainey … but not as unwelcome as she'd expected.

She'd hesitantly donned the teal dress she'd bought with Alex. Despite her misgivings, he'd been right again. It looked nice on her. Sarah even praised it as a princess dress, although it didn't hold one stitch of pink. The cream-colored heels were low enough to keep her from killing herself—or anyone else—yet still highlighted Rainey's look with a touch of elegance.

Maybe getting dolled up every once in a while wasn't so bad. Rainey's brothers wouldn't know the first thing about fashion. Birthing cows, mending fences, handyman duties? Sure. But Alex came from a very different world, and she was beginning to appreciate his particular skills more and more each day.

Dee, in all her uptown-girl knowledge, insisted all the women in the bridal party have the wedding-day stylist do makeup and hair before the rehearsal as a special treat, so not only was Rainey walking around in a stylish dress, but her hair had been curled in a rain of beautiful ringlets and pinned up in an updo that would make Sarah see princesses for days.

She stepped carefully between the tables, her heels still a relative novelty, and finished placing napkins by the elegant table settings. The room warmed with candlelight and the gentle thrum of an acoustic guitar. Even the air wafted with the scent of roses and romance.

The crowd of wedding participants went through the rehearsal without a hitch, and although Rainey found the idea of her brother, Reese, surrounded by candlelight, roses, and "dancing music" a little comical, the love between him and his bride-to-be radiated an intoxicating rightness.

They fit together, not quite like biscuits and gravy but a solid shrimp and grits. Dee's high-class style, refined but gentle ways, and more reserved nature, with Reese's country ease, tender-hearted humor, and faithful care. If her brother was brave enough to step into a marriage after the way his heart had been broken by his first wife, couldn't Rainey?

She placed the last fork down just as she heard the other guests approaching from outside. Emma had wrangled her into leaving the rehearsal early to make it to the barn venue in time to help set up for dinner, but there wasn't much her baby sister really needed except moral support. Emma buzzed around, spreading her happy charm everywhere she went. The talent she'd always possessed for hosting and cooking blended seamlessly in this first attempt.

Rainey grinned as she took in the room. Bouquets of sunflowers sprang brilliant color from the center of each table, with a frosted-painted mason jar on either side glowing brightly with candlelight.

Emma had used barn crates as stands for various flower arrangements and decorative signs, ones she'd hand painted, no doubt. White paper globes suspended from the barn's rafters by faux vines and twinkle lights lit the entire room with a magical appearance. Class and country charm.

The wedding party appeared in the doorway, a joyful procession with Reese and Dee bringing up the rear, arm in arm. The two laughed, completely smitten with each other, and Rainey's heart squeezed with thanksgiving.

She knew the scars he bore. She'd lived them too. The betrayal. The grief. And six, even four months ago, she would have never believed a second chance at romance—or maybe, if she really thought about it, a first chance at the right kind of romance—would come her way.

As if in response to her little daydream, a handsome figure stepped through the door into the farm-fashioned fairyland. Dee suggested Rainey invite him to the dinner as her date, and Rainey was more than willing to comply. As a matter of fact, Alex Murdock taking up space in her life and heart was quickly becoming a must.

She'd already secured him as her wedding date, a nice change from her usual solo attendance. If she knew him, he might even try to talk her into dancing. Her grin grew. He'd definitely try.

As if Prince Charming wasn't sweet enough, he'd asked if Sarah could be his date to the petting zoo before the wedding while Rainey completed all the matron of honor duties. He even promised to drop Sarah off at Mama's house in plenty of time for Mama to get her ready for the wedding. The man knew exactly which heartstrings to tug.

He didn't see her at first, giving her the advantage of watching the moment he did. His gaze scanned past before ricocheting to focus on her face, his look of expectancy slipping into surprise. Then, as if in slow motion, he froze, his palm rested over his chest, and his smile took an easy trip from one cheek to the other.

If someone could grow beautiful in a second, Rainey did. She couldn't ignore the transformation that occurred when Alex looked at her. Unsheathed and mesmerizing, the way he saw her—as if she were the most beautiful woman in the world—reflected in his eyes. The contorted image Gray's harsh words left behind dissipated in Alex's sweet adoration.

Love changed things.

Suddenly the wobbly heels felt like glass slippers, and she stood tall, beckoning him forward with her smiling response.

He complied, his attention resolute as he weaved around the tables and people to meet her. With his usual charm, he swept his palm to her waist and pressed a chaste kiss to her cheek, his lips slipping to her ear before he stepped back. "You're breathtaking."

His whisper spread a fiery blast down her neck and tethered her touch to his. She gripped his arm, keeping him from going too far. "I have a very good consultant..." She teased him with a raised brow. "And date."

His eyes glimmered with their mutual love for banter. "Makes it easy when the client is already a stunner." He sobered, his gaze searching hers with an unusual intensity. "I'm so glad the date idea rubbed off on you, even though it's probably not your smartest decision."

"Why are you so surprised?" She slid into a chair, and he took the one beside her.

"I don't have the best track record with fairytale endings, Rain." He gathered her hand into his and stared down at their twined fingers. "And you? You're a strong, independent woman who can certainly take care of herself. I'm not too sure I'm the guy you need."

She tightened her hold on his fingers, never breaking eye contact, hoping he felt the certainty. "I may not *need* you in my life." Her voice strengthened, resolved. "But I *want* you here"—she pointed to her chest—"I'm *choosing* you for me ... and Sarah."

His brow crinkled, and the glimmer in his green eyes glossed with tears. He shook his head and cleared his throat. "And ... um ... why is that? Why would you choose me, Rainey Mitchell?"

She squeezed his hand, adding emphasis to her words. "You do something no one else does. You make me feel beautiful in the way that matters most." Her words hushed to a whisper, and her gaze dropped to the table, away from the intensity in his eyes. "Who I am and who I want to be."

With the sounds of clinging flatware and tinkling glasses in the distance, Alex's palm traced her cheek, bringing her attention back to his face. She bathed in his look of love. Somehow, his expression, vulnerable and powerful at the same time, bridged the gap between them and cherished her without a single spoken word.

She shrugged off the intensity with a grin. "And you're an excellent k-i-s-s-e-r."

His brow tipped in his signature move. "I've been practicing."

"Indeed you have."

His gaze sobered and he tugged her close, one hand around her waist. "You are beautiful, through and through. I'd love to spend a really long time reminding you of how God has made you that way."

Alex's face blurred as tears invaded her vision, but she leaned into him, soaking in the warmth of his affection. "That sounds a whole lot like something a hero would say."

His smile brimmed, inspiring her own before he sealed their spoken and unspoken promises with a gentle touch of his lips. "Don't get your hopes up, but maybe loving you will turn this troublemaker into a hero."

Chapter Twenty-two

Alex wrestled his tie into submission in front of the mirror, his grin spreading to ridiculous proportions.

He was in love with a wonderful girl.

Actually, with two.

He and Sarah had a blast at the petting zoo on a local farm near the Blue Ridge Parkway and then had stopped in for an ice cream cone. It was difficult to simply ease into a ready-made family when he actually wanted to grab with both hands and hold on forever.

With Sarah naturally reaching up to take his hand as they walked from goat to sheep to chicken, his heart settled right into this family becoming a regular part of his everyday life. He never wanted to let go.

Home began and ended right here. With them.

He didn't need more months to sort it out through dating trials. He knew.

With a last tuck to the tie, he hummed some praise song he'd heard at church the past week, half fitting in words and half making them up. He didn't deserve all of this goodness, all of these second, third, and fourth chances, but he was beginning to understand more and more that God didn't quite work like humans did.

"I'm blown away by it, Haus." The furry fellow raised his head from his curled position on the rug by the door. "God's grace? It's mind-blowing."

Haus lowered his head back onto his paws as if the information was commonplace knowledge for a dog. Well, for a messed-up human, the very idea took his monochrome world and shifted it into megawatt color. Alex had stepped from Kansas to Oz.

One bite of a half-eaten sandwich later, he turned on his computer. He had a good half hour before he needed to leave for the church and openly gawk over his lovely date. If Rainey looked anywhere close to as beautiful as she did the night before, Alex might not be able to drum up words at all.

He checked a few e-mails, well-wishing a few worrywart students a great spring break. One e-mail brought an immediate smile to his face—they'd received another donation to TLC. And a sizeable one at that. Rainey still didn't have enough to keep the clinic running, but...

He sauntered over to the front window and peered out. The truck from the garage waited in the driveway, a new fixture in his life since the mechanic at the body shop in town took Alex up on his offer to sell Marilyn after the car accident. Alex's grin took on a double stretch. And now a colorful envelope, decorated by none other than the budding artist, Sarah Mitchell, waited on Rainey's kitchen counter to cover the remainder of TLC's need.

He'd used his private account through his father's business, so Rainey wouldn't immediately pin the gift back to him and in response try to return the check, but he couldn't help almost dancing back to his computer from sheer joy.

Why hadn't he thought of it sooner?

He paused another bite of the sandwich. Because he wouldn't have thought of it sooner. His plans and needs, his wound-licking, kept him more inward focused than outward, but, boy oh boy, what a great feeling to be there for another person. The only thing better would be adding a ring to the fourth finger on Rainey's left hand ... and those plans were definitely rolling around in his head.

Probably a bit too soon for the stubborn blonde, though.

A buzz on his right alerted him to an incoming call, and he snatched his vibrating blue cell phone. A chat with Evie dotted the day with a cherry.

"Hey, sis."

"Alex, I'm so glad you were able to answer."

Her words came breathless, igniting his alarm. "Are you okay?"

"Yes, yes. I'm fine. I just don't have a lot of time. We're on our way to you."

He froze. "What?"

"We were loaded into a car this afternoon, and the police just told me we're arriving at your house within the next hour or two."

Alex sat on a barstool. He understood her words, but the meaning wasn't sinking in.

"You're on your way right now?"

"Yes." Her voice broke. "I can't wait to see you. To hug you."

The words replayed, slowly clicking into comprehension. Realization. "Lily too?"

Evie laughed. "Lily too."

"And it's safe?"

"The police will watch the house the entire time. Yes, we'll be safe."

His chest pumped with exaggerated breaths, almost afraid to believe he'd see his sister soon. "Tonight?"

Her laugh, filled with emotions, echoed again. "Yes. Tonight. In less than two hours."

He released a chuff of air on a laugh, his vision blurring as he looked over "his" dog. "Haus and I will be waiting."

After a few more minutes of shock, the call ended. Alex released a sigh he'd been holding in since watching police sweep Evie and Lily away almost a year ago. Living with the lie of their deaths weighing his heart, engaging in secret phone calls and watching each conversation to ensure he didn't let the secret slip, carried its own unvoiced stress. Now? After so long he'd see them? Hold them?

He wiped a hand over his eyes and blinked the room back into view, focusing on Haus. "I'm gonna see my baby sister tonight, boy."

Haus barely raised an ear.

"You should show a little more excitement, man. There's going to be a five-year-old hugging all over you."

Haus' head popped up as if he understood English. Alex shrugged and stood, his tie slipping onto the counter.

Tie. Rainey. Wedding. He slammed his palm against his forehead and paced across the floor to the window and back. "No, no, no. Tonight of all nights." He took another round of pacing, his mind whirring through solutions. He couldn't leave. The wedding started in less than an hour, and Evie would arrive soon after.

He couldn't go.

He groaned and slammed his fist against the counter as he passed it. "Lord, what are you doing?"

With a hesitant tug, he unknotted his tie, picked up his other cell phone, and punched in Rainey's number. "Forgive me, Rainey. Please, forgive me."

The wedding went off perfectly. Rainey grinned at the happy couple entering the reception area, Dee adorned in a simple, elegant white gown and Reese, clean-shaven, in a classy tuxedo. A beautiful pair.

Like last night, she looked toward the door, wondering how she'd missed Alex in the congregation of well-wishers. He rarely blended into a crowd. Her face warmed with the memory of their evening kiss, and her lips tingled with anticipation of a repeat, but Alex didn't show.

She searched the room, but he wasn't among the crowd. Something was wrong.

With a quick walk to the coat room, she found her purse and drew out her cell phone. Two calls from Alex? And one message?

She slid her thumb over the message to open it.

RAINEY, PLEASE FORGIVE ME! A FAMILY EMERGENCY KEEPS ME FROM JOINING YOU AT THE WEDDING TONIGHT. WOULD YOU SHARE MY CONGRATS WITH THE HAPPY COUPLE? I PROMISE TO MAKE UP FOR MY ABSENCE WHEN I SEE YOU NEXT. FORGIVE ME.

She reread the message, then returned the cell phone to her purse. What could have happened? A sudden illness with his sister or father?

But why wouldn't he have said as much?

Had a demand from his father pulled Alex away?

Her expression must have inspired a little concern because the bride slipped from the dance floor to Rainey's side.

"You look distracted."

Rainey shot Dee a tight smile. "Who wouldn't be tonight? The wedding really was one of the most beautiful I've seen."

A rush of pleasant pink bloomed in Dee's face along with her smile. "It was like a dream."

"One of the best kinds."

Dee's gaze searched the room. "And where is your date? I know he was looking forward to spending this evening with you. He could barely contain his excitement when we last spoke."

Rainey kept her face forward, burying the disappointment. "He had some ... family emergency. I ... I just found out about it."

"Oh, what a disappointment for both of you, I'm sure." Dee shook her head, catching her breath between dances. "Things have been weird with his family ever since his sister died, so this isn't much of a surprise to me. He was distracted before, mind you, but after her death, well, it seemed the humor became more obvious."

"A defense mechanism of grief?"

"I didn't see it as that at the time. I just found him annoying. But now, looking back … definitely."

Rainey stared out over the joyous crowd, the string quartet filling the twinkly-lit room with a magical ambience. Alex had never given her many details about Evie's and Lily's deaths—only that they'd died in a car accident, and he'd been the driver. After meeting Eli Murdock and seeing the hard resentment from father to son, there was no knowing what sort of mangled healing process Alex's heart attempted to make. Humor was certainly the lesser of two detrimental choices. "I can't imagine how hard it must have been for him."

"When I was his graduate assistant, that last semester, Alex would have these moments where he would leave to take a phone call at the oddest of times. He had a period of time he gave all the teaching over to me." Dee smiled. "He even got irritable with me a few times, which, despite his many personality flaws, was unusual for him. He's not a grumpy sort."

"Grief shows itself in different ways for different people," Rainey admitted, giving the benefit of the doubt for her AWOL date.

"Of course." Dee nodded. "I wasn't as gracious as you at the time because I was too hung up on my own plans to notice anyone else's pain." Her brow furrowed. "Other than the absent professor bit, the only other strange things that happened were the mysterious phone calls."

Rainey paused, more questions than answers buzzing through her mind. Those phone calls had been happening since his sister's death? Alex referred to them as family emergency calls, so if they'd begun almost a year ago… What could they mean?

"And these mysterious phone calls weren't going on before his sister's death?"

"Not that I remember."

Reese walked out of the crowd toward them, his clean-shaven face still an unfamiliar transformation in his twitter-pated journey with Dee. He did look mighty handsome, though. So much like their dad.

"I'm pretty sure I'm supposed to have your undivided attention tonight, Mrs. Mitchell."

"And I'm pretty sure that undivided attention starts a little later in the evening."

Rainey's palm shot out. "Okay, okay. I'm happy for both of you and all, but please be merciful to my sister-brain. The wedding kiss was enough to make me squirm. Don't torture me anymore."

"Rainey Mitchell, that kiss was simply divine." Dee's hand went to the hips of her sleek bodice. "And fairly chaste."

Reese's un-whiskered grin curled, and he tugged Dee against his side. "I'll be glad to offer a do-over right now, if you want, sis."

Rainey pointed her finger at her rascally brother. "Don't even."

"Then I'm taking my wife back over here to the dance floor and practicing my new footwork." He nuzzled a kiss to Dee's cheek, and her eyes sparkled as she leaned into him. "Let's go, Doc."

Rainey slipped back to the edge of the room, watching from the fringe like she'd done the past few years. Tonight was supposed to be different, not a lonely repeat of wedding parties past, but here she stood, dolled up better than she'd ever been, alone.

She shrugged off the melancholy and tipped her gaze upward. What was wrong with her? Alex wouldn't have canceled for anything except a solid emergency. Whatever his secret, she'd choose to trust him.

And her own heart.

"Oh, Alex, I feel awful! You missed the wedding?" Evie sat next to him on the couch, her feet tucked beneath her, glass in hand. "Poor Rainey."

"It's not like we have a lot of wiggle room in choices, Evie." He tipped his head toward the police officer stationed by the front door, just out of sight from any of the windows. His thoughts swayed between Rainey's disappointment at his absence tonight and his own melancholy blended with joy at his sister's visit. He'd make it up to Rainey and someday, hopefully soon, he'd explain everything. As for his own emotions … those would be harder to curb. "Our circumstances are pretty unique, and I *had* to see you while I had the chance."

She covered his hand resting on the back of the couch with hers. "I know. I just hate it took this night of all nights. You'd been looking forward to it."

"Well, I hope to have many more evenings with Rainey Mitchell."

"From the number of photos of the two of you and Sarah on your phone, I'd say you're smitten."

His palm slammed to his chest. "Slain to the core." He ran his palm over Lily's hair, her head resting on a pillow on his lap. She'd fallen asleep almost an hour ago, but he couldn't move her back to the bedroom. Not when he didn't know when he'd get another chance to see her. "Rainey's the one for me. I just have to convince her."

"It sounds to me like she has a really good idea of it already."

Alex looked down at sleeping Lily and pulled the blanket up closer to her chin. "I hope so, Evie. She's been through a lot of heartbreak. I'd love to be the hero she deserves."

"You've changed." She breathed in deeply and surveyed him with those shimmery golden eyes of hers. Their mother's eyes. "There's this ... I don't know what to call it. Peace, maybe? Maturity. Your soul seems quieter." She chuckled and shook her head. "If that makes any sense."

"It does." His answer drew her attention back to him. "I finally stopped wrestling with God and realized I couldn't work out my life with wit and charm. Our lives are messes, Evie." He waved a hand between them, the gesture encompassing the room. "Look at this? It's a total mess. I've been irresponsible and selfish and arrogant. And this entire situation has only proven my lack of strength and control. I *need* God. I need His grace because life is messy, the future is unpredictable, and my own heart craves revenge and selfish things."

She studied him, quiet for a moment, her gaze taking on a sheen. "You've really bought into it all. Even Dad noticed."

"Did he? That didn't come through in our interaction."

Evie cringed. "Yeah, I heard it was rather explosive. Escorted out of the building and all?"

"Well, to be honest, it wasn't the first time I'd been escorted from his office."

She chuckled. "True. Your first few years of college were certainly a trying time for Dad."

"For Dad?" Alex shot a mock glare to his sister. "What about me? I had to live with the man trying to conform me into his slick and stainless steel image."

Evie's chuckle dimmed to a smile. "You've never been like him, but ... we've talked. I think he's beginning to understand how much you've really done to protect me and Lily." She squeezed his hand again. "Dad could tell a difference in you too." She looked down at Lily and gently patted her legs. "It's God in you. How?"

"He wouldn't let me go." Alex grinned, the sweet swell of love pouring like a fresh ray of sunlight through his chest. "It's going to sound trite and silly, but God caught me, Evie. I'd seen glimpses of Him for years but was too wrapped up in my own world to notice ... or care. But when I came here, He caught me. His love *wouldn't* let me go, and I understood I didn't want to go anywhere else. That's what you see in me. I'm not running anymore. I'm not spinning tires in the mud trying to find a solution to my pain." Alex shrugged. "I still struggle with being human, and my kind of human at that." His grin reflected the joy he'd found in God's love and acceptance of him exactly as he was. "But more and more, I'm not defined by the fear or second-guessing. I belong to Him."

She blinked and tears sprang a tiny trail down her cheeks. "I want that too, Alex. I *need* Him too."

One faint light glowed in the farmhouse as Rainey drove past. She slowed, almost stopped, then continued to her house. It was almost 1:00 a.m., for goodness sakes. What was she thinking? Sarah was sleeping over with Lou at Mama's, so Rainey stayed at the barn reception to help Emma clean up. She hadn't expected to see Alex at home. Hadn't he traveled to Fairfax for a family emergency?

She stilled her car in her driveway and stepped out, peering down to the farmhouse. And Rusty's pickup truck sat in the driveway? Where was Marilyn?

Something wasn't right.

Her natural curiosity bowed to some good old-fashioned suspicion. She tossed her purse into the house, replaced her heels with tennis shoes, and snatched a flashlight. She took the thin trail down the wooded path between their houses instead of the longer trek on the road. The trees shadowed the moon's glow like spindling arms along her path. She knew these woods as well as the shoes on her feet, probably even better, but tonight something felt different.

She looked back over her shoulder, listening in the dark. To be a native of these mountains and hills, the familiar sounds, and even the quiet surrounding her, usually brought comfort. Tonight, however, the silence seeped to an unnatural slumber.

She couldn't shake the feeling that someone watched her.

The night crawled with its usual shadows, but the farmhouse stood particularly dark, except for the lone light from the living room. She scanned her surroundings before stepping onto the lawn surrounding the house. If Haus had been outside, she'd have felt better. Something about having a dog nearby sent a sense of comradery, which reminded her she needed to seriously consider a visit to the animal shelter in the near future.

Rainey flipped off her flashlight and approached the house. Going to the front porch would be a bit too obvious, in the strange instance Alex was actually home and awake. She approached the window on the farthest edge of the porch, careful to slide up the steps without a creak. The drawn curtain blocked her view. Curtains drawn? Did Alex ever draw the curtains?

Her pulse skittered up a notch, and she sent another glance behind her, unable to shake the sense of someone nearby. Unmoving shadows whispered an April breeze back to her.

She really should just give up and go home.

Nibbling at her bottom lip and pausing long enough to consider her lunacy, she slipped to the next window with the same result. View closed.

The ground sloped a little downward so that by the time she made it to the third window, she could barely see above the window seal. She was ridiculous, an utter loon. And desperate. Standing outside a man's home—well, technically her family's home, so that part wasn't creepy ... much—on tiptoe in her beautiful teal fairie-dress, wearing tennis shoes, at night, and peeking through a window.

Her mama would be so disappointed. And Trigg would be laughing. So would Reese.

Emma would probably be sighing in some crazy attempt to find romance in the scenario.

Murmurs brought her higher onto her tiptoes, and the sound of a high-pitched voice nearly catapulted her through the window. By the faint lamplight and her currently unsteady position, she could make out the tops of two heads from the chins up. *Two.*

She lost her balance but gripped the window to keep from tumbling to the grass in her pretty dress. Heat slipped from her face, stinging with an extra chill around her heart. No, she couldn't have seen right.

The faint hint of a woman's laughter drilled the doubt deeper. No, no, no. She pinched her eyes closed. Her hearing and her vision were playing tricks now. She scrambled back on her tiptoes and peered to see Alex touching the woman's face. A beautiful woman with enviable blond curls.

Rainey's foothold gave way again. Her body and her heart sank to the cold ground, her thoughts battling for understanding and jabbing against the truth on the other side of the wall. How could she have been wrong again? He'd fooled everyone, even her mama.

Her fingers fisted the grass, tangling the earth until it clumped cold in her palms. She was an idiot. Again. Trusting her deceptive heart over her head. And Sarah? A sharp pain stabbed through her chest, erupting a sob. Her sweet girl loved the deceptive, smooth-talking jerk too.

Loved? She pushed herself up from the ground and threw the dirt down with an anticlimactic swish to the earth. Stupid emotions. Stupid heart. How had he tricked her so well? She squeezed her eyes closed and stumbled forward, pressing the tears inside. Alex Murdock didn't deserve her tears.

What he deserved was ... was something painful and embarrassing and probably illegal.

But mostly painful—and similar to the searing puncture spilling hurt through her middle. Alex Murdock and all those sweet dreams she'd put her faith in proved one truth. She could never trust her heart again.

Chapter Twenty-three

The faintest hint of dawn haloed the distant mountains as Alex helped Evie and Lily take their bags to the waiting unmarked car. Time flew by. He and Evie had stayed awake all night, talking, laughing, sometimes crying. Seeing her alive crippled the year-long wait a little.

After a quick goodbye, he turned to the two officers who were in mid-conversation.

"The night appears to have gone without incidence?" Calvin, the main officer assigned to Evie, said to the secondary officer, Lane, who'd kept watch on the house through the night.

"Yes, sir. Nothing of consequence to really report. Just one episode of suspicious activity."

Calvin paused in his turn and glanced to Alex, before continuing the questioning. "Suspicious activity?"

"Nothing I'd consider dangerous, just odd."

After hesitating, Calvin inquired for more information, and Lane's description turned Alex's heart inside out. "Some blonde, a neighbor from the looks of it, tried to peek in the windows around 1:00 a.m., sir, but she didn't stay very long before making her way back to the neighboring house. I didn't want to draw unnecessary attention to our situation, knowing the vital need for secrecy, so I made the judgment call to observe instead of confront."

"Oh, no. Rainey." Alex rubbed his palm against his chin and groaned. How would he ever talk his way out of this one?

"And you did not engage?" Calvin confirmed, sending a glance to Alex from his periphery.

"I was under strict orders to only engage if the situation turned dangerous, sir. A young woman in a blue dress and tennis shoes peeping through a window with no apparent weapon didn't appear a threat."

Only to Alex's future. His heart.

Calvin's steely gaze swung to Alex. "Do you know anyone who fits this description, Dr. Murdock?"

Alex's shoulders fell forward. "Yes, my girlfriend."

Calvin's eyebrows rose. "Well, I'm relieved it's someone you know, but I don't envy your task of explaining this situation."

Alex ran a palm over his face. "Me neither."

"Any idea what she saw, Lane?" Calvin turned to his fellow officer.

Lane shrugged, shadows lining his gray eyes after the all-nighter. "With the curtains drawn in the other windows, and the height of the window she may have reached, she couldn't have seen much."

"Enough to draw conclusions and maybe even recognize Evie," Alex said, glancing toward her house in the dim haze of pre-dawn.

"You trust her?"

"Emphatically."

Calvin nodded and rested his palms on his hips. "If she didn't recognize your sister, you need to keep to the script. Your niece and sister are not out of danger. Anyone who knows she's alive could be at risk. You understand?"

"All too well." Alex waved to Lily, who sat in the back seat of the car as Lane moved into the driver's seat.

"Good luck, son." Calvin's words offered little consolation.

Either conclusion ended poorly.

The sun barely dusted the morning sky when Alex jogged from his front door to Rainey's shortly after Evie and Lily left, praying with each pound of his foot to the ground. A dampness, cooled with the chill of early spring, clung to the morning air, filling his lungs and adding to the uneasy clutch in his stomach. He'd lived in a catch-22 world for almost a year, and this might be the worst scenario yet.

God, please help Rainey understand.

But every possible conclusion ended in the same result. He'd lied—and this was a woman who didn't need a man lying to her.

She opened the door, her glorious hair raining around her in a disorganized tangle and those aqua eyes more brilliant from the puffy red-rimmed skin surrounding them. She glared, shooting a million daggers at him. He deserved each one.

Yet again, he'd lost something important to him despite his best efforts. He was hopelessly caught.

His emotions dangled between running for cover and gathering this beautiful, wounded woman in his arms. How could he fix this? Rainey's jaw tightened, but beneath the tension her expression knifed through his chest with staggering clarity.

He couldn't be her hero now. He'd become the villain.

Her hand paused on the doorknob, and her face hardened to impassive. "Rainey."

"Leave. Now. I don't want to see you again."

He took another step forward, palms out, begging with every nonverbal signal he could muster. "Can't we just talk about things. Last night isn't what you think—"

Nothing prepared him for the impact of her palm against his cheek. He actually lost his footing from the force. "Don't you dare minimize my intelligence with a flimsy excuse."

He rubbed his cheek but held her gaze. "I would never minimize your—"

"I saw her, Alex. I saw your little blond family emergency. I was even pathetic enough to catch her leaving in a dark car just before daybreak."

Her accusation and the painful birth of interpretation punched the air from his lungs. She didn't recognize Evie. No, she imagined something worse. His apparent betrayal had reopened the hurt he'd hoped his love had healed. And there was nothing he could do about it.

"I know what it looked like, Rainey, but some things aren't as they appear."

Her brow etched high. "A woman didn't spend the night in your house last night?"

He groaned and hung his head. "Yes, but not in the way you're imagining."

A ruthless smile twisted her lips. "Then explain it, Dr. Murdock. I'd love to hear you charm your way out of this one."

He dared another step forward, jamming his hands in his pockets to keep from reaching for her in a vain attempt to wipe the pain from those eyes. "I can't, but I'm asking you to trust me despite what you've seen."

She laughed, a humorless, hollow sound, twisting the ache in his chest tighter. "Trust you? I didn't slap you hard enough." Her bottom lip quivered. "How could I ever trust you? You knew my past, what happened to me. And you turned around and did the same thing. You can't love me and do something like that."

"I do love you."

She sneered and looked away.

He edged a step closer. "You're the only woman I want to spend the rest of my life with. Just you."

"But you'll plan a sleepover with someone else?" Her frown deepened and she jabbed her finger into his chest, hitting at the growing ache around his heart. "I'm not into sharing."

"I know it doesn't make sense, but I promise you, nothing romantic happened last night. Nothing. I can't explain it right now, but it's true."

"You can't explain it right now?" She rolled her eyes. "How convenient! You know, you're a great liar. I actually believed all your stories about your family and your fiancée." Tears swam in those beautiful aqua eyes, stabbing a fresh wound in Alex's heart. "I believed in you."

"And I'm that same person. I've not changed." He gathered her hand into his. "All those stories were true. Real. Like what's between us."

She jerked her hand free from his hold. "You are a liar." The tiniest tear escaped the boundaries of her eyes and slipped down her cheek. His heart squeezed. "And I not only believed you, I…" Her breath shook and her gaze searched his with the faintest glimmer of hope. She leaned toward him, almost in request for an embrace he'd gladly give.

He slid his palms down her shoulders, coaxing her forward, praying her heart won over her doubt. "I promise you, Rainey, I've not done what you think I have. I wouldn't, ever."

His words jarred her from giving into the embrace. She jerked back and shook her head, spilling more tears free. "You're too good at this game, and I don't want to play anymore."

"Rainey, please."

"Leave me and my daughter alone, Alex."

She turned toward him, hand on the door, hesitating for a second as she searched his face again.

"Rainey—"

"No." She shook her head, pushed him away from the threshold, and slammed the door, silencing his plea.

He pinched his burning eyes closed and rested his forehead against the door as if his thoughts and intentions could press through the panels to reach her.

"You know me, Rainey, in your heart." His voice carried little volume, but he pressed forward. "Please know me well enough to doubt your doubts."

Rainey waited until late afternoon, checking the farmhouse every hour to note when Alex drove off and the coast was clear. Why he had that truck was beyond her. Nothing about him made sense.

If she hadn't seen with her own eyes the woman at Alex's house, heard Alex's plea, his sincere request would make her question it all. But there was no mistake. She might not have seen Alex and the woman kiss, but he'd never tried to deny it happened. He only asked her to trust him.

Did she really look that stupid?

Rainey squeezed her eyes closed. Clearly, she *was* pretty stupid. Falling for the same kind of man again. The charmer with a wayward heart.

Nothing romantic happened. How naive did he think she was?

Her steps faltered at the door, memory after memory sloshing her anger. But he didn't give away any hints to a wayward heart at all. Not like Gray, whose red flags started months before she'd discovered the truth.

The only hint came from those phone calls.

The hurt from Alex's betrayal resurrected with a fury, so Rainey dulled her mind from trying to sort out the situation. She'd survived once and she'd do it again. With a quick sweep of her hair into a ponytail, she took her purse from the counter and left the house. She was going to spend the day with Sarah, far away from Mitchell's Crossroads and Alex Murdock.

Sarah and Lou greeted her from the tire swing in the front yard as Rainey pulled up to her mama's house. She drew in a breath for strength. It would take a miracle to get in and out of there without having to divulge the entire story. Her mama held some sort of mindreading super power. Always had. Of course, she never minded Mama using her powers on her siblings. In fact, sometimes it entertained Rainey's little "do-gooder" personality, but she wasn't ready to hear about God's plan, forgiveness, or anything remotely nice related to Alex Murdock. All she wanted to do for a day was disappear—pretend the last four months never happened, and sort out a way to step back into her life without falling apart.

She hated crying.

The alarming scent of cleaner mixed with bleach burned Rainey's nose as she entered. Boxed pizza waited on the counter? *Boxed* pizza. What was going on?

"Mama?" No answer. Rainey stepped farther into the kitchen. Her mama never ordered pizza. "Mama?"

A call responded from the open door of the basement, followed by some muffled conversation. Finally her mother emerged from the stairway, her white shirt covered in dirt.

"What on earth are you doing?"

Her mother's eyes glowed with a ready smile. "Spring cleanin'. Uncle Jim's been helping me go through some of these ancient boxes downstairs, and we've made all sorts of discoveries. Did you know my granny left some love letters in a steel box?"

Rainey smiled despite her weary inward battle. "You've wanted to clean out those boxes for years."

"And now I'm just frustrated it took me so long. There's one trunk we haven't opened yet, but it looks as old as time. I think it's been good for Jim too. He has lots of memories in those boxes from when he was a young'un." She gestured with her chin toward the pizza. "That pizza place downtown ain't half bad. Don't know why I ain't tried it before now."

"You saw it as a sign of failure to feed a whole gang by the sweat of your brow, I bet."

Her mama chuckled. "I need to stop putting such pressure on myself."

Rainey smiled and took a step back toward the door. "Well, I'm glad you've finally found a cohort for your expedition." She tapped Sarah's bag, waited, all packed and ready to go. Perfect. "Well, the girls seemed to have had a great time together, as usual."

Mama washed her hands in the sink. "They're two peas in a pod."

Rainey pulled Sarah's bag onto her shoulder. "I know they're going to have a lot of adjusting to do next week when Lou moves. I'm glad they had time together today. Where's Brandon?"

"Emma took him for some ice cream. I think she's going to be hurting more from that little boy leaving than anybody." Mama opened up the refrigerator and pulled out a container. "Except me, of course."

"Of course." Rainey started toward the door. "I'll be back to pick up Lou in a few days. The girls can have a sleepover at my house, okay?"

Mama peeled back the lid of her container to reveal a fresh batch of fudge. The weeping woman's happy drug. "You in a hurry today?"

Rainey fought the pull. "Just have some things to do."

Mama looked back down at the fudge, then sliced a piece, setting it out on a little plate like a trap. "Well, I imagine you have enough time for your Grandma Ruthy's favorite fudge recipe, don't you?"

"Thanks," Rainey said and patted her stomach, "but I haven't gotten my run in the past few days, so I could do without the extra calories."

Mama waved the chocolate-covered knife. "You're an awful liar, you know that? You always have been."

"What are you talking about?"

Mama shook her head and gestured to the barstool. "I'm your mama. You don't think I can tell you've been cryin'? And the last time you turned down a chocolate sweet made in this house, you'd gotten your first, and only, bad student-teaching evaluation. So what's wrong?"

Rainey hesitated, the riptide of emotions surging to the surface, but the tender love in her mama's eyes drew the entire story out within a few minutes, complete with tears … and a few pieces of fudge.

"I can't believe I was so stupid again." Rainey hit her forehead with the heel of her hand. "To think Alex Murdock would be any better than Gray…" The wound ripped wide, releasing all the doubts into existence. "I gave up my heart. I trusted him, but I wasn't enough. Why can't I be enough?"

"Whoa there, girl. Let's set your thinkin' straight first." Mama rounded the counter and sat on the stool beside Rainey. If she was sitting down, this was going to be a serious conversation. "Good enough? The only man who ever needs to define your worth is your Savior. Not Gray. Not Alex. You are priceless in God's eyes."

Rainey reached for a paper towel to catch her tears. Priceless? Her heart failed to recognize the truth her head accepted.

"It was a fearful step you took walking back into a relationship, make no mistake, but the two situations aren't the same. Even as you told me about Alex's response, they sounded so different."

"Right," Rainey scoffed, digging in for another piece of fudge. "I caught this mistake before I got married."

"No. Gray gave off warnings, but Alex hasn't. Somethin' ain't fittin' in all this. Why didn't he make up an excuse? He just told you he *couldn't* tell you the truth, but it wasn't what you thought, right?"

Rainey nodded, taking a bite of the fudge. "How could it be anything else?" Rainey twisted the question around in her mind, sifting through possibilities. "And if it was something benign, why didn't he just tell me what it was? It was like he couldn't tell the truth, which sounds ridiculous. He's a grown man."

Mama sliced another sliver of fudge. "I can't help but believe Alex has been genuine."

"Or a really good actor." Rainey tossed her half-eaten piece of fudge onto the plate and groaned. "When will I learn? How could I have been so stupid again?"

"Stop it, Rainey." Her mom's firm response stilled Rainey's self-beating. "You're a smart woman with a good head on your shoulders. Remember *who* you are and stop listenin' to the lies. These men don't define you, do they?"

"No."

"They didn't strip you of your common sense, did they?"

She hesitated, and her mother pinned her with a look until Rainey answered. "No?"

"No, they didn't. You're still the same smart woman you were all along, so let's try and sort this whole mess out, if we can. There have to be clues? Hints? Somethin'."

Rainey dried her eyes and spun thoughts through her head. Images of Sarah and Alex emerged first. She smiled even as she wiped away a tear. "He cares about Sarah. I don't think anyone could fake it as well as he did."

Mama nodded. "I agree with you there. It came too natural to be pretend, if my eyes work at all."

And no one could have faked his poor teaching. Then he'd helped her with the grants, and the fear on his face when he thought he'd hurt her or Sarah in the car accident? No, she couldn't deny his care. A flood of warmth rushed into her cheeks at the memory of his cuddles by the fire, his kiss.

She cleared her throat and shot to her feet, reality dousing the tangible reminiscence with a sharp sting. "But how can we explain away the fact that a woman spent the night in his house? We can't ignore that, Mama."

"I ain't ignoring it. I'm trying to make sense of it."

Rainey ran her fingers through her hair and resumed pacing. "A lapse in judgement. I have a feeling he's got a track record to support that theory."

"Do you think he would have done something like this with Beth?"

The thought of his former fiancée, the photos and stories he'd shared, niggled the doubt brighter and pulled her steps to a stop. "No, I can't imagine that. He seemed to really love her ... but who can really know?"

"I reckon *you* can. I never doubted your daddy's faithfulness to me. There were other things that drove me batty about the sweet man, but not his faithfulness."

"But that was *you*." She waved her hand to her saintly mother. "And *Daddy*. You can't be compared with us regular folks."

"There you go again with your pedestals. Don't put me or your daddy on one. We both have feet of clay like the rest of the world, but I wouldn't go convictin' poor Alex just yet, either."

"Ugh." Rainey's feet started moving again. "What else could it be, then? A ghost?" She laughed. "Looked pretty real to me. A childhood friend? Why wouldn't he just say so instead of being all mysterious and weird about it?"

"That's right. Seems he'd either give a bald-faced lie or speak out the truth to save face with you. So what would cause a body to withhold information ... like he's trying to hide or protect somethin'."

Rainey stopped at the counter and pressed her fingers into her forehead. "What do you mean? Like something illegal?" She blinked her eyes wide. "Actually, at the moment I'd prefer him to be a criminal over a cheating jerk. I'd like him better."

"Rainey." Mama sighed despite the grin tugging at her lips.

"Oh, come on." Rainey slid back onto the stool, the tension in her shoulders relaxing for a moment's reprieve in the humor. "If he were harboring a fugitive, that'd be a lot easier to swallow than his choosing another woman over me, right?"

Mama paused her hand on the fudge and tilted her head as if an idea sparked in that curly-haired head of hers.

"What?"

Mama blinked back to the conversation. "Nothin', I reckon." She shook her head and took another sliver of fudge. "Just tryin' to piece it all together. One thing's for certain—you ain't going to figure out the answers by runnin' away from Alex. If you have enough doubts to make you question what you've seen, then the only way to get to the bottom of it is to talk to him."

Rainey's palms came up in defense. "Or I just need to steer clear of relationships. Label me a spinster. I'd rather have a withered-up old heart any day over a stripped raw and bleeding one."

"You won't be satisfied runnin' away, Rainey. You have too many questions."

Rainey stood and snatched Sarah's bag. "Not today. I can't talk to him today. I don't even want to look at him. I'm going to take Sarah to Roanoke for some fun and distraction."

"Listen to me, Rainey Mitchell." Mama rounded the counter and took Rainey into a hug. "Don't forget who you are." She pulled back, keeping her palms on Rainey's shoulders and locking that gray gaze into her daughter's. "You are not defined by what any man, except Jesus, thinks of you, so after you clear your head, pray, get your distance, remember who's really holdin' you, girl. Without fail. Remember whose love is faithful, then use those smarts and strong heart of yours to find out the truth."

He had the audacity to show up at church the next day. She couldn't even grieve for a few days in peace. But at least Alex had the courtesy to sit in the back, away from the family—though she wasn't sure whether that caused more rumors or not. He'd been by her side for weeks.

To add insult to injury, it seemed like the preacher was in cahoots with Alex, talking about how God uses unexpected circumstances to bring about extraordinary things ... even when the circumstances look questionable at first.

"Remember, faith is trusting in what we can't see, but what we know." The pastor's words nudged like an annoying brother.

She groaned. The world was conspiring against her well-constructed self-confidence, and she wanted to run from the church like she did when she jogged away from the Spencer dogs nipping at her heels.

Forgiveness? Unexpected circumstances? She narrowed her eyes at the preacher as if he had a hidden agenda—every word, every line somehow rattling her doubts further. She closed her eyes during the final hymn, "All to Jesus I Surrender," and breathed in a prayer.

She'd complained and cried more than prayed since yesterday. Muttered more than sought. God understood all of that, she knew, but He was the only one who provided the absolute truth, regardless of what anyone hid.

Remember who you are.

The words whispered through her soul, calming the ache with a gentle brush of love. She soaked in the truth. God, in his unfathomable love, took on anguish to give her joy, bore agony to secure her peace, fought the dragons of evil to rescue her. She was beautiful to him. Loved, eternally, by him.

She had nothing to prove ... and at the core, nothing to lose.

She surrendered.

"Dr. Alex!" Sarah ran to him at the end of the service and wrapped her arms around his leg, her smile beaming with unfettered acceptance. Oh, how Rainey half wished she could return to such blissful ignorance. "Why didn't you sit with us today?"

He ran his palm down Sarah's curls, his smile so tender it flashed doubt to life like a warning ... or a reminder. Could she forgive him?

"I came in late, princess. Didn't want to disturb the service."

"Are you comin' to Granny's with us?"

Alex's gaze found Rainey's, a question flickering to life in his eyes before dimming behind a sad smile. Her heart hurt.

"Not today. I have some things I need to see to." He looked miserable.

She stiffened her chin. He deserved it. But Rainey's hollow victory only reverberated off the hurt in her chest, swelling the pain. He was a horrible liar. Her heart hitched at the recognition, and the sweet balm of God's love reminded her.

Regardless of the circumstances, remember who you are.

"Okay." Sarah hugged him again and hopped off after Lou. Rainey attempted to pass, but Alex caught her arm in a gentle hold. "I would never hurt you, Rainey. Never."

"Then what happened?" *Please, Alex. Prove my doubts wrong.* "Tell me the truth."

His gaze fell to the ground, his jaw worked, and those green eyes came back to hers. "Sometimes people do things to protect others that may not look acceptable on the outside, but underneath it's the right choice. You *know* me. I'm not like Gray. You know I'm not."

Some whispered voice in her heart raised its volume to corroborate Alex's plea, warring against her experience, her fear. "I don't know... Alex, if you'd seen what I saw through that window."

His thumb rubbed a tender trail against her sleeve, and his gaze took on a

255

soft entreaty, turning her heart to mush. "I promise, before God and everybody, I have not been unfaithful to you in any way. I love you and you alone."

She tried to pull away. "You can't know that in four months." Her voice broke, rebelling against the lie in her own words, against her own heart.

"I can and I do." He released her with his hands, but his presence, scented with sweet sandalwood, held her close. "Don't give up on me. On us."

Her gaze shot back to his, the weariness around his eyes a mirror of hers. Her heart responded to his, despite her mind's warning. "I ... I'm not ready to talk right now."

Hope breathed to life in his expression. "That's fine."

"Maybe ... maybe tomorrow?"

He almost smiled, and tears brightened the green in his eyes. "Anywhere. Anytime."

She looked away, her mind squeezing with the struggle. "Let's meet at Daphne's. I ... I can't be alone with you."

He nodded, searching her face. Oh, how she wanted to fall into trusting him again. It would be so easy ... and so stupid. *God help me.*

"I'll see if Mom will watch Sarah tomorrow evening. We could meet late, when the restaurant isn't so crowded. Eight, maybe?" Daphne's would close at nine, and she'd have an escape plan if all these good intentions fell apart.

"I'll be there." He touched her arm again, drawing her attention back to his tender expression. "Thank you."

Chapter Twenty-four

Alex spent Sunday on another hike because giving Rainey space and trying not to comfort her almost drove him mad. The wild beauty of the mountains soothed his frustration like a prayer. Spring dawned through colors budding across the countryside in wisps of white, swirls of pale pink, and bursts of lavender.

The cool breeze was scented with damp moss and the faintest hint of honey, probably from the spindly vines Rainey referred to as honeysuckles. As he climbed higher and higher, stomping through his trapped feeling with a sense of purpose, the swelling anticipation of the view quickened his steps. Somehow, rising above the woods and tangles relieved his frustration at the situation and gave him perspective

On he walked, praying, begging, seeking clarity with every step. Before faith changed his life, he'd pumped through his pain by stuffing it deep inside or struggling on his own to fix the mistakes. Oh, the difference now... Even as his chest ached from his sister's situation and the residual pain he'd caused Rainey, Alex clung to the truth of God's love.

Where else could he go? There was no amount of inward strength to replace this sweet connection with Rainey. No human wisdom to outwit the unbelievable scenario of his sister's life. All he could do was believe this God he'd come to trust, to rely on, worked a plan beyond his comprehension.

The vista never disappointed, but today it proved even better than the last time he hiked the area. Today, he found breathing room to see a bigger picture. The forest fell away like curtains from a stage, revealing an endless ocean of gray-blue mountains. If God fashioned such a fathomless scene, complete with details of millions of trees, time-worn ripples, a myriad of plant and animal life, then couldn't He work out this seemingly impossible problem in Alex's life?

He closed his eyes, letting the breeze blow over him, through him, wrapping around him, like a hug from heaven.

You belong to me.

His fists relaxed at his sides, fingers spreading open, and he let go of the situation he couldn't change ... of the trapped life that wasn't a trap at all to God, only a piece in this grand landscape of redemption. Somehow, Evie's pain, Rainey's heartache, and Alex's catch in the middle of it all served a purpose as cosmic as the blue hues of the morning sky.

And as desperately as he wanted Rainey to trust him beyond what she could understand, God was calling Alex's heart to do the very same.

He stayed at the summit, bathing in the warmth of sunlight and contemplation, and started to understand, a little, the connection these natives had with their land. Something, or perhaps Someone, called the heart from these hills. The smooth layers of mountains, rolling to the horizon, calmed, protected, awed, and comforted, blended together like home.

Late afternoon shadows guided his path down the mountainside, and as he reached the bottom, his regular cell phone buzzed.

STOP BY AND SIT A SPELL WHEN YOU GET A MINUTE. MM

He grinned, mist spreading back into his vision. Mama Mitchell saw the truth. She had to. Either that, or she was going to take him to the woodshed, as she teasingly told Reese and Trigg on occasion for being mischief makers. His smile fell. Surely sweet Mama Mitchell wasn't mad at him too?

His other cellphone buzzed to life, reception finally coming in clearer after his long trek through the unwired wilderness.

A text from Evie? That was new.

He shaded the screen to block the glare from the sunlight.

J SPOTTED IN ROANOKE. BE CAREFUL. C CLOSING IN.

C—their code for cops.

Roanoke? Why would John come this far south unless he had another cohort for his state-to-state money laundering scam?

He hopped in his car and started back the hour-and-a-half drive to Ransom. A chat with Mama Mitchell before meeting with Rainey sounded like the perfect prelude to a serious, future-altering discussion.

"Sarah, get your winter coat from the closet and boots, okay, sweet pea? The temperature outside is dropping," Rainey said as she opened the back door of their house. The day away in Roanoke proved enough distance for Rainey to wrangle in her hurricane of emotions enough to feel like she could have a decent conversation with Alex. Whether it proved useful or not? Well, that all depended on Alex, but despite every scar Gray left behind on her heart, she wanted to give Alex the benefit of the doubt. "I'll get your knapsack so you can sleep over at Granny's tonight, okay?"

"Okay," came Sarah's sing-songy reply. "Can I wear my bear boots?"

Rainey held the door open for Sarah to enter, grinning at her adorable daughter. Would Sarah grow into a fashionista like her Aunt Emma? Rainey's grin stilled on her face. What on earth would Rainey do with a fashionista daughter?

"Of course, but put those cat boots back in the closet before you get out another pair. We're only here for a few minutes before we head over to Granny's."

The hallway held an unusual chill. Rainey flipped on the light to break dusk's darkness and stepped over to the thermostat box by the closet door. Curious. The heat should have kicked on at sixty-five degrees, but the air felt more like forty.

Sarah fumbled around in the closet, humming some song about ponies, and Rainey slipped her keys into her pocket with her cellphone, then rounded the hallway entrance into the kitchen with a view of the great room. The temperature continued to drop with each step forward through the dark house. Was her thermostat broken? If so, at least she could sleep in front of the fire tonight and sort out the problem tomorrow.

Suddenly, she froze. The dim lighting from the hallway shone into the great room and revealed an open front window, its screen removed and leaning to the side of the front porch. Her mind took in the snapshot and slowly unraveled the possibilities.

Who would…

And then she felt it, the same discomposing sense she'd carried the last few hours. Being watched. A chill crawled up her arms and descended through her chest.

Someone was in her house.

Every hair on her arms and neck sprang to high alert, every sense jolted awake, and she stepped to the kitchen entrance by the hallway where Sarah still fumbled for her boots.

Oh dear Lord, please help us.

"I knew you weren't dead." A deep voice, unfamiliar and low, filtered in from the dining room.

His dark silhouette hovered in the corner, a shadowy wraith. Her breath choked to a stop.

"You forget I still have eyes and ears in the business, people I trust." The shadow moved, almost imperceptibly. "Your brother shouldn't have visited Eli. The walls have ears, Evie. You know it."

Evie? Rainey took a step back, hemmed in on one side by the stove. "What do you want?"

Her faithful pistol waited in her bedroom on the other side of the dining room, a useless weapon at the moment. Out of her periphery, she saw her cast iron skillet hanging on its usual spot beside the stove. With a quick movement, she slid it off the nail and gripped it behind her back.

"To get rid of evidence."

The man stepped again, rounding the dining room table. Rainey's fingers tightened on the cold iron handle. "I don't know who you are, but I'm not who you're looking for."

"Do you think putting on an accent and a couple of pounds is going to trick me. I saw you with your brother. Watched you out shopping today. You'll never be safe from me, Evie."

Rainey's blood ran cold. He'd followed her all day? To Roanoke? And why did he keep calling her Evie? Alex's dead sister? She backed toward the hallway, contemplating the perfect moment to grab Sarah and run. "I am not Evie. I don't even know who that is. Get out of here."

"Stop with your games." His voice boomed with a fury that reverberated in her chest. "I'm tired of your games." The shadow loomed forward, its dark eyes and face unrecognizable but a perfect target.

"Mama?"

Sarah's voice distracted the man, giving Rainey full access to his face. With as much strength as she could muster, she swung the skillet around and aimed for the intruder's head. She couldn't be sure where she hit him, but as soon as the skillet made contact, she bolted toward the door. He dropped to the floor with a moan, still alive.

Keeping a firm grasp on the skillet, she pulled Sarah from the closet and cast a glance back.

He was still moving, crawling to a stand.

She jerked open the front door, pulled her phone and keys from her pocket, and slapped them into her little girl's hand. The man leaned against the wall, barely standing but starting forward. Rainey would never make it to the car … but Sarah could.

"I need you to be brave and do exactly what I tell you."

Sarah's wide eyes grew wider.

"Get in the car. Lock the doors and call Granny. Tell her an intruder is in the house." She pushed Sarah toward the Jimmy.

Sarah froze a moment, staring at her mother without comprehension.

Rainey grabbed for the front door to pull it closed. "Go, Sarah. Now. Back seat, honey."

Perhaps the tinted windows would keep her from his view for a little longer.

Whether it was the frantic tone in Rainey's voice or the look on her face, something spurred Sarah into motion.

The door jerked against Rainey's hold, so she jammed the skillet beneath her arm and grabbed the doorknob with both hands, looking over her shoulder until Sarah made it into the back of the Jimmy.

Her hold slipped against the strength in the man's pull, cracking the door open an inch. On the mental count of three, Rainey released the door, then took the skillet into her hands. The door slammed into the man's left shoulder, knocking him off balance but not rattling him nearly as much as Rainey had hoped.

His thick fingers grabbed around her left arm, sinking into her skin with blinding force and pulling her into the house. She stumbled forward through the doorframe, wincing at the pain knifing up her shoulder from his hold.

The man's dark eyes widened as he took in her face. "You're not Evie." He groaned, his lip curling into a sadistic snarl. "Too bad for you and your little girl."

With what strength she could pull from her right arm, she brought the skillet around like a tennis serve. It landed a perfect placement against his left cheek, sending him stumbling against the wall with a heavy thud. Rainey shook off his hold and ran down the hallway. The madman planned to kill her … unless she killed him first.

The misunderstanding between Rainey and Alex hovered in the air as he sat at Mama Mitchell's counter. Any concern of a backlash from a protective Mama Mitchell bear dissolved within five minutes of her sweet welcome.

Alex had no doubt Rainey shared details of what happened between she and Alex with her mother, but Mama Mitchell never showed her knowledge. All she did was serve him some mouthwatering salted-caramel chocolate chip cake and speak about TLC.

"Last Rainey said, she was still shy of around thirty thousand dollars."

Alex looked up from his first bite, lost for a full two seconds in the flavors falling over his tongue before her statement sank into comprehension. "Thirty thousand?" He swallowed. "That can't be right."

"Well, that's what she said yesterday while she was here."

Yesterday? One of the longest days of his life. "I know for a fact she should have a lot less to raise than that." He wiped at his mouth. Hadn't she seen the envelope on her counter beside Sarah's colorful letter? "Less than half left of that fifty grand."

Mama Mitchell's gray gaze narrowed, then she went back to slicing the cake, each piece equal in size. How did women do that? Was it a special gene or something? "I'm going to ask you a real direct question, Alex, and I'd like you to answer back with the same."

His breathing locked in his throat. "I'll try."

"Where did you get the large sum of money you gave to Rainey?"

"How did you know I gave her"—he frowned—"okay, so I wasn't the subtlest."

"Which causes all sorts of trouble for this situation with Rainey and you."

Alex placed his fork down. "What do you mean?"

"Well, you're not a deceiver, Alex, and you have a tender heart, which is as obvious as the ready grin on your face. So unless you've done something illegal…" Her gray eyes held his, measuring him for a full three seconds. "I'm going to wager that money came from a car trade-in rather than a bank account."

He released his breath. "You're really good at mystery solving, aren't you, Mama Mitchell?"

"Raising four young'uns and living with a large family gives a body some skills."

His laugh took a slightly nervous turn, so he ate another bite of cake. Had she sorted out Evie's story too?

"TLC needed the money." He shrugged. "I didn't really need the car."

She stared at him, studyin' him, as she'd say, then leaned forward and covered one of his hands with hers. "Listen here, Alex. You may not be at liberty to share the secret you carry with a lot of people, but maybe sharing it with Rainey will be a better, safer choice than not sharing it with her. For both of your sakes. She can handle the worst scare better than what she's imaginin' about you right now."

"But I'd rather she be safe, even if it means she can't be with me."

"Safe?" Her brow crinkled, and those pale eyes studied him for what felt like a full minute. "Who are you protectin', Alex?"

A tingling sound erupted from the other side of the kitchen. Alex winked as Mama Mitchell walked toward the phone, breathing a sigh of relief at the interruption. "Saved by the bell."

"Don't you go thinkin' you're off the hook, boy." She grinned over her shoulder. "I'm awful good at winklin' out news, and you're an easy read."

"Then I'd better leave while I'm ahead." Especially since Alex felt the overwhelming urge to spill the full truth within the haven of Mama Mitchell's kindness. Yes, it would probably be a safe choice, but he'd already shared more than he should have by telling his father about Evie and Lily.

"Sarah, honey? What's wrong?"

Alex stopped in his turn from the stool and met Mama Mitchell's wide eyes. Heat drained from his face.

"Mama's inside with an intruder?"

Alex jolted to his feet. "I'm on my way."

"Stay on the phone with me, sweetheart." She covered the receiver with her palm. "There's an old revolver in the desk drawer, Alex." He only hesitated a second and turned to the nearby desk. Reaching into the back of the drawer, his fingers hit onto the cool steel of the weapon. His throat tightened. He'd fired one, once, as practice...

"You're in the Jimmy? Well, you stay right there with the doors locked, just like your mama said."

Sarah! She had to be terrified, just like Lily during the car chase. He'd never forget the fear on his niece's little face.

Alex's fingers tightened around the gun, and he rushed to the door, Mama Mitchell's voice following him. "I'll call the police and Trigg on the landline. Be careful."

Chapter Twenty-five

Rainey inched down the wall beside her bed, just out of sight from the door, pistol in hand. With a practiced motion, she pulled back the slide, allowing the bullet to move into position. The click resounded in the stillness of the room, louder than the pounding pulse in her ears.

She pointed the pistol toward the only entryway into the bedroom, gripping the handle with both hands to still the shaking. The fingers of her right hand slipped into position, while her left hand supported her hold.

Squeeze, don't pull. Her father's mantra resounded in her head.

Where was the guy? He'd been moving when she last saw him.

A floor creak answered her question. He was coming around the hallway into the kitchen. She swallowed through a waiting scream, keeping the sound fisted closed. Would she have to shoot him?

She drew in a shivered breath and squeezed her eyes closed.

Keep both eyes open.

Another floor creak alerted her to his nearness. In the dining room. He was only a few steps away from her bedroom door. Her fingers searched for the trigger, gaze trained on the doorway.

Help me, Jesus.

His shadowed frame filled the doorway, and her swallow stuck in her throat. He took another step, the flash of a blade glimmering with his movements. The stench of his sweat cloaked the air as he took one more step.

Squeeze, don't pull.

The sound ripped from her, as much from the weapon as her own lungs. An angry roar exploded from the intruder in response. He doubled over, clutching his middle and slashing the air in her direction. Rainey's trembling legs pushed her into a standing position, and she tiptoed around the edges of the room, keeping the gun pointed in the writhing man's direction.

If she could just make it to the Jimmy, they could get to the police.

A floor creak sounded in the other room, and her pulse ricocheted to a stampede in her head. Did the man have an accomplice? She turned toward the door, but it was a mistake. With catlike agility, the intruder grabbed her by her ponytail and flung her against the nearby wall. She crumpled to the floor with a moan, her vision switching between blurry and dark.

He gripped her by her neck and drew her up, cutting off her airway. "You should have aimed higher," he said, his threat laced with death as the knife came into focus in front of her. "Because I won't miss."

Alex stopped the truck out of sight at the bottom of the driveway and ran up the hill. Every protective instinct within him bristled to the top, fueling his speed. Night closed in, dimming his vision as he neared the house, the revolver clutched closely to his side.

The wind hushed through the trees, deepening the chill pressing through him with its cold touch. He slipped behind Rainey's jeep and moved to the side on the opposite view of the house. Sarah's silhouette popped up behind the window.

His air pumped out in gusts of gratitude. "Hey, princess," he whispered, knowing she couldn't hear him through the glass.

She pressed her palm against the window, and he matched her motion, his large hand covering over hers. She was safe. His gaze shot to the house. But where was Rainey?

He looked back to the window and pressed his face close, trying to make out her eyes behind the dark tint. "I will be right back. Stay here."

Her little head bobbed up and down in sweet response.

He rounded the front of the SUV and ran to the back of the house, pressing his body against the wall like he'd seen in police shows. Made sense. It was harder to shoot a moving target.

The back door stood wide open, light shining into the graying evening from the hallway. Alex took the steps to the door and peered inside. Empty … and terribly quiet. He pointed the revolver ahead of him, hammer back, and stepped over the threshold.

The sound of a gunshot froze his steps, and his breath.

Rainey.

He stepped forward, back still against the wall, and scanned the great room. Empty, from what he could tell. He peered around the wall into the kitchen and dining area. A crash from Rainey's bedroom brought him to the door, the scene before him gripping him like some horror movie. A man clothed in black held Rainey against the wall, knife brandishing for a lethal blow.

Without another hesitation, Alex brought the revolver up and fired. Whether the bullet hit its mark or not, Alex couldn't tell because the man turned, eyes wide, and charged directly for him. Alex braced for the impact, the doorframe hemming him in on either side. He attempted to dodge, but the man crushed into him with linebacker force. Blinding pain erupted in Alex's side as he crashed into the dining room table before slamming to the floor.

All those years of fighting in middle and high school resurfaced, paired with a need to find Rainey. He pushed past the sting in his ribs and rammed his fist into the assailant's stomach, sending the man back so his face shone in the hall light.

John.

The fury from the past year poured over Alex, and he lunged at the man, pounding another fist into the dazed expression. John fought back, but with a weaker punch, yet he met his mark with a solid hit between Alex's eyes.

Pain exploded in his face, and the world shadowed at the fringes of his vision, but Alex kept his fists flying. When his vision cleared, John lay on the floor, trying to crawl for a knife a few feet away. Another set of steps rushed into the room. Police. Their heavy shoes beat in time with the pounding in Alex's skull. Trigg followed. Alex fell back, away from the approaching men, his muscles giving way to the tension he'd carried since leaving Mama Mitchell's house.

Lights flickered alive in the room. John moaned as the police pinned him down, his blood-covered shirt leaving a dark red stain against the floor. Trigg knelt down to Alex's side, looking him over. "Where's Rainey?"

Alex's eyes widened and he struggled to stand, but Trigg beat him to the answer, rushing through the bedroom doorway and switching on the light. Alex grappled for balance against the dining room table and then stumbled over to the bedroom door, gripping the frame. His side stung, so he pressed a free hand to the wound, fingers slicking red with blood.

How had he been wounded? By John's knife? The fall? Whatever it was, the wound proved more sting than danger.

The police struggled with their half-conscious prisoner. Alex worked words through his raw throat. "Sarah, Rainey's daughter, is in the jeep outside. She's safe, but she's there."

One of the deputies nodded and walked down the hall.

Leaning forward, Alex peered into the bedroom. Trigg was helping Rainey off the floor. Her erratic hair framed her ghostly white face. She was the most beautiful sight he'd ever seen. He leaned his head against the frame, thanking God she was safe and that John was in custody.

John. His brother-in-law.

This whole incident was Alex's fault. His stomach revolted with the realization. Had his secrecy somehow put Rainey and Sarah in danger?

He backed out of the room, unable to face the ghosts from his past he'd placed in Rainey's life. Another swell of dizziness crippled him to the floor.

"We need an EMT here, stat," someone called.

Alex tried to sit up but gentle hands wrapped around his body and tugged him forward. "Alex." Rainey's raspy voice sounded close. Her face cleared in his vision, concern tightening her features. "Oh Alex, you stupid man. You saved my life."

His grin twitched at her floundering attempt at gratitude, then he sobered. "I'm sorry, Rainey. I shouldn't have taken you with me to Dad's. I ... I placed you and Sarah in danger. My ... my brother-in-l—"

"Shut up." Her palms smoothed over his face. "You can't blame yourself for a madman. You can't." She shook her head, her gaze moving over his chest. "You're bleeding."

"The ambulance is coming up the driveway."

"Mama, Mama." Sarah ran through the room and directly into Rainey's arms. Alex sighed back against the floor and closed his eyes. The voices of police muffled in his aching head. Trigg's deep bass voice blurred, and Alex tried to ignore every part of his body screaming in protest at the assault.

Rainey and Sarah were safe. That was all that mattered.

"Alex, the EMT is here for you." Rainey's voice pulled him from the fog, and he opened his eyes, attempting to sit up. He drew in a deep breath, but the cough reverberated through all the painful spots in his chest. A moan slipped between his gritted teeth as he succeeded in rising to a sitting position.

"Oh no!" Sarah gasped and slid close to him, her lips pouting enough to break his heart. "Dr. Alex, you hurt your face."

"Dr. Alex fought the bad guy for Mama." Rainey brushed her fingers through his hair, her gaze gentling into his. "He rescued me."

His face wrestled to hold on to a smile, even if it hurt his swelling nose.

Sarah put her little hands on either side of his face and stared at him, grinning until her cheeks dimpled, no matter what his miserable face looked like. "You're Mama's hero."

His attention flipped back to Rainey, brow tipped in question.

She blinked those beautiful watery eyes and leaned in, carefully pressing her cheek against his so her words whispered near his ear. "My hero." She sat back and cleared her throat. "So get well."

More footsteps hurried down the hallway, but Alex held Rainey's gaze. "Don't forget it. I'm your hero. Sarah and Trigg are witnesses."

"Can we move on before I get sick?" Trigg stepped to Alex's side and ushered the EMTs forward. He slipped his arm underneath Alex and helped him stand. "If you keep up all this romantic talk, I might start cryin'."

Laughing hurt but he couldn't help it, and part of him didn't want to. It broke the tension and eased the residual fear still clinging to the past few minutes. He'd never admit it in front of Trigg, but there was a good chance he'd cry all the way to the hospital out of sheer gratitude.

Alex took a last look at Rainey and Sarah, gratefulness swelling from his heart to his teary eyes. Even if tomorrow she realized he wasn't the hero she thought, at least she'd be safe. And even if he couldn't have her in his life, that would have to be enough.

Mama insisted on staying the night, bringing Lou and Brandon with her, and despite Rainey's reservations, their presence proved a fantastic distraction for Sarah. After fixing the front window and helping clear broken furniture out of the way, Trigg offered to sleep on the couch, but Rainey put on her brave face and sent him home.

She'd called the hospital to check on Alex, but the nurse informed her he'd been given some medication to help him rest. Trying to see him at 9:30 p.m. after he'd had a dose of prescription-strength sleep medication wasn't the best idea, as much as she wanted to be by his side after tonight's ordeal.

Her body ached, her throat burned from the pressure John placed on it, and her mind flashed unwanted memories. She walked through the house, closing all the blinds to block out the darkness. The sweet sound of Mama reading a bedtime story to the children soothed over the tremor still alive just beneath her skin.

The police stayed long enough to get Rainey's statement and encourage her to set up an appointment with their counselor within the next few days. Mama overheard the recommendation, so Rainey wouldn't even need to put a reminder in her phone.

The house grew quiet. She brewed some coffee and settled down at the bar, her aching head in her hands. Enough pieces came together from tonight to help Rainey understand Alex a little better. Could Alex's sister really be alive? Was *she* the woman Rainey had seen with Alex?

No wonder he couldn't tell her the truth. No wonder the secrecy!

But what happened to place Evie in such a situation that Alex had to protect her "death"? Had Alex said his brother-in-law? It seemed too prime-time television to believe.

A stack of mail piled on the counter, so Rainey sugared up her coffee and drew the pile close. It was strange how something as common as going through mail found a welcome spot in her heart after such an evening. She flipped through a few bills, a couple of advertisements, then paused on an envelope with a familiar logo.

Murdock.

She slit the seal and pulled out the paper. A check fluttered from the page. Rainey's breath stopped when her eyes settled on the dollar amount on the right side of the check. Ten thousand dollars for TLC? She quickly opened the paper.

Dear Ms. Mitchell,

I'm afraid I didn't make the best impression on you during your visit to Fairfax. Please forgive my terseness. I have researched your program and am happy to support such a worthy cause. Take this small amount as the first of many donations to the children of southwestern Virginia.

I hope we have opportunity to meet again so that your second impression of me will prove much better than the first.

Sincerely,

Eli M. Murdock

Rainey stared at the check again. The first of many? Tears invaded her vision, and her shoulders sank forward. After such an evening, to have a day of sweet relief! She swiped away the tears and turned to the next envelope, a similar logo at the top but colored with bright rainbows from a young hand.

With quick work, she opened the new letter. The only thing inside was a handwritten note and a check. A check to TLC for twenty thousand dollars from Alex. She gasped and snatched the note.

So you can keep being a hero to children all over Ransom.

No signature followed the note, but she knew the writer. She flipped the envelope over—the date marked was two days before Reese and Dee's wedding. Unwelcome tears blurred her vision again, except this time, they didn't stop. The emotional roller coaster, from anger to hope to terror to fear of loss and now this? This sweet reminder of who Alex really was and had been all along?

She walked to the window and stared down at the farmhouse as if he waited there instead of in a hospital bed. Poor Alex, harboring a horrible secret and living on tenterhooks, no doubt. Then to have her doubt and accusations bombard him?

It's true, she had fair reason to doubt him, but upon reflection, he'd already proven his heart, over and over again.

"You know where he got the money, don't you?" her mama asked from the stairs.

Rainey's gaze fell on the truck parked below, and she half sobbed, half laughed. "He's such a loveable idiot, that man."

"And he needs a stubborn, headstrong, faithful woman by his side tomorrow, I'd say."

Rainey nodded, wiping at another onslaught of tears. "She plans on being there."

Mama nodded. "I think a good night's rest would do us both good."

Rainey walked to the kitchen and placed the checks together on the counter, glancing around the open room. A chill tremored up her spine as her gaze landed on the corner of the dining room where she'd first seen the intruder standing, waiting. "I'm not sure I'm ready to sleep yet."

Mama placed her arm around Rainey's shoulders and guided her to the stairs. "That guest bed is big enough for the both of us tonight. What do you say we share a girls' night like old times."

"I'm going to be okay, Mama."

She nodded, her gaze filled with understanding. "I know."

Tears stole Rainey's voice, so she merely nodded, resting her head against her mama's, walking with her—and leaving all the lights on downstairs to combat any memories hiding in the corners. For tonight.

Chapter Twenty-six

Rainey didn't know he was awake. He could tell by the way she moved about the room, looking out the lone window, adjusting the flowers she'd brought in, then returning to the chair near his bed only to stand and repeat the routine.

He'd bet she hated hospitals.

He wasn't too fond of them either, but the view drastically improved with her entrance.

Alex doubted his current appearance impressed her. He could see the bandages at the sides of his nose, and from previous experience guessed both of his eyes were blue from the residual impact.

The second time she sat down, he noticed the bruises at her neck. The memory of her crushed against the wall tensed his sore body all over. What if he hadn't arrived when he had? His vision blurred. *Oh God, thank you.*

She sat in the chair for the third time and sighed back as if she might stay for a while.

"Hey, gorgeous."

A beautiful smile transformed her worried expression like sunlight on a cloudy day. Yep, he was in love. He was thinking in imagery.

"Hey, handsome."

"Liar, liar,"—his gaze traveled down her—"jeans on fire."

She chuckled and leaned forward, taking his hand into hers. "How are you feeling this morning?"

"Like I got beat up by a criminal." He pulled his hand out from underneath hers and trailed a finger down her cheeks. "How about you?"

She shrugged. "I'm still shaken up, but I'll be okay."

"I'm sorry, Rainey. I brought this on you and Sarah. It's my fault."

"Shut up, Alex." She snagged his hand from her cheek and squeezed it, those amazing aqua eyes firing all their intensity in his direction. "This wasn't your fault. A desperate, crazy man is going to do desperate, crazy things. Stop blaming yourself and get better."

He stared back, searching for any chink in her confidence, but her expression proved beautifully resolute. "I love you."

She pretended to ignore his words, but the bloom of color in her cheeks told him she'd heard. "How bad are your injuries?"

"Broken nose and one cracked rib." He winced through a chuckle and adjusted himself straighter in the bed, even swinging his legs around off the bed.

"And the place where you were stabbed?" Rainey grimaced, glancing over him as if he might break.

"It's a mere flesh wound." He wiggled his brows at her. "I've always wanted to say that. It's hero talk."

Without warning, she took his face in her hands and with a swift but gentle touch, pressed her lips to his, avoiding his nose altogether. The soft touch moved over his mouth, matching lips to lips in a perfect fit.

She pulled away, staring at him with a lucent expression he hoped to remember forever.

"I suddenly feel ready to fight a novel full of dragons."

She grinned and kept one palm against his face, never taking her eyes from his. "I love you, and you need to know that before you start telling me Evie's story because no matter what you say or what you've had to do, I'm going to feel the same as I do right now."

"I must *really* look pitiful."

She raised a brow. "It does help your cause."

He tugged her close to his healthy side and drew in a deep breath—a free breath—without the hitch of hidden stories anymore. "It's a long story."

"We're on spring break." She rested her head against his shoulder, filling his senses with citrus and honey. "And I think I've earned a good story."

His hand swept into the hair cascading down her back. "I'm not sure how good it will be, but you've certainly earned the truth." Having her by his side, even as his body ached from a battle of nightmarish proportions, took some of the edge off the tale.

"I never was a fan of John. He set his sights on Evie from the first minute Dad hired him into the company, and he knew exactly what to do to win over my soft-hearted sister. Within a year, they'd married and in two years, Lily was on the way. John was a smart man. Manipulative. If Evie was happily distracted with a baby, then she was less likely to discover who he really was."

Alex shuddered, and Rainey pressed in a little closer. "John had been a part of some underground organization long before he met us, and my dad's company was the perfect cover and financial funnel for his operations. With John's natural charisma and strong personality, he immediately ingratiated himself with Dad. He was everything Dad wanted in a son."

"A criminal murderer? Yeah, sounds like perfect son material right there." She looked up at him. "I'll take charming, genuine, and a dorky sense of humor any day."

He pressed a kiss against her forehead. "With a nose as wide as the front of a Mercedes."

Her laugh slipped out, and she gave her signature eye roll.

"Anyway, he became Dad's right-hand man, and with Dad's nationwide contacts, John's money laundering turned into drug trafficking. Since he was a trusted part of Dad's team, John was allowed to hire people too."

"So he hired his friends to be on the inside."

"Right," Alex continued. Each added line hit a little harder and a little closer to his heartstrings. "Evie and a coworker, Seth, discovered some documents on John's desk by accident, one showing enough information to prove some of John's illegal connections, but when John walked in on the two of them in his office with the docs, he went crazy. In an attempt to help Evie escape through the back stairwell from John's office, Seth placed himself between her and John."

"And was killed in the process?"

Alex nodded. "On the way to the police, Evie called me and asked me to pick up Lily from school because she was afraid John would take Lily as leverage."

"And that's when you became involved in all this?"

"I met Evie while she gave her statement to the police and handed over the documents she'd found. Soon we learned of the scope of John's connections and crimes, but by that time John had disappeared along with about four other people who were directly connected to those documents. He left Evie penniless."

Rainey pulled back searching his face, brows scrunched low. "This sounds like a movie."

"Oh, just wait. What we experienced last night was the pinnacle of a long saga." He brushed back her hair behind her ear. "Under police escort, we drove toward one of our family's other homes, a remote place. Great idea, at the time. Unfortunately, we didn't realize the scope of John's reach and influence. Halfway to the cottage, a car started following us, shot the tires out of one of the police escorts, and started a chase. These thugs knew exactly what they were doing. Even though another police car joined the chase, the men ran us off the road, and we crashed into a river."

"And the thugs?"

"They were killed by police, later identified as two of the men cited in those documents. One officer died, one was wounded, and after the police rescued me, Evie, and Lily from the river, the cops took Evie and Lily into protective custody."

"And you were sworn to secrecy."

He looked down at their entwined fingers. "For their safety, especially when the police staged Evie and Lily's deaths."

"The police really do that? Stage people's deaths?"

"In serious situations, where there's an actual possibility innocent lives are in danger? Yes."

She sat back, eyes wide, the information almost too unbelievable to process. "So Evie ... is alive?"

He grinned. Oh man, it felt good to admit the truth out loud. Freedom. "Yes."

"And *she* was the woman who stayed with you."

He nodded. "But your reaction was normal because this kind of situation wasn't."

Rainey's shoulders fell and she looked away, shaking her head. "What happens now? Is she safe?"

"I gave my report last night and, from what I understand, John was interrogated before he slipped into a coma early this morning. Since the year after Evie's 'death,' some of the other accomplices have been caught, but it sounds like the police gained full information from him in return for a lighter sentence." He squeezed her hand. "The end is in sight, and Evie and Lily can return home soon."

"So they'll move back to Fairfax?"

"Oh, I don't know about that." Alex's grin tipped, ever hopeful. "I think she may be falling in love with some more southerly mountains."

After another report to the police and a visit with the recommended counselor, Rainey headed to Daphne's to pick up some lunch for Mama and the kids, with the distinct purpose of going back to the hospital later. Alex texted that he'd be discharged around five o'clock, and she'd volunteered to pick him up.

Rainey still couldn't wrap her mind around everything Alex had divulged. She'd never reach the bottom of his character. Everything he'd endured? The people he'd loved and protected, even his grumpy dad? And now she and Sarah were two of the beneficiaries of his generosity. The last thread of reserve dissipated from around her heart. Ever since Gray, she'd convinced herself that two people needed years and years to realize they belonged together, especially if it involved *her* heart, but Alex's character proved some things were just meant to be.

And were right from the start.

God had taught her, through her heartache, how to rediscover beauty, but more than that, He'd reminded her of who she was and where her heart truly belonged—in His hands. It just so happened, God, in his bottomless love, brought along a man to show her the best kind of heavenly love on earth.

How much He loved her stubborn heart! Even hers.

I love you with an everlasting love.

Her vision blurred as she pulled into Daphne's parking lot. She shot a praise heavenward, along with a watery smile, then headed into the restaurant. The entire room erupted with celebration as she crossed the threshold.

People from all over the community crowded every side of the restaurant. Teachers, parents, clerks, factory workers, every shape, size, and social class, crammed arm-to-arm inside Daphne's. Even Mama and the kids waited in the wings. What was going on?

Emma surfaced from the throng carrying a large envelope, her red-lipped smile larger than anyone else's. Her matching red heels tapped a staccato rhythm across the floor, with Maggie at her side carrying a vase of roses. Contrast? Definitely. Maggie with her simple style and beauty beside thrift-store classy and big-time dreamer Emma.

"What is going on?"

Emma tipped a shoulder. "Well, we'd planned this whole thing before your trouble last night, and some of us thought we should wait, but Maggie suggested it may be exactly what you need after such a tragic evening."

"What I need?"

Maggie stepped forward, placing the roses in Rainey's hands. "There's no person here who doesn't know how much you do for the kids of this community."

"We've been raising money for TLC since word came out about the center closing," Emma added, putting the envelope in Rainey's other hand.

"All total, our little community of regular folks pulled together $8, 327.00." Maggie's grin rivaled Emma's, brightening the dark brown of her eyes.

"And fifty-seven cents," Emma added, nodding to Sarah. "We don't want to forget Sarah's contribution."

And the waterworks exploded with fresh tears. "I … I don't know what to say."

"Thank you is the usual response." Emma laughed.

Maggie touched her arm. "You need to know what a difference your dream makes to so many people."

"And our community comes together to do as much as we can for our own. TLC is a part of Ransom." Emma tapped one of the roses, her caramel eyes sparkling. "And we want to keep it that way."

"Well, well, look who's up and walking like a pro."

Alex's grin started growing before he ever turned around to face his future bride, or at least, that's pretty much how he'd claimed her.

She stood in the doorway with her hands on her hips, giving him the once-over, somehow impressed with his Frankenstein-stiff movements.

He gave her the once-over right back … maybe even a twice-over or more. Her dark-blue button-up cinched her waist at her jeans, contrasting with her golden hair. "Not ready for a jog yet, but the doc said I may be in a couple of weeks."

"I'll hold you to that. We've gotten out of practice."

"Oh, don't worry. It's one of my favorite things."

"Practice?" Her brow shifted, teasing to an earlier conversation that involved kissing.

"Oh yes." He slipped a hand around her waist. "And jogging with you.

That's fun too. Oh, what about both?"

A knock at the door pulled them apart. Captain Calvin Danvers entered, a deputy at his side. "Rainey." He nodded his hello and removed his hat. "Alex. Glad to see you both on your feet and smiling."

"Thanks, Captain." Alex took his hand. "I'm guessing since you've come to see me for the second time today, you have news?"

"I do." His expression turned serious, and his body straightened with practice for the coming blow. "John Easton died an hour ago following complications from surgery to remove a bullet lodged in his spine."

Rainey released a faint gasp.

Alex slid his palm against her back, trying to take the shock. "I'm truly sorry he never made amends, Captain."

The captain's face remained impassive. "However, he did make enough statements for us to locate his contacts. Since we caught him in such a remote location, news didn't spread of the attack or arrest. Finding and arresting his accomplices has been quick and easy because his arrest came unexpectedly."

Alex released a breath he felt he'd been holding for a year. "And what does this mean for Evie and Lily?"

"We're finalizing their paperwork and setting up police surveillance for the next few months, but within the week your sister and niece should be free to resume their normal lives." He glanced to each of them and settled his attention on Alex, face softening. "I know this has been a long process for you all, and there are still going to be a few, though much less harrowing, challenges ahead with the investigation, but I'm glad to say we can see the end."

"And it's a good ending."

He nodded. "Much better than it may have been without your cooperation and your sister's patience." He turned to Rainey. "And your dozen neighbors converging at the end. How many of the local police are a part of your family?" The faintest smile brightened his stoic expression.

"Two. And one of the EMTs." Rainey shrugged. "Then there was my brother, Trigg."

Calvin pushed a hand through his hair and chuckled. "Well, I know where to look for some new recruits next time I'm in need."

"We mountain folk are a hearty, fiercely loyal, and a little scary bunch, Captain. We'd make some good additions to your team."

His grin almost crested. "And I see they already meet most of the criteria

I'm seeking too." He shifted a step back and returned his hat to his head. "I'll contact you for any further information, but in the meantime, enjoy this new freedom you have, Alex. It's been a long time coming."

The finality of the closing door hit Alex in the chest. Finished. Finally.

"Well, my hero, have you signed your discharge papers?"

He blinked his attention back to her. "Sure have."

She gestured with her chin toward the door. "Then how 'bout I take you home?"

He stood with her, groaning a little in the shift. Rainey moved to his side, and he grinned down at her. "I think you're the prettiest taxi driver I've ever met."

"Well, after all the life protecting and saving you've been doing lately, I figured you deserved the best." She winked, and he snuck a kiss right on her smile.

They moved toward the door. "I'll pay you in kisses, how's that?"

She paused and looked up at the ceiling, nibbling on her lip as if contemplating his offer. "You'd better make 'em good. We're driving in Mama's high-class Cadillac. That's a top-paying ride."

His thoughts took a dark turn. "Oh, I only make 'em good."

She stepped out of his reach and opened the room door. "Then you can pay me in full when we get to my house."

"Your house?"

She gave him a little nudge out the door to keep him moving. "Yep, I'm taking care of you until you're well enough to manage those bandages on your own. The doc said a few days."

"You're going to take care of me for a few days?" He shuffled down the hall in a wonderful haze. Maybe he was still asleep, because this dream kept getting better and better.

She pushed the elevator button, keeping her face forward. "Mmhmm, and I'm putting you in my bedroom."

Now he knew he was dreaming. *Don't. Wake. Up.* "Your bedroom?"

The elevator doors opened, and she walked backwards, her grin teasing him forward. "While I take the guest bedroom upstairs next to Sarah's."

He followed her, a puppet on a string in her presence. Oh man, he loved her. "That's painfully honorable of you."

"Just so you know, Dr. Murdock"—Rainey pressed the main floor button— "once I set my mind to something, I'm extremely passionate about my cause."

"And have you set your mind to something I need to know about?"

"Yep." She wound her arms around him as the elevator doors closed them in. "I've found my hero, and I plan to keep him."

He took her face in his hands. "Oh, Ms. Mitchell, he's not goin' anywhere." His gaze searched her beautiful, familiar face, basking in the love reflected in those eyes. "This hero's certain he's found exactly where he belongs."

"That's right." Rainey tugged him closer. "You belong right here. With me."

Epilogue

Alex met Rainey at the bottom of her driveway, the late-May morning bright with a first hint of summer sun. After three weeks of medical care and easing back into his schedule, his movements came fluid, allowing them to resume their jogs. Today, he'd pulled out the jogging shorts.

Heavens alive, the man already tempted her in ways that would make her mama blush, and now he had to show off those legs? Kryptonite for her fabulous intentions. Great legs and a ready smile did not bode well for her good-girl sensibilities.

Not thirty minutes before, she'd been thanking God for how much she loved the comradery and friendship growing between her and Alex. The fun they found in spending time together, the pleasure of simply having a conversation, the sweetness in their prayers, both as a couple and as a trio… Now he showed off his mighty fine calves, and she could hardly remember her name.

Lord, I'm so glad you love me anyway.

With a resigned groan, she stepped forward to meet him and sent God another mental thank you for giving her a man she not only liked and loved, but *really* liked. "I see you're dressed for summer already." Did her voice squeak? Seriously, could she get any more childish?

His eyes widened, and he followed her gaze to his bare legs. "It's almost seventy degrees. Besides, I love summer."

She pulled her rebel gaze from his muscular legs, but he caught her distraction, his sneaky grin angling at a devilish tilt. "You like my legs."

She rolled her eyes, heat infusing her cheeks like the summer sun scorched midday, and with a toss of her ponytail took off at a run. He was beside her in a second. "I'm glad you like my legs. I can assure you the feeling's mutual."

She sent him a mock glare from her periphery, but her treasonous lips couldn't hold the frown. "You really like to make things hard on me, don't you?"

"I'm trying to weaken your defenses so you'll marry me faster. Clearly, I have to pull out all the stops."

She laughed and almost lost her balance up the hill. "Well, you're certainly distracting, I'll give you that."

"One of the many untapped talents in my inventory, my dear Ms. Mitchell."

On they ran in companionable silence, taking in the morning breeze and birdsong welcoming the day. The weeks since the break-in and the sessions she'd attended with the counselor brought with them a slow unwinding of the residual fear associated with the tragedy, and Alex's closeness and humor sped the healing along.

They helped each other. Together. Exactly as it should be. Cute legs and all.

This one taste of such a love, wrapped in laughter and faith, for all the right reasons—even in the kissy parts, as Sarah would say—smoothed the rough edges of the past and plunged her headlong into planning her future with him. No hesitations. No doubts.

Her gaze dropped to his legs again and she grinned. *No* doubts.

"I think I need to name my truck."

"Your truck?"

"Yep, I haven't figured out a good name for it yet." They moved in unison, stride to stride, a great example of how their lives converged and journeyed together.

"Do you want a girl or a boy's name?"

His brow jutted high. "That truck isn't a girl."

Her laugh burst out. "How can you tell?"

"Women are sleek with smooth curves, like Marilyn." His gaze took a little journey down her body and back, leaving a fiery warmth spinning through her middle and a sudden need to gravitate a little closer to him. "That truck is not a girl."

"Okay, then. A guy's name." He reached for her as she stumbled on a loose rock, steadying her before stepping back into pace. Yep, he was pure distraction. "I think you ought to name it after a hero."

"That's a great idea, but which hero?"

Rainey wracked her brain through possibilities. "Hercules?"

"Hercules would work much better with a newer-model truck."

She chuckled, completely tickled by the entire conversation of naming a truck. "All right. I guess we need to think of a more ... rough-and-tumble hero name?"

"I got it." He nodded and raised his index finger like an exclamation point. "Indiana."

Perfect. She glanced at him, feigning ignorance. "Something heroic happen to you in that state or something?"

"What?" He turned fully around while running. "You don't know *the* best hero of all time? Indiana Jones?"

"Who?"

He shook his head and faced forward again. "You've had a deprived childhood, Rainey Mitchell. We really need to educate you on the finer points of classic heroes."

She caved. "A hero who has a weakness for women and is afraid of snakes?"

"I knew you had to be faking. You're too smart not to know who Indiana Jones is."

"I have two brothers who can quote every movie."

"*I* hate snakes." His grin spun to life, and he topped it off with a wink. "And you're definitely a weakness for me."

"Smooth move, handsome." She sighed and turned with him at the top of the hill to begin their descent home. "Indy it is."

Suddenly, Rainey's walkie buzzed to life. "Mama!"

Rainey slowed her pace and pulled the walkie from her side, placing it to her ear as she stared up at the house in the distance. "Hey, sweet pea."

"Are you running with Dr. Alex?"

Rainey eased her rhythm a little more and shot Alex a smile. "Why, yes I am. Do you want to say hi?"

She turned the walkie to Alex. "Good morning, Dr. Alex."

"Good morning, princess. Did you save any breakfast for me?"

Sarah's giggle echoed back. "I made a giant bowl of cocoa bites just for you."

"Mmm, my favorite."

"And I gave you the panda bear bowl this time."

Alex's palm flew to his chest, and he sighed like her little voice was the best thing in the world. Yep, Alex Murdock was a keeper. "Wow, I feel pretty special today, Sarah."

"We're having a party."

Rainey came almost to a stop and turned the walkie back to her ear. "A party? What kind of party?"

"A celebration party."

"A celebration party? What are we celebrating?"

"Dr. Alex being my new daddy."

"What?" Rainey skidded to a stop and looked up to the house. "Your new…" She turned toward Alex and nearly dropped the walkie altogether.

There he waited, down on one knee, a grin on his handsome face and a blue box in his hand displaying a beautiful diamond ring. "We can't have the party if you say no."

She laughed and brought her palm to her mouth, blinking as the haze of tears framed the handsome man in front of her. "Um … you're planning proposals with my six-year-old?"

"Actually, it was her idea." He shrugged. "Mostly." He grimaced. "Okay, I used a willing accomplice to bring in the cute factor so you couldn't say no. I'm pathetic."

She stepped close, pulling him up by his damp shirt. "Your cute factor is pretty convincing."

"I knew the shorts were a good idea." He closed in, his voice sweeping low.

She smiled against his lips, lingering close, thanking God. Maybe crying wasn't so bad. Not this kind anyway.

"Can I safely assume that's a yes? Because Sarah really needs an answer."

Rainey stepped back, tilted her chin in defiance, and raised the walkie to her mouth, all the while keeping her gaze fixed on her handsome suitor. "Sarah?"

Silence for a moment. "Yes, Mama?"

"I think Dr. Alex would be a great daddy for you." She released the button on the walkie. "And a super husband for your mama."

"Well, I don't know about super." He took her fingers into his and raised a brow as he slipped the ring into place. "But he's certainly thankful, humbled, and madly in love."

She raised their entwined hands to appreciate the new addition to her finger. The simple but elegant setting of braided white gold on either side of the round diamond showed how Alex knew her. "It's beautiful."

"Well, it had to fit the wearer." He kissed her hand and continued their walk, turning to start up the driveway to Rainey's house. "So, speaking of weddings, what do you think of a Christmas one?"

He'd given her so much, the ring merely a reflection of his heart. She knew exactly how to return the favor. "Christmas is six months away." Her grimace deepened to wrangle her burgeoning smile. "And I married Gray near Christmas. I'd rather choose a different month."

He turned to her, palms up. "That's fine with me. You've said yes. I don't care when it is as long as it happens."

She viewed her ring again, all the while keeping an eye on his reaction. "You know, I've always liked the idea of a June wedding."

He worked hard to hide his disappointment with a paper-thin grin as she slipped her fingers back into his. "June? Okay, a year isn't that long."

"Not *next* June, silly."

His smile fell and he came to a complete stop. Frozen. Studying her face with a look of unbridled shock. "*This* June? You mean, like next month kind of June?"

"Really, June is only two weeks away, so we could technically get married in less than a month."

"Less?" He blinked once or twice and stared back at her. "Is that a trick question?"

Her smile bloomed. "I like simple, Alex. All I need is a preacher, my family, and you. If you're up for it, I'd love to marry you, your smile, and your legs as soon as possible."

"Rainey Mitchell, I'd like nothing better in the whole wide world."

Made in the USA
Lexington, KY
10 January 2019